Hello Loved Ones

A NOVEL

TAMMY LETHERER

RAPID TRANSIT PRESS
CHICAGO, IL

This is a work of fiction. Names, characters, places, and incidents are the products of the author's imagination or are used fictitiously. Any resemblance to actual events, locales, or persons, living or dead, is entirely coincidental.

Song lyrics by the fictional group The Raptures taken from "Three Good Reasons" by Chicago folk band Sons of the Never Wrong. www.sons.com

www.TammyLetherer.com

ISBN-13: 978-1466459397

ISBN-10: 1466459395

Book Design by Eat Paint Studio
www.eatpaintstudio.com

To my family...
Those who came before,
for they are the roots,
And my children,
Lincoln, Boone and Genevieve,
the most beautiful of leaves.

"Facts are the barren branches
on which we hang the dear,
obscuring foliage of our dreams."

—Natalie Babbitt

Sally

Sally Van Sloeten has a father, same as anyone. Just because a mother or a sister calls a person a deadbeat doesn't make it so. Because a brother says *trust me, you're better off* doesn't mean he knows the first thing about anything. So when the Father-Daughter banquet comes along like a long-awaited signal from above, is she supposed to curl up with her ratty afghan, re-read the latest issue of Seventeen magazine and snivel *poor me, guess I'll miss out?* Damned if she'll be lumped in with this crowd of worshipers who lay their desires at the Lord's feet, then call it a day. *Whew! It's in God's hands now.*

"The gospel of John calls us to worship in spirit and in truth," said Pastor Voss, and all around Sally his flock began nodding like pigeons, flapping their bulletins against the August heat. The pastor breathed in deeply and added, with a touch of drama, "Also, of course, with joy."

Sally made another mark on her bulletin under the word

JOY. That made 43 times he'd said it. She wished he'd just shut up! It was so damn hot. The air in the sanctuary was thicker than the potato-cabbage casserole they were having for Sunday dinner. Sticky thighs were glued to worn-out pews. Swollen feet were mashed into sensible pumps. And the smell! Sally detected lilac perfume and cow manure, and each time the pastor opened his mouth it was like a sprinkle of stinky cheese. Didn't he know, didn't *God* know, that she was bursting to be set free? The letter stuck in the waistband of her skirt had to be put in the mailbox today or her father would never get it in time. By now it must be soggy with sweat. She felt it clinging to her back, and it was starting to itch.

"Turn with me to the second book of Acts, verses forty-six and forty-seven," Pastor Voss said, and while parchment pages gently rustled, Sally clenched her teeth. She'd spent every Sunday of her life sitting in the same pew at the Holland Dutch Reformed Church beside her mother Prudy, her sister Nell, and those bony, slumping, ski-slope shoulders attached to her brother Lenny. She'd long since counted every pane of stained glass, every beige ceiling tile, every flame-shaped bulb in the dusty wrought-iron chandeliers overhead. If it weren't for the Father-Daughter banquet and the fact that she was finally old enough to go, she'd have run clean out of diversions.

Everyone would be there. Not just girls from the church, but most of her classmates from Holland High, and even some from Holland Christian High School. For lots of them it was the first time they could wear high heels and make up. Sure, they'd have to suffer through Pastor Voss' lecture on how young ladies should respect themselves as God's unique gift, and look for nice young men who would do the same, but that was a small cross to bear considering they got to dance to *real* music. Not the good stuff, of course, like The Beatles, but maybe a little Donovan, or something from The Lettermen. Romantic, grown-up music. And none of it would be special if she had to take her Uncle Ollie. Her sister Nell went with him three years earlier and she said he had muck on his shoes, didn't use a napkin, and refused to dance to "Ah, Sweet Mystery of Life."

For Sally, there was no mystery. The banquet would be the beginning of life the way it was meant to be. That was why she wrote the letter.

Dear Dad, I know you don't remember me too well, but I'm sixteen now and this is the year I get to go to the Father-Daughter banquet at the church. It's an event of major portions! All the girls in town will be there. It's Saturday the 18th. Please write soon and say you'll come.

And then, because she felt strongly about this, she signed it *love, Sally.* Because, more than anything, she wanted her dad to know that she wasn't like the rest of them. She didn't hate him. She remembered the red sweater he used to wear, the way he once tickled her and threw her in the air. How his hair shone, black and stiff like a beetle's shell. The overcoat that smelled like cold air. He got bored with them, is all, with nothing more exciting to look forward to than the annual church bazaar, with its stale poppy seed muffins, pipe-cleaner refrigerator magnets, Jesus Christ nightlights and plastic rain caps that folded up to look like little purses. He probably couldn't understand why his wife had gone from a pretty girl who liked to laugh to a woman with a grim flat mouth who shared more of herself with the Lord than with anyone else. He simply couldn't bear spending half his life sitting in a church pew listening to Pastor Voss yammer on.

He was exactly like Sally.

To think he'd soon hold a piece of her! Her very heart, and yes, her sweat and tears as well. Would he smile and think back to her as a little girl, wearing pink ruffly rubber pants, shouting *daddy, daddy!* whenever she saw his car drive up? Maybe he'd be sad, thinking of all the years he'd missed with her. Maybe he lived with memories of her every day and once he held that letter in his hand, it would be too much to bear and a sob would escape him. Sally saw him clutching his chest with one hand while he held the letter to his lips with the other.

Or… Here the picture rewound itself and he was holding the letter in his hand, a frown crossing his grizzled, beaten face. He balled the paper up and threw it into an overflowing trash barrel next to his front door. He spit on it for good measure and went stumbling back inside, pulling a moth-eaten brown robe tighter around his frail, stooped frame. He sat on the one chair he owned, lit a cigarette in the dark, and wished he had moved even farther away. He cursed and vowed to chew out the mailman if he ever delivered letters like that again.

Sally heard the word JOY again and made a harsh mark on her tally. *Rejoice!* read the cover of the bulletin. *You are part of the family of God.* Bullshit. Was God going to teach her to bait a hook, or bowl a strike, or measure the hypotenuse of a triangle? Was God going to meet her boyfriends, if she ever had any? Would he walk her down the aisle, this very aisle with its dirt-red nubby carpet? She'd have to rely on her brother Lenny or Uncle Ollie and the most beautiful day of her life would be ruined. And what about her future children? They wouldn't have a grandfather.

Wasn't Sally just as deserving as the next girl? She looked across the congregation. There was Martha Malden sitting beside her father, who looked kindly and safe in a blue striped tie, the same Mr. Malden who had stood beside her in his undershirt when she spent the night with Martha back in seventh grade. He had helped them make pancakes, telling them to add a *smidge* of water to the batter. Sally had never heard the word smidge. For ten minutes he stood with them, testing the batter with his finger, again and again, and when it was just right the three of them cheered like they had saved someone's life. Sally remembered feeling stunned that a grown man would take so much time to help his daughter accomplish something so minor. Then there was Debbie Rinkema who always sat in the back pew. Her father ran the supermarket and once while Sally was standing in the canned vegetable aisle she heard him on the phone in his office saying "*I love you Deb-Deb*" before he hung up. Imagine saying those words for no reason at all! It was as if he'd said *I'll bring home some milk.* Those were the things she was missing, those little acts of fatherly kindness that, if she'd received them, might have made her a better person. And if she were a better person she might not dream of walking into the banquet on her father's arm, with girls like Martha and Debbie staring, saying so ***that's*** *her dad!*

She had to get to the mailbox! If God could really see into her heart, he must know that she regretted, just a little, calling her upstairs neighbor Miss Snootie-Patootie. It was an honest assessment, for sure. But she shouldn't have said it out loud, in front of her. Being grounded for a week was completely jeopardizing her plan. Here she sat, squirming, feeling like a mouse stuck in a sticky trap (or was it a rat?) when there came a sneeze, followed by the sound of a marble hitting the wooden floor. *Christ!* It was Mr. Van Adder's glass eye, *again.* There was a rustle through the congregation as the eyeball rolled between the pews. Mr. Van Adder was allergic to dust motes and three varieties of grass, and it was the third time in two weeks he'd sneezed his eye out. Hallelujah for a high pollen count! It was a small distraction, but she'd use it. As she started to slide toward the aisle, the rolling stopped. Mr. Dekker had the eyeball under the toe of his shoe, and Mr. Van Adder held up his hand in a gesture that said he'd retrieve it after the service. Pastor Voss abruptly launched into announcements.

"I'd like to wish Lenny Van Sloeten a happy birthday," he said. "Lenny is 18 today."

Sally was startled. She thought the pastor didn't like the Van Sloetens much. When he looked out over the congregation he never seemed to see *them*. When he called the heavy-hearted forward to pray with him at the altar and Sally was dragged up by her mother to kneel at his feet, he never touched her bowed head the way he touched the others. The Van Sloetens were poor, and their tithes didn't amount to much. Sally supposed Pastor Voss was obligated to turn his attention to those who paid for it. Maybe she was wrong.

"For those of you who haven't heard, Lenny will be working here at the church as custodian," Pastor Voss said.

Sally leaned around Nell to look at Lenny. He was tracing a vein in his forearm, flexing his fist to make it stand out. He acted like he hadn't heard the pastor and maybe he hadn't. Lenny had been deaf in one ear since he fell out of Uncle Ollie's hayloft when he was six years old.

Pastor Voss cleared his throat. "I'm so pleased to be getting Lenny's help. He's a fine young man, and..." He trailed off, as if searching for something more to say about him. "He'll be taking the furnished room downstairs so... Well, he'll be here 24 hours a day. To look after things, you might say."

What sorts of things needed looking after in their small church? That was the question on every face. It didn't matter. Everyone knew the truth. It was Lenny that needed looking after. First it was a few nights out late. Then a handful of cut classes, one or two bad grades, and a graduation ceremony that Lenny pretended to forget. Finally two weeks ago he was arrested for fighting out behind Louis Padnos' scrap metal yard. He broke Cash DeVries's nose, which was the size and color of a crook-neck squash to begin with and now looked like a watermelon split wide open, all red and pulpy with black seed-like stitches. Pastor Voss bailed Lenny out with money from the church offering plate on condition that Lenny move into the church and work it off. Of course everyone knew. At the Wednesday night prayer meeting Pastor Voss asked the Lord to be a guiding light for those struggling with hostilities and tempted toward unruliness, and Lenny's face turned nearly as stiff and red as the brand new hymnal books.

"Let's all keep Lenny in our thoughts as he begins his service to the Lord," the pastor said. "As you know, there are many forms of worship, and mopping floors is one of them."

Everyone in the first three rows swung their necks around to stare. Mr. Van Adder's good eye fell squarely on them. Tiny Mrs. Byer, barely four feet tall, craned so strenuously from her seat in the front pew that Sally saw her shiny blue hair peek into the aisle at knee-level, as if it were a fluffy bag on someone's lap. And the look the pastor gave them smacked of smugness. Sally watched him pull out a starchy white handkerchief and wipe his shiny brow. Before returning it to his pocket he examined it, the same way she examined a tissue after attacking a blemish on her face. Like he expected to see blood. She imagined that it would please him to bleed for the sake of his flock, just like it pleased him to hold Lenny up as an example.

Not that it mattered. Lenny's birthday was ruined a long time ago, seeing as it was the same day their dad walked out. *Supposedly* Lenny, only eight years old, started swinging a bat at him. Sally doesn't remember that night, but what seems obvious to her is that Lenny was a hothead even then, and hasn't gotten any better. He deserved to be humiliated by Pastor Voss. But with that accomplished, couldn't the pastor please move on? She couldn't exactly get up and walk out while he was talking about her family.

"Shit," she whispered under her breath, wiggling back and forth. She looked sideways at her mother to be sure she wasn't heard. She couldn't afford any more punishments. Once she mailed the letter, she could breathe a little easier. She could even allow herself to savor today's more immediate joy, yes, JOY. Lenny was moving out! The circumstances were not ideal, but she didn't care. Once Lenny was gone, she was getting his bedroom. No more sharing with her sister, the two of them pressed into the same sagging bed, Nell's thick legs trapping Sally to the wall. No more tripping over Nell's open books that populated every inch of the floor like little tee-pees. No more suffering under Nell's critical eye while Sally experimented with mascara and lip liner. No more discussions about the plight of African pygmies or other topics Sally cared nothing about. No more Miss Goody Two-Shoes, *that* was Nell.

She waited a few moments, then let out a loud cough.

"Choking!" she whispered to her mother. "I need a drink."

Her mother put a hand on Sally's arm and glared at her but Sally ignored her and continued coughing as she pushed her way out of the pew and hurried down the aisle. Freedom! Soon the service would be over, but for now there was no one in the foyer, so she bolted out the front door. If she was stopped, she'd say she felt faint and needed air. Anyone who remembered the time Mr. Veldeer fainted from the choir risers last summer would believe her. (And who could forget, the way his head bounced off the floor with a hollow *thwack?*)

She sprinted down the sidewalk and flung herself at the mailbox on the corner. Taking the letter from her waistband, she saw that the ink was fine but the seal had come unstuck. She licked it quickly and pressed the flap down with her thumb. It popped back open. Now what? There was a gas station across the street. Surely they'd have some tape. But she couldn't go there. Cash DeVries worked there. Imagine seeing that mangled mess of a nose up close. What would she say? *Hey, sorry my brother broke your nose. Can I have a piece of tape?*

There was a good chance he wouldn't know who she was. He was a year older, and went to a different school. He played baseball, like Lenny, and she'd seen him at some of the games, but never spoken to him.

She heard the first notes of the organ drift out the sanctuary window, which meant the sermon was over and the last hymns were starting. She hesitated. She could always wait until Wednesday to mail the letter, when her punishment was up. It was only a few days away.

No. She'd come this far. Cash probably wasn't even working today. Anyway, it wasn't like she was the one who hit him. She had nothing to do with it.

She put the letter back in the envelope and glanced once more at the church before sprinting across the street to the gas station. If she didn't hurry she'd never make it back before the Doxology.

Bursting through the door, she nearly collided with a pair

of work boots sticking out above the counter. Attached to these was a slouchy kid sprawled half off a beat-up office chair. He had long hair pulled into a ponytail and bad skin. And a red swollen nose with black stitches down the middle. *Whoa!* Lenny did that? Sally didn't know why, but the whole incident seemed a little funny at first. Lenny always talked a big game. He hit his dad with a bat when he was only eight, blah, blah, *blah.* And the way he still carried that same bat around with him everywhere he went was pretty strange, but she never thought he was dangerous. He was just her brother. Now, face to face with his handiwork, she felt afraid for him. This was serious.

Cash looked up lazily and raised one eyebrow.

"Got any tape?" Sally said, panting. She flicked her eyes over him quickly and then stared out the window. She had to act too distracted to look at him. Otherwise how could she avoid seeing that nose?

"What for?" he asked. He showed no sign of knowing who she was.

"I need to borrow a piece." Another glance in the general direction of his chest. The label on his coveralls said *Larry.*

"I suppose I could scrounge some up." He didn't move.

This was ridiculous. She had to look at him. She sighed and put her elbows on the counter. Ouch. There it was.

"That looks painful," she said.

He transferred a wad of gum slowly from one cheek to the other. "It ain't too bad."

She couldn't help herself. "How'd it happen?"

He shrugged. "Got in a fight. You oughta see the other guy, though."

Sally blinked, considering for a split second that this might be a guy named Larry who happened to work at the same gas station as Cash, and happened to have a broken nose. Then she remembered she was dealing with a teenage boy. Someone like Lenny.

"That so?" she said sarcastically. "Listen. The tape? I'm in a hurry."

"Where you going?"

"Nowhere."

"Then why are you in such a hurry?"

"I've got to get back to church." She motioned with her head. "I snuck out."

He sat up slowly, looking impressed. "What for?"

"Can I please just have a piece of tape?"

"Are you trying to mail that letter?"

She spotted a stapler sitting on a file cabinet beside a spindle of punctured receipts and a pile of oily rags. "There! That stapler. That'll do."

"Who's it to?" he asked.

She started around the counter, reaching for the stapler. "You don't mind if I come around here, do you?"

"You know the mail don't go out today."

"I know that," she said impatiently, leaning close enough that her shoulder nearly brushed his. She was annoyed at the way he wouldn't budge, or even offer to help.

"So what's the hurry?"

She tried the stapler and it clicked, empty. "There aren't any staples in here."

He stared at her. "Hold on a minute. What's your name?"

She ignored him. "Did you say you have tape? C'mon. I've got to get back."

He sighed and opened a drawer. Rifling through it he said, "Why'd you have to sneak out?"

"It's a long story." She didn't want to tell him she was grounded because she called her upstairs neighbor a Snooty-Patootie. It would sound so immature.

He stopped rifling and crossed his arms. "I'm not going anywhere."

"Do you have any tape or not?" She could see why Lenny hit him. He was extremely irritating.

"This do?" he asked, finally grabbing a roll of black electrical tape.

"Fine." She snatched it from him, tore off a piece, and pressed it down. It looked all wrong on the envelope, but that couldn't be helped.

"Thanks, Larry. You're a lifesaver." She looked down the block. The coast was clear, but any minute the congregation might start spilling out of the church. If anyone saw her she'd be grounded until her own 18th birthday.

"My name's not Larry," he said. "It's Cash."

But Sally was already out the door. She raced back to the mailbox and dropped the letter in. Soon her dad would get it and her new life would begin, the life she was meant to have. She glanced back at the gas station and saw Cash standing beside the pumps, watching her.

"Hey!" she called. "My name's Sally. Sally *Van Sloeten.*"

He snapped to attention. "Van Sloeten?" Then he sneered and flipped her off.

She laughed and ran up the steps. She felt like a new person already. Someone sassy and brave and carefree. Someone a father couldn't help but love.

The congregation shuffled out of the church, gathering to greet one another and talk about the Detroit Tigers or the boat show in Grand Rapids or some other coma-inducing topic. Sally craned her neck and saw Cash still standing in front of the station. She turned to see if Lenny noticed him, and saw him leaping down the church steps, taking them two at a time around the milling crowd. Oh no! Her brother *knew* somehow where Sally had been, and he was going to go finish what he started! But when Lenny hit the sidewalk he stopped. He pulled a red bandana out of his back pocket, tied it on his head and hooked his thumbs in his pockets. Sally relaxed. It was all part of Lenny's *too cool* act. He did it more and more lately, especially at church. Since he wasn't allowed to bring his bat, he brought the bandana instead.

She followed him. "You see Cash over there?" she asked.

He looked startled, maybe even scared. Then his face changed so quickly she might have imagined it. He shrugged and turned around.

"Who cares?" he said.

"Not me."

"Not me neither."

She nearly blurted it out then. *Guess what? I was just over there, with Cash. He gave me some tape.* Talking to Cash, actually seeing that nose up close, how could she keep that quiet?

"Boy! I guess you popped him good."

"So?" He looked at her, bored. The bandana that he thought was cool looked ridiculous. You didn't need a PhD to see that the dumb kid was miserable, same as her. But maybe it had nothing to do with Cash, or thinking about their dad, or about living in a church basement. Maybe he was just a bad kid. All his talk about how he'd take his dad's head off if he saw him again, maybe he really meant it. Sally might be putting her dad in danger, asking him back. She thought of the swollen, bloody mess on Cash's face. Who could say what Lenny was capable of? He might kill their dad and she'd spend the next fifty years visiting him in the Jackson State Penitentiary.

Oh, what had she done? She made a huge mistake, and now there was no turning back. It was just that she wasn't about to be left out of another Important Event. She was damn tired of the way people sighed over them. *Those Van Sloeten kids? The father walked out. Poor mother works herself to the bone and they just scrape by.*

Sally was in second grade before she realized that everything she wore had belonged to someone else. All those times they'd gotten boxes from the church, Sally had never imagined they were full of their neighbors' hand-me-downs. Then a girl named Patty Ann cornered her once during recess and said, "Hey! That's my old dress you're wearing." She made other kids hold Sally down while she flipped her collar around to show the tag. There were the initials P.A.L. written in black ink.

Sally punched her, just the way Lenny taught her, fingers in tight with her thumb on top. She felt a pang as Patricia Ann's tooth opened one of her knuckles. Otherwise, she was immensely satisfied with herself. But it didn't change anything. Sure, the Van Sloetens seemed presentable enough. They were like every other Dutch family in Holland, sturdy and solemn, with large bones and lanky frames, but they didn't have the bright yellow hair or blue eyes that were typically Dutch. Their colors were mouse-brown and hazel. They appeared as if through sunglasses, flat and dull. Prudy in those worn-out pumps with the heels ground down. Lenny in his dingy white shirt. Nell in a beige shapeless dress that looked like a muumuu, Sally in a stupid second-hand plaid skirt that she hated. Their father was gone and all that remained was this snapshot. Underdeveloped. Overexposed.

Lenny understood. She saw the way his eyes scanned the crowd before every one of his baseball games. She knew that he had an extra baseball glove hidden in his closet. He took it out only to oil it or tie a different ball into it, and what was that about? It was a waiting, a held-in breath; it was a body slogging through humid August air every day of the year.

Lenny was the only one Sally might tell about the letter. Imagine being able to talk, *really* talk, about her dad. Mentioning him to her mother was like being puked on. There was that *face*, and then splat, you got hit with the same old bitterness. Sally wanted to say *jeez, mom, I know you hate him. Can you just skip that part and answer my questions?* She used to think how nice it would be if, just once, her mother said *yes Sally, you got a raw deal and I'm sorry about that.* But there was only this giant wall and the bricks were made up of the same words, layer after layer. DRUNK. NO GOOD. BETTER OFF. There was no way to get past it. You needed a sledgehammer. Or a bat. Or maybe a pencil, paper and a plan.

Her mother was standing beside Pastor Voss. "It's so nice of you to join us for Lenny's birthday," Sally heard her tell him.

On the sidewalk, Lenny groaned loudly and pulled his shirttails out. The pastor ignored him. He shook Prudy's hand, and as he did, a spasm in his neck pulled the corner of his mouth down. It was a facial tick he'd developed in the last year or so, and it made him look like he was giving Prudy a secret sign: *Meet me out back in five minutes.* It always made Sally laugh because, in fact, there was something undeniably cold about the pastor. He'd never been to their house for dinner. He was probably only coming today so he could take Lenny back with him. Like a dog. Here's his leash. Hold tight or he'll run off.

Sally had to admit it was a lousy way to spend a birthday, and she was sorry for Lenny. But she couldn't help him. All she could do was smile at the red bandana on his head and wrap her arms around the front of her own orange blouse, glad for any bright spot in an unbearably drab, hot day. The Van Sloetens hadn't faded into nothingness yet.

Sally still had hope. Her dad would write back. *Sure I'll go. Sounds like fun.* Then she'd tell her family. *By the way, Dad's picking me up Saturday at six. We'll just be going to, you know, the banquet.* They'd be angry at first, but then they'd realize it wasn't such a big deal. Lenny and Nell might even thank her, once they got used to the idea. *We've always wanted to see Dad again, but we've never had the courage to make it happen.*

Talk about courage. They didn't know how lucky they were that she was the only one brave enough to state the obvious:

I miss you, dad. We all do.

Lenny

The Louisville Slugger was a very good bat. Better than a Swiss Army knife? Eight-year-old Lenny Van Sloeten couldn't decide. The knife made a nice bulge in his back pocket, but the bat...well, a Slugger was one special bat. If Lenny had to choose between them, which would he pick? With a knife you could pick your teeth or clean under your nails. You could open a can of DW40, take up whittling, kill a garden snake, or slice the legs off a frog. But a bat was part of the greatest game on earth. Lenny learned that from his father. Not that he needed his father to tell him. What he needed was someone to give him a few pointers on how to connect with the ball. Someone to play catch with in the yard. Lenny's dad never stayed at home long enough to do those things.

Richard Van Sloeten sold church tithing envelopes and his job always kept him away. It took him to Traverse City, sometimes even into Canada, where there was a string of

Methodist churches along the Hudson River. He used to tell Lenny that when you cross into Canada it's always snowing and there are Mounties decked out in red flannel uniforms sitting high atop their horses, saluting as you drive by. Mom would remind him that it's a sin to lie but that just made Dad laugh. Then he'd go away again, his trips stretching to four days, one week, two weeks. If he was gone a long time, Lenny would ask, "Where's Dad?"

"He's out on a bender," Mom would say, and Lenny was young enough to suppose that a bender was some new kind of job, better than selling church envelopes, which had always seemed like sissy work to Lenny anyway. A bender sounded important and difficult and he liked saying out loud to himself *Dad's out on a bender*, in the same way he might say *Dad's out on a round-up*, or an oil rig, or an expedition. If he hadn't already decided to be a famous baseball player he might have considered being a bender man himself.

The day before Lenny's eighth birthday, Dad came home. He'd been away five weeks, the longest ever. It was late afternoon, nearly time for supper, and Lenny was sitting with his mother and Nell out in the yard enjoying a lemonade. Sally was down for her nap. When Dad drove up, Mom's face turned hard and she looked away.

"Hello loved ones!" Dad shouted jovially. He pulled a handkerchief from his back pocket and leaned over to dust the tops of his shoes before stepping on the grass. In the sun the round toes shined like wet brown rocks. When Lenny saw the shoes his heart sank. They were new, which meant Dad was in a good mood. It also meant there was a fight ahead. Whenever he came home looking dandy Mom started in. *Don't mention the shoes*, he wanted to tell her, but he didn't want to point them out on the chance she hadn't noticed.

Dad went to Mom and pulled her up out of the chair. She let herself be kissed.

"Here I am," he said. "Stop your sulking."

"I about gave up on you."

"Never!" He smacked her cheek loudly. "You kids come here and give me a hug."

Lenny rose to greet him. Why did he feel strange? Dad was home. He wore the same brown suit, the same yellow-striped tie. He had the same smile, the same hearty laugh, but he was different too. The August heat and the way Dad appeared out of nowhere made Lenny want to rub his eyes and look again.

Lenny went over with Nell awkwardly behind. Dad gave them each a half squeeze.

"How do I look?" he asked.

Lenny squinted at him. He needed a shave. And there was a pink lump on his forehead that wasn't there before. The sight of it thrilled Lenny. Was Dad in a fight? Had he punched someone in the kisser? Maybe he'd gotten in a scrap at some roadside cafe between church visits. Lenny knew from hearing his grandma talk that truck stops and roadside cafes were dangerous business.

"What's that on your head?" Lenny asked.

Dad touched the lump like he'd forgotten it was there. "It's a beauty mark," he said with a grin. "Like it?"

"What happened now?" Mom asked. Dad ignored her.

"Aren't you hot in that suit?" Nell said.

"Now that you mention it, I am. Go fetch me a lemonade." He chucked Nell under the chin and she shuffled toward the house.

"Where were you?" Lenny asked.

"Looking for work, son. Drove down to Louisville."

"Are you done selling church envelopes?"

Dad whistled long and low. "Yes I am. Couldn't stand another minute of it."

"Were you on a bender?" Lenny asked.

Dad whirled toward Mom. "What'd he say?"

She laughed, but it was a hard sound, with no happiness in it. Lenny tried to think of a distraction. Had he done anything that day worth mentioning? He'd looked for worms under the rain barrel, drank about a gallon of lemonade, sorted his baseball cards, read the latest Spiderman. Why hadn't he done anything exciting? Why hadn't he stopped to think that his dad could come rolling in at any minute? He used to be in the habit of paying closer attention to the things he did, making mental marks next to the ones he might tell his dad about. But with the heat of August bearing down and taking all his energy, he'd forgotten.

"You *could* keep quiet for the good of the children," Dad said.

"Don't speak to me about the good of the children. I'm here raising them."

Lenny spoke up, "So were you on a bender?"

"Lenny, a bender means out drinking," Nell hissed at him. She stood with a glass of lemonade in her hand and made no move to offer it to Dad, just stood there, giving Lenny her look that said *how did I get stuck with a knucklehead brother like you?*

Lenny flushed. Of course it meant drinking. He'd been silly to think a bender was some important job. The things Mom said about Dad always came back to drinking.

"Why don't you work with Uncle Ollie?" Lenny asked. It was a question he'd asked before but he'd never gotten a satisfactory answer. He couldn't see why his dad had to go so far to look for work. His friends' dads all worked right here in Holland. Mr. Van Rhee was a tool and die man, Mr. Reidsma made office furniture, and nearly everyone else he knew was a farmer. If only his dad would stay near home, Lenny was sure he wouldn't drink so much. It was only when he went away and then came back looking dandy that things went bad.

"Do I look like I'm cut out for shit-kicking work like that?"

Lenny didn't know how to answer. It was true his dad didn't look like a farmer, and Lenny was mostly glad that he wasn't one. He disliked the smell, the sad sound the cows made, and the way his uncle was always tired from doing the chores. But in some ways he wished his dad was more like Uncle Ollie. Lenny liked the way Uncle Ollie talked. *I'm going to tell you why these cows aren't milking*, he'd say, and then he'd go and say why. Then later he would ask, *remember what I told you about the cows and why they're not milking?* Lenny found it comforting to have things laid out like that. There were no surprises.

"Do I?" Dad demanded.

"No, sir."

"Spreading manure and pulling on cows' teats are for men with no gumption." Dad stretched his arms above his head and then shook his shoulders out, as if to prove he was ready for a challenge.

"Where's Sally?" he asked.

"She's taking a nap," Nell said. She held out his lemonade and at last he took it and pulled down a long swig.

"Go wake her up."

"No," Mom said. "Unless you're planning to be gone again by dinnertime."

"I oughta go. It'd serve you right."

"Suit yourself."

"What'd you find in Louisville?" Lenny asked. He was concerned about Dad not having work. Even selling church envelopes was better than nothing. Lenny knew it was the man of the family who was supposed to have a job. If his dad wasn't going to work, did that mean Lenny had to do it? He was only eight, but he supposed it was possible. A few boys in his class had paper routes. There was no reason he couldn't get one too.

Mom lifted a glass of lemonade to her lips. "*Who'd* you find is a better question," she muttered.

Dad blew out hard, his lips tight. "You sure know how to make a man feel welcome. And *you*," he said to Lenny, "why do you have to ask so many questions? Look here. I brought you something." He walked over to his car and pulled out a bat.

"Happy birthday," he said, holding it toward Lenny.

"Wow! A Louisville Slugger!"

"That's right. World's most famous bat."

"I hope you brought a little something for the girls," Mom called.

"I'll bring them something next time. A man can't go to Louisville, home of the Slugger, and not pick one up. Besides, it's not *their* birthdays. Right, Nellie?"

"My birthday was in June," Nell mumbled. "You weren't home."

Mom patted her arm and said, "Let's go make some more lemonade."

Lenny watched Nell go inside with her head hung low. For about the thousandth time in his life he wished she were a brother instead of a sister. Then they could share the bat and he wouldn't have to feel bad about getting it. Even if she was a tomboy, that would do, but no, Nell was the most prissy sister a boy could be cursed with.

Lenny grabbed the bat from his father and set it on his shoulder. Before he could take a swing, Dad snatched it away.

"No, like this." He positioned Lenny's hand. "Feel that? That's craftsmanship. These bats have been around since 1884. The first one was made from a piece of white ash for Pete Browning. Folks called him the Old Gladiator."

"Why?"

"Because it sounded good, I suppose."

Lenny stepped away from him, eager to let her fly. Dad wouldn't let go.

"Pay attention. You're going to be the owner of a Louisville Slugger, there are a few things you need to know. See, Pete busted his bat into splinters during a Louisville Eclipse game. There was a young fella named Bud Hillerich in the stands, and he offered to carve Pete a new one. Next day, Browning went three-for-three with the new bat. That was the very first Louisville Slugger."

"Let's go over to the park and hit some pop-ups."

"Lenny, what did I just tell you?"

"You said that Pete fella was glad he ate." Lenny was being silly on purpose, to make his dad laugh. It didn't work.

"*Gladiator.* That's like a soldier. Now how many times have I told you, baseball is nothing to joke about. That's our national past time. What else is it?"

"Greatest game ever created."

"That's right."

"Are we gonna play?"

"In a minute. I'm trying to teach you something here. This is no ordinary bat. Babe Ruth used a Slugger to hit 60 home runs in '27. That's a world record."

"That's nothing," Lenny said, grinning. "I'll be hitting a hundred thousand home runs. In one game, too. Give it here."

"Repeat what I just told you."

"Babe Ruth used a Slugger."

"How many home runs did he hit with it?"

"A lot."

"Sixty. Say it. Sixty."

Lenny said it.

"What year was it?"

"1927."

"No, 1925. You've got to learn to listen, boy."

"I did listen. You said 1927." He might be deaf in one ear, but he knew how to listen. And he always made sure he kept his good ear toward his dad.

Dad shook his head. "I did not say 1927. Now get over there and give it a few swings." He pushed Lenny across the grass. "I'll go get the ball." He turned toward the house, then stopped. "Where is it?"

"Under my bed. In the box."

Dad disappeared inside and Lenny examined the bat. The pale wood was shiny and smooth, soft to his touch. He put his nose to it and breathed in deep. It smelled of dug-outs. He choked up on it.

"Hurry Dad!" Lenny yelled, hoping that after all that talk his dad hadn't lost interest. He was relieved when Dad came out with the ball in his hand. He'd taken off his suit jacket and rolled up his shirtsleeves.

"Now that model you've got there," Dad said, tossing the ball in the air, "that's the same kind Mickey Mantle used to smash one out of Griffin Stadium. What do you think about that?"

Lenny's hands felt electric on the bat. "Griffin Stadium is for babies," he said. "I'll take the bus to Chicago and hit one out of Wrigley Field. It'll fly so far it'll land in Lake Michigan." He hunched over, assuming his stance.

Dad laughed. "Lake Michigan? Why not the Atlantic? You oughta aim higher son."

A quick bitter laugh flew out the window above the kitchen sink. "You're a fine one to talk," Mom called. Her face was a flat pale circle behind the shadow of the screen. Dishes clinked faintly under the sound of running water.

"Was I talking to you?" Dad said. He did a few wind-ups.

The water stopped. Mom's voice came back louder, "Why don't you aim toward some dinner for your children? We've been out of groceries for a week."

Dad raised his voice too. "Don't start with me. Lenny and I are playing baseball."

"Throw it Dad!" Lenny wished his mother would shut up for one minute. Why was she going on about dinner? Who could eat when you had a brand new bat in your hands? If she'd leave them alone they could play and laugh and have a nice time together. His father would keep his good mood, and they might be able to settle in quietly for the evening. After all, it was the day before his birthday. He was the owner of a Louisville Slugger and his dad was about to throw him the ball.

"Mind the house now." Dad pitched and it flew high over Lenny's head. He swung anyway. He couldn't help it. The ball rolled into the bushes in the neighbor's yard.

"Damn! Sun was in my eyes," Dad said. He walked wearily toward Lenny and rested a hand on his back. "Word to the wise, son. Women are put on this earth to torment us. They can't begin to know the pressures a man is under but they bellyache like they've got the world on their shoulders."

"What sort of pressures?"

"What do you mean what sort? Does everything have to be explained to you?" He sighed. "Go get the ball."

He took the bat from Lenny and sliced the air a couple of times, making his back crack twice in little pops. Lenny retrieved the ball and then waited while his dad stretched and groaned with the bat in his hands. Finally Dad stopped swinging and looked at him. He sighed again.

"Finding work, supporting a family," he said, as if Lenny were badgering him. But Lenny had his eyes on the bat. He didn't like the way his dad was hogging it. He held out his hand but Dad didn't seem to notice. Lenny looked up at him. He put on his Spiderman face, making his mouth a thin flat line and sending all his powers out through his eyes. Lenny had big brown eyes that he could keep open, unblinking, for hours and hours, and that was the secret to the Spiderman face. He used it when he felt like sending a secret message into his dad's head, like *stop jabbering and give me the stupid bat!*

"Quit staring at me," Dad snapped.

"Sorry."

"And no more questions. Talk about pressures. *Jeez.*"

"Sorry," Lenny said again, wondering what questions he ever asked except the most ordinary kind. He never said anything about Dad's new clothes. He'd stopped asking, every time his dad went away, *when are you coming back?* He didn't once say *why are you always mad at us? What have we done wrong?* He asked him about baseball or the snow in Canada, or how long it took to drive across one whole state, or whether he knew any truckers.

"Aw, you're a good kid," Dad said. He looked over at the

kitchen window, then bent low over Lenny. "You know what they say, don't you son? Baseball's the only sport where you can go a couple months without scoring and your balls won't hurt." He threw his head back and laughed.

Lenny didn't get it. "I thought you said baseball was nothing to joke about."

Dad sighed, exasperated. "You're a serious little cuss, aren't you?"

Was he? Was it bad to be serious?

"Rich, the girls are hungry," Mom called out.

"I'm playing with my son here!"

"Sally will be up and needing some dinner."

"Goddamn it woman! I'm going." Dad dropped the bat and stomped back to his car without a word to Lenny.

"Can we play when you get back?" Lenny asked, and then, "You are coming back, aren't you?"

"I just got home, didn't I?" Dad said from behind the wheel of the car. He smiled. "I'll get your favorite food for your birthday. Sloppy joes, right?"

Then he revved the car so loudly that Lenny wasn't able to tell him that corn dogs were his favorite now, ever since he went with Uncle Ollie and Aunt Bunny to the State Fair where he ate one while he watched a man in a batting cage hit a ball going 100 miles an hour. Hit it not once, but four times. That was something exciting he could tell his dad about. Or had he already told him? The things he had actually said and the things he wanted to say were hard to keep straight. They blurred together, like the stitches on a fastball flying toward you, with you just hoping to connect.

❧

Later that day, Lenny sat on the front porch, waiting. An hour passed. How long did it take to get some groceries? He began to worry about all the things that might have happened. Dad might have had a car wreck. Wouldn't that be bizarre, to have Dad drive a thousand miles home, then get smucked pulling out of Charlie's Market? But Lenny would have heard the sirens by now. Maybe he went clear across town, to Meijer, to special order Lenny a birthday cake, and he had to wait while they iced a perfect baseball diamond on it. Knowing his dad, it would have to be made to scale, exactly nine inches between bases, or it wouldn't be right. Maybe he passed a burning building and ran in to save some poor baby. He'd be on the front page of tomorrow's paper. Maybe he had another surprise for Lenny, like a new glove to go with the bat. He might have driven to Grand Rapids because he'd want to get the best. Maybe he bumped into an old friend, someone who said *let me buy you a drink ol' pal!*

Maybe he was drunk.

Why? Why today? Couldn't Lenny enjoy one lousy day with his dad?

Lenny was no fun. Dad said it himself. He racked his brain for a good joke. Nothing. He couldn't come up with a single thing, not even a knock-knock joke. There had to be *something* that would make his dad laugh. He could do an impression of the way his gym teacher ran with her knees knocking together. That always made the kids at school laugh.

Trouble was, he was feeling far from funny. Each hour that passed and Dad didn't come back, it was all he could do to keep from crying. He'd show him. If he couldn't be funny, he'd be serious in a way that mattered. He'd break the world record for porch-sitting, if there was one. If there wasn't, there would be after tonight. He had a Guinness book in his room. There must be a phone number in it. Nell could call and have them send out their scout. When Dad came back he'd find all the neighbors gathered around, cheering for Lenny. They'd hang banners from the trees. *Way to go, Lenny! Hang in there!* Reporters from the Sentinel would scramble for an interview. Dad would have to push through the crowd. *Lemme through, that's my son!*

When he came back.

He said he'd be back. He *said.* He *said.* He'd brought the bat, hadn't he? Around and around, Lenny twisted that bat in his hand. He considered giving up his post and heading over to his friend Willie's house to show him the Slugger. Then he remembered what Willie had told him a couple of weeks earlier. Willie went to visit his grandma in California, and they went to a place called Knotts' Berry Farm. Willie bragged that he saw how movies are made.

"When you see John Wayne walking down the street, just before the gun fight, and you see those buildings behind him? They're fake. Flat as a pancake. You can walk around them and there's nothing there."

That was about the last thing Lenny wanted to hear. Now every time he watched a movie, it was ruined. Seeing his dad lately was like seeing those buildings. Stupid Willie. If he thought he'd ever get to try Lenny's Slugger, he was dead wrong.

Finally Lenny went inside and found his mother folding laundry on the kitchen table. His mother, who was always serious, always boring.

"Why'd you have to drive him away?" he snapped.

She looked at him, surprised. "I know you're disappointed."

"You don't know anything! You ruined my birthday and you don't even care."

She sighed and came around the table, reaching for him, but

he ducked away.

"I hate you! And I hate my stupid birthday. I wish I was never born."

He ran to his room and slammed the door. There was a mirror over his dresser that caught his reflection. There's the joke. Lenny Van Sloeten. *Hardy har har!* Winner of the world record for stupidity. He punched his pillow a few times, then put it over his face. One serious cry was all he'd allow, only because he was still seven. Come midnight he was done being a baby.

It was ten p.m. and Lenny was in the kitchen getting a Nehi grape soda from the icebox. Mom had gotten three bottles for his birthday. She made him promise he'd drink no more than one a day, and here he was, going for the second. Well, he needed one. He'd sat all day in the hot sun on the front porch, and for what? Just to be reminded, as if he needed reminding, that he had the world's worst life. Being a year older wouldn't mean a damn thing. Dad was probably never coming back, and even if he did, he'd leave again anyway. The way Lenny figured it, he was the man of the house now, so if he wanted fifty sodas, he'd sure as hell help himself. He was closing his hand around the cool wet neck of the Nehi bottle when the kitchen door rattled. Turning, he saw a wide-eyed, grizzled face pressed against the black window. With a shriek he dropped the bottle and it cracked open, sending a purple puddle across the floor.

"Hey there. Open up," came a slurred, furry voice. Dad! Drunk or not, here he was. Lenny should have known he wouldn't miss his birthday. He looked down at the mess on the floor and, picking his way gingerly over the broken glass, moved toward the door. He was one step from it when his mother came in.

"Stop!" she said. "He's not coming in if he's been drinking."

Leave it to her to ruin everything again. So Dad had a few drinks. So what? Chances were he'd sit for a cup of coffee and babble some nonsense about market shares or steel-belted tires. Or he might explain to Lenny the value of recognizing a sound investment. He'd tell him to keep his ears open, and Lenny would imagine that if only he weren't deaf in one ear he'd be able to locate a sound investment for his dad. If Lenny tried to tell him about how his teacher, Mr. Vollmer, passed his false teeth around the class, or about the arrowhead Lenny found at the beach, Dad might wave him away with his hand. One time he fell right off to sleep, snoring in the middle of Lenny's sentence. But other times he might listen. He might get excited at the mention of Marvin Haas' go-cart or the new gas pump at the Stop-n-Go and slap Lenny on the back as if he'd just answered the $64,000 question. Tonight might be one of those times.

"What's the hold-up?" Dad hiccuped.

"You're soused and I won't have you around the children! Go to your brother's and sleep it off."

"So I'm a little late." Dad's face mushed up against the glass.

"How could you?" she asked through clenched teeth. "It's Lenny's birthday. And you," she said, pointing at Lenny, "what is this mess?"

"I dropped a pop. And my birthday's tomorrow, so let him in."

"Absolutely not."

"Is that Dad?" Nell asked, coming in. Sally was behind her,

rubbing her eyes with a tiny balled-up fist.

"Daddy?" Sally said. She squinted suspiciously at the window.

Mom held her arm up to keep the girls out. "Your father's not feeling well and can't come in right now," she said. "Nellie, help me clean up Lenny's mess."

"You mean he's drunk," Nell said.

Dad pounded on the door. "Prudy, this isn't funny. I've got to relieve myself."

"No one's stopping you."

"Fine. I'll piss on this geranium."

"Mom!" whined Nell. "I just re-potted that!"

"One of you kids open the door," he said. He pressed his forehead against the glass so his skin looked like a piece of stretched-out Silly Putty. "Lenny. Come on, son. I came home just to see you."

Lenny started forward, forgetting the spilled pop and broken glass. They could have a real ball game tomorrow. He'd invite Willie and Mark, and the new kid from down the street.

"Don't you move!" his mother said. Lenny stopped. "I told your father I was going to start locking it." She looked toward the patch of skin on the window. "And I said no more drinking."

Dad's eyes floated up, looking watery and unreal. "Please," he said. "It's nearly nine. I want to listen to Cronkite."

"You want a newsflash? You're not getting in this house, not now, not ever. This is the last straw."

"It's past nine anyway," Nell said. There was silence. Dad's face disappeared. They waited.

Then he spoke, his voice in a sing-song. "I've got chicken cutlets."

"Mmm. Yummy." Sally clapped her hands together.

"What happened to sloppy joes?" Lenny asked, disappointed that Dad had forgotten. If he forgot that then he probably forgot about the bat he'd given him. He probably had no intention of playing ball with him tomorrow. The fact that Lenny was turning eight might have slipped his mind, too. Most likely he didn't even remember he had a son. Lenny who?

"Get back to your rooms, all of you," Mom said. "I'll clean this pop up myself."

But they didn't go. They watched the window. They heard the door creak as Dad shifted his weight against it.

"*Let. Me. In*," Dad said, angry now.

With a sigh Mom went to the door, but only to pull the curtain shut. Just then Dad said "Dammit!" and rapped his fist hard on the window, breaking it. A shard of glass, thin and pointy as an icicle, fell onto Mom's bare foot and stuck there, straight up. Blood squirted with remarkable force, spraying a fan of red specks across the floor and wall. She cried out. So did Lenny and Sally, but not Nell.

"Hit a vein," Nell said. She rushed to Mom, kneeling over her foot. The blood pulsed out again before Nell pulled the glass out and pushed her thumb over the cut.

"Throw a rag over, Lenny," she said, but Lenny was afraid to move. Now there was more glass on the floor, plus the blood and purple soda pop. Mom leaned back heavily on the counter.

"Lenny!" Nell said.

He took a giant step to the sink, grabbed a rag, and turned to throw it. Dad was already reaching through the broken window and fumbling open the lock. He staggered in and grabbed Mom's arm.

"Damn you Prudy," he said, pressing his thumb into her arm until her mouth opened in a silent gasp. *Oh no.* It was a mean drunk. Please, not a mean one. If only Lenny had known! But the mean ones hardly ever happened. Lenny could only remember two, maybe three times before when Dad had come home and gone sulking straight into the bedroom. Then the shouting would begin, but it was always hidden away, and Lenny could run out back and throw the tennis ball against the garage if it was daytime, or put his pillow over his head and his transistor radio, full static, against his ear if it was at night.

"Lenny! Give that here," demanded Nell, because Lenny still held tight to the rag. He felt slow and clumsy. Not like Nell, who looked steady and calm. She even seemed unaware of Dad right behind her, his nails digging into Mom's arm. Did she realize Dad was on a mean one? How could she not notice the loose cuffs of his shirt, or the dirt caked on his shoes, or his smell? Lenny tossed the rag into Nell's hand. Maybe he was overreacting. But there was glass everywhere, by the icebox, by the door, and blood and grape soda and who would take care of cleaning this up? Lenny pushed Sally into the living room, away from the mess, and opened the hall closet to get the broom. Before he could get it there was Nell, already grabbing it, so there was nothing for Lenny to do but watch as his mother eased herself into a chair and Nell started to sweep.

"Where'd you go, Dad?" Lenny asked. He wanted to distract him so he'd let go of Mom's arm. It worked. Dad groaned as he scraped a chair back and sat down heavily.

"Had some business. Unexpected stuff. You understand."

"You kids get back to bed," Mom said, holding the rag to her foot. There was a perfect circle of red where the blood had soaked through.

"Need a Band-Aid, Mommy?" Sally asked, her voice wavering tearfully.

"Thanks honey, but we don't have any. I'll be fine."

"Are we going to eat?" she asked, pointing to the cutlets.

"We had our supper," Mom said.

"Mayonnaise sandwiches. Yuck. I'm still hungry."

"Fry up this chicken then," said Dad, throwing the butcher's package on the table. "We may as well eat again. It's Lenny's birthday, after all."

"Tomorrow," Lenny said, but no one listened.

Mom's eyes were narrow and mean. "I'm not cooking."

Lenny held his breath but Dad only sighed and rubbed his face. Maybe it wasn't a mean drunk, after all. Dad just seemed tired.

"Cook the chicken," he said. Reasonable-like.

"I could eat a decent supper," Lenny said quickly. It didn't feel right, expecting Mom to cook with her foot hurt, but she must know that he was asking for *her*, for all of them. If Dad *was* in a mean mood, the best thing was to act as normal as possible.

"I'm going to bed." Mom started to get up.

"Yeah. It's bedtime, not suppertime," Nell said.

But they could pretend. "Hey, we could find some candles," Lenny said. "Make like a midnight birthday celebration."

"You better put something over that window," Mom said, standing.

"Sit down," Dad said, still friendly sounding.

Mom walked out.

"Prudy, get back here!" Dad yelled, his face reddening. "And cook the goddamn chicken!"

"Cook it yourself!"

"Prudy! Get the *fuck* in here!"

Mom reappeared. "Watch your mouth," she said, pointing a finger at him. "You come tooling up with those expensive shoes and act like we should all be happy to see you. You're nothing but an overgrown child, and I've got enough children to take care of."

Dad shoved the chicken on the floor. "I paid good money for this! I put this roof over your heads, and if I want a pair of new shoes, which, by the way, were *on sale*, and which I need for my *profession*, then..."

"Oh, save it." She disappeared down the hall. Dad jumped to his feet and went after her. They heard the bedroom door slam.

"You dumb head," Lenny said to Nell.

"Shut up and help me." Nell dropped to her knees and started wiping up the blood.

The sight of it made Lenny sick. "I'll put Sally in bed," he said.

"There's lots of it," Sally said, staring. Lenny had to take her hand and pull her down the hall. They passed their parents' closed door and Lenny heard the sound of drawers being slammed.

"You're not afraid of blood, are you?" he asked.

"Are you?" Sally said.

"Naw. It's messy, that's all." He put her in bed and threw her baby quilt over her, the one with silly looking cows all over it. Snoring, sleepy cows with long curling eyelashes and the words *dream a little dream*.

"I don't like messy things," she said.

"Then why are you always playing in the mud?"

"That's different. That's brown."

Lenny nodded as if it made perfect sense. "Go to sleep."

She shook her head. "Too loud."

He went to his room and grabbed his transistor radio. He hated to wear down the batteries, but he brought it to Sally's room and laid it on her pillow. She grabbed it earnestly and put it to her ear.

Lenny went back to his room and picked up his Slugger. He sat on his bed listening. He could hear Dad's voice. Something something *don't you* something *if you ever.* Then his mom, loud. *Stay. Away. From. Me.* There was a flurry of noise and a snarling, achy cry, like a cat being thrown against a wall. Lenny stood up. Why didn't Dad stop? Mom was already hurt. That blood, and the way it shot out of her foot. He'd never seen that before. She'd probably have to have a tetanus shot. Or was that only when you stepped on a nail? What if her foot got full of gangrene and had to be amputated? Then she'd be in a wheelchair and Lenny would spend the rest of his life pushing her around. He'd have to, since all this was his fault. He should have said something, *anything*, to make Dad go away. Make him go sleep it off, just like Mom said. Except Lenny didn't want him to go away.

He went to the doorway. Nell was standing in the hall, the broom in her hand. They looked at each other.

"It's her own fault," Lenny whispered. He didn't mean it. Mom did her best to provide for them, working 10 hours a day at the factory, taking in laundry from the rich folks who lived on Lake Macatawa, plus showing up at church for every single service, singing "I've Got a Mansion Just Over the Hilltop" in her clear, unfaltering way. All this, while Lenny tormented his sisters, threw spitballs at girls in school, never knew his Bible verses, and even stole bubble gum from the downtown Woolworth's. If anyone deserved punishment, it was Lenny. Come on, hit *me*! he wanted to yell at his father. But Dad never hit them, only Mom.

"What are we going to do?" Nell asked. It scared him,

hearing that. She was always the one taking charge.

"He'll probably pass out soon," Lenny said.

Then they heard it. A sickening thud, like a body hitting a wall. The bed creaking. A muffled cry. *Help.* Mom calling for help.

"Do something!" Nell said. "Make him stop!"

"*You* do something!"

"No, you. He likes you."

Lenny felt a rush of pleasure. Dad liked him. So couldn't Lenny just open the door, *hey Dad, what's up?* Couldn't he say something a man might say, like *we got ourselves a big day tomorrow, breaking in the new bat and all. How about getting some sleep?*

He still had his bat in his hand. He could carry it in, just to show Dad, just to remind him of their plans tomorrow. And if Dad didn't listen, if he didn't stop whatever it was he was doing, then Lenny would have the bat to....well, to what?

"Hurry!" Nell cried.

Lenny lifted the bat. It was heavy, unbelievably heavy. He stepped toward the closed door, tripping over the leg of his pajamas. He hiked them with one hand, and reached for the knob. Nell cowered behind him as he eased open the door. There was Dad, on his knees on the bed, his pants unbuckled. He had one hand on Mom's throat. She was thrashing, kicking at him. Dad's hand was raised. There was a bottle of vodka on the dresser.

"Stop, Dad," Lenny croaked.

Dad turned. His hair, always so neatly slicked back, was flopping over his eyes. "Get out!" he said.

"Lenny," Mom whispered. Her head was smashed sideways into the pillow. She looked at him with one eye. "Put the bat down."

"Why'd you have to mention the shoes?" Lenny asked.

"Put the bat down."

Lenny looked at the bat. He had it in both hands. A good strong grip. Mom thought he was going to use it. Why else would she tell him to put it down? He stepped forward, trying not to notice his dad's unzipped trousers, the contorted legs of his mom, or the way her dress was bunched up, binding her arms like a straightjacket. Dad's hand came down across his mom's face.

"Shut up!" Dad leaned over, grabbed the table lamp and flung it against the wall above the bed.

Nell screamed and Mom let out a long wail as pieces of the lamp fell down around her.

"Look what you made me do! You think I like this?" He pushed on Mom's throat. "Huh? *Do* you? You think I want my kids seeing this?"

Nell was sobbing, "Stop! Please stop!"

She pushed Lenny hard and he raised the bat. He had to do something. Mom couldn't breath. He started to cry, and then he swung. It was more like a practice swing than a bases loaded, full count kind of swing. It was more of a poke. The bat landed in the soft part of his father's side, just between the ribs and the hip, so there was not the crack Lenny feared. It sounded quiet, dull.

His dad fell sideways off the bed, landing on his rear end on the floor. He looked up, surprised. Mom scrambled off the bed.

"Jesus Christ!" Dad stared at Lenny, dazed. "You've been practicing your swing. I didn't mean on *me*."

"Why are you doing that?" Lenny asked. He tensed, ready to run if Dad came after him, but Dad only struggled to his hands and knees. He seemed unable to go any farther.

"Who asked you two to barge in here?" Dad said, breathing hard. "Didn't your mother teach you any manners?"

Mom stumbled to the door, crying. "I'm calling the police," she said.

Dad was trying to unwind his pants from around his ankles. "Look, I got a little carried away."

"Nell, call 911. Hurry!" Mom pulled at her dress and her hair. There was blood in the corner of her mouth. She made a quick lunge for Lenny like she was snatching him back from the edge of a cliff. He felt her shaking as she pressed him against her.

"Get out, Richard" she said, sobbing. "We don't want to see you again, ever."

Dad made an annoyed sound.

"If I leave now I'm never coming back. I'm fed up with this shit. How much is a man expected to take?"

Mom was squeezing Lenny's neck. It hurt. "They'll put you in jail," she cried. "I swear."

Dad laughed. "What do you say, Lenny? Think you can stand living here all alone with these hysterical women?"

Mom wiped her hand across her mouth. "He's survived so far. No thanks to you."

"Well?" Dad stared at him.

Lenny could go with Dad. They could ride the highways together. They could stay away from girls and there'd be no trouble. There'd be no Nell. No Sally. No Mom.

"Guess you'd better leave," Lenny said finally. For now. Not forever.

"What'd you say?"

Lenny didn't answer. He kept his eyes on the floor so the

only thing he could see was Dad's stocking feet. Where were the brand new shoes Dad was so proud of? Was he sober enough to put them up after a quick polish, or did he toss them off his feet, one behind the bed, the other in the hamper?

"Gimme back the Slugger then," Dad said. He held out his hand. Lenny hugged the bat.

"Don't torture the boy," Mom said. "Just get out."

"You're right. I'm no Indian giver." Dad leaned down so his face was level with Lenny's. Lenny saw how his head bobbed, up and down, up and down. Lenny could tap him once and down he'd come.

"You enjoy that bat son. Too bad I won't be here to have a game with you."

Nell rushed into the room. "I called. Police are coming."

Dad threw up his hands. "Great! Respectable salesman gets thrown out of his house after a long stint on the road. That's rich."

He stumbled past them in his stocking feet, wearing his T-shirt and wrinkled trousers. He stopped in front of Nell and held out his hand. She hesitated before taking it.

"Have a nice life, young lady," he said, as he pumped her hand once hard. He grabbed the suitcase that sat unopened by the bedroom door, and bumped his way through the kitchen.

"I know when I'm not wanted," they heard him mutter. "Sweet dreams, loved ones!"

The door slammed.

"Bye Dad," Lenny said, but Mom was hugging his head and his words were mushed into her stomach.

They listened, not moving, as the car revved up and peeled out.

"It's okay," Mom said, over and over. She pulled a housecoat over her dress and went to wait by the front door. When the officer arrived, she sent him away. Next, she pulled some tools out of the junk drawer and unscrewed a seat from one of the kitchen chairs. She hammered nails through the screw holes in the seat into the wood around the window, covering the hole where the window had been. It didn't cover it completely, but enough to keep a hand from reaching in.

Lenny and Nell stood watching her. They looked at each other once but it was no good. It made Lenny go all crumbly. He bit the inside of his cheek and rubbed the warm wood of his bat. The part where Dad first handed him the Slugger kept playing in his head. How could things be so good, and go so bad? How could he get that moment back?

When Mom finished, she disappeared down the hall and came back carrying Sally over her shoulder.

"What'd you wake her up for?" Lenny asked.

"Come here," Mom said. She turned on the living room light and sat on the sofa, gathering all of them to her.

"You kids are all I've got."

And there they sat, waiting. For what, Lenny couldn't say.

He tried to tell himself that he'd saved his mom. But all he could think of was the way Nell had acted when the glass went into Mom's foot. Why should she be able to move so fast, when he barely had time to take a breath? Barely had time to stop noticing how Mom's blood flung itself across the kitchen onto the potato bin—how could blood travel so far?—and here was Nell, already mopping it up. But he'd done something she couldn't. How would she like to swing a bat and hit another person? How would she like to stand up to Dad? Or live knowing she was the one who made him leave? Dad had asked if Lenny could stand living here with all these girls. What could he stand? He could stand on his head. He could stand a boiled egg on end. He could even stand a raw egg on end with a little salt. He could stand up for Jesus, the way he was taught in Sunday School. Could he stand living all alone? Or live standing on a stone? He nearly giggled like a girl. They were rubbing off on him already.

He could see the clock and when midnight came he was still awake. This was the real nightmare, this sitting. And knowing. *Come back Dad!* He felt like crying, but he'd already had his one good cry, so he was done. He was eight years old now. The man of the house.

It was a warm spring afternoon near the end of Lenny's senior year. Lenny was walking home swinging his Slugger, feeling mighty fine after a 9-2 win over the Reese Puffer Spartans. It was fucking hi-*larious* the way their third baseman thought he could read Lenny's windups. The sucker squared up for a line drive and Lenny dropped in the slider to win the game. Ding dong. And that was in addition to the triple he scored.

He sure wished people would call him Slugger. What'd a person have to do to get a nickname around here? He was just *too* talented, that was the problem. If all he did was hit in the runs, then he'd be Slugger. But he was the best pitcher the Holland High Flying Dutchmen had seen in years, too. Not a bad problem to have, considering. He was smiling over this when he ran into a girl from school named Rhoda Raymond. She was sitting in the middle of the sidewalk, her dirty bare legs blocking Lenny's path.

"Can you stop a minute Lenny?" Rhoda mumbled. She didn't look up.

"You talking to me?" Rhoda was three years younger than him, the same age as his little sister Sally. He barely knew her.

"'Course I'm talking to you. You see anyone else around?"

She was bold. Didn't she know? He was the pitcher of the varsity team. And who was she? Nobody.

"What do you want?"

"Sit down here a minute."

"I'm in my uniform, in case you haven't noticed. I'm on the baseball team."

"It's already dirty, so what's the big deal?"

"I'm not sitting on the sidewalk! Stand up if you have something to say."

Rhoda got to her feet so laboriously Lenny was sorry he'd asked.

"I've got something to tell you," she said, pushing her long brown bangs out of her eyes.

"What would that be?" he asked cautiously. *God, she's got a crush on me.* Of course he'd attract some slow-witted oddball like Rhoda. Why couldn't it be one of the pom-pom girls stopping him in the street? He always thought he might snag himself a cheerleader if they had a squad for the baseball team. Why did the football jocks get all the fun?

"I saw your daddy," Rhoda said.

It took a second to register. *Your daddy.* Those were words that didn't come his way too often. Besides, only a baby talked like that.

"What do you mean?"

"Your daddy was at my house."

Lenny shook his head. "My dad doesn't live around here,"

he said. But he had no idea where his dad lived. What if after all these years it turned out he was here all along? What if he watched Lenny play ball? What if he was there today, at the game? Wouldn't he be impressed! Lenny felt a rush of excitement before he remembered. Oh *right*. This is real life. Not la-la land.

"Maybe he was visiting," Rhoda said.

"Visiting who? Your mother?" The hair on Lenny's neck pricked up. Rhoda's mother was a loose woman. Everyone said so. She and Rhoda lived alone in a shack next to the blueberry fields. She was known to go with the Mexican migrant workers who came to pick the berries. Surely his dad couldn't sink that low.

Lenny's dad had always been a salesman. Maybe he happened by Rhoda's house trying to sell a set of steak knives, or encyclopedias, or a vacuum cleaner, or television set. The possibilities were endless. But what kind of salesman would bother stopping at those shit hole shacks out there?

"I walked in on them," Rhoda said. "I get these headaches, see, and I've got a note to go home whenever I get one. I went in and they were naked on the couch. My mama screamed at me to get out."

Lenny scoffed. "No offense, but my dad isn't Mexican. He's not your mom's type."

She shrugged. "So you say."

There was something about her face. It had a blank, open look. An honest face, you might call it. Or stupid.

"How would you know my dad, anyway? Heck, I wouldn't know him if he bit me in the ass."

That was a lie, but he was trying to make a joke of it. Goddamn it, didn't she know he was giving her an out, a chance to say, you're right, I don't know your father from Adam? Rhoda just went on looking at him, but now her chin was going all quavery. One look at that chin and his hope that this was a joke went out the window.

"Go on home, you crybaby." He gave her a little shove with one arm, not hard, but insistent. His heart was pounding. Could it be? After ten years, could he really be back?

"I thought you'd care," she sniffed.

"Are you retarded or something? I told you, my dad doesn't live around here. You didn't see him at your house. Got it?" Lenny stepped around her and started walking away. He had to remember who he was talking to, Rhoda roach-head Raymond, queen of the lowlifes.

"My mama came out looking for me in the field. She told me he was an old friend. They went to grade school together, she said. Told me his name was Richard Van Sloeten."

Lenny stopped and looked back at her, taking in her dirt-streaked legs, a crusty scab on her knee, the pitiful look on her face. Why would she say such a thing about her own mother? He got a sinking feeling. The way she looked at him was like she wanted a buddy. Like they shared something. A sickening, sleazy common bond, but a bond all the same. Except that he wasn't like her and never would be.

"Why are you telling me?"

"He's around a lot now. Either at my house or at the Torchlight saloon. Thought you might want to know."

"I don't. In fact, if I hear that you're spreading this horseshit around, I'll pound you good."

Rhoda wiped her nose with the back of her hand. "I don't like him. I don't like you neither. You're just as mean as he is."

"Get lost!"

Rhoda turned and walked away, her long tangled hair falling down her back. Lenny watched her go. She moved so slowly he wished he could whip at the back of her legs with a stick or a wet towel to get her moving. He'd like to tip her like a cow. He considered chasing her. Instead he yelled "Hey Rhoda!" He meant to flip her off, or raise his bat threateningly over his head. But as she stood looking at him, so patient, so beaten down, he couldn't do it. She waited, finally tucking a piece of hair behind her ear.

Forcing nonchalance, Lenny asked, "Was he drunk? I mean, was this guy drunk?"

Rhoda shrugged her shoulders. "Suppose so." She looked hopeful for a moment. "Wanna come home with me? Maybe he'll be there."

"What'd I just tell you? What are you, crazy?"

She shrugged again. "Just scared," she said, looking straight at him, with no embarrassment. Lenny was stunned. To admit out loud like that, to a near stranger, that you're afraid, well, Lenny had never seen that done before. He was a little impressed. Still, she was nothing but white trash. He dropped his eyes and she walked away.

So the bastard was back. So what? It was no concern of his. He'd long since given up on the babyish idea that his dad would show up saying *I've missed you.* That he would have some spectacular reason for not coming sooner. *Son, I'm dying. I wanted to spare you seeing me like this. But I couldn't stay away. Not a moment longer.* Or he'd make a gentle reference to the bad scene that had played out that last day. *I couldn't come back until I had something to offer you. Something worthy to make up for what I put you through.* He'd hand over the keys to a brand new car. *It took me ten years but I finally saved enough to buy you this car. I love you, son.*

Okay, so maybe Lenny had stayed in the room a few times when Nell was watching her soap opera. He knew how it sounded. Like bullshit. His dad was still a drunk, screwing white trash. Nothing had changed.

Everything had changed.

Lenny turned his Louisville Slugger around in his hands. It was ten years since his dad had given it to him. Ten years since he'd used it to make his dad leave. He remembered the way it had felt in his hands that night when it landed in his father's side. He remembered the horrifying thrill it gave him to see his father bent double.

Suddenly Lenny turned and hurled the bat with all his might into the street. It bounced twice and landed on the opposite side, in the gutter. He jammed his hands in his pockets and went to retrieve it. It was still in one piece, nearly good as new. Lenny picked it up and cradled it tenderly, frightened at how close he'd come to destroying the only possession he really cared about.

The only weapon he had.

There were three things Lenny wanted to be: a baseball player, a boat builder, and a hippie. He had the best arm Holland High had seen in years. ERA of 2.59. Was a hell of a slugger too. But by some freakish curse that made sure his life stayed shitty for as long as possible, the college scouts hadn't come. Now it was almost over. There was one game left, and Lenny needed to keep his head in it if he wanted to finish the year with a record 20 wins. He was still hoping against hope for a scholarship, maybe not to the University of Michigan like he wanted, but maybe to Central or Eastern. Just to play, that was his dream. Then it'd be on to the minors. The Lansing Lugnuts, maybe the Detroit Whitecaps.

It seemed like a long shot, but easier at least than becoming a boat builder. To do that you needed to go to school and learn mathematics or physics or some other icks, or else you had to know the kinds of people who hung out at the marina and hope they could hook you up over at Chris Craft boat company. He didn't know anyone.

That left the hippie thing. Being a hippie didn't take much except attitude, which Lenny had plenty of. And although he wasn't 100 percent sure about what a hippie did, he figured he'd spend the summer growing his hair and acting spacey to see if it took. He had options. Not promising ones, maybe, but there was no reason to panic. There was no reason to care about what Rhoda had said. She might as well have told him about the life stages of a dung beetle. That's how little it affected him. So why did he feel like a stupid kid standing in the doorway of a small stuffy room, heart pounding, not knowing what the hell to do? How did he explain the sudden urge he had to go out for a beer, when it was his secret vow to never go near alcohol? He knew if he did he'd become his dad. He had the same gene for being a drunk, he just knew it. He could feel it simmering in him, waiting to come to life. Still, he kept thinking about the Torchlight. A cold, frosty beer at the Torchlight sure sounded good.

You might say he'd been waiting ten years for this. Seeing his dad again. How many times had he imagined it? There had always been that plan taking up space in his head, the one so fixed that every other thought he'd had since he was eight had to crowd around it. It started with a great big IF. *If Dad comes back I won't fall for his big-guy routine. I won't listen to his excuses. I'll make him pay.* The way he saw it was like a good John Wayne movie. Lenny would sidle up beside his dad, just a stranger out of a crowd, and give him a stare. He wouldn't need to say who he was. His dad would know. Lenny would be brief. *What's your business?* (He always heard a high, whistling wind start up here.) His dad would meet his stare. *Just passin' through*, he'd say. But Lenny wouldn't blink, not once. *Let's keep it that way.* His plan never took this other stuff into account. The humiliation of his dad being with Rhoda's mom. The humiliation of people knowing. His baseball career petering out with nothing more than a whimper.

He had to show him. Now that he knew that any minute he might run into his dad — jeez, the guy in the beat-up Buick pulling out of the Amoco might be him —he had to *be* something. He had to have a story. *Whatcha been up to?* I'm taking the Amtrak to San Francisco. Expand my horizons. Or, better yet, I'm a starter for the Wolverines. His dad would be darn near awestruck at Lenny's baseball ability. Except now baseball was nearly over and his dad would miss it all.

He did have one more game left. One more chance for his dad to see him play. He could head over to the Torchlight right after practice. He knew where it was. He could walk it in less than an hour.

Only how would that work? He couldn't exactly warn his dad to stay away from them, then invite him to a ball game. His dad would have to be the one to suggest it. Lenny would shrug. Suit yourself. Then if his dad showed up in the stands, he'd pitch the best game of his life. His slider, his curve ball, his fast ball. Whoa! Wait until his dad saw his fast ball! If the wind was right

Lenny could deliver 90 mph.

He just knew that if his dad had stayed around he would have been scouted. His dad would have made sure. He might even have had a shot at the minor leagues. Hell, he might have graduated top of his class. He might have gotten a fucking Harvard scholarship, if he'd had a dad like everyone else. He wondered if his dad remembered his deaf ear. How did he know Lenny wasn't going to be drafted? He might be shipped to Vietnam any day now for all his dad knew. Would he really let his only son be blown to smithereens without as much as a goodbye?

He almost wished he *was* shipping out. At least that would be something definite. It would give him a reason to go to the Torchlight. Instead of a baseball uniform, he'd be in Army green. Just as impressive. Lenny would see his dad and act surprised. *What a coincidence seeing you here, considering I'm shipping out tomorrow.* A situation like that, his dad would have to wish him well. *Go get the gooks*, his dad would say. *And come back safe.*

But Lenny had a bum ear. He wouldn't be a soldier. He wouldn't be a boat builder either. He'd missed out on a baseball scholarship. And being a hippy was nothing to brag about. What was left for him? Who was he? If he could just sort it all out, he'd be waltzing into the Torchlight right now. Forget the Torchlight. He'd go straight to Rhoda's and knock on the door. Catch his dad with his pants down. Again.

The scrap metal yard behind the Louis Padnos factory

wasn't a good place to be at dusk. Great hulking automobile carcasses loomed high against the pale sky, leaning and moaning like living things, threatening to come tumbling down. Broken glass crunched underfoot. Headlights lay strewn about, torn from their sockets, making Lenny feel as if he was being watched. What a joke. He was nobody. Invisible man.

School was done. There was nothing to do but hang out. Hide out was more like it. He'd be remembered as one of the best players Holland High had ever had who never went anywhere. Talk about going down in flames.

He used his bat to pound a dent in an old fender. God, he loved that bat. People thought of Lenny Van Sloeten, they thought of the bat. *Hell of a pitcher, and boy, can he knock a line drive too.* Not that it mattered anymore. He was finished. Washed up. He'd let Hamilton score nine runs and there went his record. He should never have gone to the team picnic. Coach hands him a chintzy little gold trophy and acts angry when Lenny doesn't shake his hand. He's supposed to say thank you when his life's dream comes to this?

Screw the Dutchmen. Screw his small town coach for not making sure he got scouted. He didn't need them. And he sure as hell didn't need to put on a paper cap and prissy gown and get up in front of the whole school just because everyone expected it. What if Rhoda didn't keep her mouth shut? He'd walk across the stage and people would start whispering. *Did you hear? His dad is fucking Rhoda's mom! His dad is back in town and never even went to visit him.*

So he blew off the graduation ceremony. Big deal. His mom cried. He felt bad about that, but she didn't know he was doing if for her and Nell and Sally. They didn't need to know Dad was back in town. They might get all emotional. *What does it mean?*

Do you suppose he's changed? Is he thinking of us? Will we be seeing him?

They wouldn't see him if Lenny had anything to do with it. He cracked his bat against another fender. He needed to get his head together. But instead of figuring out what to do, all he could think was *why do things have to end?* Why couldn't he stay a senior forever, pitching for the Dutchmen? And why couldn't he have found out about his dad three months ago? He could have been wearing his letter jacket. *What's with the jacket?* Dad would ask. *I lettered in baseball, three years straight.*

Hell, his dad wouldn't even recognize him. Nobody recognized him, or his talent, or his plans. People only saw him when he was on the mound, and that was over. There was nothing left for him now. He had to get out of town. Except even leaving was ruined now. Lenny could never go if there was a chance his old man would show up and start beating on his mom again. It seemed unlikely, after all this time, but who could be sure? He had to protect his mother and his sisters. That had always been his real job. Now it was show time.

Okay, then. He'd start at the Torchlight, and if he had to, he'd go to Rhoda's. But there was no use getting all dewy-eyed. It was going to be hard, it would go terribly, and he'd feel like shit after. Get used to it.

He was leaning against a half rotted steel-belt tire chucking rocks through the back window of a demolished Chevy when he heard the unmistakable laugh of Cash DeVries. Cash played third base for Holland Christian. Thought he was hot shit. The truth was he was pretty damn good, and only a junior too, so he had another year to play. Lenny should have known by the empty beer bottles that he wasn't the only one coming here. Probably the whole baseball team would show up next.

He tossed a rock up over a scrap pile toward their voices. There was a moment of silence as the boys stopped.

"What was that?"

"Sounded like someone threw a rock."

"Who's there?"

Lenny threw another. Ping! It bounced off a metal barrel.

"John Thomas? That you?"

Lenny waited, still as a rail. The boys were quiet. How long would they wait? Lenny threw another in the opposite direction. Just then a voice behind him made him jump. The other kid, Martin Beyer, had sneaked around behind him.

"Over here, Cash. It's Lenny Van Sloeten."

Cash clamored over a small metal heap. "What are you doing out here?" he asked.

"Same thing you are. Whole lotta nothing."

"You're out here by yourself? That's kinda creepy."

"I'm a creepy kind of guy."

Cash and Martin both laughed. "You can say that again," Cash said.

Why didn't they like him? They were all ball players. Even blowing that last game didn't change the fact that Lenny was good. Jealous, that's what they were.

"This where you do your batting practice?" Cash asked, motioning toward the Slugger.

"What's the point now? You're done," Martin said.

"Turn me over, I'm cooked," Cash said, and the two of them laughed.

"I've got a better record than you'll ever have," Lenny said. What a stupid thing to say! He sounded like a baby.

"Sure Lenny. You had a good run," Cash said, all condescending.

"Lemme see the bat," Martin said.

Lenny hugged it close. "Not a chance."

"Didn't you know Marty? That's his blankie you're talking about. You probably sleep with it, huh?"

Lenny felt his face go red.

Martin howled and pointed. "He does!"

"What else you do with it?" Cash said.

"He humps it!" Martin shrieked.

Cash began gyrating his hips. "Uh huh…ooohh."

"You're sick," Lenny said.

"Just a little cough, is all. But thanks for your concern."

"Sick in the head, is what I meant."

Cash smiled. "Thanks."

"And you're ugly too."

Cash and Martin looked at each other.

"We're taking off Lenny," Cash said. "Have fun here all by yourself."

They were going to go laugh about him. He won 19 games! He could give them some pointers, like a mentor. So what if he wasn't all friendly-like? He could be nice if given a chance. He just preferred to wait a little, see how a person was going to turn out.

Lenny smacked his bat against a tire. "Wait a minute. Did I say you could leave?"

Martin piped up. "We don't need your permission."

"Yeah," Cash said. "It's still a free country, last time I checked."

"What's the matter, gotta run home to mommy and daddy before it's dark?" Lenny said. He ought to let them go. But they show up here at his secret spot. Make fun of him. Rub his face in the fact that Cash would probably be better than Lenny ever was.

Then think they can just walk away?

Lenny squared his shoulders. "I'll take you on right now."

"I'm going," Cash said.

"Oh right. I forgot. It's time for your medication. Poor Cash. You'll probably faint dead away if you don't get your teaspoon of cherry flavored cough syrup and chewable baby aspirins."

Cash puffed his chest out and took a step toward Lenny. "Back off!" he said.

Lenny shoved him. "*You* back off."

Cash shoved Lenny back, harder. "I'm warning you, Lenny."

"What a joke!" And with that, Lenny dropped his bat, swung his fist, and hit Cash in the nose. Cash fell backward and landed on his rear end. He looked up at Lenny as blood trickled into his mouth.

"What'd you do that for?" he asked, breathing hard.

Martin sputtered, "Jeez Lenny, you didn't have to do *that*."

Lenny took a few steps back, startled by the blood. "That'll teach you to bother me."

"I'm calling the cops," Cash said thickly. "You'll go to jail for this."

"Yeah right," Lenny said, but he was scared. Cash's nose was split down the middle.

"Go call my dad," Cash told Martin. "Tell him to get the cops."

"Go call my daddy," Lenny mimicked. "Please daddy, come save me. You're lucky I didn't use my bat."

"Come on Cash. I'll help you," Martin helped Cash up and the two of them started to run, looking back over their shoulders at Lenny like he was a madman. For a moment Lenny almost laughed. It was so easy to scare people. No one had a sense of humor anymore. Then he thought of the police and the urge to laugh left him. He jumped up, throwing his body against a pile of tires. Next he moved to a stack of cars and started to climb on it. Grunting, he pulled at a fender, an axle, a side mirror. He tried to pull the whole thing down. He'd like to topple the whole world, like to see it all come crashing down. See who'd notice then.

Pink angel food cake. His favorite. It sat on the kitchen table on a glass pedestal. But who could enjoy it under circumstances such as these? It seemed like a person might just start to relax and pow! along came the same old shit to ruin your day. God, he hated his birthday! He might have finally had a reason to celebrate, turning 18 and all. Except now he was on probation, about to be imprisoned in the church basement. And here was Pastor Voss coming to cart him off, like he was incapable of walking the six blocks back to church on his own. It was embarrassing, and the last thing he wanted was a big birthday dinner so everyone could sit there looking at him. Poor Lenny. Can't control himself. If they only knew how much he *did* control himself. He was here, wasn't he? Trapped with a bunch of do-gooders who thought they could save him from himself.

He shouldn't have hit Cash. He was sorry as soon as it happened, but sorry wasn't worth a handful of spit. Anyway, no one was sorry for him. You can bet his old man wasn't sorry for roughing up his mom, or for leaving that day and never coming back. He wasn't sorry about what he'd made Lenny do. His dad put him in a terrible position, but was he sorry? Fuck no. The bastard was screwing around across town, too busy to give him a second thought. How hard would it be to stop by and say hello?

Not that Lenny wanted him to. Really, he didn't. There was just something about his birthday that got him all confused. After all these years, he still expected to see his dad come driving up. Hello, loved ones! Only they weren't his loved ones anymore. Lenny knew that. So what was his dad doing back in town? Maybe waiting for this day. It would be just like him to stay away for too long, just for the chance to make a grand entrance.

The way Lenny had it figured, he might as well wait it out to see what happened. Sure, he'd been all set to go find him. He wasn't afraid! But why should he waste his time if his dad was going to come to him? Let him do the sniveling.

Even if Lenny wanted to go to the Torchlight, it was too late now. He was on probation. Think how embarrassing it would be if his dad knew he was living at the church. If he came driving up to the house right now he'd see Pastor Voss here and somebody would probably feel the need to blab. He could just hear Nell. *Hey Dad! Haven't seen you in ten years but guess what? Lenny's been arrested and I bet you're not the least bit surprised, are you?*

He should have gone looking for his dad the minute Rhoda told him the news. When she asked if he wanted to walk home with her he should have said *hell yes! Show me the bastard!* Should have gotten it over with. Instead he'd let it fester all summer long and now here he was again, waiting, watching the clock, the door, the street. What a way to celebrate.

Better get packed. He went and stood in his empty room, giving it a final once-over. He took his bandana off, gave his head a good scratch, and carefully re-tied it, pulling it lower over his eyes. Next he pulled on a grungy tie-dyed T-shirt he found at the beach and reached for his bat. Then stopped. It was probably time to quit lugging it around everywhere. Now that he was done playing ball, there was no reason to have it. But since the incident with Cash, he liked the way people eyed it nervously. Even though he never swung it at Cash, people were leery. He squinted at himself in the mirror and laughed.

Tough guy. He liked that. He was especially pleased to notice a big purple bruise staining his shinbone. No one would guess it was from banging into the coffee table in the middle of the night. Nell had an annoying habit of rearranging the furniture every other day, and even though he cursed her out when it happened, the bruise was beautiful now. It looked like someone had kicked him hard.

"You're not wearing that to supper, are you?"

Sally stood in the doorway watching him. Perfect. That was just the reaction he wanted. "Stylish, ain't it?"

"You look like a bum."

"After today you won't have to look at me so much."

"Don't think that thought hasn't crossed my mind." She studied him. "Hippies are non-violent, you know. That disqualifies you."

"Not all hippies are," he said. He'd seen the Democratic National Convention on TV. He'd seen plenty of long-hairs, and plenty of violence. "Some of them are mean suckers. Besides, I can be peaceful if I want to. I just don't want to."

"So you're not a hippy," she said.

"Am too."

"Are not."

"Am too."

He gave her a shove and closed the bedroom door in her face. She had a point. He might not be able to pull off the hippy thing. For one thing, they seemed so happy all the time. It must be the drugs. He wouldn't know, since he hadn't been able to get his hands on any so far. If he was ever going to be a hippie he needed to get busy in that department, but boy, would his mom take that hard. Maybe he ought to consider becoming a Jesus Freak first. Just as a transitional role. His family could be comforted by the fact that he was high on Matthew, Mark, Luke and John. Then on to full-fledged hippie. Tune in, turn on, drop out. He liked that too. But he'd do it without becoming some pansy-ass, gentle spirit. Guys like him didn't have that luxury. He had a police record now.

He heard his grandma yell to him from outside. "Get out here, birthday boy, and let us have a look at you!"

Then Nell from the kitchen. "Lenny, come say hello to Pastor Voss. Oh, and Lenny, could you bring out that chair from your room?"

He sighed and sulked out. "Why do you have to say my name so much?" he hissed at Nell. "I know you're talking to me." She started every stupid sentence that way. Lenny this. Lenny that. It made him jump, like he'd been caught doing something. He pushed open the screen door and faced his grandma.

"So! You're 18 today," his grandma said, and before the door had even shut behind him he was pulled into her bosom. She squeezed and his mouth twisted, half-open and contorted, against her shoulder. He didn't like to be touched.

"Isn't that something," she said, releasing him.

"It's not like he's accomplished anything," said Sally.

"Lenny! The chair!"

He ignored all of them and headed over to the shade tree where his grandpa was sitting. Sometimes a man needed the company of another man. Not that his grandpa ever said much. But that was the point. It was what Lenny called good sense. He leaned against the tree trunk and started swinging his bat against one of the roots.

Oh. His bat. It was pure habit that made him pick it up. He couldn't deny the comfort it gave him, and comfort was a thing in awful short supply these days. He wished he could ask his grandpa, *did you ever…* but he couldn't complete the sentence. Ever feel like you're headed for a dead end? Ever wonder why everyone is so damned thrilled to be done with high school, when all you feel is scared? Or the worst, when people tell you you're officially a man, what exactly does that mean?

This should be the beginning of things for him. Out of high school, ready for life. Except he had no idea what to do. Go to Nam and get killed? His deaf ear saved him from that. Get some piss ant job and work 60 hours a week? For what? Or go to school and learn how to do something worthwhile? No money, no scholarship. No way.

Look on the bright side. He'd have plenty of time to think up something while he was holed up in the church basement.

"Today's the big day," Sally said, startling him.

"Why do you keep following me?"

She inched closer to Grandpa and said, a little louder this time, "Yep. It's moving day at last."

The old man stared fixedly at the rose bush.

"Opa," Sally said, tapping the edge of his chair. "Lenny's moving out today."

"I don't want to hear it," Grandpa said indifferently.

Lenny smiled. His sentiment exactly. He looked at Sally and she smiled back. She wasn't so bad, really. Lenny would even miss her. She seemed to look up to him, no matter how much he screwed up. She was all right, Sally was.

"I guess I'll go move into my new room," she said.

Scratch that. He wasn't even out the door and the world was being rearranged as if he'd never existed.

"What's your hurry?" he asked.

"It's my room now. What do you care?"

"I just might be back, you know. This job isn't permanent."

Grandpa jerked his head up. "You'll be back."

Lenny scowled. "Then again, I might never come back."

"That's right. You're 18 now," Sally said. "If the job doesn't work you can go live somewhere else."

"His place is here, with his family," Grandpa said. "When he has a family of his own he can leave home. Until then he oughta stay put."

Lenny knew Grandpa meant he could move out when he was ready to get married. But the way he said it sounded like once he *had* a family, he could leave them. Just like his dad.

He couldn't imagine having a family of his own. He'd had a few girlfriends, though he never cared much about any of them. There was a mousy girl named Beattie he used to walk home from school who wore braces and covered her mouth with her hand whenever she smiled. She moved to Texas last year. Then there was a group of girls in Lenny's class who liked to play spin-the-bottle out at the beach, and he'd gotten pulled into the game a few times. He remembered how he'd bragged about it to the guys on the team and, in the same breath, called the girls names like *fat cow* or *sewer mouth.*

Sure, he'd like to be married someday, in the same way you'd like to go see Montana, or swim in an ocean. It was something other people did. He'd probably screw it up.

"I'm not the marrying type," he said flatly.

"That's right," Sally nodded. "Too violent."

"Lenny's just kicking up some dust," Grandpa said. "Perfectly natural for a boy his age."

"Grandpa, he *broke* someone's *nose*."

Grandpa chuckled. "Yessiree bob." He got serious. "You shouldn't have done *that*, Lenny."

Lenny sighed again. Didn't he know it? It was getting harder and harder to remember the satisfaction of that moment when his fist landed on Cash's nose, especially with the pastor hovering over there at the side of the house like a big black vulture, and his last moments of freedom ticking away.

"You ever think about Dad?" Sally said, and *bammo!* there was that feeling again like he had a target on his forehead and everyone was taking aim.

"Why the hell would you ask something like that?" he snapped. She was sharp all right. Like she was reading his mind.

"I don't know. Your birthday and all."

He didn't answer right away, too angry that she would bring it up like this. He thought they had an unspoken rule to leave the topic alone.

"What about it?" he said finally.

"You ever think about him coming back?"

Grandpa piped in. "Your mother drove him off. She figured with the church's help she could raise you kids alone."

"Is that the way it happened, huh?" Lenny said. No one wanted to acknowledge that an eight-year-old boy could drive his dad away, but Lenny knew the truth.

"See, the thing is," Sally said. "I'm planning to…" She stopped and chewed her lip. "Well, I'm taking him to the banquet with me."

Lenny whipped his head around. It must have been his bad

ear. It was crazy, what he thought he heard her say.

"I wrote him a letter and invited him," she said.

Just like that! Like she was talking about a friend or a teacher or even a local celebrity! Didn't she know that their dad and all the bad memories wrapped up with him belonged to Lenny? You don't go messing with that. Not without asking.

"Have you lost your mind?" Lenny asked, incredulous.

"I put it in the mailbox this morning. During church."

Grandpa shook his head. "That's ill-advised, if you ask me."

"How'd you know where to find him?" Lenny was going to kill Rhoda, that little piece of trash! He should have known it would get out. People just had to talk, didn't they?

"Frannie let me use her phone to call the V.A. in Grand Rapids. She said her mom never checks the phone bill. They gave me his address in Kalamazoo and I mailed the letter today. Mom doesn't know."

Kalamazoo? But Dad wasn't in Kalamazoo. He was here, in Holland. Could it be that what Rhoda said wasn't true? Or maybe he lived in Kalamazoo and just drove down every once in a while to shag Rhoda's mom. Now he wished he'd asked Rhoda for the details.

"He won't write back," he said, hoping he was right. Jeez! Here he was worrying about how he might ask his dad to a baseball game—baseball! His dad's favorite thing on earth! — and Sally invites him to a stupid banquet? So now if he showed up it would be because of *Sally?*

"You don't know anything!" Sally said vehemently.

"I know it's about the stupidest thing you've ever done." He was shouting. He looked around frantically, convinced his dad really was driving up. Everyone, including Pastor Voss, was looking at him, perfect reminders of the trap he was in.

He punched at the air. "Dammit Sally!"

He'd rather die than have his dad see him for what he was. A prisoner. A janitor. A nothing. If only he didn't have to work at the church! What if he said *screw it* and left now? Would the police come after him? He ought to just take off, hitchhike out West. He'd get caught for sure, standing out on the highway all day. He needed a train or a bus. Which meant he needed money. He'd have to steal it.

That was a problem. Breaking a kid's nose was one thing, especially a rat like Cash. But stealing, that was just plain wrong. Look how long they'd scraped by with Prudy working two jobs. They'd never taken food stamps or any other government hand-out. Just clothes from the church, but that's what churches were for.

He picked up his Louisville Slugger and leaned toward Sally. "If I ever see his face around here I'll take this baseball bat and hit a home run against his head." Lenny swung and it purred through the air. Let them all think he was a hothead. If he was mean it was because he had to be.

Sally ducked. "Why do you have to be like that?" she asked.

Good question. She'd never understand. He wished there was another nose he could smash, since he turned out to be so good at it. He settled for a big black beetle unlucky enough to be crawling up the nearby tree. He leaned over, held his bat out straight, and ground the bug into the bark.

"Splat!" he said, and laughed.

"You're probably what's keeping him away," Sally said.

His laugh petered out. "Let's hope so." But it hurt to hear. He always believed she thought more of him.

"All I can say is, thank God you're leaving!" Sally ran inside, pushing the screen door so hard it knocked back against the wall before slamming shut with a whine and a whack.

"Whatever happened to being nice to the birthday boy?" Lenny asked sullenly. As if being the birthday boy had ever meant a goddamn thing.

Grandpa sucked his teeth loudly but said nothing. From across the lawn the rest of his family studied him like he was some species they'd never seen. They didn't call over *everything okay there?* They didn't care to hear his side of things. They just stared, too hot and fed up with him to bother being nice. Hell, they probably hated him. The lowly, dying beetle sure did. On the tree trunk the damn thing's legs were still twitching, like he was trying to kick Lenny for what he'd done.

Prudy

Prudy Van Sloeten watched her daughter Sally sulk into the house. Let her go. And her son Lenny, standing over there with his face screwed into a scowl. She was tired of both of them. Of course she loved her kids. But lately she was seeing them differently. It was like working on some chore, like ironing or repainting the front steps. You think you've done a fine job, and it's not until you fold up the ironing board and lug it back to the front closet, or rinse out the paint brushes and hammer the lid back on the paint can, that you notice your mistakes. A rumpled cuff you missed, a corner piece of wood that shows raw when the sun strikes just so. That's how it was with her kids. Now that they were nearly grown, her job nearly done, she was seeing her mistakes. Nell so serious and plain, old before her time. Sally miserable and searching. Lenny a common criminal. She'd done a bang up job, all right.

She turned to Pastor Voss. "Don't mind them," she said.

That was dumb. If it weren't for her kids, he wouldn't be here at all. She only went to him because she didn't know what else to do. She hesitated. "I suppose I should thank you, pastor."

"Prudy," he said quietly, "you *can* call me Phillip."

"I don't think that's a good idea."

He sighed. "Whatever you say."

That tone! It had been awhile since he'd used it with her, but it still infuriated her.

"So I'm calling the shots now, huh?" she asked.

"Prudy..."

"You offered to help with Lenny! If you don't want to..."

"I never said that."

She didn't know why she was snapping at him. She knew her role. She'd practiced it long enough. But she was feeling unhinged. Maybe it was the heat. Or having him here. Or her son turning 18 and moving out. Maybe it was the wondering, what would her life be like once her kids were gone? Without them she was nothing. Never mind the hard work she'd put into raising them, the years of scrimping and saving and praying. Now Lenny was the bad kid. She was the bad mother.

She blamed Pastor Voss. This man she'd once slept with, this man she'd *loved.*

"I'm sorry," she said. "This is difficult for me."

He sighed. "It doesn't have to be."

"Of course you'd say that."

"Look, you're the one who wanted me here today."

It was true. He didn't need to be here. Certainly she'd dreamed many times of having him back in her house, sitting down to dinner with them, but never like this. Not because she couldn't handle one of her kids.

And it wasn't just Lenny. He was a kind of catalyst, like

the expensive nylon stockings she had pulled from her husband Richard's suitcase all those years ago, the ones that were not her color. She wore sand or suntan. These were dark taupe, darker than any white woman would wear. Prudy wasn't surprised, but seeing them set something fluttering in her, something reckless and vengeful. So when Pastor Voss came to pray with her about her failing marriage, she wasn't totally unaware of the possibilities. The poor man had just lost his wife, dead from a bee sting at the church picnic. Prudy considered herself a good Christian, but she couldn't get over how unnecessary that was. Why didn't the fool woman know she was allergic to bees? Or if she knew, why didn't she wear one of those Medic Alert bracelets? She didn't have to die.

It was all just so pathetic! Prudy had a husband who drank too much. So what? With two small kids, Richard always on the road, never enough money, she had felt sorry for herself. Unappreciated. Angry. This allowed her to serve the pastor homemade cookies and coffee on a silver tray and not feel guilty. She smiled at the way he settled himself awkwardly on her sofa, the way he nervously picked at the creases of his trousers and clasped his hands together in a way she found endearing. With their Bibles open before them, she took his hand in prayer. And when he began sobbing one night, she leaned into him, her arm tight around his shoulder. She closed her eyes and told herself she enjoyed their first kiss, that sudden, awkward, sloppy kiss. When it went on from there, her slip folded casually over the chair, his white tank-style t-shirts beside, what then? What on earth was she telling herself then?

This is love! That was the main thing. *The Reverend Phillip Voss, a man of God, choosing me!* And he needed her. What a difference it made to be needed.

Then she got pregnant.

When she told Phillip he looked like he'd jump out of his skin.

"Does Richard know?" His eyebrows knit together, making a little tee-pee on his forehead. She hated that look! So helpless and pleading. So lacking resolve.

"What does Richard have to do with it?"

"He *is* your husband."

"A fact you were happy to forget on a few occasions!" Here's where it started, the *oh-NO!-this-is-not-the-way-this-goes* feeling.

"What I mean is..." He started pacing like an animal. A weasel, or an over bred dog. "He's been home a few times over the last two months. It could be him."

"Twice he was so drunk he passed out without touching me, and the other two weren't at the right time."

"I don't see how you can be sure. Can't you have some kind of test?"

"I don't need a test!"

"Yes, but can't you have one?" he said, speaking patiently, as if to a child.

"Why are you so surprised?" she asked. "This kind of thing can happen when people have sex."

"*Please!* Don't talk like that. I thought you'd taken care of everything. I thought you were careful."

"I was, but..." Then she realized. "You don't think I did this on purpose, do you?"

He stopped pacing. "Did you?"

"Are you out of your *mind?*" Yes, she wanted a life together, Phillip and her and Nell and Lenny living peacefully in the parsonage, a husband kind and steady who didn't drink, or leave her so high and dry she had to dig through an underwear drawer or under the sofa cushions for change to buy a loaf of bread.

"I would never wish for a baby under these circumstances," she said.

He held his head in his hands. "This could ruin me."

"What about *me?*"

"Nothing has to change for you. You can have the baby." He paused. "With Richard."

"I don't want to be with Richard!"

There was that pleading, weak look again. "He's mostly gone anyway."

"What are you saying?"

"I don't know! I'm in shock!"

"You expect me to go on living with him? What about his drinking?"

"Maybe he can get help. Isn't that why you came to me in the first place?"

"This isn't about him anymore."

Phillip took a deep breath and put his hands on her shoulders. "All I'm saying is let's not act hastily. Let's think this through."

She pushed him away. "What is there to think about? Don't you love me? Don't you want to marry me?"

"Yes, but…" He was actually squirming! Only two days ago she'd been in bed with him, close enough to feel his heart beating on her cheek. And *now!*

"Things aren't so bad, are they?" he said. "The way they are?"

"Phillip, my God!"

She knew then. He did not love her. Most likely never had. Most certainly never would. Talk about a fool woman! What did she expect? Some kind of knight in shining armor riding in on a white horse to carry her off to the church? *Darling! Grab your two adorable children! You're all moving into the parsonage with me. The church board? They won't care that you left your husband when I explain to them the pure, redeeming blessedness of our love!* Not Phillip —soft, quivering, sloppy-kissing, cookie-crunching Phillip.

"What am I going to do?" she said. "I can't pretend this baby is Richard's!"

"I need time to pray on this. Please Prudy, I want to do what's right."

"I'll send you a birth announcement, how's that?"

She stormed out and he didn't come after her. The coward! She hated him and she hated herself.

It only got worse when Richard came home, all hugs and kisses and cash, enough cash for her to open a savings account at the First Trust Bank.

Maybe Phillip was right. Maybe it wasn't so bad. Richard was her husband, after all. It was just the drinking she despised, not him. If she could figure out a way to make him stop, everything would be alright. And there was Lenny and Nell to consider. For their sake she had to try to make it work.

But before she could tell Richard she was pregnant, he got drunk and came home railing about some bartender at one of his haunts.

"He knows damn well what I drink, but he always does this stupid 'what'll you have?' routine. Every other guy gets the nod. 'The usual?' Not me. *Me* he treats like a fucking stranger passing through. Like I'm not welcome in my own hometown."

"Really, Richard," she said. "You're overreacting."

He whirled on her and struck her in the face. "Don't

patronize me!"

She fell back, stunned. He'd never hit her before. All the times he had stumbled in, dead drunk, and she had forced coffee down his throat, undressed him, shoved him under the shower, put him in bed. All the times she had listened to him mumble and complain and act like an overgrown baby, a royal pain in the ass. Where did this come from? Why now? It was almost as if he *knew.*

"Talk to me like that again and I'll fucking punch your lights out," he screamed.

She ran to the bedroom and locked the door. It was her fault! She should have told him right away. He never would have hit her if he knew she was pregnant.

She had to get out! She would call Phillip. This changed everything. Richard's drinking was one thing, his beating her was another. She wasn't safe, for God's sake! Phillip had to care about that.

If only she weren't pregnant! Then she could leave Richard, maybe move in with her parents for a while. Wait things out. A year, that's all. She and Phillip could start dating. Do it the right way, out in the open.

She never called Phillip. And by the time she went to the doctor, Richard had come after her again. It wasn't bad, just some bruises on her arm. But she didn't know what to do. What did women in this situation do? Where did they go? She couldn't tell her parents. They didn't believe in divorce under any circumstances. Prayer. That was their answer for everything. Prudy couldn't stand the humiliation of telling her older sister Bunny. Bunny had a wonderful husband, a brand new farmhouse, a pair of adorable twins. Her younger sister Flookie would understand, but she wasn't capable of giving any practical advice. Maybe another pastor could help, if she could find one. The thought made her cringe, remembering Phillip hiding under her sheets, laughing, giddy as a ten-year-old. *Oh Pruuu-dy, where* ***are*** *you?*

When she undressed in the doctor's examination room, she made sure to hide her bra and underwear under her clothes. Maybe some women would just fold them neatly and lay them on top. That made sense, since they were the last things to come off. But hearing the doctor's step outside the door made Prudy want to shove the white cotton under her dress, as if it was a kind of surrender flag and what she was giving up was her good reputation. Showing her soft side was something she couldn't afford to do. Not with marks on her arm and a bastard baby in her belly.

Unless he asked. If she said a prayer, this was it. *Please ask.*

The doctor glanced at the bruises. He cleared his throat and asked how she was feeling *overall*, stressing the word like it was some kind of code.

"Terrible," she said.

"Well." He patted her arm. "It'll pass. Get plenty of rest. And congratulations."

She started to cry. He gave her a sympathetic smile, his hand already on the doorknob. "You can get dressed now."

She stopped. This was how it was going to be. No one would help her. No one cared. People liked things neat and tidy, by the book. They liked to go about their business. Making sales. Writing prescriptions. Having affairs. Saving souls.

It was up to her to make things right.

When she picked up a knitting needle, she made herself think of her condition in terms of a parasite, or an illness. Once she was better, she would be able to set things in motion. Contact a lawyer. Prepare the children. Besides, as she tentatively placed the knitting needle between her legs, God would ultimately decide whether it would work or not. She wasn't going to act foolishly. One gentle poke was all.

The next morning she started to bleed.

The things she remembered about that time were brief but sharp, like the pains in her belly. Nell, five years old, pushing open the bathroom door, seeing Prudy on her hands and knees, blood on the tiles. *Want me to bring you a Kotex?* Two strange men in white. A towel behind her head. An IV in her arm. Phillip's face, slick and red, his hair a mess. *Prudy! Are you okay?* Her voice, so strange. *It's better this way.* Talk of blood type. The stranger holding the knitting needle. Hadn't she hid it!? His whistle, *looky here!* Phillip's gasp. *How could you?* Someone stern. *Why don't you remove the girl?* And the shame. Oh, a flood of it! The thundering voice inside. *What have you done?*

Prudy didn't know if it was miracle or curse, but the baby was fine. It was everything else that died. In the hospital she saw it immediately. Phillip could barely look her in the eye. When he said her name, his jaw jumped in a nervous spasm. Later she heard her sister Flookie pacing the hall, whispering with him. Heard him. *I don't know what possessed her.* Heard Flookie slap his face. *Get out!*

He would never forgive her.

Not that she deserved it. Still, it was hard to bear, those first few months. She was just home from the hospital when

Nell—dear, capable, overly responsible Nell, who had called the ambulance and then, inexplicably, called *Phillip!*—Nell said to her, "Do you love Pastor Voss?" Stunned, Prudy stared at her. She pulled her bathrobe close around her throat.

"Why would you ask such a thing?"

"The way he talks to you is…strange. He calls you Prudy."

Prudy tried to smile. "That doesn't mean anything."

"But he's over here a lot. He's your friend."

"He's not going to be coming over anymore," Prudy said finally.

"Why not?"

"It's complicated."

"I understand lots of hard stuff. Mrs. Bareman always says so."

"I know you're the smartest girl in your class. But this is different."

"Different how?"

"Nell please! Stop badgering me. I can't stand it!"

Nell looked at her a long moment. "The Lord was watching over you, wasn't he, Mom?"

With this, Prudy burst into tears. Nell went to the counter and got a Kleenex. When she held it out, Prudy grabbed her arm. "You love me, don't you, Nellie? No matter what?" How she'd sobbed in the strong arms of that child!

As she stood now in the stifling August heat beside Pastor Voss on this strange sad-happy occasion of Lenny's birthday, she knew she'd never stop paying for what she did. She had accepted that. It was the pretending that had grown so tiresome.

"I can't live like this anymore," she said quietly.

Pastor Voss didn't respond. She began to think he hadn't heard her. She glanced at him and saw that he was fixated on a spot somewhere above the neighbor's roof.

"I can," he said, nodding. "And you can too."

She turned to face him. "I won't."

He smiled calmly, but not before she saw it: he steeled himself. He must have prepared for this a very long time ago.

"You obviously have something to say," he said.

As if she could explain sixteen years of disappointment! He'd never understand all the mornings she'd laid in bed alone, imagining Mrs. Rozema next door in her spanking new green kitchen, wrapped in a silky floral robe with her face already applied, smiling across the table at her husband, who sat with rolled-up sleeves, enjoying one of those expensive toaster pastries that came individually wrapped in silver foil. He'd wipe his mouth appreciatively and come around to his wife's side of the table to wrap his thick arms around her neck, pressing his cheek against hers, whispering *I love you* in her ear.

Or her other neighbor, Mrs. Beyer, up at 5 a.m. every day, breakfast dishes already dried and put away, the picture of efficiency. And Mr. Beyer, before he died, rocking on the front porch for hours, placing a loving hand on his wife's arm when she came out to drape a blanket over his knees.

It should have been Prudy, past, present and future. Oh, the hopes she used to have! She'd never told Phillip about the time she was sixteen and competed in the Miss Clover Honey competition at the Allegan County Fair, how she'd stood on a wooden platform waving to the crowd while a matronly woman pinned delicate wings to the shoulders of her dress. She didn't get the little silver crown with a honey bee and clover embossed on the front. That went to Cissy Vorquist, along with a $300 scholarship and a chance to travel all over Michigan handing out samples of Clover Honey in tiny plastic spoons. Prudy was first runner up and all she got was a 32 oz. jar of Clover Honey that had already crystallized on the bottom. No, Prudy never mentioned this to Phillip. Considering Mrs. Voss' untimely death, the bee connection seemed too cruel and ironic. But it played in her head like a nursery rhyme, or a radio jingle. *The bee that stung Mrs. Voss, that caused her death, that made her husband sad, that sent him to Prudy, that made them sin, that started a baby. My, what a bee! A Clover Honey bee!*

It was too late to talk about the two of them. But Sally, that was different.

"I've been thinking about the banquet," she said. "Sally's 16 now. She wants to go."

"Oh God, Prudy. I know where you're going with this, but we agreed!"

"Sixteen years ago! Do you even realize, Phillip? Sixteen *years* have gone by. Your daughter is almost grown."

"I knew it was a mistake to come here. You're ambushing me."

"Oh, *please*. You had to know this would come up now. You're responsible for the Father-Daughter banquet. Hasn't that been bothering you?"

"Of course it bothers me, but we decided—"

"*You* decided."

"We *both* decided that it would be best if she never knows about us."

"She badgers me constantly about Richard, asking where is he? What's he like? I can't take it."

"What do you want me to do?"

"Take her to the banquet. Spend some time with her, for Pete's sake. Make her feel like she's not missing out."

He shook his head furiously. "It's playing with fire, if you ask me. Because we decided…"

"Stop saying that, would you! You're like a broken record. People make mistakes. I'm telling you—"

"Come and get it!" Nell, beaming, flushed, called them to the table. Well. It was probably better left unsaid. Because he wouldn't like what she had in mind. The Reverend Phillip Voss was going to take poor, fatherless Sally Van Sloeten to the Father-Daughter banquet. Then he was going to tell her that the reason she was poor and fatherless was because he was too big of a coward to claim her as his natural daughter. Only then would Prudy find out if she was doing the right thing. She hardly knew what the words meant anymore.

Nell

The Van Sloetens rented the first floor of a green wood frame house that was a ten minute walk from the church. Nell made it home in five. Pastor Voss was coming for dinner on account of Lenny's birthday, and she wanted everything to be just right. Forget the usual potato-cabbage casserole. She'd prepared a new dish called Impossible Cheeseburger Pie that was featured in the latest issue of The Ladies' Home Journal. *This tasty twist on an old favorite makes a pleasing lunch when served with a crisp green salad and tall glasses of chocolate milk*, read the caption. She had decided against the chocolate milk and went with lemonade instead. She'd brought in some daisies from the yard, and rearranged the living room to create an inviting *tableau*. That was a French word that conveyed the mood she tried to achieve in each of her arrangements. Her mother told her she was wasting her time, that they'd rather eat outdoors, but Nell had listened to the weather report and knew there was a sixty percent chance of rain.

Nell couldn't remember the last time the pastor had been to their house. It bothered her, his never coming. That's why today was so important. Nell filled three pages of her diary planning for his visit, list after list—possible outfits, menu ideas, topics of conversation. She might say something literary. *Oh! Let me just get my copy of War and Peace out of your way.* Or perhaps something in French. *C'est la vie!* Or philosophical. *One never knows, does one?*

Maybe it wasn't right, the way she thought of him. It might even be sinful. She'd known the pastor since she was a kid, but lately she was thinking of him in a more *mature* way. As in he was a man. She was a woman. At first, she was ashamed. *Dear God take these lustful thoughts from me*, she wrote in her diary. *Or at least direct them toward someone my own age*. Then she read the novel Jane Eyre and discovered she wasn't the first person to fall for an older man. If Jane was allowed to love Mr. Rochester, couldn't she love Pastor Voss? He couldn't be more than 40, and she was 21. The two of them *ensemble* wasn't out of the question.

Things got off to a bad start. Thanks to her mad dash home, she had sweat running down her back and two large crescent-shaped stains under her armpits. She had to change clothes, check the casserole, refill the ice trays, toss the salad. Would the pastor notice all her hard work? She wished he'd come inside and talk to her. She imagined the two of them chatting while she flitted about the kitchen. *Loved your sermon today, pastor! So joyful!* Him sitting at the table in a bathrobe while she scrambled him some eggs. Leaning against the counter draining his coffee before he hurried off to work. *Bye hon!* Snaking his arms around her from behind. Lifting the hair off her neck, his breath hot and close.

"Come on in," she called out the screen door. "Lunch is served!"

But everyone was lolling about in the heat, looking like the last thing they wanted was a good hearty meal. Her mother and the pastor stood alone, making no move to come in. It was exactly as she feared! Her mother was monopolizing him. Even from inside she could see his face twitching as they talked. Did anyone else notice the way his tick revved up when he was talking to her mother?

She stood at the window, watching. What were they *doing* out there? Grandma came huffing in, followed by Grandpa and Lenny. Sally slouched in from the bedroom. She heard Aunt Flookie coming up the front steps. Still the two of them stood there talking. About what? Something troubling, the way it looked. Nell didn't get it. They weren't especially friendly with each other. Mostly they seemed to ignore one another, in a way that, well, it reminded Nell of high school, the way the popular girls would walk past this or that boy with their noses in the air all week long, then on the weekend, there they were, sneaking behind the bleachers with them. And just like in high school, she got a strange and hollow pang in her stomach watching it. It was almost as if there was something between them. Something married people had. Familiar, but disdainful.

If only she understood that sort of thing! She had no experience with boys. In high school, the boys used to talk to her in the hall, but only to ask for help in algebra, or would she talk to Cathy in homeroom and see if Randy stood a chance? She'd never been on a date. As far as she knew, no one had ever had a crush on her. It used to bother her. She tried the *How to Turn Heads!* advice from the magazines, the egg whites in the hair, olive oil on the skin, head up, shoulders back, heel-to-toe steps. Nothing. People were always perfectly pleasant with her. But the *va-va-voom!* That's what she lacked.

Her mother didn't have it either. Not anymore. She might have been a looker when she was young. Now she was hard and brittle and plain. Except, was that *lipstick* she was wearing? Nell squinted out the window. Prudy had certainly freshened up, same as Nell, but why should that mean anything? Why should it make Nell grip the counter top with a hot surge of jealousy? Her mother didn't have designs on anybody. She'd made it clear over the years that she wasn't interested in remarrying. *You kids require every ounce of energy*, she always said. Still, Nell couldn't get past the feeling that maybe, somewhere in her past, her mother had felt something for Pastor Voss. It was nothing more than an odd notion, the kind that makes you pause and purse your lips, considering. Hmmm. *Maybe*. Then you shake your head. Nah. Couldn't be.

"Mother, coming?" she called.

Nell turned and surveyed the table. Everything was just as she'd planned. She wouldn't spend another minute worrying. This was her day to shine.

Then Aunt Flookie came waltzing in.

"I think I'll expire if I don't get some food," she said, crunching noisily on a pickle spear that appeared from nowhere. "Let's get this show on the road!" Flookie's real name was Frieda, but no one called her that. Whenever she met someone she'd say *call me Flookie. I'm available, if you know anyone.* Unlike Prudy, Flookie dated anyone and everyone, mostly men that she met at the bowling alley or the truck stop or the Circle R Chicken Ranch where she worked as night manager.

She dumped a foil-covered platter on the counter and said,

"Pigs-in-blankets."

Nell sighed. "You shouldn't have."

"Hey, no problem. I drove right by the Certi-Saver."

"No really. I'm not serving those with lunch," Nell said firmly.

Flookie's eyebrows, already arched and over-tweezed, inched up higher. "Why not?"

"I have the menu all set," Nell said through tight lips. "It's from a *magazine*."

"Well la-di-da! They happen to be Lenny's favorite." Flookie pulled the foil off and set the plate on the table.

"Flookie!"

But here he was, coming through the screen door. Nell planted a bright smile on her face before snatching Flookie's plate off the table.

"Welcome, pastor!" she said. "Make yourself at home."

He stood looking at her, his hands rumbling around in his pockets.

"Gosh, this weather!" she said. "We sure could use some rain!" *Dumb*. She sounded like her Uncle Ollie.

"Sure could." He cleared his throat. "Might I trouble you for a glass of lemonade?"

Nell practically leaped at him. "Or would you prefer ginger ale? I think there's some iced tea, too. And there's some frozen orange juice. I could mix that up. Or chocolate milk?" Nell stopped. She was going overboard.

"Just the lemonade," he said. "Milk doesn't agree with me."

Thank goodness she hadn't served the chocolate milk! It was so sensible of her. Could he see it too? Did he think about their compatibility? Did he realize that she could do such a good job of taking care of him?

The two of them were cut from the same cloth. She imagined a sheet hung out to dry, their shapes taken from the center like perfectly matched paper dolls. They were a pair, weren't they? Her, so rooted in her faith, reading her Bible every day, so sure that she was called to serve the Lord. And him, tirelessly spreading the Word, but without a loving woman at his side. Why, with the right support, who knew how far he could go? Together they might build a ministry in Africa, or the Philippines, or wherever else heathens lived. Just think how they could change the world!

She gestured grandly toward the table. "Please sit down. I've got eight places set out here. One for you, and me, and Mom and Lenny and Sally and…" she trailed off. She didn't need to list every last person. "Why don't you sit at the head here?"

"No, no. Let Lenny sit there."

"Yes, of course," Nell said, her smile so big it made her face hurt. Why couldn't she have been born a smiler? They were the lucky ones. Sweet, open faces that people couldn't help loving. Perfect, white teeth, pearly pink gums, cheeks that slid effortlessly up and down. She had always hated that she was so serious. If only she could be like that flighty woman Daisy, who worked at the church and was always hovering around the pastor, always touching his arm and whispering things behind her hand. Ha, ha! No! *Really?* Ha, ha, ha! What could possibly be so hysterical?

Responsibility was no laughing matter, and the pastor had to see that no one was more responsible than Nell. She'd taught Sunday School for two years, and in September she'd be starting a job as crossing guard, employed by the *police department.*

They took their seats and began passing the dishes amid the usual murmurs. *Smells divine. What a treat.* When everyone was served Grandpa cleared his throat and said, in a voice that was much too loud, “What’s doin’, Lenny?”

“What?” Lenny said, with a screwed up face. Grandpa was sitting on his bad side.

“He said, what’s doin’?” Grandma repeated. “He’s wondering what your plans are.”

“Oh.” Lenny looked uncomfortable. “Work off my debt. Why?”

Aunt Flookie cleared her throat. “Your situation is all too clear, hon, but what are your *plans?* That is to say, your *prospects?*”

Lenny set his fork down abruptly. “You all know I’m taking the custodian job at the church. You want to know which toilets I’ll be scrubbing first?”

Nell cringed at Lenny’s rudeness, but the pastor laughed, good-natured. How she loved him! And how he might so completely love *her*, warts and all. Because wasn’t Lenny a kind of wart? And her absent father too. Yet here sat Pastor Voss, ready to break bread with them as if they were all perfectly normal.

“Why don’t you tell them what some of your duties will be?” the pastor said.

“You mean how you want me to make crepe paper flowers for the banquet? For chrissake, it’s not exactly man’s work.”

“Crepe paper never killed anyone,” said Prudy.

“Speaking of decorations…” Here was Nell’s chance. She was already on the decorating committee for the banquet, but it wasn’t enough. She wanted to be in charge of so much more, so when the night came and the banquet was a smashing success, she would get the credit.

“Maybe you need me to help out with the caterers? Or

something else behind the scenes?" The thought of doing anything behind the scenes with Pastor Voss made her cheeks burn.

"You've already done so much," he said.

If he only knew! He ought to see her diary. She'd laid out three different scenarios for the night of the banquet. The first she called Humble Servant. *Wear: jeans, colorful head scarf (think Doris Day), no make-up. Motto: cheerful efficiency! See to every last detail. No complaints! Smile always. Offer to help. That Nell! Some gal Friday!*

The next was entitled Woman In The Wings. *Complete all work well in advance. Stay all night beforehand if needed. Make an entrance. Where's Nell? Emerge from the shadows in the peach chiffon from the display window at Steketees. Beg, borrow, steal for this dress.* (She scratched out *steal* and wrote *just kidding.*) *Motto: transformation. Girl to woman. Lights dim, HE takes your hand, leads you to the dance floor, whispers 'It's like we're meeting for the first time!'*

Her third plan she called Distressed (But Not A Mess). *Let him see you sweat (not literally!). Take every opportunity to ask his advice. Build him up! Compliment! Show him you've got his back but HE IS IN CHARGE (very important for men). Motto: Mature, pragmatic, equal partner.*

She still had plenty of planning to do. For now, all she could do was look at Pastor Voss, shrug in what she hoped was a dainty way, and say, "If you like I can come by this week and go over a few—"

Lenny interrupted her. "I'm finished," he said, tossing his napkin on his plate. "Can I be excused? I've got business." He scowled long and hard at Sally.

"You've barely touched your food!" Nell said.

"No offense, Nell, but I don't see why I can't have a normal cheeseburger. It is my birthday, which everyone seems to have forgotten."

"What you've forgotten is your manners." She tried to keep her voice light. As for the smile, she couldn't keep it up. Anyway, she probably looked like a crazy lady.

"That's right, Lenny. Sit down," said Prudy.

He groaned. "I don't see why everyone's on my case. Why don't you ask Sally what she was doing this morning?"

Sally's head shot up. "Lenny! Shut up!"

"Why? Is it a secret?"

"You know it is!"

"Because you never said it was a secret."

"What's a secret?" asked Prudy. "Sally?"

"What's she talking about?" Grandma asked. "Speak up, Sally."

Sally sighed. "I suppose you'll all find out soon anyway. It's about the banquet."

"What is it?" Nell asked, instantly protective. She felt like it was her banquet.

There was a long pause. Sally bit her lip and looked nervously at her mother.

"You gonna tell or should I?" asked Lenny.

"Okay! I invited Dad to the banquet," Sally said in a rush.

Everyone paused, their eyes on Sally, except for Grandpa, who kept chewing. Grandma set her fork down and folded her hands in her lap.

"Richard?" Prudy said finally. "Invited him how?"

"Don't worry, there's no way he'll show," Lenny said.

Prudy put her hand up to stop him. "Can you please tell me what you're talking about?"

“I wrote him a letter.”

“Why?” Nell asked. She couldn’t imagine wanting *him* back in her life. She’d said it a million times because she believed it: they were better off without him.

“Because I wanted to!” Sally cried. “What’s it to you anyway?”

“Maybe we don’t want to see him!” Nell cried. How was she supposed to have the night of her dreams with her father there? He’d turn it into a nightmare! To him she would always be a dull, clumsy, overweight little girl. If he showed up, she’d become all those things. In front of Pastor Voss.

“You don’t have to see him,” Sally said.

Nell didn’t know where to begin! “Sally, he’s trouble. We’ve told you—”

“Shut up! He never even liked you!”

Nell gasped. There it was, her secret, out in the open. Her own father hadn’t liked her. How could Pastor Voss ever love her? How could any man?

“Sally!” Prudy said.

Sally crossed her arms. “I’m sorry Nell, but there’s no way you can understand.”

“Neither do I!” said Prudy. “Why would you do such a thing? Behind my back, no less.”

Grandma was shaking her head. “Sooner or later, like I’ve always said,” she muttered.

“You don’t have to tell me *over* and *over* and *over* what you think of him. *God*, I know by now! But I’d like to find out for myself. I just might like him!”

Prudy put her head in her hands. Then she looked up at Pastor Voss. “You see?” she said.

He flattened his lips and said carefully, “Let’s not overreact.”

But Prudy began to cry. They all stared at her, shocked. Prudy didn't cry, and certainly not in front of a *guest*.

"Mom!" Nell hissed. Her lovely meal! All her plans! If her mother had an ounce of consideration, she'd pull herself together.

"Prudy, really," mumbled the pastor.

"I should have known this would happen," Prudy said, wiping her napkin across her face.

"Well. You should have," Sally said stubbornly. "It's only natural that I would want to meet my own father."

"Oh God," Flookie said, dropping her fork on the table.

"Richard was a very good dancer," Grandpa said thoughtfully. "That's one thing you might like to know."

"How is that relevant?" Prudy snapped.

Nell wanted to die. What must Pastor Voss think of them! Could they possibly draw more attention to the fact that they were a broken family? That they always had been and always would be? Could they manage more perfectly to send him running from their house, thanking his lucky stars that he only had to see the Van Sloetens three times a week at church? Could it get any worse?

The pastor made a little humming noise. "Prudy, why don't you tell Sally *your* suggestion regarding the banquet?"

Prudy sniffed and turned to Sally. "Pastor Voss and I were talking earlier and we thought it would be nice for the two of you to go to the banquet together."

Sally's mouth fell open. "Me… go with him?"

Flookie was staring at Prudy. "Hon, do you really think that's a good idea?"

"It's a terrible idea!" Nell blurted. Talk about worse! This was disaster. She wasn't about to stand by like a *nobody* while her sister got a date with the pastor. Especially when Sally wouldn't even have the sense to enjoy it.

Pastor Voss ignored them. "What do you say, Sally? Would you be *my* date?"

Sally was shaking her head vigorously. "I'd look like a charity case," she wailed.

"What about Uncle Ollie?" Nell asked frantically. "I went with Uncle Ollie."

"No way!" Sally said.

"So he's good enough for me, but not you?" Nell sounded petty and mean-spirited. Better to roll her eyes at the pastor, as if to say *we adults have so much to deal with, don't we?* But she couldn't manage it. This was all wrong! Pastor Voss escorting Sally to the banquet? Where did *that* idea come from? It made no sense at all to Nell. Neither did the idea of having her own father at the banquet. When it had been her turn, Nell had considered the possibility of going with her Dad for maybe a split second. She knew it would never happen, and she'd made peace with it. Peace like a river. Well, maybe not a river. A trickle, for sure. Over time, a gurgling little stream of peace.

She didn't appreciate Sally damming it all up.

The pastor spoke patiently. "Let's just suppose your father doesn't respond. Why not come as my special guest? If you like, I could ask a couple of other girls. Dora De Jonge comes to mind. Her father broke his leg. Then there would be a group of us. How would that be?"

"Listen, nothing personal," said Sally, "but there's no way I'm going with you. I *have* a father."

Prudy's hand hit the table. "You are *not* going with Richard!"

"Why not?"

"I expect you to accept the pastor's invitation *graciously*. Or you'll stay home."

Aunt Flookie raised a finger. "Prudy, could I talk to you in the kitchen?"

"Flookie, this is not your concern."

"Oh! So I'm the bad guy now?" Flookie snapped.

"All this hollering's giving me indigestion," Grandpa said.

"What about my letter?" Sally asked. "If he writes back…"

"He won't," said Lenny.

"He better not!" said Prudy. "You think I need this right now? On top of everything else? First Lenny, now *you*. Thank God I've got one sensible child!" She motioned toward Nell.

Sally glared. "That's right, I'm not Nell."

"At least I'm not so selfish," Nell said.

"You're just jealous!"

"Sally, I'm warning you," Prudy said.

"If he comes back here, it'll just upset everyone," Flookie said.

Lenny raised his voice. "Would everyone stop worrying? He won't write back."

Prudy whirled on Lenny. "Don't tell me not to worry! You do *nothing* but cause me worry."

He shoved his chair back hard. "Aw, screw it! Screw everything! I'm going to the beach. Call the cops if you want." He stormed out.

"Aren't you going to stop him?" Grandma asked.

"Stop him yourself if you're so damned concerned."

Pastor Voss sighed. "Let's all just slow down here."

"You *want* me to go with my dad, don't you?" Sally asked him. "Isn't that the whole point of the banquet?"

He frowned. "I think we should consider what your mother wants."

"It's not *her* banquet! It's mine!" She pushed her plate away and stood up. "Nobody cares about me!"

She stumbled out of the room.

"I give up," Prudy said.

Nell squeezed her eyes shut. What was that expression? It's not the hardships that matter. It's how you handle them.

"Teenagers are so…driven, aren't they?" she said cautiously. "It's nice to be grown up. To move on to new things." She stole a glance at Pastor Voss but he was studying his hands, his chin tucked into his chest.

"What about Lenny's cake?" Flookie asked. "Shame to waste it."

Prudy wiped her eyes.

"It's just like Nell said. Teenagers are a handful." She looked at the pastor. "You wouldn't know unless you live with one," she added, a hard edge in her voice.

Pastor Voss stood abruptly. "I must get back," he said curtly. "Thank you for a lovely meal, Nell." He took her hand and shook it. It happened so fast! Before she could begin to memorize his touch, he'd let go and was shaking her grandpa's hand.

"Prudy, you'll keep me posted," he said, and was gone. Out of there nearly as fast as Lenny. All she could do was stare after him thinking *No! Not like this!* She wanted to walk him out. To give him that parting smile that he could carry with him like a fresh, clean handkerchief (which, as his wife, she would make sure he always had). But she hadn't gotten to do or say anything especially charming, and now it was too late.

Oh, the two of them together was just impossible! And she wasn't being cute about it, like Betty Crocker when she named her recipe Impossible Cheeseburger Pie. She wasn't being sappy or melodramatic, like Nat King Cole when he sang *how sweet a kiss could be...impossible, impossible for me*. She was stating a fact. No fancy recipe or silly banquet was going to change that. How could she manage it? How could she rearrange everything so she was front and center? How could she achieve the wonderful *tableau* she imagined, the one that looked so comfortable and warm?

Flookie shrugged. "What do you say? Cake or no cake?"

Prudy stood up and left the room without a word.

"Oh for God's sake!" said Nell. "Pass it over!"

That's right. Slop a little pink icing on something bland and spongy and shove it down with a fork. Nell wished every ugly thing could be glazed over the same way. A little sugar here. A little lipstick there. It seemed unlikely. She sighed and pushed the dirty plates out of the way. Later she would scrape her beautiful meal into the garbage to be forgotten. Thrown out. Left to rot. She took the cake, cut four squashed, misshapen pieces, and handed them over to Flookie and her grandparents. Just passed them down, without the sprinkle of red sugar or the little crown of Lifesavers like she planned. Passed them over the way the church passed down second-hand clothes to the Van Sloetens. The way a mother passed a bad son off on the Lord. The way a silly girl might say to a certain man *please pass the salt* when what she meant was *give me your heart. All I ever want is to be yours!*

Sally

Sally, why didn't you tell me about the letter? asked her mother. Did you ever stop to think this through? asked her sister. Her brother just rolled his eyes and said *you're pathetic*.

Really, they didn't have to take it so hard. Couldn't she have *anything* to herself? It wasn't as if the banquet had to be any of their business. If she were just a few years older she might go on a date with someone they didn't like. They couldn't stop her. They could only watch out the window while she jumped into Mr. Unlikable's car and peeled out. Of course she would never date someone who didn't come to get her at the door, but never mind that now. The point was, her decision didn't have to affect her family. If they were so upset about Sally bringing her dad to the banquet, they could go hide in their rooms that night. Let them pace the floor, brimming with questions. She wouldn't tell them a single thing! Afterward, she'd breeze in with a mysterious smile, breathe a happy sigh, *nighty-night, sleep tight.*

But how lonely that would be. She had to admit, she was caught up in the hoopla. It was hard not to be, listening to the other girls go on about dresses and hairdos and how to do the box step without looking at their feet. If Sally got to go to the banquet, she'd want to dissect every detail with her mother and sister. That was half the fun. But she would also want to say *see? Wasn't this a great idea? I got my father back and you didn't!*

What they didn't understand was that, beside the banquet, Sally had nothing else in her whole life to look forward to. Sometimes she thought about college. Only because her best friend Frannie was planning to go, but her dad was a professor at Hope. That meant she got to go for free. And even though Frannie tried to tell Sally that it wasn't impossible for her to go too, *(My dad can help you! There are scholarships! If you'd just bring your grades up a tiny bit!)* it seemed a lot easier to get a dad than a college degree. Besides, when she mentioned it to her mom, *guess what? Mr. Valkema says...* she got a flat look. *Don't count on it.*

Sally hated that downtrodden acceptance. *This is my lot in life and I thank the Lord for it.* She thanked the Lord that her dad was going to come and save her from all that.

If only he'd write back!

She sat on the front porch watching for the mailman, even though she didn't expect anything today. It had only been a few days since her letter went out. But since she was still grounded and had nothing to do, she waited. And considered.

What would she do if a letter never came? For one thing, she wouldn't go to the banquet. She remembered the way the girls at school had made fun of Nell when she went with Uncle Ollie. And Pastor Voss, that would be even worse. One would elbow the other *why is she here with **him**?* The other would hiss *because she doesn't have a dad, stupid!* Then they'd puff up, all proud of their ability to be kind to poor Sally.

No sir. She didn't spend years acting like she could care less to go and blow it in one night.

She would wait exactly one week. Then she'd shrug. *That silly banquet? Oh, I lost interest in that a long time ago*. She'd go straight in, crack open a book and concentrate on bringing up her grades.

When she finally saw the knobby white knees of the mailman round the corner, she jumped up and ran toward him.

"Gizzy! Got anything for me?"

He smiled and flipped through his bag. "Sure do."

Already? Could it be? That meant her dad wrote back the second he read her letter. Like he'd been waiting to be invited. Oh, she should have done this years ago!

"Give it here!"

Gizzy frowned at her. "No, ma'am. No can do."

"Are you kidding?" she asked, jumping up and down.

He shook his head. "It's my job to put this in your box. Federal offense to do otherwise."

"I've seen you hand mail to plenty of people."

"Adults maybe. Not children like you."

"Why not?" she asked. Could she wrestle it out of his hand? He was a very large man.

"There could be something in here you don't want your mother to see. Something from the school, for instance."

She rolled her eyes. "Gizzy! School hasn't even started yet."

"All the same. I believe I'll keep my cautious ways." He walked past her.

"If it's got my name on it, it belongs to me," she said, running beside him. "Give it here!"

"Why don't you go have a seat on your porch? I'll be along shortly."

She groaned and stomped her foot. A stickler for rules. She hated that in a person. There was nothing she could do but watch his wide backside waddle away. How could a person who walked all day stay so large? She should have brought a cookie out. She bet if she held a cookie in front of his face, he'd drop his bag in a second.

At last he thumped up her stairs. "OK now," he said, dropping a bundle of envelopes into the black box beside the door. "Patience is its own reward."

She snatched the letters up and flipped through them. There! Written in strong black ink: **Miss Sally Van Sloeten**. She started to pry one corner open, ever so slowly, then stopped, her mouth suddenly dry. In seconds her whole life would change. She watched Gizzy walk away. Not just ordinary Gizzy, but The Man Who Brought the Letter. Years from now, they would reminisce together about this day, thinking back with a happy sigh about how he helped make her dream come true. He would tell everyone that it was people like Sally and her dad that made his job worthwhile, and she'd laugh and slug him affectionately in the arm. She imagined the reunion soon to come. First the banquet, then Thanksgiving and Christmas with her dad. They could even invite Gizzy. Dear, sweet Gizzy. Her heart filled with gratitude, until she saw him stop in front of the Blakes' house and wipe his nose with the back of his bare arm.

She ripped open the envelope. Inside was a white piece of notebook paper.

Dear Sally,

Thank you for your recent letter. It was a pleasure to

hear from you. It sounds like you're doing very well. I've thought of you often. It's very kind of you to invite me to your banquet. Unfortunately I will be traveling at the time. Perhaps next year. Say hello to the rest of the family.

With love, your Dad

She stared, then read it again. It was like some kind of *business* letter, the kind of thing they practiced in typing class. *Dear madam, we're sorry to inform you that your qualifications do not meet the current needs of the company.* As if she were applying for something. As if she were some stranger! She lowered herself slowly to the steps, her knees weak. It sounded like he dictated it to someone! His new daughter maybe? The one who worked with him, side by side, every day. *Honey, will you jot down a quick note for me to someone named...uh, let's see...Sally?*

She should have known. She'd gone and put the cart before the horse. That's what her mother would say. Don't count your chickens before they're hatched, or some other tired phrase that had nothing to do with flesh-and-blood, heart-pounding situations.

Why did her mother always have to be right?

She read the letter a third time.

It was a pleasure to hear from you.

I've thought of you often.

With love.

She focused on those two words, letting them soothe her. But if there was comfort there, it was short-lived. Was he mocking her? She'd signed her letter with *love*. She'd meant it!

She looked at the envelope. The postmark read Holland,

Michigan, which made no sense, since her dad lived in Kalamazoo. How could he send this letter from Holland, unless he was here, in town? For a moment she entertained a wild idea. This was all a set up! Her dad's idea of a surprise. *When I said I was traveling, I meant to you! And here I am!*

How wonderful it would be if he drove up right now. *Ha, ha*, he'd say, tumbling out of the car. *Got you!* All her worries would dissolve as they shared a laugh. What a way to reunite! The two of them instantly at ease, bonded by blood. She looked around, but the movement that caught her eye was her mother, looking out the window. Prudy dropped the curtain as if she didn't want Sally to see her.

Sally quickly folded the letter and hid it under her shirt, hoping her mother hadn't seen, but knowing she had. She stood up, ready to bolt. She needed time to think! But Prudy was at the door.

"Well?"

Sally looked away. "Well what?"

"Is that a letter from him?"

Sally didn't answer.

Prudy studied her a moment. "I'm sorry, honey."

Sally tried to think of something flip, something to make her mother believe she hadn't seen her with a letter in her hand. She couldn't do it. Disappointment pressed on her too heavily and she sagged. "You don't even know what it says."

Prudy blinked and folded her arms around her waist. "Why don't you tell me."

"Oh, take a guess!" Sally pulled the letter out and threw it at her. "It's just what you predicted."

Prudy picked it up and read it.

"I'm so sorry," she said again.

"Sure you are. You're sorry, I'm sorry, everybody's sorry!"

Folding the paper carefully, Prudy said, "Never mind. You did what you felt you had to do. Now that you have your answer, you can just put him out of your mind."

Like Sally could pluck the thought of him from her mind, drop it in the garbage can and let the lid fall.

"He could have rearranged his schedule!" she said.

Prudy pursed her mouth. "Sally, really."

"And this envelope doesn't make sense! Look, this was mailed from Holland. Not Kalamazoo. That means he's *here*."

Prudy sighed and shrugged. "I'm sure he passes through here all the time. For his work."

All the time. Which meant that Sally was no more meaningful than the scenery out a car window. *There's the Tastee Dawg, the turn-off to Tunnel Park, my children's house.* Did he ever wonder about her or had he stopped years ago? How does a person *do* that?

"You're only making me feel worse," Sally said.

Her mother didn't hide her impatience. "What difference does it make where he is? He's not a part of us anymore."

"He's a part of me!" Sally said. Only he wasn't. She had built him up from nothing.

But this letter wasn't nothing.

"I have to see him. Face to face. I have to talk to him and make him understand."

"It won't do any good."

"How do you know?"

Prudy looked around the porch, like she was searching for words. With a great heave, she threw up her hands. "Honey, he's given you his answer."

"But it's only because he'll be away! Anyway, forget the

stupid banquet. He can come another time and we'll go to…I don't know, the drive-in or something!" Somewhere the other kids would see them.

Prudy reached for her. "I told you, you don't have to miss the banquet. You'll have a nice time with Pastor Voss. We'll get you a beautiful new dress."

Sally shrugged her away. "You don't understand anything!"

There was a long pause. "I tried to prepare you for this. I know it's painful to realize that your father…" Prudy stopped. It was almost as if she was going to cry. Sally looked at her sharply. "…that he isn't really interested. But you have to let this go for now."

"Of course you'd say that!" She pushed past Prudy, through the front door, and threw herself down on the sofa. Could it really be over, in the space of five minutes? Her mother would love for her to settle for this tiny crumb. Well, I tried. Move on to the next obsession. In a few years Prudy could say *remember when you were so gung-ho to find your dad? Oh, I hardly knew what to do with you!*

But Sally had actually heard from him! She wasn't about to let go of that. Besides, if she didn't make something happen, what would her life be like?

When her mother followed her inside Sally turned her head into the pillow, then snapped it back.

"And *another* thing," she said. "I might just go to college, so you'd better get used to it!"

Prudy looked at her, surprised. "That would be wonderful."

Wonderful? Things were changing already.

Sally had never been eager for Vacation Bible School to start. Who wanted to spend all day in the sweltering church basement watching Mrs. Regneres' bouncing bosom while they sang *This Little Light of Mine*? But this year was different. Sally's light was a full glare, lighthouse beacon, guiding her father home to her. She wasn't about to let her mother or anyone else blow it out. In fact, while Nell and all the other young people were memorizing the New Testament, Sally would be busy. She had to get to Kalamazoo. A letter was so impersonal. Face to face was the way to go.

You might say her new plan was her mother's fault. You hear from your runaway husband after ten long years and all you can do is give your daughter a pat on the arm? *Sorry dear, I guess I'll go mop the kitchen floor.*

Prudy only cared about saving face. That's why she wanted Sally to go to the banquet with the pastor. She was just embarrassed about Lenny. She probably thought if everyone saw Sally at the banquet with Pastor Voss, they would think he was some special family friend. Then Lenny's situation would look more like a favor than a punishment.

She was using Sally for her own selfish reasons. Why shouldn't Sally be selfish too?

Sally would go straight to Pastor Voss and ask him for some money. *My mother is too embarrassed to ask, but I really need a new dress if I'm going to the banquet.* She'd offer to work it off, like Lenny. She wasn't above scrubbing a few toilets. It was just another thing she and her dad would laugh about. *Did I ever tell you how my daughter got the bus fare to Kalamazoo?*

If all went well, she'd be at the Greyhound station later today. Wouldn't her mother love that! Prudy liked to warn that bus stations were full of drugs and drifters. But Sally would manage. She had her dad's address in her pocket, along with a five dollar bill and five ones left over from the twenty her Aunt Flookie gave her on her birthday. Anyway, did Christopher Columbus worry when he stepped aboard the Santa Maria? Did Moses worry when he led the Jews out of Israel? Did her own brother worry when he threw his cap and gown in the garbage and said *the hell with it, I'll do what I damn well please?*

Besides, what other way was there? She didn't know anyone who had a car except Aunt Flookie, and Flookie couldn't keep a secret about anything.

"Hurry up Nell!" Sally was waiting in the back yard, watching Nell climb the stairs to the second floor to get Mandy, the neighbor girl.

"Mrs. Veenstra?" Nell called through the screen door. "We're leaving for church now."

Mrs. Veenstra came to the door with an open lipstick tube in her hand.

"Is Mandy ready?" Nell asked.

"She's not feeling too good. I'm not sure she should go."

Sally twisted her toe in the grass and pulled her dress away from her armpits. It was going to be another hot day.

"She'll be fine," she called up, hating this snootie-patootie Mona Veenstra and all her different shades of lipstick. Sally had only one color and it was too pale. She longed for a bright red, or burnt umber. Today a peachy keen or frosted ice would have given her some confidence. If Mrs. Veenstra weren't so unfriendly, Sally might have borrowed something from her.

As if reading her mind, Mrs. Veenstra carefully put the cap back on the lipstick. She crossed her arms and looked down at Sally.

"I don't know," she said. Mandy appeared in the doorway

behind her wearing a pink ruffly dress and heavy pink stockings. Glancing back, Mrs. Veenstra saw her and shifted her weight just enough to block Mandy from Sally's sight. Sally sighed and put her hands on her hips. The woman treated *Mandy* like a tube of lipstick. She used her only to make herself look good.

Sort of like what her own mother was trying to do by sending her to the banquet with the pastor.

"Would you like to go, Mandy?" Nell asked gently, leaning toward the girl.

"She don't know what she wants," Mrs. Veenstra said.

Nell frowned. "Last week you said—"

"I've been thinking about it, and I'm not sure I like the idea of her going to church. I don't want her brainwashed or nothing like that."

"Oh, *please*," Sally said. "*I'm* going, aren't I?"

Mrs. Veenstra looked at her coolly, her nose in the air. "Still grounded?"

Sally was tempted to call her another name. Super-bitch, maybe. But the last thing she needed was another punishment, so she only smiled.

"Aren't you working today?" Sally asked. Mrs. Veenstra was the beautician at the Restful Slumber funeral parlor.

"I've got two heads this afternoon. Hair only."

"You'll be needing us to take Mandy then."

"She can always come along with me. She sits quiet in the corner while I work."

"Scared stiff," Sally muttered. Nell gave her a mortified look.

"Is that a crack about the departed?" Mrs. Veenstra snapped. "Because that is not respectful."

Sally sighed. "I'm going."

"Wait." Nell turned to Mrs. Veenstra. "I'm sure Mandy will enjoy Bible School. We do lots of fun stuff, like draw and sing, and today we're making..."

Sally stopped at the edge of the yard. She couldn't stand hearing Nell talk in that sniveling way. She would never be a sniveler. It was probably a rule. No snivelers allowed on Greyhound buses.

"We'll have her until three," Sally interrupted loudly. "You can take the day for yourself. Get someone to do your hair, maybe."

Mrs. Veenstra stood straighter. "I don't let anyone touch my hair," she said. "I do it myself."

"Your nails then. There's a new manicurist down at Swanky. My Aunt Flookie says she's the best and she ought to know. You've seen Flookie's nails."

Mrs. Veenstra pointed at Nell. "You should talk to your mother about her. She's very rude." Then she held her hands out, examining them.

"Go on, then," she said after a moment. She reached for Mandy and pulled her away from the door. "Don't make them sorry they asked you."

They all watched Mandy come out silently and descend the stairs with slow perfect steps. She moved like a bride down the aisle, step together, step together, making sure both feet touched each stair. Sally might have laughed —it was comical, wasn't it? A girl trying so hard to be prissy —but she didn't. There was something wrong with Mandy. She never played with other children, and she hardly ever smiled. Without a word, Mrs. Veenstra went inside, letting the screen slam behind her.

"She'll be back about three," Nell called after her, as though she wanted to establish that, as the eldest, *she* was in charge.

"Jeez, I thought you were going to take all day," Sally complained. "We do lots of fun stuff," she said, mimicking Nell's tone. "You could say anything in that mush mouth voice of yours. Tell her we pull the wings off flies and spray paint the stained glass. It's not like she's listening."

Nell ignored her. "Would you like to take my hand?" she asked Mandy.

Mandy nodded and took her hand, then reached for Sally's too.

"The way to deal with that woman is to remind her what *she's* getting out of it," Sally continued as they walked up State Street. "That's all she thinks of anyway."

"Sally! Be quiet."

"What? Mandy knows I'm right."

"You shouldn't talk about her mother like that."

"*Step*mother. Imagine making a child sit in a mortuary with a bunch of dead bodies! It's no wonder Mandy acts half dead herself."

"*Sally!*" Nell leaned over Mandy, patting her shoulder. "She didn't mean anything."

Mandy was silent.

"Cat got your tongue?" Sally asked. The poor girl was going to grow up to be just like Nell, resigned to her lot in life, letting herself get walked on.

Then, abruptly, Mandy said, "How old are you when you die?"

Sally and Nell looked at each other.

"Much, much older than you. You have nothing to worry about," Nell said.

"But how old?"

"It depends." Sally laughed. "The meaner you are, the longer you live."

Mandy seemed to consider this. "Mona is 33," she said.

"Sweetie, Mona is too young to die," Nell said.

"Jesus died when he was 33," Sally said.

"That's different. He was killed."

"My other mom was killed," Mandy said.

Nell's brow furrowed. "Yes, but that's different too. Your real mommy died in a car accident."

"If my stepmother dies and goes to heaven," Mandy said, "she'll meet my real mom. Then my real mom will yell at her for not being nice to me."

"I wouldn't worry about Mona being in heaven," Sally said.

Nell stopped, her hands on her hips. "Could we *please*—"

Sally shrugged. "Sorry."

Nell shot her a warning look. "We're going to have such fun today!" she said, patting Mandy's shoulder. "Now tomorrow," she added brightly, "you'll come with *Sally*."

"Yippee," said Sally.

Another glare from Nell. "Because I'll be starting my training at the police station. When school starts you'll see me every day on the corner in my uniform."

"Crossing guard extraordinaire!"

Nell snapped, angry now, "Why are you being so difficult? You've always loved Vacation Bible School."

"Says who?"

Nell gaped at her.

"No really. What makes you think I love it?"

"Don't you?"

Sally frowned. "Doesn't it seem a little pointless?"

Nell seemed genuinely surprised. "Why no! It's a chance to be joyful together."

“Joyful? Who’s joyful?”

“Well,” Nell sputtered. “What would you rather be doing?”

But something had caught Sally’s eye. There, across from the church, was the Texaco station. Leaning over someone’s windshield was Cash DeVries. And parked beside the building was a beat-up brown Chevy Impala. The type of car a teenager might drive. A car that was so much more comforting than a Greyhound bus.

“I’d rather be talking to *him*,” Sally said and before she could stop to consider what she was doing, she was running across the street.

“Sally!” There was a pause as Nell watched her go. Then, “You didn’t use the crosswalk!”

By the time Sally reached the asphalt lot of the station, Cash had gone back inside. She slowed to a walk. With the glare of the sun on the window, she couldn’t tell if he was watching her or not. She took a deep breath and pretended to be fascinated by the words *high octane*.

Nell was still yelling when Sally opened the door. A little bell rang. Cash was behind the register counting money and didn’t look up. She was disappointed. It’s awkward when you’re being watched, but even worse when you’re not.

She waited as he flipped through the bills. The station smelled of motor oil and air freshener and ....dill pickle? Glancing around, she saw a half-eaten pickle sitting on a napkin on the counter, the big kind that you get from a barrel at carnivals. She could see his teeth marks in it. She looked away, embarrassed.

"Hey," she said.

He raised his head, a five dollar bill poised mid-air. "What do *you* want?"

How could she put this? Will you drive me out of town? Are you and your car for hire? Maybe she should talk about Lenny. *My brother asked me to say he never meant to mess up your face.* But she didn't want to think about Lenny. He'd blow a gasket if he knew she was here.

She shrugged. "I dunno."

"So you're a Van Sloeten. Which means you're that cocksucker's sister."

She tried not to wince at his language. "Yeah, well. Kinda funny, huh?"

He pointed to his nose. "Does this look funny?"

"Listen, I'm not the one who did it, so don't get mad at me."

"What makes you think I'm mad? Because you'd know if I was mad."

She rolled her eyes. *Ooohh*, she felt like saying. *You're so dangerous*. But she made herself smile.

"Anyway, thanks for the tape. That was a real lifesaver."

He set the pile of fives down and scribbled something on a pad. "That's what you came to tell me?"

She looked around, stalling. "You're probably wondering why I was mailing a letter on a Sunday."

"Not really."

"You were curious about it before. Remember? You reminded me that the mail wouldn't go out."

"That was before." He stared at her. "Today I'm not interested."

Sally stepped closer to the counter. "I was afraid I'd change my mind about sending it. I've sort of been working up my nerve to write to this particular person."

His eyes were an odd color. Not really blue, or green. More like gray. A very dark gray. They were pinned on her, flat and indifferent. "I don't write letters myself," he said.

"Don't you want to know who I was writing to?"

"Why should I care?" He took a pile of ones out of the register.

Sally scuffed the toe of her shoe against the concrete floor. "Anyway, I'm just glad for the help."

He said nothing, just stood with the money in his hand, looking at her.

"Otherwise...my letter wouldn't have gone out."

"So you said."

"I just thought you might be curious. That's all."

"I'm trying to count this money."

"Oh." She hesitated. She could just hear his next words. *So why don't you run along?*

"Is that your car outside?" she asked.

"Yeah."

She might as well blurt it out. "How would you like to drive me to Kalamazoo?"

He didn't answer. Only stared.

"I need a ride to Kalamazoo." She put her hands on her hips to express her determination. He raised his eyebrows slightly. For the first time, Sally noticed the sexy pin-up girls on the wall behind him. Blushing, she said, "It's not what you're thinking."

"How do you know what I'm thinking?" He slammed the register drawer shut and leaned forward on both elbows.

"I'll pay you," she said quickly.

"How much?"

She thought of the money she'd saved from her birthday.

"Ten dollars?"

He laughed. "Is that gonna cover my hospital bill when your brother comes after me?"

"Lenny has nothing to do with this."

He shook his head. "Thanks, I'll pass."

"I can understand you might be scared of him…"

"Scared! If that fucker could be trusted to fight fair, I'd take him on right now!"

Sally looked nervously out the window. Lenny was just across the street. Nell might be with him now, ratting her out. He could come charging out any second, a ball of crepe paper still in his hand.

"Never mind Lenny. He doesn't tell me what to do. Besides, he's on probation now."

Cash seemed to consider this.

"So what's in Kalamazoo?" he asked.

"My dad."

"What's he doing there?"

She didn't want to admit that she had no idea exactly where her dad was or what he did. Her mission would seem too vague and he would refuse. She motioned nonchalantly with one hand. "He travels around giving motivational speeches to college kids and community groups. He'll be in Kalamazoo, and since it's so close I thought I'd go see him."

He narrowed his eyes. "Why doesn't he come see you?" he asked.

Oh, if she could answer *that!*

"He's just so busy. Sometimes they even tape him, and play the tapes in mental hospitals, or...or...in offices, or at Sears or Penney's. You know, for the salesgirls."

Those eyes. Didn't he ever blink?

"Why do you keep scratching your arm?" he asked.

"I don't," she said, but there were white fingernail marks crisscrossing a large red spot on the inside of her elbow.

"Are you nervous?"

She shrugged. She didn't want him to think she was a square. "I'm not supposed to hang out in gas stations," she said. She'd never been told this specifically, but she supposed gas stations were the same as bus stations. Pretty much any kind of station was off-limits.

"Then I'd imagine you're not supposed to ask people to drive you to different cities, either."

She scowled at him. "What's it matter to you?"

"It doesn't. I'm just making an observation."

"I'll worry about myself."

A car drove up, and the bell in the station clanged. He straightened.

"You don't have to lie, you know. Everybody knows about your dad." And he walked out.

Sally's face burned. *Everybody?* Even kids from different schools? What was there, some kind of extensive telephone tree designed to protect all the cool kids from the losers? Those Van Sloetens, from Holland High? *White trash.*

No. Of course Cash would know about her family because of Lenny. He had gone and made another enemy, and now Sally had to suffer the humiliation of it. It wasn't the first time.

When he walked back in she thrust her chin out. "Do we have a deal?"

He rubbed his hands together and made a tragic face. "It sounds pretty flaky to me. I mean, you just mentioned mental hospitals. For all I know you could be an outpatient. Your brother is crazy enough."

Sally sighed.

"Plus, this thing about gas stations. That's troubling. If I were to give you a ride in my car, we might need to stop at a gas station. It's sort of hard to avoid."

She gave a little stamp. "Stop it. I'm serious. I need to get to Kalamazoo. *Today.*"

He frowned. "Well, Queenie. In case you didn't notice, I'm working."

"I'm offering to pay you. You could use ten bucks, couldn't you?"

He stepped around her and his arm brushed against hers. Sally stiffened. Had he done that on purpose? There was plenty of room in the station. He didn't need to be bumping into her.

"It's a fucking inferno in here," he said, lowering a flimsy plastic shade. "Look at you, all sweaty." His eyes shifted to the front of her blouse. She didn't like the way he was looking at her. She didn't completely hate it, either.

"How old are you anyway?"

"Sixteen," she said. Old enough to handle herself. Maybe if she didn't have an older brother, she might be more wary of him. Imagine her friend Frannie here, talking to Cash like this! She'd probably pee her pants. Not Sally. She knew this mean-like-James-Dean act.

"Kalamazoo is a long way, you know," he said.

"Only an hour. Haven't you ever been there?"

He nodded. "Sure, I toured the Kellogg's factory in 5th grade. Didn't you?"

"Of course. But besides that. Have you driven there by yourself?"

"No. Why would I?"

"How am I supposed to know? What I'm asking is if you can get us there. Can you follow a map?"

"I'm not a moron."

So he'd do it! "How soon can we go?"

He cracked his knuckles. "It just so happens I'm off tomorrow. I have every Tuesday and Thursday off, in case you're interested."

"Not today?"

"Like I said, this here's what's called a job." He said it like she was retarded.

She sighed. She hated to wait, but it was her only chance. She had to take it.

"Okay, tomorrow then."

"You still paying me ten bucks?"

"What do you need it for? Since you have a job."

"I don't like to waste my days off." He started thumping his hand on the counter, as if suddenly bored with her. "How long is this going to take, anyway?"

"I don't know. It depends if my dad is home." It was a big IF. A gargantuan one. Ignoring it was like ignoring an elephant.

Cash examined his fingernails, which were filthy. Seemingly satisfied with their condition, he turned his eyes on her. *All* of her. "I might be persuaded," he said.

Sally crossed her arms in front of her and gave him the most level look she could.

"Cash. Whatever your name is. I'm serious about this. No funny business. I've got to see my dad. What do you say?"

He gave her a slow smile. "I say a test drive is in order, see if we're compatible. The owner will be in soon. Wait ten minutes and I'll drive you home."

"What does it matter if we're compatible? We don't have to

talk, long as you get me there."

"If we're compatible I won't charge you the ten bucks."

She might need that money. In case of emergency. "Oh, all right. Only you can't take me home. I'm supposed to be at Bible School all day."

"Whatever you say," he drawled. "You're the boss."

That's right. She tried to act boss-like as she walked outside to wait by his car, but her insides had gone all jittery. Was she really going to drive away with this guy? It hardly seemed possible, yet here she was, leaning against the black hardtop of his Chevy. She looked it over. How did he ever get a car? Did his parents give it to him? Maybe he saved up. He must be more responsible than he looked. She felt a twinge of admiration. And relief. She'd be fine with him.

Still. If they didn't get moving, she might lose her nerve. Ten minutes was an eternity. Plenty of time for Lenny or Nell to come over here. Lenny would read the situation all wrong. He wouldn't realize that Cash's Chevy Impala was all that mattered to Sally. He'd assume something else. His chest would puff out, he'd stare at Cash and say in that overly incredulous way *Are you **kidding** me? Are you **trying** to mess with me?*

Well. She was free to have her own friends and form her own opinions. About Cash and about her dad.

Finally she heard the door clang and voices inside. A moment later the owner came out with Cash. He was a burly man with a gray bristly mustache that stuck out over his upper lip. He looked at her and said something to Cash. Certain assumptions were being made, she could tell. She should explain herself, *it's not what you think*, but how many times could she say that? Maybe she wasn't a boy-crazy, hormone-charged teenager, but was the truth much better? The man looked at her sideways before disappearing.

"Hop in," Cash said, coming around the car and opening the passenger door. With his free hand he pulled the rubber band from his ponytail so his hair hung loose, just touching his shoulders. Ready for adventure. That's what that movement says. She felt an unexpected thrill. *Ready or not. Here we go.*

No sooner had she climbed into the car when he leaned in the open window and planted a quick kiss on her cheek.

She jumped. "Well! I hardly know you."

He grinned. "What better way to get to know a person?"

"But..." He'd got it all wrong. He actually thought she was that kind of girl! He shut her door and went around to the driver's side. Should she get out? She put her hand on the door handle.

"What's the matter?" he asked, slamming his door behind him. The noise startled her and she jumped again. "You've been kissed before, haven't you?"

She felt her face burn as the realization sunk in. Every other sixteen year old girl in the history of the world had been kissed, except her. Could he tell? He must have noticed her frantic look because he laughed and said, "Just a quick kiss like that don't mean nothing. It's like a friendly hello. Like in Europe. Hell, I kiss everyone like that."

"Oh. In Europe," she repeated stupidly. Calm down! It was just a peck on the cheek. But it was real! She touched her face. A boy's lips had touched her face!

"That's what they do in Paris and Spain and places like that," he continued. "Everybody's kissing everybody. All the time."

Maybe *she* had got it all wrong. "It's just that you weren't very friendly in there," she stammered.

Cash continued to grin at her. "I can be real friendly."

She tried to breathe normally but it was hard with him looking at her. Maybe ugly was too strong a word. If you looked past the purple swollen nose and underneath all that horrible stringy hair, there was a decent enough face. Bad skin, but if he washed a little that might go away. And when he smiled, well, it was a little like flipping on a light. His mouth went crooked but his teeth were shiny and straight. And was that a dimple on one cheek?

Not that she was noticing. She folded her hands primly. "I hate to mention this, but well, Lenny looks out for me pretty good."

His smile slid away. "What's that supposed to mean?"

"It means this is just a ride. That's all."

He snorted. "Well, Jesus! Is this a problem or not? Never mind Lenny. That's what you said."

She stared out the window. "I'm just saying, if anything happens to me…"

"You want a ride, or not?"

"Of course." She kept her hand on the door handle.

Cash started the car and revved the engine up a few times. Exhaust blasted loudly from the tailpipe. It may as well have been a bullhorn. *Hey, look over here! This girl's headed for big trouble!*

"Can you just *drive*!" she said, looking around. She figured Nell was over in the church basement acting all bossy and in charge, but she still expected her to come looking for her if she stayed away too long. Nell lived for moments like this, when she could call Sally young lady and drag her by her ear.

Cash glared at her before beginning a variety of driving activities that Sally didn't quite follow. He straightened the mirrors, polished the chrome center of the steering wheel with his shirttail, adjusted the radio knobs and squinted at the gauges.

She tried to relax but her foot was tapping wildly. A test drive! What a stupid idea. More like a chance to blow everything.

"Come on," she whispered between clenched teeth.

"Ready?" Cash said.

She rolled her eyes. She was more than ready. She would never be ready. She didn't know which and she didn't care. *Just make it happen.*

They pulled out of the lot and headed toward downtown. Cash didn't say a word. Confined to the car seat, with both hands on the wheel, he seemed suddenly self-conscious. It was just as she thought. *Harmless.*

"Why do they call you Cash?" she asked.

He shrugged. "I got to be a bat boy one time at a Tigers game. Met Norm Cash face to face." She heard the pride in his voice.

"You're called Cash just because you met Norm Cash? That's weird."

"Well, I play ball too. Same position."

Sally nodded, but she didn't understand. The way boys mooned over ball players was a mystery to her. She had nothing to compare it to, unless she counted the way she imagined her dad. Meeting him would change her life too, the way Norm Cash had apparently changed Cash's. Maybe they had something in common. She stole a glance at him and he had a gentle, pleased look on his face, probably remembering his moment at Tiger Stadium.

He wasn't so bad. Better than a Greyhound bus.

He turned to her. "You ever get stoned?"

She nearly choked. "No! Why? Do you do that?" God, he was a drug dealer! He'd force her to get high, then they'd be arrested and she'd be sent upstate to some juvenile hall!

"No," he said, making a face. "I don't touch the stuff. I was just wondering."

"Why would you wonder that?"

"Hey, chill out." He put a hand on her knee.

She slapped it away. "What are you doing?"

"What do you want me to do?"

"How about drive?" She looked around. They hadn't gone far. She could easily walk home.

"You know the great thing about having wheels?" he said. "Is I could probably go right now and find half a dozen girls who'd like to take a ride. That seat you're in is in demand."

She didn't buy that for a second. But. His car was awfully important to her. Without it she'd be waiting at the bus station. And who could say what kind of sexual pervert might accost her there?

"I'm sure you're a real Casanova. What's your point?"

He looked at her quickly, then looked away. "You're not bad looking."

She couldn't help it. She was flattered.

"What I mean is," he said, "I like your style. You're easy to talk to."

"You call this talking?" If he thought she'd get sucked in with a little flattery, he was wrong. This was no joyride. And it wasn't about *dating*. She was on a mission to get to her dad, to bring him to the banquet, to sit with all the other girls and listen to Pastor Voss talk about dating and—oh, so it didn't make much sense! Here was that dumb old cart rolling ahead of the horse again. See how behind she was? See how desperately she needed a dad?

Cash gave a weary sigh. "O-*kay*," he said, like he was resigning himself to a *conversation*. "So what's this business with your dad all about?"

There was no way to explain the mishmash in her head. Or heart. "None of your business," she snapped.

He stepped hard on the brakes and jerked the car onto the gravel shoulder.

"What are you doing?" she said.

He glared at her. "Test drive's over."

"*Fine*. Drop me at the Greyhound station."

"You're taking a bus?" he said finally.

"If I have to." She meant it, too. She wasn't turning back. No matter what.

They sat in silence. Then, "We can leave in the morning. Eight o'clock."

She hesitated, but only for a second. "Make it nine. I have to pretend to be at Vacation Bible School."

"No way," he said. "I want to be at the beach by noon."

She'd have to sneak out while Nell and her mother were getting dressed. It was risky, but what choice did she have?

"Eight-thirty then," she said.

"Fine. But I gotta have the ten bucks."

So they weren't compatible. That's what he was telling her. Well, so what? As long as her dad liked her, that's what mattered.

"Some of it's in quarters. Got a problem with that?" she snapped.

To her surprise, he started chuckling. He pulled the car into the street and drove back to the Texaco.

Before the car had fully stopped she had her door open. "I'll meet you at the station," she said.

"Wait," Cash put a hand on her arm. He leaned over and kissed her again on the cheek. "That's one of those European good-byes. Classy, huh?"

She stared. She didn't know much about boys, but this seemed crazy. *He* was crazy. Did he have a crush on her? How would she know? She thought of Debbie and Patty Ann and their crowd and how they were always swooning and shrieking around the bathroom mirror, overcome with the same contagious disease. Did you *see* him? Did he see *me*? Oh, I could just *die*! Boy crazy. Strait jacket, loony bin crazy. She was beginning to understand. Boys made girls crazy because boys were, in fact, crazy.

She managed a faltering smile and tumbled out of the Chevy. She smoothed her skirt and headed quickly across the Texaco lot toward the church. He was watching her now. She'd bet on it. She was no longer sure that was such a good thing.

She wasn't so sure of anything, really.

Lenny

The Torchlight Tavern was a tiny, triangular shaped place across from the water treatment plant. It was 4:30 when Lenny walked in. There were three men inside. One was the bartender. The other two chatted together in the corner booth. They all glanced up at him, but didn't show much interest. He adjusted his bandana and tried to hide his relief. He'd been worried someone would stop him, knowing he didn't belong.

The jukebox against the wall attracted him. He sauntered over and studied it awhile. Finally he dropped a dime in and chose B19: Creedence Clearwater Revival, *Susie Q*. He imagined a long-legged girl wearing a thin dress held up with those little stringy shoulder straps. What they called Cajun. If he hadn't settled on going to San Francisco or Chicago, he might head down to Cajun country. Of course, he didn't know if they played baseball down there. It might be too swampy.

He leaned against the warm sloping glass of the jukebox

and focused on the vibrations tickling his chest. He was just a man—yes, a *grown* man now, a legal adult—hanging out in a bar, enjoying the atmosphere. No one knew him. No one would guess he was a kid in search of his dad.

He still couldn't believe he was here. Go. Don't go. Back and forth, round and round. He was tired of trying to make sense of it. Was it really so easy? Write a few lines on a piece of paper, drop it in a box, and a couple days later you get what you thought was gone forever. Love. That's how his dad had signed his letter to Sally. *With love, your dad.*

All for a stupid banquet. Think how many baseball games Lenny had pitched! It never once occurred to him that he could send a simple invitation and poof! there his dad would be, waving at him from behind home plate. But the *asking.* That was the problem. Like trying to tackle Mount Everest when the highest you've ever climbed is Mount Baldy in Saugatuck. You have to train. Start small. Here's how it might have gone. You see him around town. Give a shrug in his general direction. Maybe a mumbled hello. After a while some eye contact. Finally, *finally*, might come *hey you maybe want to toss the ball around?* You don't send a letter out of the blue that pretends to be about some silly event but might as well spell it out in big block letters. *Please come back.* Come back and be my dad.

Or do you?

Sally was the only one who could do it. Blissfully ignorant, that was Sally.

The song ended, and as he stared at the stack of 45's inside the glass, all he saw were the holes in his plan. Face it, he didn't *have* a plan. He'd started out so sure of himself. Keep the deadbeat away from his mom and sisters; that was the job he'd been handed, like it or not. But with Sally confusing everything, he found himself imagining all kinds of scenarios. He might tell his dad how much the banquet meant to Sally, maybe get him to go with her. Or he might say *people are talking. Go back to Kalamazoo and leave us alone*. He just didn't know. He figured it'd come clear to him once he saw the old man. He looked around again and realized he'd never really believed he'd find his dad here. So now what? Walk out? What kind of a loser goes into a bar to listen to one song and then leave? He ought to order something. Act normal. But what was normal?

He fished in his pocket for some more change and walked casually to the bar. It'd be embarrassing, but he would ask for a Coke. He waited what seemed ages for the bartender to turn around. Now that Lenny was no longer on the pitcher's mound, he was feeling more and more like he didn't exist.

I've thought of you often.

Who did his dad think he was, writing a lie like that? The worst part was that Sally was dumb enough to believe it.

"Gimme a beer," Lenny said roughly, surprising himself. He hardly recognized his own voice. Without a word the man reached into a cooler and grabbed a long neck bottle. He lodged it expertly under a metal lip on the bar and popped the cap.

"Seventy-five cents."

Lenny gave him three quarters plus an extra dime. The man nodded at him and turned away. Done. Nothing to it. Lenny took a long swig. It wasn't bad. He liked the bitter edge. The warm trail it made inside him. And beer was innocent enough. Not like the hard stuff. He drank more, quickly, then he went back to the jukebox and picked out two more CCR songs. He was looking for a third when he felt a quick rush in his head.

Was he drunk? Had he let the monster loose? God*damn* it. What happened to his vow to stay away from alcohol? You think he could control himself for once. It should be easy. *Hello to the rest of the family.* See how easy that was?

The door opened and a square of sunlight flashed against the floor by Lenny's feet. He looked up, startled, but it was only an old man wearing a dirty ball cap and baggy t-shirt. Lenny took a final swig and turned back to his music. As the bass kicked in on the second verse he started to hum.

The man took a seat at the bar and began drumming his fingers noisily. He couldn't keep the beat. Lenny was distracted from the music. The man began singing loudly, "I put a spell on you. 'Cause you're *mi*-ine."

This went on through two verses. Wouldn't you know? A simple pleasure and even that had to be ruined. Lenny sighed and kicked the jukebox with his toe. Obviously this little visit wasn't going to accomplish anything. Except to leave him hankering for another beer. Had this been his moment? His fork in the road? He saw himself wasting away on skid row. *If only I'd never set foot in that bar.* Thanks Dad.

He couldn't stand it.

"Hey! Who sings this song?" he called.

"That's the CCR," the man said, swiveling on his stool.

"Let's keep it that way."

"What's that?"

"I said, you ain't no Fogarty, so shut up." He shouldn't talk that way. He might get thrown out of the place. Maybe that was exactly what he wanted.

The man laughed but resumed his singing. Screw it. Lenny set his beer down and headed for the exit sign.

"Hey kid, come over here," called Mr. Killjoy.

"Fuck you," Lenny muttered. He had his hand on the door.

"Is that any way to talk to your dad?"

Lenny froze. He'd heard that voice loud and clear, with his good ear, but he could so easily pretend he hadn't. Because this wasn't the way. His dad was not an old man. He was tall and thin and good-looking and he was going to come waltzing in here wearing a sharp suit and polished shoes. Lenny would be wearing his letters, or his jersey at least. *God!* Why hadn't he worn his jersey?

The man waved his arm. "Come on over here."

One push and he'd be out. Out of here. Out of town. Outta *sight*, man! He'd drop out so far that all of this would be nothing but a memory. Because he didn't need it. He still had a few things that nobody could touch.

He glanced over his shoulder. Everyone was looking at him. Even the two men in the corner booth.

"Come on! I won't bite."

The cool thing would be to throw out some snappy line. *Old man, I'd never be related to the likes of you.* Chase it with a perfect sneer. Stride, stride, out the door.

But.

He turned and took a few slow steps, close enough to see that this man had shaky hands and a sunken spot on his forehead. He looked about sixty. Lenny squinted. He didn't know how, but someone could be playing with him. It could be that Rhoda got together with some of her lowlife friends to trick him. *Send in a bum from the trailer park and tell him he's his dad! What a riot!*

Should he play along?

"Heard you been asking around about me," the man said.

That grin. That eyebrow, and the way it shot up while the other one stayed still. Lenny used to practice that in the mirror.

Hello, loved one!

"I'm not buying you a drink," Lenny said. See, he should have had a plan! What kind of first words were those? But wait. Technically his first words had been fuck you.

Richard laughed and turned to the bartender. "Hey, this here's my son. Leonard Van Sloeten. Goes by Lenny."

Lenny felt another rush. Of course his dad knew his name. But hearing him say it out loud like that made it real. He hadn't forgotten him.

"Get him a beer," he said.

"I don't drink," Lenny said abruptly. He hoped the bartender wouldn't snitch.

Richard nodded and smiled. "That's admirable."

"What are you doing here?" Lenny asked.

"What's it look like?"

"I mean here in Holland. Why are you back?"

"It's my hometown, ain't it? And far as I know, there ain't no warrants out for my arrest." He said this to the bartender. Both of them laughed loudly.

"So I heard you might be coming for me," his dad said, once his little joke was over.

"Heard how? From who?"

"Margie's girl Rhoda said she ran into you. Said you seemed interested in seeing me."

That little shit. "Why would she say that?"

"I guess you gave her that impression."

"I did not!"

"Women have a way of knowing things. That's why they're so goddamn hard to live with."

Lenny had already had enough of that easy smile. "How would you know?" he said.

His dad raised his glass. "Touche." He pulled down a couple

swigs of his drink. "I've been hoping that someday you'd want to see me again. You know, I follow your team. In the paper. I always make a point of looking for the Dutchmen."

Lenny tried not to look shocked. His heart began to thump. He dug his hands in his pockets to hide a sudden shakiness. "That's all over with now that I'm graduated."

"Graduated already? Good for you. Got big plans now?"

But Lenny only shrugged. Anything he said his dad would shoot down. He should just go ahead and tell him he'd been picked up by some farm team. His dad would never know any different because once Lenny walked out of here he'd most likely never see him again.

Unless. What if this was only the start of something? What if his dad stayed around and they continued to meet? And what if his dad wanted to meet just because he thought Lenny was a ball player? Dad could never resist ball players.

"What have you been doing all these years?" Lenny said.

"Knocking around, trying to make a buck. I've done all right for myself."

"I can see that."

Richard sat up straighter and patted his hair. "I'm a little beat up maybe. Lost some of my shine. What about you? Fill me in."

As if Lenny could lay out his life like that, in 50 words or less, like a fucking essay. *How I Spent my Fatherless Years.*

"What do you care?"

"Now, son—"

"Don't call me that."

"Well, you are my son. Nothing's going to change that."

"Wish I wasn't."

His dad nodded. "That's fair," he said. "Come on, pull up a

chair."

Why'd he have to be so reasonable about everything?

"Do my legs look broken to you?" Lenny asked.

The pleasant look on Richard's face dropped away.

"They look good enough to walk your ass out the door," he said. "What'd you come here for if you're just going to give me grief?"

Do it, Lenny told himself. Walk away. You've seen enough.

"I wanted to talk to you about this Sally thing."

"Sally?"

"She's your daughter."

"I know who Sally is."

"She got your letter."

"What letter?"

Lenny sighed. "Oh, for chrissake."

His dad tapped his forehead. "See this little cave in my head? There's a steel plate in there. Souvenir from a bar brawl a few years back."

Lenny put his hands on his hips, waiting.

"What I'm saying is that I'm not always as sharp as I used to be, but I think I'd remember if I wrote Sally a letter."

Hold on. Hadn't Lenny seen the letter with his own eyes? Hadn't he read it about twenty five times, even sneaking into Sally's room to look at it while she was in the bathroom?

"You didn't write her a letter?"

"Nope."

Lenny blinked. That would mean that those words, they weren't real. There was no *thought of you often*. No *with love*. This bastard in front of him was the same bastard he'd always been.

"So who did?" Lenny demanded.

Richard shrugged. "Johnny Carson?"

It was no joke. Who would do such a thing? Nell? His mother? Lenny shook his head. It *was* strange how that letter came so fast. And was mailed here in town. Lenny had just supposed, like the rest of them, that his dad was passing through Holland, on the way to somewhere else.

"Did you get the letter she sent you?" he asked.

"What's she writing me for?"

Lenny paused, shaking his head, trying to clear it. "She wants you to go to the Father-Daughter banquet with her," he said finally. "At the church, week from Saturday."

His dad swirled his glass around. There was nothing but ice cubes in it. He tilted his head back and put one of them in his mouth.

"I always liked Sally," he said, after sucking awhile on the ice. "But her and Nell and your mom, they're better off without me." He paused and looked at Lenny. "It's you I've missed."

There was a real beauty, right over home plate. No signal. No wind-up. No time to plant your feet. Lenny felt a quick sting of tears. Horrifed, he looked away. He could not think of a single thing to say.

"C'mon!" his dad said, reaching over to slap Lenny's arm. "We had some good times!"

This ought to be interesting. "Like what?" Lenny asked.

"Remember listening to the ball games on Saturday afternoons? Fenwick Park, the '52 series, and Babe Ruth, the greatest player ever lived. Hit—"

Lenny finished, "Sixty runs in '27. World record."

"Hey! Will you listen to that? He remembers!"

His dad was looking at him with a happy grin. Was that all Lenny had to do to please him? Recite a stupid baseball fact?

"Yeah, I remember all right," he said.

"He remembers," his dad said to the bartender. He kept shaking his head. Suddenly he snapped his fingers. "How 'bout that bat I got you? That was one fine bat. Cost me a pretty penny, if I recall."

"Yeah, the bat."

"Still got that bat?"

"Oh, it's around somewhere," Lenny said, looking away. Aw, what the hell. He'd come this far.

"You remember me whacking you with that bat?" His eyes darted quickly to his dad's face to catch his reaction. He expected him to become angry.

"Well, you got me out," was all his dad said. "That's what you wanted. I'd probably still be married to that woman if it weren't for you."

"You are still married."

His dad laughed. "Is that right? Don't tell my new wife that!" This made the bartender laugh too.

"You're married again?"

"I was, but that didn't work out either."

Lenny felt an odd relief. They were right about him all along. Still. He'd hoped for more. He'd always thought if he ever met his dad again, he might be glad to know him.

"So it was me who made you leave, then." Matter of fact.

Richard stopped smiling. "What do you think?" He leaned far off his stool toward Lenny. "Do you really believe an eight-year-old kid swinging a bat is enough to make me walk out on my family? I could have broken that bat over your head."

"Not in the condition you were in."

"You did the right thing. I don't blame you for it. I was a drunk and a bum."

Lenny looked him up and down. "Looks like not much has changed."

"Now I'm just a bum." He motioned to the bartender. "Right, Merv? This here's just Coke. Merv's the only bartender in town who won't serve me a drink no matter how much I beg. He's a pal."

"So you're done drinking?"

"Well. I do my best. One day at a time. You know, the usual bullshit."

Lenny looked at Merv. Merv smiled at him, but Lenny turned away.

"Now sit down here." His dad grabbed a nearby stool and pulled it over. "You're making me nervous hovering like that."

Merv popped opened a Coke and poured it fizzing into a tall glass on the bar. It looked mighty inviting.

Should he? Guess he owed it to Sally. He hesitated a moment, then sat.

"All right," Richard said, laughing. He slapped him on the back. "What do ya say? Shake your old man's hand."

Lenny looked at the outstretched hand but didn't move. To talk was one thing but to touch was another. A handshake signified a truce, or an understanding. Lenny wasn't about to let ten years go with a handshake. Instead he scooted his bar stool farther away.

"So where do you live, anyway?" he asked. "Sally sent a letter to you in Kalamazoo."

"We playing twenty questions now?"

"I'm just trying to work this out."

Richard looked at him wide-eyed. "Ah! Watson's on the case!"

Lenny scowled. "You know, the banquet is a big deal to her.

And obviously someone's messing with her. Don't you care at all?"

His dad nodded. "You're right. You say someone's impersonating me? That ought to piss me off."

"Damn straight," Lenny said, moving quickly from disbelief to disgust. It didn't matter which of them had faked the letter. It was a mighty low thing to do. Cowardly. Desperate even, but he wouldn't think about that.

Richard studied his empty glass for a moment. "She really wants to take me to this thing?"

Lenny shrugged. "All the girls are worked up over it."

"Pastor Voss still in charge over there?"

He nodded.

"Panty-waist. I never liked the man."

Lenny couldn't help allowing a small smile.

"So what did I say in my letter?"

"That you can't come."

His dad smiled. "Prudy's that afraid of me showing up, huh?" He drummed his fingers on the bar. "Hmmm. That's reason enough to go."

Too late Lenny remembered his job. Keep Dad away. Now he realized this was the fork in the road. This was the path that would bring Richard straight to their door.

"Well," his dad was saying. "That's not for me. Tell her I'm sorry but I don't usually attend church activities."

"*You* tell her." His decision was made. He was no saint, but writing those false words to Sally? That was just wrong. Sally deserved more. Maybe she'd share a dance with her dad. Maybe she'd tell him to fuck off. She should get to decide.

He reached for the Coke and took a long swallow. His dad might take some convincing, but that was okay. He had another dime in his pocket. He might pick one more song from the jukebox, long as he was here. Or maybe, if the mood struck him, he'd tell his dad about Cash's broken nose, just to see if he'd laugh and maybe slap him on the back once more.

Prudy

A mother is a woman prepared, her purse packed with necessities. A safety pin, Kleenex, throat lozenges, bobby pins, a packet of Saltines, aspirin, breath mints. A crisp five-dollar bill for emergencies. Dimes for the payphone. Prudy imagined a roving mother patrol. *Dump your bag, please. What, no Band Aids? No mini sewing kit? And what's with the packet of crumbs?* Still, she'd get plenty of points. Because the ability to anticipate disaster is what counts.

Richard coming back and taking Sally to the banquet. *That* would be disaster. Prudy would do whatever she needed to avoid it.

It was too bad she didn't have any more sick days left. If she didn't have to be at work, she'd take Sally to the department store for a new dress. Still, as she slipped on her shoes and reached for her bag, she felt a sense of accomplishment. And relief. As if she was finally able to let go a breath she didn't know she'd been holding.

Let's just get this over with. That was the thought that pushed Prudy to pick up a pen. Not that it was easy. She hesitated a long time before writing *with love, your dad*. It seemed wrong. But necessary.

The risky part was assuming that Richard would never write back, but the man she had known would never take the time to write. He might think about it for a few days, he might even pull out a piece of paper or search the drawer for a stamp. He might start talking as if he had actually done it when he hadn't. *My daughter and me, we keep in touch.*

And of course there was the fear, what if he had changed? Ten years was a long time. He might be sober. Successful. He might have become the man she imagined when she married him. He might like to have a daughter now, the same way he would like picking up a bargain suit, or getting a good trade-in on a car. *Hey, got me a sweet deal on a kid. She's practically grown, lives an hour away, and thinks I'm the cat's meow!* How unfair that would be! He skates away to happiness, leaving the rest of them wallowing in misfortune.

Fine. Let him stay away. To be safe, she'd watch the mail like a hawk. Or get a post office box. Something. Anything. Because the sooner Sally gave up her hope of Richard coming back, the sooner she'd see that going to the banquet with Pastor Voss was better than not going at all.

Once they were there, together, the truth could come out. Surrounded by all the other girls with their dads, Sally wouldn't take it so hard. See, you have a dad too. He's right here. He's been here all along.

He's ready now.

So maybe he wasn't ready yet, but he would be. Like it or

not.

Did Phillip think she enjoyed this? All the years of torment. The hours spent arguing with herself: *The truth cannot come out.*

What if it does?

My daughter will hate me. My kids will never forgive me.

Here an annoyed tsk tsk—*yes, but what about Sally? Doesn't she deserve to know?*

Here confusion. Did she? Did anybody deserve anything? What does it mean to be deserving?

And here clicked in that finger-wagging, hands-on-hips part of her. *Phillip deserves whatever comes of it. Getting off scott free all these years!*

Why is it the men who get to walk away?

No, it was time. Sally had to be told that Phillip was her father. The truth might stop there, with the three of them. No one else had to know. Except that her sister Flookie, she'd known for years. That she'd managed to zip her lip was something that still amazed Prudy. And what about Lenny and Nell? Shouldn't they know? And what if Sally told her best friend Frannie?

Face it, everyone would find out.

Prudy had an affair! With a pastor! She has an illegitimate daughter.

Well, look at Robert Van Oldebekking, from church. When he confessed to a gambling problem, no one condemned him. He mortgaged his house and lost it. Two years later, he and his wife and two kids were still living with his brother and Robert was still singing in the Sunday choir.

Would anyone stand by her?

She'd have to leave the church. How she'd miss Amelia Rozeboom and Sandra Van Ark from the prayer circle, and old

Mrs. Vorst on the organ. She'd known them for years! Or else—and the more she considered this the more she believed it—she would be forgiven. *Just as I am without one plea, but that thy blood was shed for me!* Adulterous, deceitful, cowardly. But who did Jesus die for, if not the likes of her?

Imagine kneeling before the Lord with her soul laid bare! Standing before the faithful, being truly welcomed by their outstretched arms.

I was lost but now I'm found.

What about Phillip? What would happen to him once everyone found out Sally was his daughter? He'd probably lose his job. He'd have to move away and Sally would lose him.

Found, then lost.

Was that what she wanted?

Maybe she ought to leave it alone. Hadn't she made it this far? There was the time when Sally was five years old, right after Richard left for good, when she kept saying *where's daddy? I want daddy.* It was hard on all of them, especially Lenny. *He's not coming back*, he'd say, patiently at first, until he finally yelled *can't you get it through your thick skull?* Later she heard him crying in his bed.

Hadn't Prudy wanted to drag Sally over to the church right then and tell her *never mind that daddy. Here's another one. Your real one.* She thought she might be able to make things right while Sally was young, before she got to the age where she could suffer the way Lenny was suffering. It was too much to hope that Sally might take Richard's leaving well, like Nell. Even as a child, Nell had a knack for turning adversity into a life lesson. The most emotional Prudy ever saw Nell was the time Sally was seven and delirious with fever. It was the middle of the night. Prudy was so scared she called Phillip and made him come over. Poor Nell came shuffling down the hallway in her nightgown, and when she saw the pastor she started wailing, certain he was there because Sally was dying. It was then that Prudy knew there was no halfway. Phillip was in, or he was out. Anything else was too confusing.

Now here was the banquet. It was always visible, a storm cloud on the horizon. The fact that Phillip allowed it to continue for so long had always astounded Prudy. Tradition or not, it was his church. Why didn't he make the church board put their money toward something else? A carnival maybe, or camping trip. Was the banquet his way of punishing himself? Or worse, did the tragedy of it fail to register with him?

Maybe he'd been waiting, just like her, for Sally to turn sixteen, knowing they'd be forced into something.

There was a right way for this to happen: Phillip would tell Sally. Alone. Prudy couldn't bear to see her first disbelieving look. Besides, Phillip was used to serious discussions. Preparing someone for death, or plumbing the dark depths of a sinner's soul, it was all in a day's work for him. If he could make Sally understand their affair there might be a chance for forgiveness.

Afterward, Sally would come to accept Phillip. Maybe even be proud of him. He was an important man, a leader, and a far cry better than a deadbeat drunk. Sally might even want Prudy to marry him. How would Prudy explain? She couldn't very well tell her that Phillip was no more attractive to her than their slouchy, stuttering garbage man. In fact, she couldn't believe she'd ever enjoyed his touch.

There was no use remembering those other feelings. The hopefulness, the tenderness, the longing. Anyway, what was love but a different kind of storm cloud? Heavy with confusion. Ruinous. Here, then gone.

Nothing but clear skies, please! As she dressed she found herself whistling. She had the nine to six shift today at the factory. This year would mark her ten year anniversary at John Thomas Batts. Fifty hours a week on the line assembling wooden hangers. She'd get a silver watch. Since they weren't allowed to wear jewelry of any kind to work, the employees joked. *Hey boss, how many years before I get my tiara?* But it meant something. When Prudy got hers, she planned to keep it in her underwear drawer with her wedding band and a $50 savings bond her parents gave her on her wedding day. Maybe wear it to church.

The long hours didn't faze her anymore. Factory work helped her mark time. Every half hour broken by a whistle. Rotate stations. You fall into a rut. You start to think the unanswered questions of life will maybe slip away, leaving you in peace. Then one day you wake up and it's like some giant alarm clock is clanging in your head. Move it! Now's the time! Go, go go! You spring into action the way you would if you were late, with that same feeling. How could I be so careless? What's wrong with me!

Thank God she was up. And ready. For better or worse, something was going to happen. She stuck her head in Sally's room to wake her. What she saw on the pillow was a head of dark hair. Not Sally's.

"Lenny!" she said. "What are you doing here?"

He groaned and flopped over. "Trying to get some sleep."

"Where's Sally?"

"How would I know?"

"You're in her bed."

"It's been her bed for a week. It was mine a lot longer." He pulled the sheet over his head.

She went and knocked on the bathroom door. She could hear Nell humming in the bathtub.

"Where's your sister?" she called.

"Haven't seen her."

She sighed and went back to the bedroom.

"How long have you been here?" she asked Lenny.

He groaned again.

She reached over and pulled the sheet back. "Lenny!"

"I came home to get some breakfast," he said groggily. "The bed was empty so I got in."

She slapped his leg. "Get back to the church. You're supposed to be working."

Prudy looked around, annoyed. Where was Sally? Prudy wanted to tell her that she could walk over to Steketees today to look at dresses. Nell would be hurt. When she went to the banquet, she wore a dress that she and Prudy made from some nice organza they found on sale. A new dress was a luxury they couldn't afford. But what Nell wouldn't know was that Prudy was going to make Phillip buy Sally's dress. *Thanks for sixteen years worth of hand-me-downs*, she'd say, handing him the receipt. *It's time you spring for something new.*

Her next thought surprised her. *This is going to be fun.*

She went to the kitchen, calling Sally's name, half expecting her to be sitting at the table eating breakfast, ignoring her, in full-blown surly mode. She wasn't there.

Prudy went out the screen door into the yard.

"Sally?"

It was 8:30 a.m. Prudy was lucky to pull Sally out of bed by now.

"Sally?" Hurrying now, she went back in the kitchen. Nell came in toweling her hair.

"I can't find her anywhere," Prudy said, an ominous feeling taking hold of her. Did she really think that by writing that letter Sally would give up on her dad?

"She'd better not forget about Mandy," said Nell. "She's supposed to take her to Bible School today."

"She must be upstairs, then," Prudy said, relieved. She went back outside and climbed the steps to the Veenstra's apartment. But when she reached the landing, the door opened and Mandy tripped out as if she'd been pushed. Before Prudy could speak, the door slammed shut.

"Mandy! Sally's not with you?"

Mandy shook her head.

Prudy's heart skidded. "Hold on there," she said, breathless. She turned and hurried back down the steps, calling over her shoulder, "Just sit there and wait a minute, honey."

In the kitchen, she found Nell at the sink.

"Where could she have gone?" Prudy asked. "To Frannie's maybe? Or Deb's? She wouldn't go to the church this early, would she?"

Nell shook her head. "Like I was trying to tell you last night. She skipped out on the whole first morning. She ran over to that gas station and we didn't see her again until song circle started."

Right. Nell had told her. But she hadn't really listened. She'd been dead on her feet after her shift at the factory. Besides, with Nell it never stopped. Sally did this. Sally did that. Prudy couldn't keep grounding Sally for every little thing.

Lenny shuffled in, frowning. "The gas station? Was Cash there?"

Nell nodded. "Yeah, he was there. She went to talk to him."

"What for?" Prudy asked.

"She was going on about finding Dad."

Face to face. Those were Sally's words.

"Does Cash have a car?"

Lenny threw up his hands. "Don't look at me. We're not exactly buddies."

"Well where *is* she?" As if repeatedly asking would produce an explanation. *Of course, I forgot! She's taking a jog. Or she's having coffee next door with Mrs. Beyer.* Only she didn't jog. She didn't drink coffee.

How about: *she ran away? She's lying dead on the highway.*

"She doesn't do this sort of thing, does she? While I'm at work? She doesn't just disappear, does she?" This might be old hat in her household, Sally gallivanting around while Prudy had her head in the sand.

Lenny shrugged.

"You watch her, right Nell? You would know."

"Maybe she'd go to Frannie's," Nell said, "But not this early."

Frantic now, she told Lenny, "Get over to the gas station and see if this Cash kid is there and if he knows anything."

But Lenny slouched against the counter. "I'm not talking to Cash! I'm on probation, remember?"

"You don't understand. Your sister could be halfway to Kalamazoo by now."

"Yeah," he said. "Nice going."

Prudy stared. "What?"

"I know about the letter, okay?"

Something in her started to sink. "What about the letter?"

"I know Dad didn't write it."

"What are you talking about?" How could he know? Had he somehow seen her mail it?

"Come on," he said. "I know you did it."

Nell was looking at her closely. "Mom?"

Prudy made a face. "Why would I write Sally that letter?"

"Because you don't want Dad taking her to the banquet," Lenny said.

"That's true, but—"

"So you should have known it would just make things worse."

The look he gave her! She didn't have to admit anything. "What makes you think you know so much?" she said.

"Never mind." There was disgust in his voice. Just wait, she thought. Wait until it all comes out.

"I was trying to spare Sally's feelings!" she cried.

Lenny rolled his eyes. Nell sighed, disbelieving.

"Is this about making her go with Pastor Voss?" Nell asked.

"Let's just start looking for her," Prudy said. Here it was. The unraveling. She should have sat them down a long time ago when they were still children. *I have something to tell you.* When they would have loved her with a child-like faith. Then none of this would be happening.

"But I've got my training this morning!" Nell said.

"How much training do you need to stand in the middle of the street with your hand up?" Prudy snapped, not meaning to hurt her, but really! What was wrong with them? Didn't they realize that Sally would never take off without permission? She wasn't that kind of girl. Or maybe she was. Was there a side of Sally that was hidden to Prudy? Maybe all her children lived separate lives. Maybe they laughed with one another about how gullible their mother was. Was that why Lenny and Nell didn't seem worried? Or was it because, despite their ages, they truly were still like children, not understanding the disasters of the world?

"Look for her yourself," Lenny said, striding away.

"Please!" she called after him. "I'll be late for work."

"Go ahead," Nell said. "I'll call her friends."

Prudy shook her head, hating herself for snapping at Nell. She reached over and touched her arm. "No. You can't miss your first day. Get over to the police station."

"What are you going to do?"

"I've got to call Phillip," she said, realizing too late. She'd never called him Phillip in front of her kids. The look on Nell's face, the surprise and confusion, the quickly downcast eyes, made her squirm.

"Go on," Prudy said, wishing she could explain, just a little. But there was no way to prepare any of them. Anyway, wasn't being prepared overrated? Her kids would stand by her. They had to. All they had was each other.

Thanks to her.

Nell

There ought to be a word for that feeling of being pulled two ways at once. If there was, Nell couldn't think of it. *Torn*. That was close, but too willy-nilly. Indecisive people were torn. No, she was stuck equally between two angers, not knowing which was worse. Why did Sally have to pick today to pull such a stupid stunt? Did she bother to think how she would ruin Nell's big day, her first day with the Holland Auxiliary Police Department, training for a job that was not easy to get, thank you very much! And what about her mother, ruining her big night with Pastor Voss by butting in with that fake letter? Why, it was downright deceitful! And Prudy was the most honest, the most moral, the most *Christian* person Nell knew. Besides Pastor Voss.

Nell understood her mother's reason for lying. Nell was afraid too. She didn't want to have her dad back again, tamping her spirits down every time his eyes flicked over her. No one wanted all the bad feelings he was sure to bring. She imagined him standing in their living room, a Santa-like bag slung over his shoulder, bulging with slights and sounds still freshly wrapped after a decade. *Whew!* he'd groan, spilling it all over the floor. *Here we go! Some insults, a little foul language, and this big box here? Insecurities!*

But what she'd decided, with a little help from her trusty diary, was that she could take it. If her dad's coming meant that Pastor Voss was freed up for her, then she would be on Sally's side. What better way to show a little grace under pressure? It would be hard, but with the proper planning, she could manage some cool lines, something Lauren Bacall-ish, to show the pastor her backbone. When she wrote that in her diary —*show him your backbone* —it caused her to spin into a reverie *tres risque*: him standing in the doorway of the bedroom on their wedding night, thoughtfully giving her space to undress, her naked back toward him as she perched on the bed.

So please, butt *out*, Mother! Let Sally do her thing.

Except.

Who knew it would come to this? Running away! She still thought Sally might be off sulking somewhere, just to throw a scare into Prudy. Still, she couldn't help but worry. Worrying seemed to be her full-time job, along with shopping and cooking and washing, and watering the grass, and supervising homework, and keeping track of the bills. Now here was another worry: she might lose her new job if she missed today's training.

She needed to get dressed, but she was too aware of her mother dialing the phone in the next room. Dialing Phillip. *Phillip!* Nell should be the one calling him that, not her mother. Why was she calling him Phillip, as if...Oh! She was making too much of it. She was prone to that. Still, she stopped in the hallway outside the kitchen and listened.

There was no greeting, just *Something's wrong! Sally's missing. You've got to help me find her.*

Pause.

She wasn't in her bed. I can't find her anywhere.

Pause.

She's not at Bible School. She's gone to Kalamazoo to find Richard!

Then, an angry burst: *What does it matter? She was upset.*

Pause.

Now begrudging. *She got a letter saying he wasn't coming.*

Then impatient. *Listen, I wrote it. I probably shouldn't have, but I thought it would make her realize...*

Don't you start pointing fingers!

Nell's hand flew to her mouth. She heard her mother draw a deep breath.

Fine. Start at the Texaco. Find out if Cash DeVries has a car. She might be with him. I'll call her friends.

Pause.

They'll dock my pay, but what can I do?

Next a sudden, muffled sob. *Oh God, Phillip. It's all going wrong!*

Nell slipped into her bedroom, heart pounding. Yes, all wrong! She couldn't understand why he was the one her mother called. What was he supposed to do? Better to call the police. Or Nell could make a report in person, as soon as she got there.

Why wasn't she going?

She kept thinking *wrong, all wrong!* You don't call your pastor by his first name. You don't yell at him like it's all his fault. You only talk like that if you don't see him as a pastor. If you see him as a man.

She reached for her dresser and held on tight with both hands. She couldn't seem to make a move. *Torn*. That's what she was. Between ignoring or admitting something she'd known for a long time. *For such a smart girl, you're a real idiot*, she said, giving herself a hard look in the mirror. So they had a thing. An affair. So they were once *in love*.

It didn't change anything! Nell had plenty to offer. A great new job, impeccable domestic skills, solid character. Above all, faith in the Lord.

She clasped her hands and bowed her head. *Please bring Sally home safe. Please make things normal again so I can have the chance to find the love I know you want me to find.*

How she'd looked forward to today! To the white gloves, the stiff blue hat with the shiny black brim, the orange vest with the sewn-on badge that said Holland Auxiliary Police Department. Once she had her uniform, people would notice her. They'd have to, otherwise she'd be run down in the street! But what about *now*? She needed to be noticed now!

It seemed to her that misbehaving brought the most attention. Do a thousand good deeds and don't rock anybody's boat. *Splish splash!* That was the size of the thanks you got. But screw up and it's *Mayday! Mayday! All hands on deck!!*

Nell heard her mother blow her nose, then the sound of the phone being dialed again. Her mother would be calling Sally's friends now. It wouldn't do any good. Someone had to go after Sally.

Without a word, she went out the front door and down the sidewalk toward the church. She'd find a way to explain to Sergeant Van Zandt. He liked her. She'd seen that right away when she applied for the job. He gave her the once-over and immediately saw her for the no-frills, no-fuss girl she was. She liked to think it was her posture. But people with good posture showed up for work.

All she could do now was hope for a second chance.

She'd gone three blocks when she heard a strange clacking noise behind her. She turned to see Mandy running after her, dressed in ruffles and strappy shoes. Mandy! Nell had forgotten all about her. Sally was supposed to take her to Bible School today.

"Wait!" Mandy cried.

Nell groaned and shook her head. "Honey, I can't."

Mandy's face fell.

"Oh, honey, come on," Nell said. She couldn't send her back to Mona. And she didn't have time to bring her into the church. She'd just have to come along. "Hurry up, now. There's been a little change of plans. Just follow me."

"I thought you had training," Mandy said.

You thought wrong, Nell very nearly snapped. What had come over her? I *thought*. I *thought*. I thought it paid to be good! What if she was wrong?

What she needed was a good long session with her diary to sort things out, although she'd reflected plenty and had nothing to show for it. She was certain now: she'd die a spinster's death. She'd become one of those old dried up parishioners clutching a large-print Bible, volunteering for every committee imaginable, wanting so much to be noticed, never realizing that being ever-present only makes a person into a fixture, requiring no more thought than a light switch or a folding chair.

"Something's happened to Sally," she managed to tell Mandy, because tears were threatening. Crying was another thing she did not do! "I have to help her. I have to show them…."

There would be other jobs. Anyway, what was a job

compared to a life? A life was a collection of defining moments. She thought of the rocks she collected whenever Aunt Flookie took them out to Lake Michigan, each one worn down and spit out by the ever-changing tide. You had to look to find the good ones.

If Pastor Voss wasn't willing to look, what was she supposed to do?

When she got to the church with Mandy in tow, she found Lenny sitting on the steps, staring over at the Texaco.

"Did you find anything out?" she called, flipping her thumb toward the gas station.

Lenny gave her a glum look. He hesitated. "Owner says Cash was there but left. With a girl."

So they were right. She motioned for Lenny to follow her as she hurried past the church to the parsonage. There in the driveway sat Pastor Voss' Ford Galaxie 500. She went over and peered in the window. Just as she suspected, the keys were dangling in the ignition.

"Get in," she called over her shoulder. The driveway was behind the house. The room above them was probably the pastor's bedroom. *Bedroom!* She couldn't bear to think of all the wonderful mysteries that room would hold.

Lenny stopped. "He's letting us drive his car?"

"Shhh!" she said, looking quickly toward the open window. "Just get in! You too, Mandy."

Mandy obeyed but Lenny was frozen in place.

"You're stealing Voss' car?"

"It's not stealing," Nell whispered. "Just borrowing."

He made a face. She could tell that he didn't believe she'd do it.

"Come *on*," she said, exasperated. Lenny of all people

should understand. Obviously it took some rabble-rousing to be the center of attention. Well, she could rabble rouse with the best of them.

She opened the driver's side door with sweating palms. She was an okay driver, but not what anyone would call confident. She was climbing in when Lenny ran over and pushed her.

"Are you crazy?" he said. "I'm already in trouble, remember?"

"So stay here. I'll go alone."

"Go where?"

"To find Sally."

"You don't even know where she is!"

"I've got Dad's address," she said. Lenny said nothing and Nell knew he'd seen the same slip of paper. Sally had it taped to her bedroom mirror, just daring someone to take it down.

"You're taking her with you," he said, pointing at Mandy sitting in the back seat. As in *sure you are*.

Nell flashed the girl a bright smile. "Don't worry Mandy. I'll have you home soon."

"I don't have to go home all day," Mandy said. "Mona said so."

"Then we're good to go." Nell pulled the door shut quietly and rolled the window down for some air.

Lenny leaned in. "Wait. This is not a good idea."

"When did that ever stop *you*?"

"I don't steal cars!"

Nell looked over her shoulder. "Mandy, I'm not really stealing. You know that, right?"

"I don't care if you steal or not. I know you're a good person."

Nell smiled. Everyone else would know it too.

"Will you let me go?" she said to Lenny. "I haven't got all day." Prudy might be heading over right now to join forces with Pastor Voss. She didn't want to get caught just sitting here.

"You'll get arrested!"

Nell hesitated. She didn't believe that, but she knew she could lose her job. And she hadn't even tried on the uniform yet! But better now than after she got to know all the kids. *What happened to that nice crossing lady? Oh, didn't you hear?*

She turned the key and the car purred to life. She put it carefully in reverse.

Lenny jumped back as the Ford started to roll. "For chrissake!" he hissed. He ran around the front and flung open the passenger door.

"Will you a wait a goddamn minute and tell me what your plan is?" he said.

"I just told you!"

Didn't he get it? Having a plan was not the point! If she found Sally no one would care about how she did it. If not, well, this was the kind of impetuous mistake—a momentary dance with the devil!—that would require hours of counseling with a spiritual leader.

He managed to get in the seat and shut the door before she was out of the driveway. He stared at her as she turned and braked, shifted into drive, pointed the car down 17th Street and stepped on the gas.

"This is stupid," he said. "Why not just let them go to the damn banquet together?"

"Fine by me," she said, her knuckles white on the wheel.

"Bullshit! If it's fine with you, what are we doing in this car?"

"They'll thank me when I get Sally home safely."

"Sure, Mom will love this. Now she'll have a daughter charged with grand theft auto."

"I'm not doing anything for Mom!" It came out like a snarl. Nell took a breath. "I want Sally to be happy."

Lenny looked at her suspiciously. She tried to concentrate on her movements but it was hard. Her hands were where *his* had been. She was sitting where he sat. Every sag, every lump in the car seat was put there by the pressure of his body.

"Is this the way to the highway?" she asked, breathless.

There was a long pause. "Pull over," said Lenny.

"No. You're not stopping me."

"I *said* pull over. You drive like shit."

"Stop it, you're scaring Mandy."

But when Nell glanced in the rear view mirror she saw Mandy smiling.

"No, he's not," Mandy said.

"Nell!" Lenny grabbed the wheel.

"Oh all right!" She coasted to the side of the road. Whose robbery was this anyway?

Lenny jumped out and ran around. "Move over."

She moved, not wanting to admit she was relieved to have him drive. As long as she got credit for the heist. That's what she'd call it in her diary. *Today I pulled a heist.*

He got in and revved the engine a few times before pulling back into the street. They were going faster now. As far as Nell knew, he drove a lot less than she did, but he knew what he was doing.

What was *she* doing? With someone else at the wheel, she was overcome with uncertainty.

He gave her a quick glance. "You don't mind if Dad goes to the banquet?"

She sighed. "No."

"Even if it means you have to see him?"

"Lenny," she began, then stopped. Everything was so complicated. It wasn't a question of minding. It was about *sacrifice.* About enduring what you don't want, to be rewarded with what you do.

"Ok," he said, like something was decided. He spun the wheel sharply, making a U-turn in the intersection.

Mandy flopped to one side in the backseat. Nell clutched at the armrest. "What's going on?" she cried, alarmed.

"Sally won't find him in Kalamazoo because he's not there. He's here, living with Rhoda Raymond's mom. I've seen him."

"*What?* Why didn't you say so earlier?"

He shrugged. "Didn't see the point."

Nell gaped. "I hope you see it now!" she said. "Now that your sister's run away!"

"How was I supposed to know she'd do something so stupid?"

"You should have told me!" She tried to imagine Lenny with their dad. "Have you talked to him?"

"Yep. That's how I knew he didn't write that letter."

"What did he say? What's he look like?"

"You'll see for yourself. Since we've got the car, we may as well put an end to this whole mess. We'll go get him and then find Sally. Once the two of them are hooked up it'll either work out or it won't."

They were flying down James Street, out toward the blueberry farms. Nell saw the pavement whiz by and felt dizzy. It was all too fast.

"Just drop Mandy and me off," she said, hearing the panic in her voice. "We'll get a bus home." She wasn't ready! What would she say? What would he say? Would he recognize her? Should she comb her hair?

Lenny was shaking his head. “No way. You started this.”

“I’ve got to get Mandy home!”

“You should have thought of that before.”

Mandy leaned forward and rested her chin on the front seat. “I don’t want to go home,” she said.

“Lenny, please!” *Don’t make me go back there!* He wouldn’t know what she meant if she said that. She hardly knew herself, except that it felt like he was pulling her back to a time when she hated everything about herself. She didn’t have room for that anymore, not when she was gearing up for love.

Lenny drove faster, his face set in a grim line, and soon they were rolling to a stop outside a group of weathered white shacks. How could Lenny do this? Just drive right up, cool as a cucumber! There were cats, scads of them, circling the yard and a row of navy work pants hanging from a line. Further back there was a man sleeping in a chair, a hat covering his face, his brown arms hanging heavy to the ground. A *migrant* camp! Her dad lived *here*? Nell tried to speak but her throat was dry. It was as if she expected to see some lurching, drunken monster rush out, with an army of Mexican fruit pickers close behind, their tin buckets clanging on their belts, their purple-stained fingers reaching, clawing, closer…closer…. She squeezed her eyes shut and thought of the quiet cool order of the police station. Right about now Sergeant Van Zandt would be looking over his roster, *looks like Van Sloeten’s a no show.* She was about as far from where she’d planned as a girl could get.

Well. When you start your day by stealing someone’s car, what do you expect?

Lenny sounded the car horn. The sleeping man didn’t move.

"He should be here," Lenny said. The way his eyes darted around gave him away. He wasn't so cool. For some reason, this calmed her a little.

"Have you been here before?" she asked.

He wouldn't answer.

Nell reached back for Mandy's hand. "It's okay, Mandy. Everything's fine." Mandy was perched on the edge of her seat, her head bobbing, birdlike, as she took it all in.

Hello. That was all Nell needed to say. She didn't need to smile, or shake hands, or cry or give anything away. Just hello.

A man came out from between two shacks. He walked straight to the open window of the car and leaned in. He was rumpled and easy and could have been any stranger on the street. Except he wasn't.

"Who have we got here?" he said, nodding at Mandy. Mandy! What did she have to do with anything? Didn't he recognize *Nell*, his own daughter?

"I'm a friend of Nell's," Mandy said, and Nell held her breath. Now he knew. *Hello, it's me.*

He gave Nell a long, thoughtful look, followed by a solemn nod. "Of course, there you are," he said. "What brings you kids out this way?"

That was it. The big moment, over and done. Nell wondered if she ought to feel slighted. She didn't. What was there to say, anyway?

"We need you to come with us," Lenny said. "Sally's run off looking for you."

"Aw, dang." Richard pulled at his face. "Let me guess. Kalamazoo?"

Lenny nodded. "Get in."

Richard stepped back, his hands on his hips. He cocked his

head and chewed the inside of one cheek thoughtfully.

"Hang on," he said. He disappeared behind one of the houses.

Nell looked at Lenny. "You want to fill me in?" she said.

Lenny licked his lips and fidgeted. "I ran into him at the Torchlight. We had a drink."

"A drink?"

He shrugged. "Okay, a Coke."

"But how…"

"That's it! End of story."

Sally was writing to him, Lenny was drinking with him. Where did that leave her? Stunned and sweaty in a car with nothing but a black mark next to her name. Just a foolish girl who thinks stealing a man's car will make him love her! Her dad would see right through her.

If she were another kind of person, one of those smiley, jokey types, she might still turn it around. When Richard came back she might push her hair up with her hands and bat her eyes. *Long time no see*, she could say with a grin. She wrenched the rear view mirror around and squinted at herself. At least she looked fairly nice, considering she'd expected to be on the job today. That was how the officers talked. *How 'bout Zoerhof? He still on the job?*

"Mandy, I'll ride by you," she said. She got out and moved to the back seat, smoothing her skirt carefully. At least her dad wouldn't be staring at the back of her head.

In fact, when he came back wearing a clean blue shirt, he hardly looked at her. Just like old times! He slid in beside Lenny, threw an arm over the back of the seat and said, "Whose car is this?"

"Never mind," Lenny said.

"Shoot! You're doing all right for yourself, nice ride like this. American made. Solid choice."

"It's not mine. I borrowed it."

"Still, must be a pretty good friend, let you take this out. I'm glad to hear you've got friends."

Lenny gave him a cool look. "Nell stole it."

Richard laughed. "Come on!"

"It belongs to Pastor Voss," Lenny said. "Nell stole it."

"Are you kidding me?" He looked at Nell in a surprised, admiring way. She felt a flash of pride. Maybe there was something to this trouble making.

"Let me out then," he said, "I don't need to be tangling with the cops."

"Like I do?" said Lenny.

"If we let you out we won't know where we're going," Nell said. Like a ringleader. She liked that.

"I'll give you directions."

"Lenny's no good at directions," she said. *She* was, but she didn't say so. As long as her dad was here, they might as well do what Lenny said. Find Sally and get this over with. Besides, the opportunity might arise to tell him about her crossing guard job. Today was no more than a tiptoe on the wild side. She was no delinquent. She wanted him to know that.

Anyway, Richard didn't seem very intent on getting out. He heaved a big sigh and his face settled into something close to amusement. A moment later they were flying up the ramp onto US131 toward Kalamazoo.

The air from the open windows whipped through the car and seemed to whip Mandy into life. "Someday I'm going to live with Nell and Sally and their mom," she shouted. "My dad can visit me because he'll be right upstairs."

Nell looked at her, surprised.

"Nell takes me to church and we make things, like boxes out of milk cartons, and picture frames out of Popsicle sticks. Stuff like that."

"She's a chatterbox, huh?" Richard said. He nearly had to shout too. "I like kids who keep quiet. You were always quiet, weren't you Nell?"

"I never got the sense you liked me any better for it!"

Richard cupped a hand to his ear. "What's that?"

"You never liked me any better!" This was silly, yelling like this. It wasn't ladylike. She rolled her window up and motioned for Mandy to do the same.

"Awww," her dad said, seeming very close now in the relative quiet. "Why do you go and say something like that? 'Course I liked you just fine."

"That's not the way I remember it," she said. Petulant. That's how she sounded. The shouting felt better.

"I take it you don't share Sally's sentiment about getting to know me."

"That's right."

"Like I told Lenny, I don't blame you. Anyway, look what a mess I am." He seemed as proud of his downtrodden state as he used to be about his good looks.

"How about you, Mandy?" he said. "You like me just fine, don't you?"

Mandy looked at Nell. "If Nell says I like you, then I do."

"That ain't something you ask someone else. Either you like me or you don't."

"She doesn't know you from Adam," Nell said.

"Neither do we, really," Lenny said.

"That didn't stop you all from coming after me, did it? I was having a relaxing morning."

"Nell and me ain't been able to relax for weeks, what with Sally bitching and moaning about this banquet."

"What have you been telling her about me?" Richard asked.

"We tell her the truth," Nell said.

"Nell always tells the truth," Mandy said. "She's a Sunday School teacher."

"What a surprise," Richard said dryly. "Your mother's got you whitewashed pretty well, huh?"

Whitewashed? "I suppose your way of life is preferable," Nell said.

He chuckled. "How about you, Lenny? You into the church thing too?"

"If Voss has anything to say about it, I will be. He's got me pretty boxed in."

"Ah! One more soul for the book of life! That peckerwood."

Nell gasped and covered Mandy's ears. "Watch it!"

Richard just laughed again. "It's a wonder his pecker don't fall off."

Lenny perked up. "Why?"

"He was sticking it in the organist and who knows who else at his last church. That's how come he lost that job and ended up here."

Nell bolted upright. "That's not true!"

"Are you kidding?" Lenny said.

"First Reformed, White Plains, Michigan. It's on my circuit. Or was, I should say."

Nell shook her head violently. "No! That would have been more than ten years ago! And your… your *head's* all bashed in. You don't know *anything!*"

Richard shrugged. "Sorry to burst your bubble."

She looked frantically at Lenny. He didn't seem the least outraged. He was *enjoying* this.

"Why should we believe you?" she cried. "You aren't even in the same *league* as Pastor Voss!"

"I'm no saint, it's true. But I don't pretend to be one, neither."

There was no reason to believe such trash. And yet. What if the man she'd known and admired for nearly half her life was not what he seemed?

"Please stop talking about him," she said. "It's upsetting me."

The sound of a siren wailing in the distance made them all look quickly at each other.

"You don't want to be upset, you better hope that's not what I think it is," Richard said.

Lenny whipped his head around to get a good look behind them. "Nell! What did you get me into?" he said.

Nell turned and saw a Michigan State Police car approaching. The dumb luck! A Holland cop wouldn't be so bad. One of her own. But a state cop!

"Pull over!" she cried. She'd surrender willingly. Lock me up! I masterminded the whole sordid affair. Even the inadvertent use of that word—*affair*—delivered a quick stab of pain, like touching a raw nerve.

Lenny cursed as he brought them to a stop. A squad car pulled up behind, flashers pulsing in the sun.

"What's wrong?" Mandy asked.

"Nothing," Nell said. "Just a misunderstanding." Her heart was beating so loudly she was sure everyone could hear it. Lenny's eyes flitted nervously in the rear view mirror. Richard's thumb danced wildly on the back of the seat. They waited but the officer didn't get out of his car. Nell looked again and saw him talking on his radio.

Richard sighed. "Kids, you may as well know. Trouble follows me. This situation here, it's just the sort of thing I've come to expect." He sucked his teeth. "But goddammit!" he cried, slamming his hand on the dashboard.

Finally they heard a door slam and the crunch of boots on gravel. The officer loomed large next to Lenny.

"Afternoon, son. I'll need a driver's license and registration, please."

Lenny had neither, but he made a show of patting his shirt pocket and the pockets of his jeans.

Richard cleared his throat. "These here are my kids," he said. "They're taking me to see my mother."

The officer leaned over and squinted at him. "Is that right?"

Nell knew she should say something, if only to shut Richard up. The truth! Tell him the truth!

"These three kids are yours?"

Nell squeezed Mandy's hand. She'd be charged with kidnapping too!

"We're headed to Kalamazoo. I let my son drive for a spell."

"I'm legal," Lenny said quickly.

"Well son, maybe you are. Maybe you're not," the officer said, rubbing his jaw. "But I'll tell you what's peculiar. I've got a report that this car is stolen. It belongs to the Reverend Phillip Voss."

Nell had missed her moment to come clean. Now she'd be called uncooperative.

"You see..." Richard said. "Voss loaned it to my son. Lenny works for him."

The officer turned his stare on Lenny. "He reported it

stolen."

"The pastor gets bad headaches," Nell blurted. "From the heat." She was in it now. Was this how criminals were made? With a series of missteps, split second lapses of judgment? When you see how hard it can be to do what's right, is it with relief that you say *oh well, may as well go whole hog?*

Richard said, "What she means is that he may have forgotten. Right honey?"

His eyes, wide and kind. His voice, soft, forgotten. *Honey.* Yes, just like that, sticky and sweet, pulling her toward uncertainty. She was nodding before she realized it.

But she caught herself. "The truth is," she said. The *truth.* "I borrowed the car. I had to. My sister ran away and we're going after her."

The officer looked at her, unimpressed. He turned back to Richard. "You got an ID?"

Nell waved her hand at him. "It was me! I took the car!"

The officer ignored her.

Richard sighed and pulled a battered wallet from his back pocket. He rifled through it, then handed a license over.

"Sit tight," the officer said. He ambled back to the squad car.

"Man!" Lenny exploded. "Should I take off?"

Richard laid a hand on his arm. "Cool it. Just keep it cool, cat."

"Are we going to jail?" Mandy asked.

"One of us is," Richard said.

Lenny sneaked Nell a look. All right, all *right.* So this wasn't their dad's fault. But then you *could* argue that everything was his fault. How dare he spread such lies about Pastor Voss! And with that cock-sure way he had that made her nearly believe him. She hated him! He started *whistling*, as if a run-in with the cops was such a lark. It didn't make sense. And neither did this thought, sudden and unwelcome: this time with her dad, was it all she was going to get?

"I wonder what they're doing in Bible School," she said wistfully.

"Probably singing," Mandy said. "You want to sing, Nell?"

Nell gave her a thin smile. "Maybe later, honey."

The cop came crunching back. "All right. I think I understand the situation."

"Of course!" Nell said, relieved. "It's all just—"

The officer's hand shot up, silencing her. "Step out of the car, Mr. Van Sloeten. I'm taking you in."

Richard groaned. "What for?"

"Mr. Voss wants to press charges."

"Listen, I'm just along for the ride here. You can't pin this—"

"You can tell me all about it at the station. Come on. All of you."

"Where are you taking us?" Nell asked. "Back to Holland?" *Hello Sergeant, no I'm not late for the orientation. Yes, these are handcuffs.*

They climbed into the squad car, unshackled, which was a relief. She was packed in tight between Lenny and her dad, with Mandy on her lap, but she was able to turn enough to see the pastor's Galaxie 500 out of the corner of her eye. Already it had a lonely, abandoned look. Had she really been riding away with her father? She felt a pang, empty and needy, like hunger. He'd called them *his kids*. She couldn't say why such simple words should come echoing back like a voice bouncing off a canyon. Or why she felt the urge to answer. *You were wrong about me.*

"What about...?" She stopped, her finger floating uselessly in the air. Never mind the car. It shimmered in the heat, a shrinking speck on the horizon. It hurt her neck to watch it disappear. She turned to the highway stretching ahead, a silver rope pulling her back. Back again. To the only truth that mattered: she wasn't going anywhere. Forget the new job, the joyous reunion, heroic rescue, or redeeming love. She'd let herself get carried away. Too late she felt the thrill of it. Too late common sense returned. This is your place, it said. Stop hoping for more.

Prudy

There was a reason Prudy didn't go rushing off half-cocked to the church to look for Sally. Only what was it? Shouldn't she be running, shouting, searching, *moving*? Stay by the phone. That's what Phillip told her. Like in the movies. But that was for kidnappings. Waiting on a ransom call. This was different. This was just a stupid teenage stunt.

Sally was making her point all right. And when she came home Prudy would make hers. I run this family, she would say. *Not* you.

Prudy dialed Sally's best friend Frannie, rehearsing her words in case Mrs. Valkema answered. *By any chance have you seen Sally?* she'd say, apologetic. (Prudy doesn't know where her daughter is? Doesn't she keep an eye on her?) But there was no answer. Next she called the Texaco station, but that phone rang unanswered too. She thought about calling Flookie. *You won't believe what Sally's done!* And she ought to call Cash's parents, but that would be awkward, considering what Lenny did to Cash's nose. She'd never met the DeVries, and she didn't feel like having to apologize for her son when she was worrying about her daughter.

Face it, it would be embarrassing, having people know. Maybe that's why she wasn't marching out the door. If Sally was at Bible School, Prudy didn't want to look like one of those overbearing mothers by showing up hysterical. She didn't want to be square. When Sally came home, right as rain, people would guess the truth: Prudy didn't know what she was doing.

Oh, what was *wrong* with her? Why care what anyone thought? Her daughter was gone! She grabbed the phone and called the police. The officer listened to her like he'd heard this story too many times. Teenager? Last seen with a boy? Ho-hum. She tried to say all the right things to convey that this was The Real Deal. But was it? It didn't matter. The report was made. Except that she wasn't able to tell the officer what Sally was wearing. Asleep on the job. That's what she'd been. Asleep for years. When she hung up and went to Sally's room, the things she saw only proved it. There was a purple skirt that Prudy had never seen lying in a heap on the floor. And on the dresser a bottle of nail polish. Since when did Sally paint her nails? And three Nancy Drew novels stacked beside the bed. Prudy had no idea whether Sally had read them or not.

Well, *someone* had to work! There was no one else around to support them! And now she'd be late. *Dammit Sally!* What if she was in an accident? Or buried in a cornfield? Or worse, what if she just vanished, and they had to live out their lives never knowing *where* she was?

She grabbed her purse. She'd go to work. When her morning break came she'd call the church and Mrs. Regneres would tell her Sally was making faces at the grade school kids when she was supposed to be singing the Lord's praises. Or she would say *Sally? No, she's not here and I was just saying to Mrs. Droost, aren't we missing Sally's cheerful smile?*

Prudy threw her purse back down and squeezed her head in her hands. Phillip said everything would be okay, but what did he know? Was he prepared to speak at Sally's funeral?

She went to the kitchen and grabbed a dishrag from the sink. She wiped the table roughly. This would all turn out to be nothing. Just a crush. Sally sneaking off to see Cash before Bible School. The fact that Lenny hated him probably made him more appealing to her. Or Cash might have nothing to do with anything. Maybe Sally left early to visit Lenny in his new room. To rub it in. That would be like her. Except Phillip would have found her and called by now.

Could Sally actually get herself to Kalamazoo and locate Richard? If she did, she'd learn that he never wrote that letter. She'd *know.* And then what else would she discover?

Prudy had to find her!

Sally

Okay, so it wasn't exactly the greeting she was hoping for. As odd as the whole European cheek-kissing thing had been, Sally had found herself reliving it a few hundred times during the long sleepless night. So when Cash leaned over and shoved the passenger door open the next morning, without so much as a hello, she was surprised. His face had the doughy, squinty look of someone who's just rolled out of bed.

"Hey," she said, instantly somber. The care she'd taken with her hair and her clothes seemed silly. It was her dad she wanted to impress. Not Cash.

He grunted and stepped on the gas before her door was shut.

"Not a morning person, huh?"

"I'm here, ain't I?" he said, and his voice was gravelly. She couldn't say why, but it set something fluttering in her stomach.

"I knew you would be." A lie, but he seemed to need an encouraging word. She didn't want him changing his mind.

Cash cranked up his radio. Sally recognized The Doors. She wasn't allowed to listen to this kind of music at home, but she heard it around. She didn't know enough to talk about it, though, so she said nothing as they headed for the highway. Instead she fidgeted with her purse, unzipping it to check the contents one more time. There was her dad's letter, of course. And her ten dollars. A stick of gum, and the wadded-up wrapper of a Dum-Dum sucker. A flier from the skating rink about a high school skate-a-thon she'd never get to go to. And, the thing she was most proud of, her library card, with her name typed in bold ink. An identity.

Maybe she should have left a note. Soon her mother would realize she was gone and what would she do? Yell? Cry? Sally had never done something so drastic. She didn't know what would happen. Anyway, wasn't this all her mother's fault? Keeping a child from her father, well, it must be a breach of civil liberties or some such thing.

At the edge of town she turned and took a quick look back. She was really doing it! She was on her way to Kalamazoo. She wasn't surprised—she'd never doubted her determination—just a little stunned that it was happening so fast. Without a hitch. Her only regret was that she'd waited so long.

But. What was she going to say to her dad? *I know you said no to the banquet, but won't you reconsider? I came all this way to meet you! Aren't you glad to see me?*

His face would break into a reluctant smile. Of course he'd be glad! Who could resist such a gesture?

Only a mean, no-good, heartless drunk.

"You hungry?" Cash asked.

"Not really."

"How about we get some breakfast?"

"I'd rather get to my dad's house right away." The way she figured it, her dad might take day trips to other towns. In which case he'd be home mornings and evenings. Or else he might work at home for stretches of time. She had to hope today was one of those lucky days.

"What's your hurry? You've waited this long. Besides, it'll be an hour before we get there. I'm starved."

"Eat on your own time, why don't you?" she said irritably. "I'm paying you to do this for me."

"Jeez, I ain't your slave. And you ain't paying that much."

"It may not seem like a lot to you, but it's all I've got and I don't have a job like you do."

There was a pause. Cash cleared his throat. "Speaking of payment..."

Sally dug the money from her purse and flung it on the seat. "Take it. It's all yours."

"A deal's a deal," he said defensively.

She glared at him. His mood seemed to lighten.

"You're sure crabby today," he said. "Here I go and invite you to have breakfast with me. You might try to be polite."

"You're the crabby one."

He smiled. "Let me get some food in me and I'll perk right up."

"Forget it."

They drove in silence for a few minutes.

"Did you hear that? That's my stomach growling," Cash said, grinning now.

Sally said nothing.

"I feel a little weak, too. And with this heat —"

"Oh all right!" She was feeling a little weak herself. "What did you have in mind?"

Cash motioned with his head. “There was a billboard back there for Stuckey’s. I could go for some biscuits and gravy.”

She made a face.

“They’ve got other stuff too.”

They pulled off at the next exit and rolled to a stop in a parking lot that was nearly empty. Sally was dubious. But she was also hungry after listening to him carry on. She’d been too nervous to eat breakfast. And as much as she hated to waste time, she supposed she needed some fortification.

The waitress brought two laminated menus covered with greasy finger smudges. Cash whistled cheerfully.

“See? This is great. The two of us, just relaxing, enjoying a quick bite together.”

“You don’t get out much, do you?” Sally asked.

Cash’s laugh was low and he drew the end of it out in a long *ahhhh*. He looked at her as if she was very clever and she had to admit this was a tiny bit nice. She allowed a smile.

“Truth is,” she said, “I don’t get out much either.”

“Sure, we might as well have some fun today. It doesn’t have to be all business.”

He was right. Here she was, sitting in a restaurant about to have a meal with a boy. And he’d invited her. When she thought of it like that, it was pretty much a date. Her first date. She felt a blush crawling up her cheeks and looked at the menu.

“Maybe I’ll have a waffle. And some orange juice.”

He whistled. “You’re a big spender. I’ll have to stick to the side order of biscuits and gravy.”

“*I’m* a big spender? I thought—” Wasn’t he buying her breakfast? She had never dated before but she wasn’t so dumb that she didn’t know an invitation when she heard one. Besides, girls shouldn’t have to pay. Decent boys didn’t allow it.

"You thought what?"

"I don't have any money," she said. "I just gave it all to you."

"Why are you talking about ordering then? Do you expect me to pay?"

Your face burned. "You asked me. Like a date."

"I never said it was a date. For chrissake, it's breakfast!"

"When a boy asks a girl to eat out, it's a date. That means you pay."

"That'll blow every last cent and I'll go home with nothing."

Sally set the menu aside. What a jerk! He was rude and obnoxious and didn't deserve to be enjoying the company of a respectable girl like her. She had no reason to feel embarrassed. But she did. This might just qualify as the most embarrassing moment of her life.

Then the waitress was there, her pen poised to take their order. Sally stared at the tabletop. If she sat statue-still, it would be like she wasn't there.

"So you're not having nothing then?" Cash said.

She didn't answer.

"You want me to give you kids a few more minutes?" the waitress asked.

She barely shrugged.

"So I've got to eat while you sit there staring at me?"

This wasn't working.

"You said you're not hungry anyway, right?"

"I'll just go sit in the car, how's that?" she hissed, her voice low, as if the waitress wouldn't hear. "In fact, as soon as you're done feeding your face, you can take me home."

"Aw, you don't mean that. Come on, I'll share some with you."

"I don't like biscuits and gravy."

The waitress was tapping her pencil on her pad.

"But I came here especially for that," he said.

"So get it. I don't care."

"Fine," Cash said. "I'll take a side of biscuits and gravy."

The waitress gave her a sympathetic smile before she turned away. Sally jumped up out of the booth.

"I wish I'd never laid eyes on you, Cash whatever-your-name-is. I hope you choke on your damn biscuits!" She rushed to the back of the restaurant and pushed her shoulder into the door marked *fillies.* There was no one else around. She banged her fists on the bathroom stall. She hated Cash. She hated the entire male population. Most of all she hated her father. If it weren't for him she'd never be in this position. If he had stayed around she'd be having her first date in a nice restaurant with a boy who wore brown penny loafers and a red garnet class ring. Instead she was stuck miles from home with a boy she hardly knew, on her way to meet a man she knew even less. She could just imagine Cash sitting in the booth with that stupid grin on his face, laughing at her, the same way her father would laugh when she showed up at his door. Well, she wasn't turning back. She wouldn't speak one more word to Cash. He was like a taxi driver. A hired hand. That's how she'd treat him. She looked at her hands. They were shaking. Taking a deep breath, she made herself lean back against the bathroom wall. *Cool it!* She opened her purse and took out a skating rink flier. *Rollin' Thru the Night! Hey Teens! Turn Your Wheels for the Tots! Have fun and earn money for the Shriners' Children's Hospital. August 31, 9 PM to 5 AM. Prizes! Refreshments! Music and Games! Pick up your pledge forms now!* She read it again, then once more. She looked up at the ceiling and saw three globs of dried toilet paper balls stuck to the tile. After what seemed ages, she dumped the flier in the garbage can, ran a hand through her hair and marched out of the bathroom, back to the booth.

Cash was gone.

Stranded! How *could* he? Now she'd have to call her mother and tell her that she'd been left on the interstate. She'd have to sit in the restaurant for a good hour, with no money, hoping the waitresses would be kind. *Relying on the kindness of strangers.* It was something she'd never had to do. Her heart began to race. Think! *Think!*

She spotted a phone booth at the edge of the parking lot and started toward it. Maybe she could reach Aunt Flookie at the beauty parlor and ask her to come pick her up. She might even convince Flookie to finish the trip to Kalamazoo. Flookie knew her dad. She was chatty and friendly and even if she hated Richard she'd flash that tight, bright smile and call him *Hon'.* Hobnobbing, she called it. It was her special talent. And if Sally caught her in a generous mood, if she'd just met a new fella or had her hair frosted, Sally might persuade her not to tell her mother.

Then she remembered. She didn't have a dime. She'd have to reverse the charges. Some ditz at Swanky would answer. *Sally? There's no Sally here.* And Sally would have to shout over the operator and it would be chaos. Absolute *chaos.* Like what was happening inside her. Her ribcage felt squeezed, and it was getting harder to breathe. What was she going to do?

Boom. Ba-ba *Boom.* She heard music. Like a car radio. She turned and saw Cash's car, parked behind the building. And there he was, sitting with the door open, his legs up on the open window, singing along with some discordant, bass-heavy tune. When he saw her he raised one hand in a lazy wave.

"Thanks a lot!" she said, marching over. "You scared the hell out of me."

"Serves you right."

There was not a bit of remorse in his tone. He acted like he could take or leave her. Was she so easy to disregard? Was she just someone to be tossed away without a second thought?

Of course she was. She felt her chin wavering.

"Hey there!" Cash jumped up and grabbed her by the arm. "Don't make a scene," he said, looking around the parking lot. She let him pull her into the car.

"You have to admit," he said. "It was a pretty good prank."

She slouched in the seat and turned her face away. It was hot in the car. Her knees were shaking and her head hurt. She closed her eyes. He could sit there forever, or drive if he wanted. She didn't know what she wanted.

Then he said, "Hey, I'm sorry about that. I would never act like that on a real date. Honest."

"Like you said, it wasn't a date. My mistake."

"But I can see how you thought that."

"That's not what you said earlier."

"I was hungry. But I'm sorry, OK?" He was turned toward her, his stringy hair tucked behind his ears. He seemed sincere.

"You've probably never even been on a real date," she said grudgingly.

"Maybe we can have one."

"I'm not allowed to date."

"We've already established that you do things you're not allowed to do."

She already had something of a reputation with him. She sat up straighter.

"I'd never date you anyway."

"Okay, sure. But slide over here a little, why don't you?"

She glanced at him. He had one hand slung over the steering wheel and the other lay casually on the seat between them. His forearms were long and ropey, like branches of a tree.

"I wish you'd be serious."

He leaned closer. "I am serious. Give me a kiss."

"That's not what I'm here for."

"Sure you are, you just don't know it."

"Stop it. I have to find my dad. That's all."

"So you said. Then what?"

Maybe he was right. Maybe there was a reason she hadn't gone to Aunt Flookie in the first place. Or ended up at the Greyhound station. Maybe Cash wasn't just part of God's plan for her. Maybe he *was* the plan.

"I'll tell you what," he said. "He'll say nice to meet you, have a nice life. We'll drive back home. You'll never see or hear from him again. But I'll still be here. See what I mean?"

She didn't answer. *Have a nice life.* How could she do that, without a dad to love her?

"Gimme your hand," he said.

How dangerous could it be? She reached over and he fit his fingers between hers in way that made her stomach drop. It was the novelty of it, that was all. You could even call it an experiment, because she really couldn't stand him.

Except didn't his hand feel nice? Warm and heavy and just the right size.

"You got a raw deal, that's for sure," he said quietly, and gave her fingers a gentle squeeze. Oh, how she'd misjudged him! He understood, in a way no one else did. She was so used to feeling alone when it came to her dad, she hadn't seen this blessing unfolding. But they were in this together. That's what his hand said to her. And he was all she had.

They drove, a sudden shyness between them like a passenger. For one moment she allowed herself a strange, incredible thought. Soon she'd have a dad *and* a boyfriend! She knew it was unlikely, but it gave her boost, so that when they stopped at a filling station in Kalamazoo for directions and she heard the attendant tell Cash *just turn at that light, go maybe five, six blocks, and there you are*, she didn't panic. And when they pulled up in front of a house—his house!—she was able to stop herself from blurting *just keep driving!*

There it was. Pale blue, small but nicely kept, with a neat row of hedges in front and grass you could bounce on. The home of a respectable family.

"Hey, don't be nervous," Cash said. "I'll do the talking if you want."

"No." She was ready. Seeing the house helped. *Here's* what he's moved on to. *This* is where he pretends he doesn't have a daughter named Sally.

They knocked on the front door and after a moment an attractive young woman answered. She wore a large wedding ring on her finger. Sally took a deep breath. Hadn't she expected as much?

"I'm sorry," the woman said. "We don't entertain door-to-door solicitations." She had a soft voice with a southern drawl.

"Do we look like we've got something to sell?" asked Cash hotly. Let *him* do the talking? Sally made a gurgling sound in her throat as she tried to think of something to say.

The woman studied them with wide blue eyes. She had

to notice Cash's purple nose, but she was polite enough not to stare. "You look like those high school kids with the magazine subscriptions and what not."

Why did she have to be so pretty? The girly type. That's what her dad liked. And Sally hadn't even brought lipstick! She managed to thrust her hand out.

"I'm Sally. I'm here to see my dad."

She steeled herself for a reaction. A cool bitchiness maybe, or the door slamming in her face.

"Your…dad," the woman repeated.

"My….*dad.*" Sally stared at her, waiting. Anger flared in her and took her by surprise.

"Oh! You're Richard's daughter!"

"Is he here?" *Just try to keep him from me. Just try!*

"I'm sorry. Please come in," the woman said, with a welcoming gesture.

"Nice digs," Cash muttered as they stepped into the foyer. He was right. It was like stepping into a television set. The room was painted a canary yellow that you only see on advertisements. The very air glowed from some inner, uncontainable happiness. There were soft pastel rugs on the floor, gauzy curtains at the window, and in the middle of it all was a baby in a playpen.

"Oh," Sally said, staring at the cutest baby boy she'd ever seen. He was dressed like a miniature man, in overalls and a red plaid shirt. She put her hand on the back of a chair to steady herself. "What's *his* name?"

This was going wrong. She was shaken when what she wanted was to be bright and bubbly for her dad. But poor Lenny! He'd been replaced. They all had.

"This is Willard." The baby let out a squeal and started

banging something against the playpen. The woman hurried over and lifted him out. “And I’m Aurelia.”

Sally glanced at Cash. What kind of name was that? But he only raised his eyebrows at her like he was impressed. It wasn’t fair! What right did she have to be so classy and poised? To have everything yellow and soft and clean? This…this… *Aurelia* got a lovely house and a cute little baby and *her father* for a husband when back in Holland Sally’s mother struggled to raise three kids on her own. They had *nothing*, and this woman had everything.

“How long have you known my dad?” Sally said stiffly.

“Only a few years.” Aurelia jiggled the baby on her hip. “But I haven’t seen Richard in some time.”

Sally’s jaw dropped. “He left you too? And the baby?”

The woman’s face opened in a slow *oh!* She started to smile, but a deep voice barked from the hallway.

“Who’s there?”

A man stood in the adjoining room, hugging the wall as if he didn’t want to be seen. Her dad? Sally stepped forward.

“It’s Richard’s daughter,” Aurelia said quickly and Sally froze, confused.

“Who’s the quiet one?” the man asked.

“That’s Cash,” Sally said slowly. “He’s my…” Friend? My driver? *Just some guy I met.* “He plays ball for Holland Christian.” Stupid, but it seemed like a guy thing to say.

The man jerked his head. “Are you staring at me?”

“Marvin! It’s all right.” Aurelia went to him and took his arm. She led him into the living room in such a way that Sally realized. The man was blind.

“This is my husband, Marvin.” She placed him in a chair and set the baby in his lap. He made a face as the baby squawked and tried to grab his nose.

Sally nearly squawked too. "Aren't you married to my dad?"

Aurelia laughed. "Richard is our tenant," she said. "He rents the cottage out back."

"Whoa," said Cash softly.

"I see," said Sally, before catching herself. Was that rude to say in front of a blind man? Besides, she didn't see anything.

"He's been gone, what would you say, honey? About three weeks."

But that would mean— "What about my letter? I wrote to him here at this address, and he wrote back."

Aurelia went to the foyer. "We keep his mail for him," she said, holding up a cardboard box. "He gets it whenever he's back in town."

Sally looked in the box and saw it immediately. Her letter, on top, unopened.

She reached in her pocket and took out the letter from *him*. From him! She opened it. *With love, your dad.*

She felt slow and stupid. "So who wrote this?"

Cash took it from her and read it. "You've been had," he said quietly.

She felt a wave of nausea and wished she could sit down. Her mother. It had to be. Who else would go to such lengths to keep her from her dad?

"Can I give him a message?" Aurelia asked. "When I see him?

Sally shook her head. A slow burn began behind her eyes, but she would not cry. Not in front of Miss Southern Hospitality and her creepy, blank-eyed husband. Did she have a message? Only one thought popped into her head. *Where have you been all my life?* Like a line from a movie. She tried to think of something else, but Marvin cleared his throat.

"Don't touch anything over there!"

Cash had turned his attention to the wall, where four guitars were leaning in stands.

"Those are valuable," said Marvin.

"Where'd you get this Fender?"

"Cash, *please*." She wouldn't leave it to these two to tell her dad anything. They'd reduce this trip to a *by the way…* moment instead of the brave and bold statement it was meant to be.

"Do you know where he is?" she asked. "Where can I find him?"

"I believe he's in Holland."

"Holland? But I live in Holland! Was he going to see me?" Her heart leaped before she could remind herself. He. Never. Read. Her. Letter. There it was, in the basket. Proof positive. Yet a part of her believed that he *just knew* she was looking for him.

"Um…" Aurelia pressed her lips together and gave her a soft look. " I don't know dear. He goes there quite often."

Sally stuck a hand in her hair and pulled, like she could straighten out her confusion of thoughts. There was a bright side. There was no pretty wife, no replacement baby, no bouncy green lawn that he preened over.

"Maybe my mom called him and told him about my letter," she said, beginning to pace a small patch of the carpet. "And he told her what to say to me. He told her to let me down easy." She stopped and pulled her letter from her purse. "That's why she wrote *this*."

"I thought they didn't talk," said Cash.

"Maybe they do!" Sally turned to Aurelia. "Does he ever say anything about my mom?"

"He talks about a place called the Torchlight," Marvin

interjected. “I get the impression it’s a favorite hang-out.”

“That’s a bar,” said Cash.

Sally swallowed hard and said, “Is he, you know, a drunk?”

“What’s it to you?” Marvin growled from the couch.

Aurelia snapped her head around. “Stop it!”

Cash touched Sally’s elbow. “Let’s go.”

Sally nodded and they backed toward the door.

“Thank you,” Sally said. Aurelia turned, looking flustered. She opened her mouth to speak but Sally had the door open. “Thank you. Goodbye.”

They hurried out to the car.

“Jeez!” said Cash as he started the engine. Sally couldn’t wait to get out of there, but there was Aurelia, hurrying down the walk toward them. She bent over, putting her elbows on Sally’s open window.

“I just wanted to say, I believe Richard has mentioned you once or twice. My husband didn’t realize....” She patted Sally’s arm. “Good luck.”

Sally gave her a thin smile. Maybe she wasn’t so pretty, up close. Maybe Sally had only imagined that the air in there was super-charged with happiness. Maybe at this very moment her dad was standing in *her* living room, finding out that she was gone, simply vanished and no one knew where, and his heart was racing and he was thinking that ten years was such a long time. Much too long to be gone.

Prudy

Prudy was pacing her front porch, convinced that if she kept looking down the block she'd see Sally round the corner, when the phone rang. It was Phillip.

"You heard?" he said.

Her heart lurched. "Heard what?"

"My car was stolen."

She was confused. "That's terrible, but—"

"Prudy, it's *Richard*. Richard was in my car."

"Richard? Stole your car?"

"It looks that way."

"Was Sally with him?"

"I don't know. The police told me he had some kids with him. I think Lenny was driving."

"How could that be? Isn't Lenny at the church?"

"I don't know."

She made a frustrated sound. "He works for you now.

Shouldn't you know where he is?"

He sighed. "I'm not at the church, am I? I'm here in my kitchen talking to you. And then I'm going to the police station."

"Why are you yelling at me?" Maybe he wasn't yelling exactly, but he sounded like he wanted to.

"I have an appointment at the funeral home in Burnips this morning," he said. "How am I going to get over there?"

"This is not my fault!" There was a long pause. "Phillip?"

"I'll see you at the station."

Prudy ran the seven blocks to the police station. Her side ached, but each time she slowed the questions came faster. How on earth could Richard and Sally end up together in Phillip's car? What had he done to her? And *Lenny*? What did he have to do with any of this?

The desk sergeant looked up as she burst in. "I'm Mrs. Van Sloeten," she said, trying to catch her breath. "You found my daughter?"

He checked a piece of paper in his hand. "A state trooper pulled over a Richard Van Sloeten. Your husband?"

She nodded. "Estranged."

"He was with his kids in a stolen car on US131."

"What kids? My kids?"

"Are you missing more than one?"

"I have three kids. Maybe he's taken all of them."

He removed his glasses. "Has he threatened to take them?"

"No! I haven't heard from him in years. But why would he steal a car? That's bad, right? It's got to be bad."

"They should be here any minute. Why don't you have a seat?"

Not more waiting!

"Was my son Lenny in the car? Pastor Voss said something

about Lenny."

The sergeant shook his head. "I don't have a complete report yet. Just be patient."

"Could you at least check—Nell Van Sloeten. My oldest daughter. She should be upstairs for the crossing guard orientation. Can you see if she's there?"

He frowned. "I'll check." He ambled down the hallway and poked his head in another room. She heard the door open behind her and Phillip came in. He was sweating in a dark suit. Before she could speak to him the sergeant returned with a concerned look.

"She was on the roster but didn't show."

"Phil, he has all of them!"

This was a kidnapping! What did Richard want with her kids? Had Sally's letter touched off something crazy in him?

"Calm down," said Phillip, taking both her hands in his. "Let's just wait and see."

He hadn't touched her in sixteen years. Not even a handshake. Something terrible was happening.

"The stupid banquet!" she said, shaking him off. "That's what started all this."

Phillip sighed and gestured toward the row of chairs. Reluctantly she sat and he settled himself beside her.

"Speaking of the banquet," he said after a moment. "It obviously means a lot to Sally."

"You think?" She knew sarcasm wouldn't help, but neither did stating the obvious.

He cleared his throat. "You know, we could let them go together."

"Richard is not her father. You are!"

Phillip's startled eyes flew to the desk, but the sergeant was on the phone. He shifted his weight and put his arm around the back of Prudy's chair.

"Don't you think it might be damaging to Sally, at this late stage, to—"

"Don't try to weasel out of this!"

He lowered his voice and spoke reasonably. "If they go to the banquet, she could find out for herself what sort of man he is. And then…" he trailed off.

"You just don't want her finding out what kind of man *you* are," Prudy hissed.

He rubbed a hand slowly over his face. "Okay, I admit it. I'm scared. I don't want to lose everything."

"I've already waited too long. Whatever happens to her, it'll be my punishment. I know that."

"But is this the best way to help her?"

"The truth has to be the best way."

He leaned close and looked in her eyes. "Listen to me. We're doing the Lord's work, Prudy. You've raised three good kids. The church has grown."

She made a disgusted sound. "That lousy little church hasn't amounted to anything!" It wasn't true. The church had been her life. But she wanted to hurt him.

His face turned hard. "Then why haven't you left?"

"You'd love that, wouldn't you?"

He slapped his thighs and stood up. "I don't know why you had to stick around!" He threw his hands in the air and raised his voice. "Why should I have to look at you every week? Why do you have to be a constant reminder to me?"

Prudy saw the sergeant glance at them. She tried to speak calmly.

"*Because*, Phillip…." God, she saw it now. She thought he'd forgive her! That someday they'd be together! When they were old and the kids were gone and nothing else mattered. Now she understood part of her fear. If Sally was gone, her connection to Phillip would be gone too.

"You know what?" she said angrily. "You're a selfish prick."

"You're the one being selfish!" He knelt in front of her. "Make your peace with God! That's what matters. That's what I've done."

She stared at him. "That gives you the right to treat people like shit? Because you've worked it out with God? I don't think God operates that way."

He shook his head. "I didn't mean it that way. All I'm saying is that you're asking for trouble."

"I've already got trouble!" she cried.

He sighed heavily. "I struggle with this too, Prudy. If you only knew."

Her eyes narrowed. "You're going to be struggling a whole lot more. I'm done with this. I'm going to set things straight, no matter what happens."

"What do you want? Money? More time? I can do that."

"You've had sixteen years and you haven't done anything. You barely acknowledge us. You think the church doesn't notice?"

"I'm helping Lenny, aren't I?"

"You made me crawl to you for help. You made me beg."

He stood and turned away. "That's not true."

"You think it'll be easy for *me* when the truth comes out?"

For a long moment she looked at his back. When he faced her his hands were clasped tightly in front of him.

"I won't let you do it," he said tightly. "I'll resign right now, this afternoon. I can be gone by tomorrow."

He would too! Only a fool would be surprised. She was obviously a fool.

"Go ahead and run," she said bitterly. "You've still got to live with yourself."

She got up and went to the window. A state trooper car was pulling into the circular drive in front of the station.

"Let's see what happens with Richard," he pleaded. "That's all I'm saying."

But she wasn't listening anymore. She lunged for the door.

"Ma'am, sit down," the sergeant said sharply, coming around the desk. "Let us process this, please."

Prudy stopped. Outside, the state trooper had the car door open and was helping a man out. The sun shone on a balding forehead. *That's not Richard!* But then he straightened and she saw the way he rolled his shoulders back and planted his feet. He surveyed the cracked concrete sidewalk and rows of wilting, yellowed box woods like he was looking at a red carpet lined with cheering fans.

It was him.

She grabbed the back of a chair, unsteady. Ten years became as fresh as ten minutes and the old fear sprang up. Not gone at all, just waiting for this ambush. But she was safe here, surrounded by cops. Why was she afraid?

She watched the trooper lead Richard by the elbow up the walk. Lenny climbed out the car, then Nell. She was holding a girl's hand. Mandy? Mandy Veenstra?

Where was Sally?

They came in and Prudy grabbed Lenny's arm.

"Where is she?"

Then she was face to face with Richard. There wasn't time to be stunned, or to ask *my God, what's happened to you?*

"What have you done to her?" she cried.

"Hello, Prudy," said Richard. He grinned at Phillip. "How's it hangin', Rev?"

"Hello?" Prudy said. "Hello? Where is my daughter?"

"She's with Cash," said Lenny.

"We tried to go after her but it didn't work," said Nell.

"We would have found her too," Richard said, "if we hadn't been pulled over."

"But—" Prudy looked at the desk sergeant. "I thought you found my daughter."

The sergeant looked surprised. He looked at Mandy.

"Isn't this your daughter?"

"No! I told you she's sixteen! I described her this morning when I called. What's wrong with you people?"

It was clear. God in his infinite justice had brought all of them together for this moment. For tragedy? Life lesson? Another chance? Yes, *please!* Just one more chance to do things right. She would never forgive herself for picking up that knitting needle so long ago. But God, you let her live! You wouldn't take her away now!

"Take that one back to holding," the sergeant said to the state trooper, pointing his chin at Richard. "The rest of you sit down here and we'll sort this out."

"Stop telling me to sit down!" Prudy shrieked. "Do you know where Sally is or don't you?"

She looked at Richard's back disappearing down the hall. "Richard?" she called, but he shrugged. He didn't care either. No one seemed to care.

She turned to Lenny and Nell. "How do you know she's with Cash?"

"Someone saw them together this morning," said Nell. "We

had to go after her!"

"Is that why Richard took my car?" Phillip asked.

Nell's cheeks were red and she didn't look at him.

"He didn't take it," she said. "I did."

Prudy and Phillip looked at each other, shocked.

"So what does your father have to do with any of this?" Phillip asked.

Nell shrugged. "It seemed like a good idea to get his help."

"But how did you know—" Prudy began.

"I've seen him around," Lenny mumbled. "I didn't want to tell you."

The desk sergeant hiked his pants up with one hand. "So the girl you reported this morning is still missing. Is that right, Mrs. Van Sloeten?"

"Yes, she's missing! Aren't you listening?"

He put both hands up, meaning *calm down*. "Who is this little one?"

"This is Mandy Veenstra," Prudy said. "Our neighbor."

"I brought her along," Nell said. "There wasn't time to take her to Bible School."

The sergeant's eyebrows shot up. "Do her parents know where she is, or will I be dealing with another hysterical mother?"

Mandy let out a whimper. "Tell Mona I didn't do anything wrong. I didn't!"

Nell hugged her tight. "Please leave Mona out of this," she said. "She's not expecting Mandy home until this afternoon."

"Who is the person you think your daughter is with?"

Lenny spoke up. "She's with Cash DeVries. He drives a beat up '62 Impala. By now he's probably driven my sister into a ditch while you sit here with your thumb up your ass."

The sergeant squinted at him. “Didn’t I see you in here recently?”

Pastor Voss put a hand on Lenny’s arm. Lenny yanked it away. “He’s doing his community service for me, at the Dutch Reformed Church.”

The sergeant was nodding. “Yeah. Cash DeVries and Lenny Van Sloeten. Simple assault, wasn’t it? Now you and your sister are stealing cars, huh? And you’re looking for DeVries. What is this, some kind of family feud?”

“They’re just trying to find Sally,” Prudy cried.

“Which is more than we can say for you,” Lenny sneered.

“Watch it, kid.”

“Come on, now,” Phillip said.

“Well, what are they doing to find her? We just told him who she’s with and where they’re going.”

Phillip nodded. “He’s right. Are you looking for her?”

“What reason do you have to believe she’s in trouble?” the sergeant asked. “It sounds like she’s out joyriding with her boyfriend.”

“No!” said Prudy.

“And he’s not her boyfriend. She barely knows him,” Lenny said.

Pastor Voss stepped forward. “It’s rather involved, sir, but it doesn’t seem like Sally is acting rationally. She was very intent on finding Mr. Van Sloeten.”

The sergeant nodded. “Let me get on the horn. We’ll see what Van Sloeten says about all this. Then we’ll talk about the car.”

“Great,” Lenny said. “Now I’ll be locked up for breaking parole.”

“What about me?” Nell asked. “I’ll lose my job!”

They were interrupted by a different police officer coming in. He looked at Prudy. "Your husband would like to see you."

His words jarred her. Richard was still her husband. After all this time, had anything really changed? His absence had been a hole she stepped around, never bothering to fill in. You forget about it until it trips you up.

She was told to leave her purse at the desk and follow the officer to the holding room. Richard wasn't under arrest, so they could talk in an open room while the officer waited outside. Prudy took a long shaky breath. She had always imagined seeing Richard again. But in a chance encounter on the street, with her looking smart, on someone's arm. Of course Richard would look as good as ever. He'd most certainly be with a woman, but Prudy would be prepared. She had just the right sort of pitying smile for whatever poor sap fell for him. But for *him* to pity *her*?That wasn't part of the plan. Still single? Raising delinquent kids? Wasting your time at that church?

She stepped into the room and he turned and smiled. She saw a black gap where his left canine tooth had been.

"You're looking good," he said.

"You're not."

His smile faded and his eyes narrowed. He peered over her shoulder. "Where's preacher-man?"

"He's talking to the sergeant."

"Go tell him I didn't take his fucking car. It was your kids."

"*My* kids," she repeated. It seemed true. How could this man possibly be the father of Lenny and Nell? How could she ever have loved him? He looked so busted up, so *old*. It took her off guard. He'd gone downhill without her. It made her sad.

"Why would I take it?" he said. "I was minding my own business. Tell him."

She cleared her throat. She needed to be in control. Or at least sound like it. "He won't press charges as long as you promise to leave us alone. Especially Sally." *If they ever saw Sally again.* She turned her face away.

He studied her. When he spoke his voice was gentle.

"Prudy, she's fine. She'll be back and she won't even understand why you're upset."

"Stop it!" she said. She couldn't stand one more of these stupid men who didn't know the first thing about raising a child! Treating her like *she* was the one out of touch.

"Just tell me if you know anything. Have you talked to her at all?"

He shook his head. "No. But I'd like to."

Of course he would. *Now* he wanted Sally? And Phillip didn't. Perfect.

"You think you can just show up after 10 years and…and…" She tried to stop herself, but she was losing it. Her words came out ragged and ugly. "…and take all her *love*?"

"You're overreacting," he said.

That's right. There was that unraveling sensation again. She had to keep it together! She needed a tissue. She had one in her purse, but she didn't have her purse.

"Where did they find you, anyway?" she asked.

Richard smiled and brought his hands together. He still had a way of moving that was graceful.

"Lenny found me a couple of months ago."

About the time of his graduation. She felt the heat of that moment, sitting in the stands when they called his name. *Not present.*

"He didn't tell you," Richard said. It was an accusation. "I gather he gives you some trouble."

“Nothing I can’t handle,” she said angrily.

He smiled. This time there was nothing graceful in his look. “You look like you could handle a few things. You got yourself a man?”

“None of your business.”

He leaned forward and grabbed her hand. “Aww, *Prudy!* You’ve missed me, haven’t you?”

There was unexpected comfort in his touch. She closed her eyes. For one blessed moment she didn’t feel so alone. Then, suddenly, he stepped close and she felt his breath on her ear. One hand went to her waist, his fingers pressing gently into the soft spot above her hip.

“You must be drier than a bone,” he whispered.

She gasped and pushed him away. “What’s wrong with you? Your daughter is missing and —”

She stopped. Not his daughter. She should tell him. Right here. Right now. But that would change all that he believed, and she couldn’t do that yet.

Sometimes believing is all a person has.

Sally

Sally clutched the letter in her hand. *It was a pleasure to hear from you. I've thought of you often.* She still couldn't believe these weren't her father's words. He didn't know anything about the banquet or about her invitation. He wasn't feeling flattered that she reached out to him. And he certainly wasn't dreaming of seeing her again. How she hated her mother for making her hope!

"I'm feeling kind of sick," she said.

Cash shot her a quick look. "If you're going to lose it, do it out the window."

"Bet you think we're all crazy, huh?" she asked.

"Nah." He reached for her hand. She hesitated a second before taking his. Was he just being nice so he could make a move on her?

He cleared his throat. "Doesn't it make you think about throwing in the towel? I mean, if your mom wrote that letter, it's because she sure as heck doesn't want you seeing your dad."

He was right. This would be the time to give up. That's what her mother wanted her to do. She'd never understood Sally's feelings about her dad. Never wanted to hear Sally talk about him. Never had one good word, not *one*, to say about him. But *this*!

"It's not her decision!" Sally said angrily. "It's mine."

"But she might have good reason. What do you really know about the guy?"

"He's my dad. That's all I need to know."

Cash frowned. Great! Now he was jumping on the bandwagon? He was supposed to be on her side!

"Just drop me off at the Torchlight," she said. "I'll run in quick and—"

"Whoa there," Cash said, "That wasn't part of our deal."

"But—" Sally stopped. *But we're holding hands!* How idiotic that would sound!

"You don't even know when he'll be there. Christ, it's not even noon yet."

"Just swing by anyway, ok?"

"Let's go to the dunes," he said eagerly. "Some of my friends will be there."

She took a deep breath. "I...I can't. I don't have a swimsuit."

He let out a laugh and her cheeks burned. Oh, right. Teenagers didn't go to the beach to swim. He looked at her pointedly but she couldn't think of anything to say. Abruptly he dropped her hand. Flung it, really. She pulled it back to her lap and cursed herself for ever letting him touch her.

He moved restlessly in his seat. "This is such a waste of my time."

"I thought you might do it as a favor, because we're..." she paused, "...friends."

He acted like he wasn't listening. He tapped his thumb on the steering wheel, keeping the beat with some private tune. She wished she could rewind him like a cassette tape. The truth was she *wanted* him to hold her hand.

"I thought you liked me," she said.

He glanced at her. "Maybe I was starting to, but right now I could go either way." He brushed some dust off the dashboard with his fingers. "Anyway, you don't like me."

No, she didn't. She couldn't wait to get out of this car. So why did she have the feeling that once he dropped her off, she'd miss him? Was it just the touch of his hand on hers? Or was it something more?

"Well, you move kinda fast, don't you?"

He shrugged. "Life is short. Besides, there's only two weeks of summer left."

"Let me guess. You have a girlfriend at school."

"No. I don't want one neither."

"Then why were you talking about you and me dating?"

"When did I say that?"

"When we left Stuckey's. You said we could consider today a real date."

He shrugged again, as if she was boring him immensely.

"Dating someone don't mean you're boyfriend and girlfriend."

"Oh." Was this something everyone understood? She could see that to call a boy your boyfriend after one date might be premature, but what about after two, or three? And what about holding hands? That meant something, didn't it?

"What does dating someone mean?" she asked.

"It means you have fun together and want to hang out."

"How's that different than being boyfriend and girlfriend?"

"Definitions are unnecessary." He wore a squinty look and kept turning his head back and forth like the plain houses and brown scrubby lawns they were passing were simply fascinating. "They create expectations."

"My only expectation was that you get me to my dad."

He was scowling now.

"Why don't you get your brother to go?"

"I'm not telling Lenny anything about this! And I don't want you to either."

"Hey, I have no desire to talk to him." He lifted a ropey arm to adjust the mirror, then laid it coolly on the back of the seat. "But you and me can still hang out."

Sally rolled her eyes. "Yippee."

He flashed her a hot look but she didn't care. Did he think he could insult her and not get a little payback?

"You're no prize, you know," she added.

He pursed his lips. A moment later they slowed for a red light and he turned to face her.

"I've got feelings too," he said, with a look so like a hurt little boy, open and unflinching, that Sally was instantly sorry. In a burst of spontaneity, she leaned forward and planted a kiss on his cheek.

"Hey!" There was that grin, transforming his face. "That was nice! Do it again."

She couldn't see that it would harm anything. She leaned toward him and right before her lips made contact, he turned his head. Just like that, without a moment's notice, she was having her first kiss. An honest-to-God, lip to lip, someone-likes-me *kiss!* It was so much easier than she ever imagined. And nicer. The softness of his mouth surprised her. She felt a scratchiness above his upper lip and a warmth on her face as he exhaled from his nose. She squeezed her eyes shut tight, vowing to remember this her whole life through.

"You smell good," he murmured, pulling away.

How did she smell? She wanted to ask him, but that would definitely not be romantic. Instead, she'd check the soap in the bathroom the minute she got home and use the same kind every day.

She ought to thank him. Not just for the compliment, but for giving her this gift. *Finally!* She'd been kissed! But before she could speak he swooped in again. This time he put his hand on the back of her head and moved his mouth around hers so that what might have been one little kiss grew into five, ten, more kisses until something in her belly went rubbery. Was this making out? Dear God, she was *making out* in a *car* with a *boy*! She knew she had to make him stop, but this was an even bigger compliment. She must be good at this! Look how eager he was for more!

"Green light," she mumbled, putting a hand on his chest and pushing him away. He sighed and stepped on the gas. They got on the highway and rode a while, that quiet between them again, only this time the air really was super-charged. No mistaking. They shared something special. She looked over and he was smiling too.

She leaned her head out the open window. The sun was on full bake but the heat no longer seemed oppressive. The air rushing by lifted her hair and rustled the letter she held in her lap. She looked at it again. Yes, her mother did a terrible thing. But maybe she deserved a break. As long as everything turned out okay, what did it matter?

What did anything matter now? She had a boyfriend! Her

very *first*! Her stomach fluttered. So Cash wasn't her absolute ideal. Her father wouldn't be ideal either. That didn't mean she couldn't appreciate them for what they were.

Suddenly she was dying to know *everything* about Cash! His favorite subjects in school. Did he want to be a mechanic? Did he have any brothers or sisters? She'd even talk baseball. *Anything.*

"How long have you worked at the Texaco?" she asked.

He shrugged. "Not long."

"You like it?"

Another shrug. "It's okay."

Well. The wind was whipping too loudly to talk anyway. And Cash seemed to prefer the radio. He cranked it up and they listened to song after song as the miles spooled out, until Sally began to feel that old feeling close in on her. Hey! Here I am! She checked her reflection in the side mirror just to be sure she was there.

But every so often he would flash a quick smile—that *smile!* How she lived for it!—and she was reminded, this was a *companionable* silence. They had plenty of time. That's what his silence was saying.

So she couldn't explain the fear that gripped her as they drove into Holland. They came to a main road that led to opposite sides of town. A right turn would take her home. A left would take them out over the tracks.

Tentatively she said, "About the Torchlight..."

He groaned. "Then can we go to the beach?"

She tried to imagine herself at the beach with him. Would they sit on the sand, hold hands and talk, or would he expect her to go back in the bushes, where the easy girls went? Was she one of those girls now? Maybe it was the same as her journey to her father, the thing she knew when she first set foot in Cash's car:

there was no going back.

"Maybe just for a half hour or so."

He turned the wheel left. "This better be quick."

Sally sat staring at the squat concrete building. There were no windows. Just a beige brick wall, a blue steel door and a neon Schlitz sign.

"Go ahead," Cash said.

She didn't move. "I can't."

He rolled his eyes. "Oh for chrissake."

"You go in first." If she could follow him, she wouldn't be so scared.

He shook his head. "I'm not going in. You get your ass inside or I'm leaving you here." He put his foot up as if to push her out of the car. "Go!"

"You'll wait, right? No more practical jokes."

He killed the motor and gave her a sugary smile. "I promise."

She still didn't move. "What should I say?"

"The same thing you were planning to say in Kalamazoo."

That was different. Then she thought her dad had read her letter and he would know immediately why she was there. Here, face to face with him, she'd have to explain everything. And what if he was drunk, or with his buddies? What if they made fun of her? What if she became tongue-tied and couldn't get her story out and looked like some stupid, awkward loser? Or worse, what if he denied knowing her?

Cash sighed. "It's hotter than hell just sitting here. And I don't got all day."

She opened her car door. She'd never expected it to be easy. She crossed the gravel lot and pulled on the steel door. It was so heavy she thought it was locked. She tried again and it opened with a loud sucking sound. Inside, the room was so dim all she saw was the exit sign shining over the back door. Then a TV playing in the corner. She stood blinking a moment. A man at the bar turned.

"I don't know anything about it," he said loudly, holding up both hands.

She looked behind her. "Uh…"

The man leaned forward and squinted at her. She walked toward him cautiously.

"Nope, not here," he said. "Someone beat you to him."

"To who?"

"Richie. Another kid was in here the other day. They left together."

"How do you know why I'm here?"

"Ritchie Van Sloeten, right? His son came in for him."

"Lenny? Are you sure?"

"How many more of you are there? Just so's I can mark my calendar." He laughed.

Lenny and her father, together? There had to be a mistake. Her dad could have other sons, maybe an army of them, from countless different women.

"What did the kid look like?" she asked.

"Tall. Scrawny. Wore a bandana and a mean scowl."

That was Lenny all right.

"He wasn't carrying a baseball bat, was he?" She imagined Lenny charging in, swinging away like a madman. But there was no sign of trouble here. And the bartender wouldn't be acting so casual if there had been a fight.

"Not that I could see."

She hesitated, afraid to ask. "Where did they go?"

"Didn't say. If you want I'll tell him you were here."

She shook her head. Now what? It should be simple. Go find Lenny. But she had a sinking feeling, like she'd just waded into quicksand. Like the faster she moved, the faster she'd be pulled under. What was she going to find out?

"Hey. What you want with him?"

She took in the dismal surroundings. What did she want? A father who hung out in a place like this?

"Just wanted to catch up. You know, on old times." It was a ridiculous, old-lady thing to say.

She hurried out, squinting in the glare of the sun, and threw herself into the car.

"I've got to get home."

"What's the matter?"

"My dad's been with *Lenny*."

"I thought you all hadn't seen him for 10 years."

"I don't know what's going on. Just go!"

"What about the beach?"

"I can't. I've got to find Lenny."

Cash made a sound of disgust. "This has turned out to be one hell of a wild goose chase. You couldn't have talked to Lenny about this before we went chasing all over?"

"I did talk to him. Sort of." She was thinking of his birthday, just a few days ago, when she told him about mailing her letter. *He'll never write back*, he'd said. So sure. It came at her like a kick in the gut. *He knew.*

"Can you get me home?"

"You're awfully bossy."

She sighed. "Listen, Cash. I'm sorry. We'll go to the beach some other time. *Please*." She motioned for him to hurry up.

"*I* want to go today. You said we'd go."

What a child! She turned on him.

"Do you have any idea what I'm going through? My dad is with my *brother!* You know, the one who's always talking about how much he hates him and how he'll beat his head in if he ever sees him again. My mother has been lying to me, and—oh, can't you see? It's like everyone is in some secret plot against me!"

"Jeez. Calm down."

"Then stop being such an asshole."

"Right. I'm the asshole. I spend my whole morning driving you around, wasting my time, and I'm the asshole. Anyway, you said we'd go to the beach, so it looks like you're a liar."

"Circumstances have changed. I have to get home. Go to the beach by yourself."

"Damn right I will."

"Fine." She wouldn't be bullied. She stuck her chin out and ignored him as he snorted and huffed and threw the car into gear. When she stole a glance at him she saw that he was playing the same game, his jaw thrust out like a tough guy. It wasn't as if she didn't want to go to the beach. She knew it was what the cool kids did. But she didn't have the energy for him anymore. Not now.

When they pulled up in front of her house, Cash didn't look at her. Abruptly he leaned across her—*for a hug?* she wondered, because it was just the kind of backwards, unpredictable thing he'd do— but he grabbed the door handle and pushed hard.

"Better go find daddy."

Her cheeks burned as she climbed out. "Don't you want to..." she began, but the car peeled away, kicking up a shower of gravel. She felt it sting against her ankles. Then came the sting of tears. What did she do wrong? Why was everyone in such a hurry to lie to her, or leave her in the lurch? She was likeable, she *was*. And deserving. Only no one seemed to notice.

As she walked up the sidewalk to her front steps, she counted. One. Two. Three. It was a habit she got from her mother, who always told her to count her blessings. *When there's trouble ahead, count it out.*

One. *I'm home, safe and sound.*

Two. *I had my first kiss!*

Three. *I'm not starving in Africa.*

It was no use. This time there was too much trouble ahead. She eased open the door, believing for one split second that the house might be empty. Maybe her mother thought Sally had gone to Bible School early. She'd be at work like usual. Nell would still be at her crossing guard orientation, and Lenny, the one she most needed to see, didn't live with them anymore. But her mother wasn't stupid, and Nell lived for moments like this, when she could help bring the hammer down on Sally.

Steeling herself, she stepped inside and came face to face with Pastor Voss. She blinked, surprised. Then groaned. Was she going to have to live in the church basement too?

"Prudy, she's here!" She heard relief in his voice. Her mother rushed out from the kitchen with Lenny and Nell right behind. There was a pinched look on their faces that relaxed when they saw her. Wow. They were really scared for her. She hadn't expected that.

"Where were you?" her mother asked, her eyes raw.

She heard Nell say *Thank God!* And from Lenny something about Cash. She looked at him. *Liar.* At her mother. *Liar.* And why hadn't it occurred to her before? *Nell* could have written the letter. Sally no longer trusted any of them.

Her mother gave her a shake. "Where were you?" she repeated.

"Looking for my dad."

"Are you *crazy?*"

"Why didn't you tell me?" she asked Lenny. "You've seen him and you didn't tell me!"

He glared at her. "Who knew you were going to go running off?"

"Did you go to Kalamazoo?" her mother cried. "Is that where you were?"

Sally was silent. *I don't have to answer anything. She's the one who needs to explain.*

Prudy threw her hands up. "The police were out looking for you!"

Police? So it *was* bad. "What did you expect me to do?" she said. "You were no help!"

The pastor stepped forward with his hands out. Like she was some crazy lady. He spoke gently. "We were worried. Everyone here cares about you."

She looked at her mother. "Why does he have to be here?"

Prudy looked stunned. "Sally!"

"I just don't see how this involves the church."

Lenny spoke up. "I agree."

Prudy's jaw clenched. "I'll speak to you alone, in your room, right now."

But Sally stepped back. "What's the matter?" She pulled the letter from her pocket and waved it in front of her mother. "You don't want anyone to know about *this?* The letter that *you* wrote. How *could* you?"

Let her try to wiggle out of this one! Instead, her mother

seemed to deflate. She closed her eyes for a moment. Then nodded. "I'm sorry. It was a mistake. But I'm only looking out for you."

"That's it? That's your explanation?" There had to be something her mother could say to take away this crumpled-up feeling. *I called your dad and we discussed it. He asked me to tell you….* Or *He wrote that himself. Really! In fact, he desperately wants to come but I talked him out of it!*

It was nothing but her mother's mean-spirited way of bending Sally to her will. She wasn't allowed to have her own ideas, her own plans. Her own *heart*. She wished she'd never come back. It would serve her mother right if she disappeared and Prudy spent her life knowing she'd driven her away. And talk about a double standard.

"What about Lenny? He's seen him!"

Prudy didn't answer. She seemed to be considering something. She worked her hands together. Stared out the window. Finally she sighed.

"We've all seen him," she said.

Sally looked at Lenny. Nell. The pastor. They all wore the same hang-dog face. "When?"

"Lenny and Nell stole my car this morning when they learned you were going to Kalamazoo with Cash," Pastor Voss said.

"We've just come from the police station," Prudy said. "Lenny broke his parole. Nell almost lost her new job."

Sally didn't understand. "Why would you do that?" she asked them.

Lenny snorted. "You think I'm going to let you take off with Cash DeVries?"

Nell shot him a dirty look. "We wanted to find you," she

said. "We went and got Dad and he came with us."

Went and got Dad. It sounded so cozy, like they were stepping into the next room. *Hey Dad! Dinner's ready!*

Suddenly paranoid, Sally thought: what if they saw him all the time? Maybe they got together secretly, without her, for holidays and special occasions. Those Sunday afternoons she spent at Frannie's house, were those their special family days?

"I had to beg for a ride to Kalamazoo from a guy I hardly know who, by the way, likes me. That's right, *likes* me. Or at least would if I didn't have such a psycho family. And I get all the way there just to find out that my dad knows nothing about me or my letter, and then I have to walk into a creepy looking bar and have some stranger tell me that Lenny was there with his dad." She stamped her foot. "What's going on?!"

"I'd like some more answers myself," Prudy said. "But all you need to know right now is that your father is not someone you're going to be spending any time with."

"You've all seen him! Why can't I?"

"Your father hasn't changed," Prudy said. "Tell her Lenny."

"This is fucked up," he grumbled.

"You can't keep me away from him! It's not fair."

She saw her mother look at the pastor. As if this had anything to do with him.

"I don't think that's a good idea," Prudy said.

Sally would explode if she had to hear that one more time. It was like a broken record. "I want to hear it from him!" she shouted. She was out on a limb now. Either she'd see her father or she'd come crashing down. "Why won't you listen to me?"

But who was the one not listening? He doesn't love you. He never did and he never will. That's what her mother was trying to tell her.

Prudy put her head in her hands like she didn't know what to do. Sally wavered, remembering what Cash said, that her mother might have good reasons for what she did. So why couldn't Sally accept that and let it go?

Then Pastor Voss made a strange, guttural sound that startled everyone. He was over by the window, lifting the curtain with one finger. "Prudy, you'd better come here."

Prudy went to the door and opened it. Sally followed and, craning her neck, saw a dark-haired man sitting on the porch steps. The man stood, chuckling.

"This is better than the soap opera they play down at the Torchlight," he said, turning.

Sally stared. Could it be? After all this he shows up on her doorstep, like a present dropped from above? She pushed past everyone and through the door until she was standing before him. She took in his rumpled clothes, watery red eyes, the strange dent in one temple. Maybe he wasn't so handsome like she imagined, but she looked awful herself, all sweaty, her face blotchy from yelling. It didn't matter. She'd know him anywhere.

Her mother took her arm and pulled her back. "Richard, I thought we agreed."

He cocked his head and smiled. "No, we didn't really. As I recall, you left before we could reach an understanding." Then, natural as could be, he said, "Hello Sally. I hear you've been trying to track me down."

She gave Lenny a grateful look. That's what he was doing at the Torchlight. Helping her. Why didn't he just say so?

"Suppose so," she said, suddenly shy. How much had he heard? He might think she was a nutcase, ranting like that. And what about him? She might find out very soon that he was a nutcase too, only it would be too late. She couldn't very well shrug and play it cool. *Oh, hey. Nice to meet you*. Big yawn. She was committed now.

She considered hugging him, just to break the ice. But not with her mother standing there. Instead she stared at him.

"I can't believe it."

"Kids, you all go inside for a bit, and let the pastor and I speak with your father," Prudy said.

"I'd rather stay," Lenny said.

"Me too," Nell said.

Prudy sighed, exasperated. "What do you want, Richard?"

"Aren't you going to invite me in?"

"No." Prudy moved as if to block the door.

Another chuckle. "Lenny told me about this banquet thing."

"Does that mean you want to go?" Sally asked.

"You're going to the banquet with Phillip," Prudy said.

"Pastor Voss," Nell added quickly.

Sally sighed. Was her mother really going to keep this up? Even now? "It's a *Father-Daughter* banquet."

"Dammit, Phil! Say something."

The pastor took a deep breath and shuffled his feet.

"What's there to say?" Richard answered cheerfully. "It sounds like fun."

"And I'll be there to look after her," Nell said hesitantly.

"Yeah, what's the big deal? Now that he's here," said Lenny.

Sally watched her mother eagerly. It felt good to have everyone on her side. It was her mother's turn to accept it. Sally won! She was getting exactly what she wanted!

"Honey, I know you're angry with me," Prudy began.

"Can you be here Saturday, seven o'clock?" Sally interrupted.

"It's a date." Richard gave Prudy a triumphant look, then

narrowed his eyes at Pastor Voss. "Well, love to stay and chat, but if I'm going to shine up, I'd better get my suit to the cleaners." He reached over and tugged on Lenny's t-shirt. "Anybody want to loan me some money?"

Lenny's jaw dropped.

"Aw, I'm kidding!" He winked at Sally and hopped down the steps.

Sally heard her mother's hard angry breathing and the sound of Pastor Voss smacking his lips. Never mind them. She clung to the railing and watched her dad disappear down the sidewalk, praying that he'd be back. But of course he would. Imagine it happening like this! He walked right up to her house and singled her out. And not because of her letter. Because he wanted to. Like it was meant to be. She wanted to jump around so every person she'd ever met could see. I did it! He's here! She felt ten feet tall.

Nell

Dear Diary:

First of all, nobody's perfect. Second of all, I DO NOT hate the sinner. Only the sin. Assuming there was sin, which I am by no means ready to believe.

Nell stopped with her pen poised, remembering the way Pastor Voss had looked in the police station, his face wrinkled with distress. It wasn't just his car he was worried about. He cared about her, too. It was obvious in the way he pleaded her case with Sergeant Van Zandt, convincing him to keep her on as a crossing guard. *She's a remarkable young woman.* Those were his exact words! When she heard them she knew.

There was no fighting her love for him.

With an explosive sigh, she threw her diary onto the floor,

which wasn't like her. And let it lay there, which was even less like her. Her whole life was unlike her now. It had gone all topsy turvy. Maybe it was just the world seeping in. Far away, soldiers were dying in the jungle. There were assassinations in Atlanta and Los Angeles. Riots in Detroit. Heads busted in Chicago. Her brother breaks a nose. Her mother lies. Sally runs away, and she steals a car. Where would it end?

Fortunately, Nell was worldly, in her own way. No one would guess it from looking at her, but she was what you called *savvy*. For example, she was no longer unnerved by the possibility that her mother had had a relationship with the pastor while she was married. That she might even have *slept* with him. Because Prudy was a just a practice run for Pastor Voss. Whatever spark was between Prudy and him was in Nell now, a full blown flame. She just had to find a way to make him see. She needed him to fulfill her role in life. Oh, she wasn't one of those sappy doormats who *has* to have a man. She was no feminist either. It was simply a practical matter. She was meant to be more than someone's sister, or daughter, or wife. She was called to spread the word of God and in order to do that, she needed a man of God. The fact that she loved him—in spite of everything, she loved him!—was icing on the cake.

Finally she picked up her dear friend, dusted off the cover and turned the tiny key in the lock before tucking it into her dresser drawer. She took the fabric Sally had chosen for her dress and studied the peachy-orange sheen of it as she spread it carefully on her bed. *Can't you buy me a dress?* Sally had asked their mother. *Nell can make you one, same as she did for herself. Take it or leave it.* Then Prudy went on banging things around in the kitchen, which seemed to be all she'd done lately.

The bodice was almost finished. There was just some

pleating across the front that needed to be done by hand. Nell worked the needle in, out, in, out. It made her think of sex. She bit her lip, ashamed. If she was going to make it work with Pastor Voss, she had some work to do on herself. Pure of heart. Clean of mind and body. That should be her focus. But that wasn't so easy for a savvy person. She could only hope he'd appreciate that about her.

There was so much about her to appreciate! Her own dress hung on the back of her closet door. Look at that craftsmanship! Her seamstress abilities were quite remarkable. She could whip up costumes for the yearly Christmas pageant, sew sashes for the Christian Youth Crusaders, make curtains for the rectory. *Darn his socks*. It was that pesky va-va-voom she was worried about. Could she make herself attractive enough? Could she get him to dance with her at the banquet? Would he notice that she was surprisingly light on her feet? Or would he be too busy watching her father for signs of disaster?

It was a mixed blessing, all right, having her father back. It left her *amour* in the clear. But to what end? Would she have any chance to shine with her dad in the room? She felt little pinpricks of hurt thinking how her dad had stood on their porch and never said one word to her. It was all about Sally.

She paused in her stitching. There was something to the way Sally went about her little escapade. Boldly. Unafraid. Nell admired it in a grudging way.

She stood abruptly, letting the dress fall at her feet. Why wait for the banquet? Did she really think that in one night she'd impress Pastor Voss so much that he'd suddenly fall madly in love with her? One way or another, she'd have to tell him of her feelings, and there was no better time than the present. She hurried to her dresser and studied her face.

"The squeaky wheel gets the grease," she whispered. Maybe it wasn't *exactly* apt, but close enough. First savvy. Now squeaky. Because Sally wasn't the only one who deserved to be heard.

Nell's heart was pounding so loudly she almost couldn't hear her own knock on the pastor's office door. She heard him call *come in*, so she gripped the doorknob and turned. Her palm was slick, causing her to fumble a moment before she could push it open.

"I hope I'm not disturbing you," she said in a shaky voice. She cleared her throat and tried to breathe. No one liked a shrinking violet.

"No, no." Was that a look of disappointment on his face? Maybe he was expecting that dunderhead Daisy, with her crimson fake nails and witch-cackle laugh.

"If it's about my car," he said, "you really don't have to say any more. I'm not angry with you."

"I'm not here about that." She stopped. Should she keep standing, or sit down? She couldn't very well throw her heart down on his desk without some kind of preamble.

"I thought I'd come see if there are any last minute details you need help with," she said.

He had his glasses off. It made his face seem over-exposed. He blinked.

"No, I think everything's under control. Mrs. Dekker always sees to that." He rubbed his lenses clean with a handkerchief and put them back on.

"I've checked the decorations," she continued. "Everything looks wonderful."

Why didn't he ask her to sit? Because he didn't want her to stay. She should go. In fact, what on earth was she doing here?

Had she lost her mind? She'd never been alone in a room with a boy, never mind a man. Yet here she was. Something had brought her to this moment.

"Are you happy with the way things have turned out?"

He stared at her a moment. She wondered if he heard her.

"Oh, yes. Of course. Everything's lovely."

There was another pause, like he was waiting for something from her. This was it! Say it! But she couldn't speak.

"Well," he said finally, and shuffled some papers into a pile in front of him before standing. "I need to go unlock the back door for the florist delivery. I can walk you out."

No! She stepped quickly in front of the door, blocking his exit.

"All the girls are looking forward to dancing," she stammered. "Will you be dancing?"

He smiled and punched his hands into his pockets. "I'm not much of a dancer."

That's right. Steer the conversation. You can do it.

She gave him what she hoped was a coy look. "Oh, but you shouldn't miss out. If you like, I'd be happy to dance with you."

He looked embarrassed and didn't answer. Maybe he really did think of her as a delinquent for stealing his car. Maybe he lumped her with Lenny. Two troublemakers. He might have forgotten all the work she did for the banquet. He certainly wasn't giving the impression that he was on top of things. *On top of…* Oh! Her cheeks flamed. This wasn't the time for sexual thoughts!

"You know, about the car. I can't tell you how sorry I am for that."

"I understand why you did it."

"I don't want you to think I would commit a crime so

casually. I'm not that kind of person."

She saw a look of patience settle over him. She also saw the effort it cost him. "Of course not," he said, and she thought *no, not politeness! Anything but that!*

She forged on. "I'm the kind of person who… well, I have some very specific goals."

He nodded. "Your mother mentioned you'd like to be a missionary."

So he knew! This was a good start.

"Yes, but if there was a way I could serve the Lord right here, in my own community…" She stopped and gave him a very direct look.

"There are many ways to serve the Lord," he agreed.

She rushed on. "I admire the work you do. It must be very lonely, and terribly hard, leading the church all alone, without someone at your side."

Now his brow furrowed.

"You've done a wonderful job!" she added quickly.

But he was shaking his head in a way that made her heart sink.

"Nell, I haven't done a wonderful job. I've failed miserably. If only you knew how badly I've failed."

"Don't say that! Because…" she took a deep breath. "Well, I know all about you and my mother, if that's what you're referring to."

His eyebrows shot up. "What do you know about Prudy and me?"

"I remember the way you used to come over all the time. I know you had feelings for each other." She reached out and touched his arm. "It doesn't matter to me. That's over."

He stared at her hand. “What are you saying?”

Her words tumbled out. “I have feelings of my own. For you. Loving feelings. And I know you don’t feel the same about me. Not yet. But I would be very good for you.”

He took a step back and pressed his fingers to his temple. “Oh, no, no.”

“I’m 21 now! I’m ready to be married and start a family.”

“Nell, I’m flattered. But please, don’t say any more.”

He didn’t take her seriously! He saw her as a girl, not a woman! She wouldn’t let that keep them apart. She grabbed his shoulder and half stepped, half fell toward him. Pressing her eyes closed, she kissed him awkwardly. Frantically. She couldn’t even be sure she accurately hit his lips. Quickly he pushed her away with a terrible sound—was it disgust?—that Nell would never be able to get out of her ears.

“I’m so sorry for the hurt I’ve caused your family,” he cried, anguished. “Your mother and your sister. And you. Even Lenny.”

He lunged for the door.

“Don’t go! I’m pouring my heart out here!”

Looking back, he said, “You may soon feel very differently about me, Nell. And I won’t blame you. In the meantime, I can hardly bear to look at you.” He turned away. “At any of you.”

She watched him go, too stunned to move. And if there was any squeak to be heard, it was only the wheels flying off her heart.

Sally

If ever you need a best friend, it's at one of the biggest moment in your life. And this—finding your father!—was up there with the best of them. So was a first kiss. And Frannie knew nothing about either. She wasn't due back from vacation until the day before the banquet. Which, for Sally, was torture. She had to tell *someone!*

So she called Patty Ann, who she couldn't stand, and pretended to have a question about school supplies. *Um, I lost the list Mrs. DeLong mailed us. How many notebooks do we need?* She sounded like an idiot, but she didn't care. Nothing could ruin the satisfaction of saying *thanks! See you at the banquet!*

Nothing could hide the surprise in Patty Ann's voice. *You're going?*

Yeah, with my dad. Bye now!

She could practically hear the rumor mill churning out the news. There was only a brief period of panic when she thought *why did I do that? What if he doesn't show?* She'd drag a stranger off the street, that's what. She had to have *this one night*. Maybe it was silly, but she thought of the banquet like an elevator, letting her off on a different floor. And wouldn't she enjoy the view! Once she was there, she might never need to leave.

To calm her fears, she tried her dress on fifteen times a day, along with the pair of white pumps Aunt Flookie was loaning her. She set her hair in curlers and wrangled it into various styles, turning the bottom up in a flip, or under in a bob, before shellacking it with Aqua Net. The whole time her mother hovered nearby, babbling at her in an annoying way. *You know I think you're beautiful, don't you? I've always been so proud of you.*

Then she started in with this *remember when* routine.

Remember when you were three years old, and you copied every move I made? You wanted to be just like me.

Or *I remember when I was young like you. I didn't always make the best decisions. But things have a way of working out.*

Sally knew darn well when someone was trying to buddy up to her. But if her mother felt bad about trying to keep Sally from her dad, couldn't she just say she was sorry? Instead she went on sniveling, not giving Sally a moment of privacy, until Sally wanted to scream *Mother! I don't really have time to traipse down memory lane!*

Then, after all of Prudy's weepy, *you're-my-whole-world-Sally* drivel, when the big night came she refused to even wait with Sally in the living room. Even Nell didn't stick around. She'd announced that morning that she wasn't feeling well and wouldn't be going to the banquet after all. But when Mrs. Dekker called from the church and said they desperately needed her help, she threw on her dress and left, looking grim. Sally sat on the nubby plaid davenport, alone, fingering the lace doilies her mother draped over the armrests to hide the threadbare spots. She found a loose thread in the cushion and slowly pulled, knowing her mother would squawk if she saw her. She didn't care. Let everything come loose. All the resentments and grudges and stubbornness they were so bound up in. Sally wanted to be free of it all.

Besides, she didn't want to admit it, but she'd expected so much more from her mother. Prudy was still single, after all. So was her dad. They'd loved each other once. Why not again? Not that she'd spend all night playing matchmaker. She planned to enjoy herself. Just a girl and her dad, out having fun. The idea of getting to know him was like a warm sandy path before her. She couldn't wait to take her shoes off and dig her toes in.

When the bell rang she rose, hating that she had to answer it herself. She wished they had a stairway in their house so she could descend it slowly in her new dress, a picture of loveliness, just like in the movies. Only it wouldn't be some dumb immature boy standing at the bottom gaping up at her, it would be her father, and he would be so proud of her. She reached for the doorknob. *As long as he's presentable, that's all I ask.*

She opened the door.

Richard stood there grinning, and though there was no hiding the gaps where his teeth were missing, his face was clean and shaved. His slicked back hair was freshly cut, and his clothes! Sally couldn't hide her surprise. He actually looked handsome in a gray jacket with black pants and shiny black shoes.

"Good evening, my lady," he said with a mock bow.

"Oh! You look wonderful!" And *sober*, she thought.

"What did you expect?" He looked at her with a wide-eyed, hurt expression. Sally didn't know if he was joking.

"I wasn't sure," she admitted. "I'm just glad you're here."

He grinned again and took his hands from behind his back. In one he held a wrist corsage in a box. It was a small pink rose surrounded by baby's breath, with a purple satin bow, and it was the most beautiful flower Sally had ever seen. The other held a box of chocolate-covered cherries. Sally didn't happen to like chocolate-covered cherries, but she'd eat every last one, and when she did she'd remember how thoughtful her father was, and how perfect this night was.

Because it was going to be perfect. She knew it with a certainty she hadn't felt before. She knew it by the easy way Richard smiled at her, by the perfect cinch of his necktie and the way he smelled of aftershave. She took his gifts with mumbled thanks and stepped aside to let him in, and that's when he patted her shoulder, gently, two times.

She hesitated briefly, then threw her arms around him.

"Thank you for coming!"

He held her a moment, his breath warming the top of her head. He's my dad, she thought. *My dad.* She knew that whatever happened, whether her friends made fun of him, or her mother was angry with her, or Nell and Lenny thought she was a selfish fool, this moment was enough.

"Sorry," she said, pulling away.

He shrugged. "I have that effect on the ladies." He looked around the empty living room. "Where's your mother?"

"Um…she's not coming out."

He pursed his lips and nodded. "Nice to see you too, Prudy!" he called loudly. "Oh, yes! We *will* have a wonderful time. Thank you!" He rolled his eyes at Sally and gestured toward the door. She looked back only briefly, hoping to see her mother. How much more perfect this would be with her blessing. But that was one blessing she couldn't count. Anyway, she wasn't interested in tallies right now. She wanted to be a giant slate, wiped clean.

They crossed the porch together and headed into the night. Richard walked with such a jaunty gait that his suit coat swung open and Sally caught a glimpse inside: a silver lining, shiny smooth. A label with a name she couldn't read. A pocket, mysterious and warm. Underneath, a beating heart.

This must be the feeling the other girls thrived on when it came to boys, this decision to love a person before knowing a thing about him! Or the knowledge that whatever you learned wouldn't make a bit of difference. Call it love. Or butterflies. To Sally it was heavenly.

"Your mom got a boyfriend?" he asked.

Sally laughed. The idea was so preposterous. She was about to tell him when a sudden pang made her close her mouth. Her mother didn't deserve that. And maybe it would help to keep him guessing. So she said, "She thinks this sort of thing is silly."

"Your mother was hooked into this sort of fuss too, when she was your age. You know she almost won Miss Clover Honey?"

She allowed a wry smile. "I've heard."

"A banquet such as this isn't any more silly than a beauty contest."

"You knew her for a long time, huh?" Was this where he'd start bad-mouthing her?

But he looked thoughtful before he said, "Long enough to screw up her life. And yours."

It was like cold water splashed on her face, hearing that.

Well, good. No bitterness. No idle chit chat either. She could almost hear her brain slide into a higher gear. Just give me a moment to rev up, it said. This was so different from the family she'd known, where no one ever wanted to talk about anything.

"You're here now," she said. "We can make a fresh start." *All of us.*

Richard cleared his throat. "Sally, I have to be honest with you. I don't know that too much will change after this. I'm not the sort of guy you want to start counting on."

But she was cruising now. "Don't say that! I don't believe what everyone says about you and you shouldn't either."

He groaned. "You're not going to start talking about self-esteem and faith and that kind of shit, are you? 'Cause I've heard all about how much Jesus loves me."

"No. I'll leave that to Nell."

"Let's leave it period. Some of the best preachers around have given up on me. I'm what you call a modern man, and the church doesn't deal with modern."

"What exactly is a modern man?"

"I make things happen on my own terms."

Sally liked the sound of that. "I'm modern too," she said.

He slowed and put a hand on her arm. "No, I'm a real son of a bitch," he said. "We should at least admit that to each other."

How she loved him! Each time he admitted something about himself it was a like a shutter rolling up with a snap. Here I am. Come in. Look at the mess in here.

She wasn't afraid of it.

"I don't believe that."

"Then you're the only one. What's the buzz about me anyway?"

Buzz? More like a roar. Lazy, selfish, mean-spirited,

conceited, good-for-nothing drunk.

"Stupid stuff," she said. "People around here don't know what they're talking about."

He snorted. "Anyway, what do I care?" But he looked like he wanted to give somebody's face five good reasons why he cared. Okay. So maybe inside him there was a kettle on a back burner and it was set to boil.

She'd be careful with him. No sweat. But how come when you tell yourself that, you start to sweat? On top of that, she tripped.

"First time wearing heels?" he asked, catching her with one arm.

"No." She sounded defensive, but it embarrassed her that he'd guessed. Besides, if he'd been around he would know that it was her first time.

"You must have been surprised to see Lenny again," she said, to change the subject.

"You could say that."

"I still don't know why he tracked you down like that. He hates you."

He gave her a *well-thank-you-very-much* face. He knew it, though. She could tell.

"He was concerned about you, I guess," he said after a pause. "Just like Nell was concerned about you when she took Voss' car."

"They weren't worried about me. They just wanted to keep me away from you so they didn't have to see you again."

That look again. "Is that so?"

Could it be he really didn't know these things?

"I don't mean to make you feel bad."

"Don't worry about me."

"They just have memories, is all. They find it hard to believe a person can change."

"Not like you, huh?"

She shrugged.

"Well, they may just be right. On the other hand, I probably mellowed a little over the years."

Sally didn't want to ruin things, but this talk of Lenny and Nell, well, it was like they were standing behind her tapping her on the shoulder. *Why don't you ask him about the time he smashed the window? Or the time he made us take our Christmas tree out to the curb on Christmas Eve because we didn't wait for him before decorating it?*

"Lenny says he's the one who made you leave," she said, careful to keep her voice normal. "Is that a fair assessment?" *Assessment?* She sounded like a school teacher. In fact, those words might be something she'd heard the principal say to a boy he caught fighting in the hall.

Richard made that sound that when you see it in books it looks like *hmpf*, with all the vowels sucked out.

"Lenny was a kid," he said.

Remember, clean slate. But there was that tap again.

"What was it made you leave, anyway?"

He rubbed his hand over his face. "Aw, who can remember that far back?"

"Nell can. And Lenny."

He stopped suddenly. "So listen here. You want to have a good time tonight, or not?"

Sally nodded.

"Then let's not rehash all that unpleasantness. I don't see it doing anyone any good."

Now the darn tap was like a pair of hands around her

throat. Whether the hands came from Lenny or Nell, or from somewhere inside herself, she didn't know.

She took a breath. "I just would feel better knowing the particulars."

His jaw tightened. "And I'd feel better dropping it."

"I was just wondering why you never wrote, or called."

He sighed. "Prudy thought you kids were better off without me. Why should I argue with her?"

Three reasons. And she was one of them.

"Don't you feel bad about it?"

"I could spend time feeling bad about a lot of things, but who wants to be miserable?" He faced her, his hands on his hips. "Now if you want to make yourself miserable over seeing me tonight, I'll just go."

"No, no, please!" She pulled his arm. What was it with her parents, that neither could say those simple words? *I'm sorry.* She'd feel so much better. She ought to tell him, but asking for an apology...well, it was like someone handing you a glass of warm water on a hot day. It tides you over, but it's not real enjoyable.

He softened. "Why do you think I'm here, huh?"

Sally smiled. Of course he felt bad. Who wouldn't feel bad after being thrown out by your wife and son and being alone for ten long years? And here Sally was picking on him, making him dredge up the feelings he probably worked so hard to hide. She would not ask for more than he could give. She would not wreck it!

"Mom doesn't date," she said.

"How about you? Anyone special?"

She thought of Cash. "There's one boy I like all right."

"Does he treat you good?"

Hmm. There was the way he pretended to ditch her at Stuckey's, the way he'd gotten mad when she wouldn't go to the beach with him, the way he peeled out without saying goodbye after they had kissed.

"Not really."

He laughed. "Then you must be madly in love! Hell, boys around here aren't good enough for you. You never want to end up with someone you knew in high school. It's the kiss of death. Look at your mother and me."

But Sally didn't want to think anymore about her mother, or Lenny or Nell. She wanted to talk about boys, or school, or whatever ordinary things a father and daughter talked about. She wanted to have fun.

"So tell me about your friends," he said. The connection was there, between them! In their DNA. "Will they be surprised to see me?"

"Frannie is my best friend. She knows everything now. She'll be there with her dad, Verle, but he doesn't talk much. Then there's Debs and Patty Ann. They're ok sometimes, but mostly they're stuck up. You know, all giggly and snooty-like."

"They give you a hard time?"

Sally shrugged. "They give everyone a hard time." She smiled. "But once, in second grade, I split Patty Ann's lip open when I socked her in the mouth."

He laughed again. Sally loved the way it sounded, like a big round bubble that came out in a burst and hung in the air. She could reach out a finger and pop it.

"Why'd you hit her?" he asked.

"She made fun of my clothes." She said this as if it were funny, when it had been anything but. She wondered, did he have any idea how bad off they'd been without him? If he did he didn't show it.

"Lenny taught me how to make a good fist," she said. That was another thing her dad might have taught her if he'd been around. The old sadness started seeping in and she had to will it away. Was every conversation going to be a reminder of something she never had?

Something seemed to change in him, too. There was a gloominess when he said, "Yeah. Lenny's a born fighter. That much I know."

Were they both remembering Lenny's bat, and the way he'd hit Richard with it that night ten years ago? Sally wished those years weren't separating them. It was such a wide gap. Whatever they said to each other now was no more than throwing rocks in a hole.

"Are you still drinking?" she asked. She might as well throw the boulders first.

He laughed. "You've been dying to ask, haven't you?"

"So what if I have? It's a big night for me, in case you haven't noticed."

"I haven't had a drink in, oh, at least seven or eight days, so don't worry. I'm good and sober."

She tried to hide her shock. "Seven *days?* Is that a long stretch for you?"

"What are you, my sponsor?"

"Oh, so you go to….those meetings."

"Didn't I just say I'm sober? If that's not good enough—"

Here was a balancing act that had nothing to do with her shoes.

"No. Of course it is."

They walked without speaking until they got to the church. There was a knot of girls in fluffy dresses out front. And the

Texaco station across the street. If only Cash could see her now! Wouldn't he be shocked? If he hadn't dumped her off like he did, she might have called him to let him know how everything turned out.

Wait a minute. Why should she want anything to do with Cash? Look at her! She was as pretty as any other girl, and twice as sensible. Which of these girls would have the gumption to do what she'd done, locating a father who'd been gone for ten years? Now that he was back, things were going to be different. She might stand a chance with one of the popular boys, like Roy Westveer or Jimmy Dorn. Still, she kept looking over at the station as they approached. She heard someone say *Hiya Sally.*

It was Patty Ann and Debs, walking arm in arm in that childish way they had, as if everyone didn't know they were the best of friends. Sally's mouth went dry. If her dad was going to be ridiculed, it would begin with them. Everyone else would follow.

She swallowed. "Hi. Here's my dad." So she blurted it out. Who could blame her?

Richard tilted his head back and looked down his nose at them. "These the ones you told me about?"

She nodded. He took Debs' hand, leaned in close, and said in a voice you'd use with a five-year-old, "High school is not the slightest bit important in the grand scheme of things. You girls realize that, don't you?"

Their faces went slack with surprise. Patty Ann recovered first.

"Sally just talks about you constantly," she said sweetly. "In fact, she never shuts up."

"I do *not,*" Sally said. Prissy-ass bitches. If she did talk about her dad, it wasn't to the two of them.

Richard laughed. There were those gaps, where his teeth were missing. She wished he wouldn't open his mouth quite so much. But she was awful to be so picky. It wasn't like any of the other dads were Hollywood handsome.

"I'm just giving you girls a hard time. I know you can take it. Look at you! Top of the food chain, that's for sure." He gave a long whistle.

Debbie and Patty-Ann smiled uncertainly and ducked away. Richard took Sally's arm.

"Don't worry about the losers in this hick town," he whispered. "They'll wind up married to the football players, with nice houses and a bunch of kids and they'll be bored and miserable their whole lives."

"Actually…" That first part sounded pretty good to Sally. But she could see what he was trying to say. Wasn't she just telling herself the same thing? Aim higher!

Inside the foyer they found a table covered with name tags. She half expected to be left out, to find that they wouldn't be getting the same treatment as everyone else. But there they were. *Richard Van Sloeten. Sally Van Sloeten.* See, he belonged here, same as anyone. She handed his name tag to him, then peeled the waxy backing from hers and pressed it on her chest. People were bustling around them, and they were briefly separated by a whirl of glittering, giggling girls smelling of perfume and hairspray. He caught her eye over the top of a dark-haired head and smiled, then reached out a flat hand, meaning she should give him her balled up paper for him to throw away. How thoughtful he was!

"I'm surprised old peckerwood hasn't moved on yet," he said, pointing to the plaque on the wall that said *Reverend Phillip Voss.*

"Excuse me?"

"Voss. That's my name for him. You like it?"

"Why do you call him that?"

He snickered like a kid. "I'll tell you later."

She couldn't help it. She laughed too. The things he said! His attitude, the way he walked, the way he rolled his shoulders, and looked around with those sparkly eyes like he was looking to take on the world. Maybe he was a little rough around the edges, with the dent in his head and the missing teeth, but he seemed fresher and more alive than anyone else. She hoped it would rub off on her.

The banquet was in the Fellowship Hall, which was a nice name for basement. Sally's breath caught as she looked around. Why had she never appreciated the 4-H Club? They'd worked a miracle. The tables were covered with white cloths and crepe paper flowers (Lenny should be proud!) and giant ribbon bows hung from the backs of the metal folding chairs. Long pieces of fabric covered the ugly ceiling tiles and billowed gently in the breeze from the fans. Candles flickered everywhere and gave it all a gently, dreamy look. The only bright light came from the corner, where there was a painted backdrop of a starry night behind a white swing. For a dollar Mrs. Dekker, the church secretary, would take a Polaroid. Finally Sally would have a picture of her and her dad! She could tape it on her mirror in her bedroom.

"Want to get one?" Sally asked, motioning toward the swing. She didn't want to seem too anxious but there was no line yet, her lipstick was still fresh, and if they waited Mrs. Dekker might run out of film, or break the camera. Anything was possible.

Her dad was surveying the room with a beady-eyed look. "Sure," he shrugged, following her over.

"Well!" Mrs. Dekker squinted. "Who's this?"

"My dad," Sally said proudly.

"Oh!" Mrs. Dekker was startled. "Of course."

"Nice to see you, too," Richard said, his voice heavy with sarcasm. Sally stared at him.

"She knows me!" he hissed as they took their places, Sally on the swing with Richard behind her. "I saw her every month for years when I sold tithing envelopes here."

"She's like eighty-something. She didn't recognize you."

But he was scowling. "It's bullshit."

"It was ten years ago!"

"Shut up and smile," he said, slapping a hand on her shoulder.

The flash went off before she was ready and Sally feared the moment was ruined. She didn't want to be punished for the past any more than he did. But couldn't they make a fresh start without trampling on anyone's feelings?

Mrs. Dekker handed her the Polaroid and Sally watched the milky white square intently, waiting for their images to appear. Again, she expected to somehow be left out. There would be a strange smudge where her face should be. Or her dad wouldn't show up at all. Something to tell her this wasn't really happening.

Then there they were. A little blurry, their smiles unsure, but visible. Real. She gave her dad a happy, goofy grin and tucked the photo in her purse.

"C'mon," she said, "There's some people over there I want you to meet."

She dragged him across the room, an electricity crackling in her ears. This was just so perfect! It had to be the greatest reunion in the history of reunions! She ought to call the Sentinel and tell them to send their best reporter. Surely it was front page news.

"That's Stanley," she said, pointing to one of the boys lined up against the wall. "See, the boys work as waiters. Isn't that fun? Anyway, we're in homeroom together. You can talk baseball with him. He's a big fan, like Lenny." She knew she was talking a mile a minute, but she didn't care. In fact, seeing the boys just made her more giddy. Could they tell from looking at her that she'd been kissed? Were they noticing her dress, or her mysteriously mascaraed eyes? Did her legs look more shapely in heels?

"And over there, that's Myrna, she's the brainy one, so you can use big words all you want. She knows them all. But be yourself, of course."

"What am I, a goddamn puppet?"

She stopped. Where was the easy grin, the bubble-like laugh, the cocky tilt of his chin? He had his hands shoved in his pockets and his eyes were shifting uneasily. She was reminded of an animal in a cage.

"Sorry." Now that they were in the middle of the room, she felt the eyes on them too. Curious eyes. Confused, calculating, *judging* eyes. She straightened. It was okay. She'd expected as much. All the same, when she saw Frannie waving at her from across the room, she nearly went weak with relief.

"Frannie!" Sally squeezed past some people and hugged her friend before introducing her dad.

"Doesn't Frannie look great?" Sally said.

Richard seemed to be collecting himself. He gave his tie a quick cinch, and with a hard blink flipped some switch in his face. There. A smile. He cocked his head and said, "Next to you, dear, all others fade."

So maybe he was a little thoughtless. Because Frannie *was* plain, there was no hiding it. But he was only trying to make Sally feel special. How could she blame him for that? She'd just have to help him think about his words before he said them.

How exactly would she do that?

"Let's sit," he said, and she nodded.

"Well?" Frannie whispered, pulling on her elbow. "How's it going?"

"Good. A little overwhelming."

"You look marvelous. Really happy."

Of course she was happy. This was what she'd wanted. She had her dad at her side. Her best friend too. Maybe even a boyfriend waiting in the wings. Who could say? The banquet was supposed to be about dating. Now that she was *experienced*, she had reason to pay attention tonight.

The tables were arranged in two long lines, and they chose seats at the end, near the back wall, across from Frannie and her dad. Richard made a big deal out of pulling Sally's chair back.

"Allow me," he said.

He had charm all right. Enough to fill a bowl. She'd collect it all and bring it out later, when she was alone. Munch on it piece by piece.

"Valkema," Richard said to Frannie's dad as he sat down. "You connected with the Valkemas in Traverse City?"

"I don't believe so," said Frannie's dad. "Do you …travel up there often?" Sally thought he was going to say live up there, but Mr. Valkema was kind enough to know better. There was something awkward about acknowledging that Richard had been gone so long.

"My work takes me all over," Richard said.

"What line are you in?"

"Salesman, through and through. Used to work for the paper mill in Muskegon. I was their top man in raw materials for a while. Good pay, but I couldn't stand the smell. It gets in your hair, your clothes, everything."

It was just so normal then, with a capital N, listening to the two men talk. Sally could almost believe she'd been doing this for years. By the end of the night she'd be rolling her eyes and saying *Dad!* all exasperated-like while they went on and on with their man talk. The weather, car parts, layoffs, union strikes, home repairs, the price of gas. Outwardly she'd be slouchy bored, but her insides would be on the edge of her seat, taking in every word. Her dad was just one of the guys, and sitting here with him, like this, she was just another kid. She breathed a silent prayer of thanks that her dad was so chatty and easy to be with. And that Frannie's dad was sweet enough to treat him like anyone else.

It wasn't until she saw Pastor Voss working his way down the table, shaking hands, that she felt uneasy. Peckerwood greets deadbeat dad. What would happen?

Her dad stood and extended his hand. "It's such a pleasure to be here," he said. "This is really a wonderful event you've got here."

"Thank you." Pastor Voss looked surprised too.

"We are definitely enjoying ourselves. No doubt about it. Aren't we, Sally?"

She nodded. What was with the Mr. Jolly routine?

"I thought you couldn't stand him," she said, when the pastor had moved on.

"He knows how I feel about him."

"So why were you nice to him?"

He sighed patiently. "It's called playing the game."

She considered this. "You're not playing a game with me, are you?"

"Why would I do that?"

It was a silly thought, but if he could so easily fake it with the pastor, could he be faking it with her too? Was he was only pretending to like her? Was he suffering through this night out of a sense of obligation? She would hate that. She'd rather she'd never met him than to have him smiling and laughing the way he was and then rolling his eyes and shaking his head when he was alone.

He must have seen her worried look because he put his arm around her shoulders and gave her a warm squeeze that chased away her doubts. Such casual affection! No wonder he didn't fit with her family. He was a whole different species.

"Here comes Nell," he said, nodding toward the kitchen. "She doesn't look happy."

It was true. By the look on her face, you'd think someone had died. When she walked by their table Sally reached out to stop her.

"What's wrong?" Not that she really wanted to know. She didn't want Nell spoiling her night with her usual list of complaints.

"Pull up a chair," Richard said. "Tell us why you look so down."

Nell sniffed. "I just came to make sure everything looks good. The way I planned it." She looked at their place settings and nodded as if she was very satisfied.

"Well," Richard said, "what happened? Somebody burn the meatloaf?"

Nell didn't laugh but Sally did. They obviously shared a sense of humor. When Nell didn't answer, Richard jabbed Sally's shoulder.

"Better not tease her. She's liable to go hotwire ol' Peckerwood's car."

Nell's eyebrows buckled from some internal tremor. She turned abruptly and walked away.

"You know, you might want to watch what you say," Sally said. "She's…" How to explain Nell to a guy like him? She didn't want to make her sound stodgy. "Well, she's sensitive about people thinking she's done something wrong." It didn't come close. All it did was remind her how little their dad knew them.

"Thanks for the advice," he said, sounding not at all grateful. He chewed his lip a moment.

"What is it about women, anyway, always trying to improve a guy? Now if Nell had invited me tonight, no way. I can see she knows how to turn the screws. I never expected it of you. Christ! You're only 16."

Sally hoped no one had heard. "No one's trying to turn the screws," she said quietly. "Whatever that means."

"Is it my fault she walks away? She can't take a joke."

Sally sighed. This was like walking into history class and seeing the homework assignment on the board: pages 200 through 275. So much to do! On top of everything else, how would she ever manage? Because it wasn't just her own relationship with her father that mattered. She'd need to fix the whole family, and the thought was pure exhaustion.

"Here comes our dinner," he said. What his tone said was *let's get this over with.* The boys were coming forward with trays and pitchers of water and the girls started tittering. Predictable. And annoying. Although it was cute the way they hammed it up, setting the plates down with a flourish and a bow. Someone turned on the music. The candles cast a lovely glow. After dinner there would be dancing. This was still *her* night. She made herself smile as Roy and Stanley set plates before them. Baked chicken. Mashed potatoes. Green beans with slivered almonds and a big fluffy dinner roll. She picked up her knife and fork and daintily sawed into a breast. Her father was already chewing. And making a face.

"What's the matter?"

He set his fork down. "It's dry."

He'd been gone too long. Too long away from teenage girls with sensitive feelings, and small town events, and knowing what it was like to have your whole life in one room.

"Hey Stanley!" he called. "You think you could bring this back to the kitchen and try to find me something that doesn't taste like a piece of firewood?"

Sally froze. So did Frannie and Mr. Valkema. Everyone at their table had their ears on hyper-alert, listening. Sally wanted to slide under the table.

"You want me to throw it out?" Stanley asked.

"Unless you have a starving dog back there, yes." Richard handed him his plate.

"You want another piece?"

"Something different please."

"They don't have anything different," Sally mumbled. Somewhere along the way had he failed to notice they were in a church *basement*?

Richard smiled at Stanley. "I'm sure he'll find something, won't you?"

"Yes sir." Stanley took his plate away.

"Even a free meal should be edible."

"It's not free," Sally said miserably. "Mom paid for the tickets."

Richard sighed. "You want the finer things in life, you have to ask. Don't settle for second best."

"What do you know about the finer things?" she snapped. With his missing teeth and dented head. Living in a migrant shack, hanging out in bars—these were the finer things?

Richard was smiling after Stanley. "I like that kid. He's okay. Why don't you date him?"

Like she could just decide and have anything she wanted. If she could do that, she wouldn't be having this *oh, no, oh please, please no!* feeling. She'd be sitting where Frannie was, Miss Sally Valkema, beaming at her dad while he picked chicken from his teeth. Loving everything about him. Here she'd been so afraid of her dad coming across as not good enough, she'd never expected him to act like *he* was too good for everything. She never expected this arrogance.

What exactly *did* you expect, you idiot? That your brother and sister are completely nuts? That they talk trash about him because for some twisted reason they enjoy being fatherless? And your mother, what's her angle? Is she addicted to working 12 hours a day? Proud of being called a divorcee?

She shook her head, remembering the hug she had shared with her dad. That hug said it all. It reminded her of their bond. Face it, she was *better* than her family! Uncontaminated. Open-minded. Modern. She could make this work.

"Ladies and gentlemen!" Pastor Voss stood beside a podium on a little riser, with a microphone in his hand. The lights came up.

"Welcome to the Twenty-Seventh Annual Father Daughter Banquet. While we enjoy this wonderful meal, I'd like to say a few words." He held up one hand. "I promise to be brief."

No. Take your time. She could sit through hours of his

drivel now, as long as it took the spotlight off her and her dad. Everyone would make fun of the way he'd sent the food back. She stole a look at Frannie, who smiled and gave a little shrug that said *welcome to the club*. That's right. Other kids were always griping about how their parents embarrassed them. It was even kind of funny, when you thought about it. So when Stanley returned with a plate without chicken, just extra potatoes and beans and another roll, Sally tried to give him the same elegant shrug. *You know how dads are.* He actually winked at her! In less than two weeks she'd had her first kiss and been winked at, by two different boys. She wasn't an outcast. She was just in the club.

"Girls, as you know," said the pastor, "you are here because you have reached an important new phase in your life. You stand on the brink of womanhood, a time of new opportunities, as well as greater responsibility.

"Many of you look forward to dating, and this can be an exciting time in your life. It can also be a confusing time, filled with heartache and temptation. Above all, it's a time to rely on your relationship with the Lord."

Maybe she wasn't relying enough on the Lord. Where was her gratitude that her dad was even here at all? God loved her father, and so did she. Thank you, God! Thank you for my dad!

"I would encourage you, young ladies, to be particular in your choice of young men. What qualities will you look for in a potential mate?"

Why couldn't he just say boyfriend? Were they supposed to be thinking about marriage already?

"You might ask yourself, is he responsible?"

Cash? She didn't know.

"Does he hold a job?"

Yes.

"Is he serious about his schooling?"

No idea.

"Does he show respect to teachers or other authority figures?"

She doubted it.

"Does he attend church regularly?"

Probably not.

"And finally, does he respect your virtue?"

That one made her squirm. She looked at her dad and he patted her knee. *We'll sort all this out*, the pat said. *I'm here now.*

Pastor Voss continued. "We see in the papers every day stories of lost youth. In San Francisco and New York, young people are seeking love without standards. Society has ruined our understanding of love. It preaches the opposite of love, which is selfishness. It tells us that it's all right to pursue anything that feels good. But whatever causes us to sacrifice our morals is not love. Real love is like God, holy and perfect."

Though Sally was in the back of the room, the pastor seemed to be looking right at her. As if she were the one running around with a zillion boys. He ought to be directing his comments at Patty Ann.

"The gospel of Samuel reminds us that love is patient. Lust requires immediate satisfaction. Love is kind, lust is harsh. Love does not demand its own way, lust does. Lust may feel like love at first, but when physically expressed, it results in self-disgust and hatred of the other person."

Did that explain Cash's behavior the day he dropped her off? Was he disgusted with himself for kissing her? This dating business was all so confusing, not to mention embarrassing. Did the other girls feel funny listening to this with their dads?

Or was it only hard for her because her dad was practically a stranger?

"For yourself," he went on, "you must possess purity, a commitment to home and family, and devotion to the Lord. And fathers, in these unruly times, it is your job to guide your daughters through the temptations and pitfalls of this age, to help them recognize good character and Christian values, especially in their dating partners."

Sally glanced at her dad. He rolled his eyes and smiled.

"Fathers, it is your job to set the rules, to enforce those rules, and to make sure your daughter chooses young men who will meet the standards of your family. You are to be her example. Through your own marriage you teach your daughter what she should seek in a mate."

Sally winced. Couldn't the pastor be more sensitive to the fact that not everyone here was Ward Cleaver? She leaned back, ready to shoot her dad another loving glance and maybe another roll of the eyes. What she saw made her gasp. Richard had a small silver flask in his hand, and he was hastily splashing a clear liquid into his fruit punch.

"What are you *doing?*" she hissed.

"Relax," he whispered, slipping the flask expertly back into his breast pocket. He gave her an easy smile and a wink. Oh, why did sparkly people have to be so dangerous? The tactless comments, the bad manners, she could handle all that, but not *this*! Not drinking!

"Fathers, question your daughter's dates. Be involved. And girls, don't be angry with your father when he advises you. Proverbs 23:22 says 'listen to your father, who gave you life.' Remember he's doing it because he loves you."

He loves you. More like he loves you *not*. How could her

dad do this? Did anyone notice? Would they have to leave? Her thoughts were racing so fast, it was a moment before she noticed the quiet. The pastor had finished. But why wasn't anyone clapping or moving? Oh. He was only pausing. But the pause grew longer. His eyes were downcast. He held the podium as if dizzy. Maybe he was sick. Maybe the whole lot of them would get food poisoning. She could only hope! That at least would overshadow everything else.

At last the pastor looked up. Straight at her.

"A daughter is a gift from God," he said quietly. "Treat her as such and your reward will be great." He continued to look at her. Sally stared back at him, growing uncomfortable. He coughed and looked away.

"I believe the ladies will begin serving cake now," he said.

Sally turned on her dad.

"I thought you weren't drinking!" she whispered.

He put up his hands. "Sally, *honey.* This doesn't change anything. Believe me."

She wanted to believe him. She knew that some people drank when they were having fun. Maybe he just felt like celebrating.

"So, you notice how that fucker was staring at me?" he said.

"I thought he was looking at me."

"Why would he be looking at you? No, he was making it obvious that he doesn't want me here. And everyone else noticed, too."

Her cheeks grew warm. "Maybe they noticed what you put in your drink."

This made him sigh. "Would you get off my case? Just a smack or two keeps me sharp. You want me to be at my best, don't you?"

"Yes, but…" she faltered. "People just won't understand, that's all."

"So what? They'll all have something to gloat about. A bunch of fucking saints, aren't they?"

Sally blinked hard and saw Frannie watching her. Sweet Frannie with her plain face and warm smile, sitting beside her overweight dullard of a father.

"They're not so bad."

"Listen, I'm going out to have a cigarette. I'll be back in a jiff." He leaned over and gave her shoulder a squeeze. "This is fun."

Watching him go, Sally realized that she couldn't let him wander around on his own. She grabbed her purse and started after him. A hand on her arm made her stop.

"Sally, could I speak to you a moment?"

It was Pastor Voss.

"Just leave him alone, okay?"

She pulled away from him and made her way around the crowded tables, her eyes glued to her dad's back, suddenly fearful that if she looked away, he'd disappear. She saw him step out the back door that opened onto the church parking lot. It shut with an ominous thud. Rushing forward, she put her hand on its cold metal bar, ready to push, then hesitated. There he was. Through the cloudy square window she could see his head bowed, the quick flare of a match, a curlicue of smoke. She sighed and leaned heavily against the wall.

Looking out the small window, Sally could practically hear her dad's cigarette crackle as he took a drag. He was so close, yet here she was, invisible to him. She wanted to knock hard on the glass, to wave wildly and *make him look*. She told herself that if he would only look, if he would raise his eyes and break into a smile, she would be satisfied.

She waited, standing on tiptoe until her feet and calves ached and she had to stop. This was ridiculous. She opened the door and he cut his eyes at her.

"You checking up on me?" he said.

"Why don't you come in?"

"Sure. I'll be right there." He exhaled. " Go on."

"I'll wait for you."

"For chrissake," he muttered, tossing the cigarette aside. "I gotta go to the john."

As he moved around her, she smelled the alcohol.

"What happened?" she asked, sounding plaintive. She must have made him mad, or somehow let him down.

He pulled at his face. "I just don't know why you gotta be breathing down my neck. I said I'd be right back."

She felt her knees shake. "I'm afraid you'll drink."

He gave her an indulgent smile. "Hon, if I'm gonna drink, you ain't gonna stop me."

The buzz of the crowd was coming through the walls. All the girls in fluffy dresses. The dads in neckties and aftershave. This was her moment. She couldn't let it be ruined.She took a deep breath. "Well. I love you, okay?"

He went on smiling at her, like she hadn't just handed him a slice of her heart.

"Of course you do, hon." He cupped her cheek. "Now get yourself back in there, you crazy kid."

Slowly Sally returned to the main room, her head feeling strangely hot. People had left their seats and were milling about, waiting for the tables to be cleared and moved aside to make room for dancing. She'd look for Frannie, that's what. Sensible, comforting Frannie. But as she scanned the crowd, Pastor Voss approached, blocking her view.

"I need just a moment of your time," he said solemnly. "Please. It's very important."

Sally sighed. "Fine. Have your little I-told-you-so." The old Sally would never talk this way, but she was irritated! Maybe her dad had rubbed off on her. She could hear what he would say. *This is such bullshit!*

She followed the pastor up the back stairs to a small study behind the sanctuary. He shut the door and turned to her and the look on his face made her stomach drop.

"Did something happen to my mom?" she asked.

He shook his head. "Sally, I have something to tell you and it will be very hard for you to understand. But I want you just to listen."

"Is it Lenny? Where is he?"

"It's nothing like that. Everyone is fine. What I have to say, I say because I care about you." He paused and looked at her meaningfully. "More than I care about any other church member."

She stepped back, an uneasiness washing over her. Was he some kind of pervert? This was something else the old Sally would never do. She'd never have that kind of thought. But she was changed. Her dad had changed her. Cash had changed her. Even her mother and her sneaky fake letter had changed her. She glanced at the door. If he came any closer she'd run.

"Please, just listen. Years ago your mother and I were..." He paused again. For someone who spoke in front of a crowd every Sunday, he had trouble getting to the point. Still, hearing him mention her mother made Sally breathe a little easier.

"We were romantically involved," he said and his head started bobbing on high speed.

Jesus, she thought. Not Jesus as in *Dear Jesus help me out here*. More like the letters stitched into Aunt Flookie's needlepoint. They were hidden, sort of. But when you stared at the right colors, there it was: Jesus. Once you saw it, you didn't know how you missed it; the strange formality between them, the way his face twitched when he spoke to her. It made a crazy kind of sense.

"Okay," she said slowly. Her mom had been alone a long time. And Sally was modern now. "So?"

He began pacing and spoke like he was explaining something to himself. "It was after your dad left your mother. *After*. Then he came back, but you see, at the time it seemed as if he'd gone for good. So you see, we thought..."

She had a flash of her mother married to him. She would have been a pastor's kid. Thank God that hadn't happened! Everyone knew how strange PK's were.

"When—"

"You weren't born yet. That's what I'm getting to."

So this was ancient history. She supposed she should care, but she was more worried about getting back to her dad. Anyway, the pastor seemed bothered enough for both of them.

"What you're saying is that you had an affair," she said, trying to help him. "My mom was still married."

"Yes! Yes, that's right." Like they were playing charades or something.

"So my dad came back and you broke up." What did this matter now? He was stealing valuable time away from her and dad, and for what? A game of true confession?

"We did break up, but as a result of our....time together, your mother became pregnant."

Sally felt herself go still.

"You got my mother pregnant?" she finally managed. "But…what you said tonight… that crap about love and lust and Christian values—"

"Everything I said in my speech is true. It's what I believe. It's just that people stumble from time to time."

"Stumble? Into someone's *bed?*" She had a quick flash of him falling, naked, on top of her mother, and cringed. "Don't tell me I have a half brother or sister out there somewhere."

He sighed. His look was pleading and watery. "She was pregnant with you, Sally. You are my daughter."

She stared a moment, stunned, then laughed, the same way she'd laughed earlier when she thought of her mom dating. *Oh sure, tell me another one.*

His eyebrows climbed higher on his forehead. *Plead, plead.*

"No!" She turned away. "I think I know my own mother." But hadn't she already seen that her mother wasn't what she seemed? That she would double-cross her own daughter?

"She put you up to this, didn't she? She's jealous of me and my dad, and so are you."

He made a face. "Nobody's jealous of you." As if that were the stupidest thing in the world, that anyone would be jealous of Sally Van Sloeten.

She didn't have to take this! She knew who she was now. She was just like Richard. Free-spirited. Unique. For the first time in her life she fit somewhere. She wouldn't let some crazy-talking weirdo ruin it.

"Listen, I'm sorry your wife died and you don't have any kids of your own. But you can't go around stealing other people's daughters for yourself."

"Why would I tell you this if it's not true? A man in my position—"

"Because you hate him, that's why!"

He pressed his lips together and waited. It was an *I-shall-not-be-moved* look. Her anger turned to panic. She had to get out of there.

"When my dad hears what you're saying, you'll be sorry. He'll beat the living shit out of you."

He grabbed her arm.

"No one has to know about this, Sally. Especially not now, not tonight. Let's give it time to sink in, and you can decide how you feel about it, and what kind of relationship you want to have."

"Let go of me! I don't want any relationship with you! I want my dad."

"Stay for just a minute. I'll have someone send your mother in."

This startled her. "She's here? Why would she be here?"

"To help you understand this."

"There's nothing to understand!" Sally had a Polaroid in her purse! More than that, there were the images burned on her heart. That first hug. The corsage. The way Richard pulled out her chair. All the promise she saw in his eyes.

"I am so sorry, Sally. I should have told you a long time ago."

"That's right!" she cried, as in *Ah ha! I've got you now!* "Why wait for tonight?"

"I don't have a good answer for that."

Richard must be truly dangerous for him to lie to her like this. He must have done something so terrible that the pastor and her mother would lie to make Sally think she wasn't related to him. Maybe he was a murderer. Or on the lam. What else could explain this?

Unless it was true.

But that would mean that there was no one pining away for her from afar, wondering what she looked like, hoping she got good grades. *Missing* her. It would mean that the person who was supposed to love her more than anyone in the world was there all along doing….nothing. Choosing every day to ignore her.

The pastor spoke gently. "What I can tell you is that I care about you. Very much."

She put her hands over her ears. "Shut up! Just shut up!"

"Sally, *sshh!* Do you want the whole church to hear you? Let me get your mother."

She ducked away from him. She had to go! Out, anywhere, away from this crushing sense of doom. But before she could escape, there was a thud and Richard stumbled through the door.

"There you are," he said.

She stopped, seeing him with new eyes—a beaten-down, disheveled, loudmouth mess with a flask in his pocket who, face it, was not what she had hoped. He was a stranger. She didn't know what to do.

Richard put his hands on his hips. "What's the problem here?"

"Get her mother. She's in the kitchen," Pastor Voss said.

"*You* get her."

Pastor Voss reached for her again. "Sally, please. Let's not do or say anything until your mother is here."

Richard took a couple of threatening steps. "Voss…"

Sally felt a fury rising in her. "Why did you leave us? Why? None of this would be happening if you weren't such a loser!"

He stopped. "What the hell brought this on?"

She wiped her hand across her face. There were tears on her

cheek. "Is it true? What he told me?"

Richard looked confused. "Would someone tell me what the fuck is going on?"

Sally pointed at Pastor Voss. "He says *he's* my father." Her breath was locked in her chest along with the small hope that Richard was about to clear all this up. But she could see the possibility pulsing in his temple.

"I am her biological father," Pastor Voss said quietly.

Richard swayed on his feet. He looked dazed. *Drunk*. He looked *drunk*.

"You're nuts."

"It can't be a surprise to you," the pastor said. "You had to know."

"Know *what?*"

"While you were gone, in '52, Prudy and I were involved."

Richard's face twisted. "You were screwing my wife? If I'd known, buddy, you wouldn't be standing here."

A voice from the doorway. "Let's all calm down here." There stood Prudy, her face pale and puffy, her arms rigid by her sides. Sally saw her and knew. She asked anyway.

"Is it true?"

"Did this piece of shit knock you up?" Richard said.

"It was a difficult time for Prudy," said the pastor. He seemed bolder, now that Prudy was there. "You were drinking a lot."

Prudy came into the room, shutting the door behind her. "I went to the pastor for help. We never planned—"

"I oughta bust your face!" Richard yelled, and Sally couldn't tell if he meant the pastor or Prudy.

"Immature prick," said the pastor, his voice thick with disgust. "You'll never change."

Richard smiled. “Spoken like a true man of God.” With that he lunged and tried to get a headlock on the pastor, but Voss was too quick for him. He sidestepped Richard and then gave him a shove, sending him to the floor.

Richard rolled over and just laid there, flat on the floor, panting. “Jesus Prudy, how could you do it?”

Prudy flared. “At least I could remember his name afterward!”

“You think fucking a whore is worse than fucking a preacher?”

“Stop it!” Sally cried.

The pastor stood over Richard breathing hard. The two of them looked at each other for a moment, then Voss reached out a hand and Richard let himself be pulled up.

Once he was on his feet, Richard said, “How do you know Sally is his, anyway?”

Prudy pointed. “Just look at her.”

Everyone stared at her as if she had some indelible mark on her skin.

Richard rolled his shoulders a few times and rubbed his face.

“Christ, I thought we were having a good time here.”

Prudy had her hands pressed to her face. “Sally? Say something.”

Sally was having trouble breathing. If only everything would go back to normal. Only what was normal? She’d never been normal. Never been wanted. Or loved.

“I don’t care what the truth is,” she said. “I don’t want any of you.” She pushed past them and ran out the door.

Sally flew down the stairs, wanting only to be alone. She ducked into Lenny's tiny room. Where was he? She felt a sudden, fierce kinship with him that made her swallow hard. Her *half* brother! But he'd always been on her side.

She heard heavy, uneven steps in the stairwell, then loud breathing in the hallway as someone passed by. Her dad. No. *Richard.* She didn't know what to call him. And she didn't know whether to let him go or stop him. If he was looking for her, people would start to talk. She wished he would just leave.

Suddenly a loud screech pierced the air. Feedback from the microphone. Oh *God!* It was Richard, trying to say something to the crowd. Sally rushed into the main room to stop him but it was too late.

"Excuse me, listen up folks!" Richard said, tapping the microphone. "I've got a little news about your dear pastor, the Reverend Phillip Peckerwood Voss." He was enunciating every word carefully. "Turns out he's fathered a bastard child. That's right, my dear Sally, right over there…" The room went deadly quiet. Every eye was on her like a pushpin holding her in place. "…who I thought was my own, is actually a result of your pastor having an affair with my wife."

Someone yelled from the back. "He's drunk!"

"Yes, I am," he said, slurring. "But I speak the truth. And she is still my wife."

Pastor Voss and Prudy appeared next to Sally.

"You are still my wife, Prudy!" Richard yelled.

The pastor walked slowly toward him. "That's enough," he said quietly.

Richard gave a welcoming wave. "The adulterer would like to say a few words!"

Pastor Voss tried to take the microphone from him but

Richard twirled away and laughed, "Let's give him what he deserves! Who's with me?"

Sally heard Frannie's voice. *Dad, stop him!* As if gentle Verle Valkema could save her. Nothing could save her now. Her life was over. She stumbled toward the exit sign, the crowd parting to let her through, person after person stepping back reflexively, afraid to touch such disgrace.

"I love ya, Sally!" Richard called after her.

But Sally, whoever she was, was long gone.

Somehow, over the pounding of her heart, Sally heard Richard calling her name as she tore out of the church. She didn't want his pity, if that's what he'd offer. Or worse, *nice to meet ya!* A handshake and a wave and he'd be back at the Torchlight telling everyone *remember that girl came looking for me? Turns out she's no relation of mine.* They'd slap his back and shake their heads, laughing *close call Richie!*

How could she ever face him? How could she face any of them? He must think she was so childish, the way she'd fussed over bringing him to this stupid banquet. The way she'd wanted to parade him around for all her friends to see. Look at my dad! I have one and isn't he snazzy? Doesn't he love me?

And she could have loved him. She could have had exactly what she wanted, until Pastor Voss ruined it all. How she hated him! And her mother! Imagine her *sleeping* with him. Sally would never forgive her.

She pushed through the outer doors and took the steps two at a time, amazed she didn't fall and break her neck, not caring if she did. All the other girls would be dancing, super charged with scandal. Forget their carefully crafted steps, every one of them would be content to stand like a stick in their fathers' arms. Oh my God. Oh my *God*, they'd repeat like a bunch of dumb cows, while the sensible dads murmured things like *the excitement's over, let's just enjoy ourselves.* But really little pinball words like *yikes!* and *holy cow!* would be lighting up their brains. *Wait until I tell Margaret about this!*

She'd show them. She'd run away. She could go to Detroit and live in a home for runaway teens. Or Kalamazoo. She remembered Aurelia, with the blind husband and chubby baby. If Richard was going to stay in Holland with his shack-up sweetie, then maybe she could go to Aurelia's and live in that rented room. She could watch the baby, or help with the husband. She could clean house and cook.

But somehow Sally knew it would be different. Not the sunny, sitcom scene she remembered. Aurelia would have makeup caked under her eyes and spit-up on her shoulder and the baby would be screaming and even her husband in his blindness would make it to the door quickly enough to tell her to scram.

The night was still and dark, lit only by the Texaco sign across the street. She headed for it, desperate for a place to hide, and the alley behind the station was the closest place. When she saw the hood of Cash's '52 Impala poking out from behind the building with its driver's side window down, she felt something hopeful and clear stir in her. *When God closes a door, he opens a car window.*

She got a quick glimpse of someone behind the counter as she went past the station window toward the back alley. Now she could hear Richard calling her name from the church steps, then the tumble of other voices, rising and falling, turning this way and that, finally fading away. She leaned against the cool cinder block wall and tried to catch her breath. There was a crunch of shoes on gravel and Cash rounded the corner. The light from the Texaco sign shone through his stringy hair, turning it to a halo.

"What the hell are you doing?" he asked.

"What time you closing up?" she said, her words coming in spurts.

"I been closed."

She reached down to take off her heels. The gravel would ruin her nylons, but she didn't care. "Then what are doing here?"

"I don't know. Hanging out." He looked over at the church. "What's going on? I saw you go in with your dad."

My dad. It sounded so natural when someone else said it. Other people said it all the time, probably thousands of times in a lifetime, because other people had dads.

She fought back tears. "He's not...never mind. Can you drive me somewhere?"

Here's where he'd tell her to go to hell. She should have gone to the beach with him that day! She should have let him kiss her again instead of bossing him around. Finding her dad had been so important, she'd gone and ruined everything else.

"How many times you gonna come begging a ride from me?" he asked.

She pressed her hand into her side where a stabbing ache was starting. "Believe me, this is the last time. After tonight I'll never bother you again. I promise."

He was looking her up and down.

"Quit staring at me!" she snapped. "You never seen a girl in a dress or what?"

"You look different."

If only he knew! She was different all right. Ruined.

"Can we get out of here?" There were voices in her head. Mostly slippery starts that went nowhere. Why—? How—? And the loudest one: Go! Go! Just Go! The voices were hers, but who was *her*? Sally Van Sloeten? Sally Voss? The person she thought she was didn't exist anymore.

"Go get in, then," he said finally. "I'll just lock up."

She hobbled over the asphalt. What the hell was she doing? She wanted Frannie. Why didn't Frannie and Mr. Valkema come looking for her? They would know exactly what to say to get her through this. She could stay with them until she sorted things out. Maybe Mr. and Mrs. Valkema could even adopt her, and she and Frannie could be sisters. She'd visit her family on weekends and they'd bring out all her favorite foods like peace offerings. In return she'd tell them how wonderful it was to live with the Valkemas. A *real* family. That's how she'd refer to them, casually, so they wouldn't guess she was rubbing it in.

But Frannie and her father were in there, and she was out here. With Cash.

Why was God punishing her?

The car door opened and Cash threw one long leg in. He draped his elbow over the steering wheel, looked at her and sighed.

"So? You gonna talk?"

A panicky feeling rose in her. She couldn't say it!

"You know Pastor Voss?" she managed.

Cash nodded. He was listening, but in that prickly way that said *I may or may not be interested.*

She could do this. Pretend it was a story about someone she once knew. She cleared her throat.

"He just told me that he had an affair with my mom. He says

he's my father."

Cash's eyebrows shot up. "Holy shit. That's fucked up."

She went on, her voice unsteady. "Then my dad, I mean *Richard*, who by the way is already drunk, went and announced it to the whole church."

Cash whistled. "Wow." He started shaking his head. She knew that shake. The pity shake. If she was tired of it before, she'd get it tenfold from now on.

"So why did Richard come tonight if he's not your dad?"

"He just found out too."

"What are you going to do?" he said.

The panic rose again, but she pushed it away.

"I don't even know if it's true."

"Why would they say it in front of everyone if it's not true?"

Oh. So tactless. You don't just come at a person with a question like that. It was a challenge. Worse, it was two fists raised, daring you to deny you're about to get your ass kicked.

"My mom's trying to get back at my dad, that's all," she said, thinking *here's what I'll do! Simply refuse it!* "He used to beat her up," she said, "And then he left us on our own. She's probably been plotting something like this for years."

He frowned. She could read his thoughts. *Uh-huh. Right. Sure.* He chewed on his lip and stared out the window toward the church. When he turned to look at her it was *bammo!* Right in her eyes. "What if it's true?"

She flinched. "If it's true that means that for sixteen years he's never wanted anything to do with me. It means that my mom would rather watch me make a fool of myself instead of tell me the truth."

There it was. No sugar-coating. Cash's quiet nod verified what on her own she would never believe: even this was possible.

"What kind of people would do such a thing?" she asked.

"Cowards," he said finally. They sat a moment, quiet. He put his hand carefully over hers. To her horror, she felt everything caving in. Like a landslide.

Her voice grew thick. "Maybe Pastor Voss thought I was going to be different. Maybe he was planning to tell me, but then I was a disappointment to him. He probably doesn't even *like* me." She was turning messy, embarrassed at how she sounded as she tried to talk through tears. Some cries were graceful enough that you could still make your mouth work. Others were all-out wails that used up every part of you. For these it was best to save your words. She hugged her knees tight and cried.

"Sssh," Cash said, probably thinking *pull yourself together woman!* Certainly not understanding that a thing could be bigger than all your efforts.

"Just imagine what my mom's been thinking every time she looks at me! She's probably exhausted having to pretend. It's a duty, like going to work."

"Nah," he said. But it was weak. He didn't know any better than she did.

"I'll show them!" she cried. "Where are the tracks? Over by the junkyard? I'll throw myself in front of a train!"

"Hey now, wait a minute."

"I'll drown myself in the lake! What about pills? Where can I get my hands on some pills?"

"Come on. You're overreacting."

Maybe. She didn't *want* to die.

"But wouldn't it be worth it to see the looks on their faces?" she said. "Assuming I *could* see them from heaven. Assuming I'd go to heaven. If I kill myself even God won't want me."

It was clear. She had no one.

"What's wrong with me?" she whispered.

He squeezed her hand.

"I might as well tell you," he said. "I didn't have to work tonight. I was waiting over here to get a look at you."

She turned her head and sniffed. "Why?"

He smiled, shy-like. "You *know*."

"Are you saying you like me?"

"You know I like you."

If he thought she knew that, what other great mysteries of life might she unravel? Sally No-Name cures cancer. Or explains the great pyramids.

"I don't know anything! Isn't that obvious?"

It was the wrong reaction. She'd left his declaration hanging and now his jaw took on a hard edge.

"Well, why didn't you say so before?" she said, embarrassed.

He sighed again. She was wrecking this too. She didn't mean to. She was only trying to sort it out. Did he see something in her that couldn't possibly be there?

How long before he realized his mistake?

She lunged forward and threw her arms awkwardly around his neck, feeling the solid thud of her body on his. His head knocked back against the car door as she buried her face in his neck. She nearly apologized, but didn't. Everything was a tug of war. A hanging on for dear life. Every inch counted. There was the inch from his neck to his ears. Then to his cheek. And another one to his lips. A kiss was nothing now, a small gift to this person who liked her *even now*.

"Thank you," she said. She understood what he was telling her. *I'm here. Now and always*. It didn't matter that those weren't his exact words. Why, just saying what he'd said, who knows how much courage he had to stockpile for that?

He laughed, happy. "Let's get out of here."

She nodded. From now on she'd put him first. Nothing she wanted mattered. She'd had her turn.

"Let's go to the beach," she said recklessly. Whatever he said! She was ready.

He rubbed his chin. "You know, that sounds great, but I've sort of got a curfew. I have to have the car back by ten."

He was supposed to be there for her always, not just until ten.

"It's almost ten now," she cried. "I can't go home!"

He turned to her eagerly. "You can come to my house and stay in the garage. My parents go to bed early. They'll never know."

"But how will I get home?"

"I thought you didn't want to go home."

He had a point. Still.

"That's a terrible plan," she said.

"You got a better one?"

She had nothing. No plan. No money. No ties to anyone. Spending the night in a garage sounded terrible, but at least her mom would never find her there. She'd be out all night looking and that was a satisfying thought. Sally may have started this journey but someone else had released the brakes and if everything spun out of control, it wasn't her fault.

"All right, go," she said, and he surprised her by laying hard on the gas. She gripped the armrest tight as they peeled out into the street. There it was, then. Decided.

Cash lived on Beeline Road in a little house surrounded by tall scrubby pines. In place of grass there stretched a carpet of rust-colored pine needles over dirt. They pulled into a long, unpaved driveway and Sally saw a tire swing off to one side. She tried to imagine Cash as a kid, laughing and twisting, the ground carved out under him where he dragged his feet. She loved a tire swing. She might have gone over to try it, if the circumstances were different. Now she'd probably never do those kinds of silly things again.

He pulled into the garage and turned off the car. It was ten on the dot.

"Be right back," he said. See, Cash's parents cared enough to wonder where he was, to make rules for him. That said a lot about a person.

He came out carrying a pillow and a can of 7-Up.

"Sorry I don't have anything stronger. My parents don't drink."

A pang of disappointment surprised her. She'd never had a drop of alcohol in her life. Suddenly she craved a taste. More than a taste. She wanted to blur the edges off everything.

"How about some music?" he said and she nodded. He flipped the radio on. WLIT. Soothing Sounds of the Night.

"Won't you run your battery down?"

"Aw, I can jump her."

"What if your parents come out?"

He studied her a moment. "You're kinda uptight. You know that?"

"I just don't want any trouble. Haven't I got enough?"

"Well, they're asleep. And I deliver the Sunday Sentinel, so they expect me to leave early in the morning."

Convenient. Maybe she *could* relax a little.

He pointed with his head. "You wanna move to the back seat? It's more comfortable. I mean, if you're going to try to sleep."

"I'm fine," she said quickly. She wasn't that relaxed. Or stupid enough to fall for an amateur trick like that. But when he gently took her hand again it was so comforting. Not tricky at all. She gave a small squeeze, another thank you. Silent this time. She couldn't go on gushing *thank you! thank you!* all night. He wasn't donating a kidney or anything. It was Saturday night. He was bored. She was available. That was all.

He started kissing her. Okay. It felt like more. It felt like he was telling her she was special. Oh, the way his lips said so much without speaking! Who needed words? Words were too much, or never enough.

His mouth grew harder on hers. He was good at this. He'd done it before. She was probably one of many. Didn't he say it himself? *You're no different than anyone*. Now she wanted him to stop. Not that it mattered. Look where wanting had gotten her. Wanting her father had ruined her life. It had brought her to Cash, to these hands of his that were moving on her with a purpose, like they were asking for something. *Gimme, gimme, gimme*, said his hands.

She pulled back. "Cash, wait."

He stopped immediately. His features were soft in the dim light. His eyes moist and truc. Hc was respecting her virtue! Just like the pastor said.

"What am I going to do?" she asked. "Shouldn't I be *doing* something?"

"All you have to do is let me cheer you up."

"I don't think I can."

"Shhh. You need a friend, don't you?"

"You're probably the only friend I have now."

"Okay then."

She was beginning to love his sly, secretive smile. So much that she hardly noticed his broken out skin anymore. Even his stringy hair wasn't so bad. She remembered her first impression of him. Grime and oil up to his elbows, packed under his nails. She never thought she'd let him touch her.

"You look really… clean," she said. She was noticing it for the first time.

He was hurt. "I do wash, you know. Once a month at least."

Oh the effort he was making! For her. He *did* think she was special. And maybe, if she was like everyone else, it was in the good way. The normal way. Because everyone else did these things with boys. This is what they laughed about in the bathroom at school, huddled together in front of the mirror mushing their lips around like applying lipstick was a strenuous event. Engage face muscles. Ready, set, pucker!

"I don't know what I would have done if you hadn't been there," she said.

"Why don't you show me how much you appreciate me?"

His hand sneaked up her side to the front of her dress. Whoa! She pushed it away but it came back. Okay. No big deal. She was sixteen, after all. And it wasn't *unpleasant*. No. Far from that. His lips were on her neck. He whispered her name as if he had a wonderful secret to tell her.

"Yes?" she answered.

But he only pulled his head back and smiled at her. Oh. It was one of those sweet nothings.

"Relax," he said as the other hand moved lower. "Everything will be fine."

She wasn't silly enough to believe that. What she did

believe was that something was happening here. A turning point had been reached. One that deserved contemplation and introspection. She just didn't feel up to it. Besides, it was all clear to her now. No one would ever love her unless she *made* them.

She put her hands on his face and kissed him. She let his hands wander. It felt…important. Even welcoming, like someone had just taught her a secret handshake. She saw herself standing shoulder to shoulder with the bathroom bimbos. She'd have a sly smile of her own now.

But then the Lord's Prayer began playing in her head. It was reflexive, something she did whenever she felt pure hatred for God. A way to remind herself: The Lord is my *shepherd.* The Lord *is* my shepherd. She also did it when she was afraid. Which was now. Because not only was the handle on the car door starting to press painfully into her back, something else was beginning to press into her leg. She knew what it was and what it meant. The words from Pastor Voss' sermon were still fresh in her head: beware of lust versus love. Well, why should she listen to a thing he said? The *idea* that he would stand up and preach to her, that he would tell her or anyone how to behave! She saw it now—everyone did this sort of thing. Even him. There were no rules, only moments of fleeting relief. Take them where you can!

I shall not want. Anything. Anymore.

She arched her back away from the door. Cash mistook her movement for desire and pulled her hips further down the seat.

He maketh me lie down.

He moaned a little, like he was in pain. It must be that body part. It must hurt being in such a state. She felt responsible, like she should do something, but she had no idea what.

"Are you all right?"

"Move down more," he whispered. She scooted a little. He seemed more comfortable, but it was still pressing on her.

Thy rod and thy staff, they comfort me.

She giggled, though nothing about this was funny. She felt him working her panties down her legs. No, not at all funny. How could she allow this to happen? All he had to do was lift her dress and there she'd be, naked and shameful. She could just see her virtue huddled in the corner of the girls bathroom, not getting the respect it deserved.

"Stop," she said, but it wasn't forceful enough, and the rasping of her voice in the steamy, close air embarrassed her. So did her nakedness, but… at least it was dark, and her panties had already been lowered. It was done. And if she made him stop, then what? He'd throw her out. Make her walk home in the middle of the night and she'd never see him again. She'd be back in school, everyone laughing and whispering. *You hear about Sally? Illegitimate. Bastard baby.* This brought a sobering thought.

"Is… is everything, you know, taken care of?"

His voice was silky smooth. "It's your first time, right?"

She nodded. First time! What was she *doing*? Panic surged through her again, but she found if she waited it out, a dull, heavy feeling soon followed. How she welcomed it!

"Then there's nothing to worry about," he said.

"What do you mean?"

"Nothing can happen the first time. There's skin or something there. My brother told me."

She realized she didn't care, so she did nothing. *I didn't plan it! I didn't!* She wanted God to know, as if it earned her points. Yes, it was all a game, and she wanted in. She would not be a poor sport. She stayed very still while Cash wrangled his pants down, her eyes glued to the metallic letters on the dashboard: *Impala.* She felt his thighs press against hers, solid and warm, and the sticky cool of the car seat against her bare backside. His hand was there then, in the dark, prying her open. Then came pain. Much, much more pain. She felt it all the way in her ribcage, stabbing at her heart. Oh, she had no idea! She swallowed tears. There would be no blessed union on her wedding night. No standing at the altar in a white gown. But she had no father to walk her down an aisle anyway, so what did it matter? What did anything matter?

"You're all I have now," she whispered, tears dripping from her eyes into her ears as a burning rose up through her belly.

"Okay, okay."

He was moving on her now, and as he did his leg bumped against the radio and made it jump to the next station on the dial: WJOY. Sally knew it well. It was the religious station Nell listened to at home. If Nell only knew what Sally was doing! She wouldn't ….Oh! *Breathe. Breathe.* The pain was lessening. She wouldn't think about that. She concentrated on the music. It was a song she knew, a folksy ballad by a band called The Raptures: *Dear Mary, trust me for what I'm about to do. I've got three good reasons and one of them is you.*

There were three reasons she shouldn't be doing this. Three hundred. Three thousand. There was her mom, Nell, even Lenny. There was Frannie and Mr. Valkema and God. There was Mandy, who looked up to her, and Mrs. Dekker, who used to babysit her, and Aunt Flookie, who always told her she'd go far.

Cash seemed to finally notice the change in music. He reached over to turn the dial back.

Electric guitar. *Hello, I love you, won't you tell me your name?*

His leg bumped the dial again.

Violin. *You can stand on the mountaintop and wonder why the sky's so blue. There are three good reasons and one of them is you.*

He fumbled with it again. Static.

"Goddamn AM radio!" he exploded.

"Just forget the stupid music." Her voice sounded far off, like someone else's.

"Fine." He turned it off, but then there was only the sound of his breathing and a clicking noise from the engine. And the pain. And the dark void of the garage. Beyond it a piece of black sky through a window pane. Not blue. Only black. Like a sinner's heart.

"Turn it back on," she said, and now there was an unmistakable sob in her voice. If he noticed he didn't show it. He managed to get the electric guitar going again.

"I love The Doors," he said, as reverently as a person might say *I love you.* Sally knew the song but could not have named the group, just like Cash could never name The Raptures. The differences between them were measured by a radio band, vaster than the airwaves. As he became more feverish she had a quick image of her mother with Pastor Voss. Was this the way it was with them? *Disgusting.* Cash was like a rabid animal now, moaning and gyrating. Finally he finished with such a shudder and moan, she wanted to say *oh come on! Aren't you being a little dramatic?*

This must be the hatred Pastor Voss spoke of.

"Get. *Off.* Me." Her teeth were clenched. The windows were steamed and the air was suffocating.

"Wow." He was damp and musty smelling. "Are you okay?"

She pulled her dress down. "I've got to go."

"What do you mean? Right now?"

Where were her shoes? She felt along the floor. Nothing.

"I'll be fine. I just need to..." She found the door latch and pulled. There was nothing graceful about her as she stumbled out of the car.

She ran down the long dirt driveway in her bare feet, not caring how dark it was or that she'd walk half the night to get home. She had knowledge that would cut through the dark like a fog light. The girls at school were all fakes. That was one thing she knew. They'd never done what she just did. If they had they wouldn't be looking in the mirror, all aflutter with anticipation, acting like their future was still worthy of curled hair and a powdered nose. They would know how useless it is to giggle when there's nothing more to lose.

Nell

It must have been three a.m. when Nell began rearranging the living room furniture in her head. Call it a compulsion, but a fresh room always made her feel reborn. Trouble was, she'd tried everything. The davenport had been under the window, against the wall, even angled in the corner. She was out of possibilities. She had only one idea left: she'd seen a magazine photo of a rug hung on the wall, like a tapestry. She might try that. Squeezing her eyes shut, she flopped over in her bed and tried to see it. Instead, she saw herself bending over the armchair, trying in vain to push it out of the way. Pastor Voss was sitting in it, laughing. *Heavy, huh?*

She punched her pillow and prayed for sleep. Pastor Voss, Sally's *father?* It was straight out of a soap opera, but even her beloved *Days of Our Lives* wouldn't stoop to such depths. Viewers would revolt. *You call this entertainment? This kind of trash doesn't belong on the airwaves!* And here she was living it.

If you can call it living when you're dying of embarrassment.

She felt tears welling again. Don't even think about crying, you dumb cow! You think Pastor Voss is worth crying over? It was just that…well, she'd really believed she had a chance with him. She kept remembering a picture of a missionary family she'd seen in the church newsletter. Standing in front of a thatched hut was a father, mother, sister, brother, and they were holding hands in a circle, so no one was loose on the end. Four ventricles of a heart. She wanted it. The safeness of belonging. The sense of purpose. It was a dream that had always kept her going. Now it seemed she was destined to be alone, and she was afraid. What if she got cancer? What if she died a slow painful death, with no one at her side? What if, and this was a thought she hardly dared admit, what if there was no God? What if she spent her life devoted to a faith that in the end was as false as Pastor Voss?

If she had a best friend she might be told to stop being such a downer. *You're only twenty-one! You've got your whole life ahead of you.* But the humiliation! The confusion as she tried to work through it all. Pastor Voss was a philanderer, just like her dad said. He had an affair, created a life, then walked away. No, not away. Only as far as the pulpit, where he stood before them every Sunday and *preached* to them.

She sat up in bed, too restless to lie there any longer. She simply couldn't believe that Sally was his daughter. It was like being fourteen, when she'd first heard President Kennedy talk about sending a man to the moon. She supposed it had to be possible if the President was so excited about it, but that didn't mean it would ever happen. It was just too farfetched. And yet. This was no mystery of science. Sperm meets egg and voila! The bang is so big it sends you spinning into another universe.

It could have been worse. Let's say Pastor Voss had taken Nell in his arms and kissed her with a passion that was criminal, like Warren Beatty and Faye Dunaway. *What a relief to know you feel the same! I thought I'd die of desire!* They'd agree to marry. They'd rush off to find Sally and Lenny, and most important of all, her dad. *I'm engaged!* The pastor would try to hide the truth but it would come out, somehow, and wouldn't that be worse? To have a fiancé and lose him in a matter of hours?

But what if she didn't lose him? What if she stood by him?

You mean you don't mind that I slept with your mother and fathered your sister?

Darling, I forgive you.

She was disgusted with herself for allowing such a thought. She knew there would be no forgiveness, that she'd never go back to that church, to those people she thought cared about her, who only gaped when she dropped a plate of pie, their eyes and ears too glued on her father's drunken rant to come to her side. Still, a film in her head played on: Pastor Voss delivering his next sermon. *Um, you may have heard a little something about my illegitimate child. It is truly heartbreaking. But nothing like the heartbreak I feel over her sister Nell. Because of all this I can't love Nell in the way I would like. It wouldn't be right.*

Then a scene with her dad. What was it he had said? *Pull up a chair.* Like he cared. Like he wanted to know her. If they saw each other after this, they'd both be thinking the same thing. Nell was his only daughter. For good or bad, she had him all to herself.

What a funny thrill that gave her. What terrible guilt that followed.

She'd never wanted her dad back. Not before and certainly not now, after what he'd done. It turned out just as she predicted, and although she normally took satisfaction in being right, this time all she felt was a disappointment she didn't understand. Anyway, this wasn't about her. Think of Sally. How much worse it was for her, being rejected by not one, but two, fathers. And her mother. The shame Prudy must feel was punishment enough. She didn't need Nell turning against her.

But how she hated her mother right now. She didn't know if she could ever get past it. Maybe she could dump her anger into her trusty diary. Lock it up and throw away the key. But the thought of writing anything down ever again seemed useless. In fact, diaries were for babies. Look how much time she'd wasted pining away like a moonstruck teenager. It was time to grow up. She might not be destined for missionary work, but there were other worthy careers. She could be a teacher. Maybe even a real police officer. There were no women on the Holland force, but couldn't she be the first? How unexpected *that* would be. *There goes Sergeant Van Sloeten. When I think of how I used to gossip about her, well, I'm just glad she doesn't hold a grudge.*

At least she had her job. Crossing Guard was no career, but it was a foot in the door.

When the clock said five, she got out of bed. Today she'd curl her hair. Wear make-up too. She'd be the best darn Crossing Guard the department had ever seen. When the high school kids came she'd nod at them with a small, professional smile. They'd come to respect her, over time. Next would come the middle-schoolers, the boys with the boys, the girls with the girls. They were still young enough to admire a uniform, and Nell hoped that one day they'd greet her by name. She'd love to be called Miss Nellie. Then, around nine, the real fun would begin. The little ones would come skipping and laughing with their mothers, decked in ribbons and ruffles and stiff little overalls. *Hey know what? I'm Batman! My cat's name is Sheba. Can I blow on your whistle?* The young mothers would smile. And even if one whispered *did you hear about her family?* someone would defend her. *Aw, it's not her fault. Besides, she's so sweet and she does an excellent job.*

As luck would have it, the day was terrible. Wet and windy. Nell left early, and when she got to her corner, her feet were damp and chilly. The first teenager to come by was a hulking, overgrown boy who seemed to glare at her.

"Monday mornings," she said ruefully. "Rough, huh?"

He grunted.

She took out the clear plastic rain hood that was rolled expertly into her pocket and carefully put it over her cap. A group of kids were crossing when she saw her mailman Gizzy approaching the intersection on his bike. He was slowing for the red light.

"Hey Gizzy!" she called, thankful for at least one friendly face. He looked up and waved. As he did his bike wobbled. He must have braked too hard, and the road was wet. The bike began sliding out from under him, into the intersection. What happened next was so fast that Nell could only blink and watch. A car swerved. There was a crunch of metal. The bike flipped over the curb, and Gizzy landed on his back in the street.

Nell started flapping her arms and blowing her whistle. What had she done? This was no welcome wagon! She was on the job. It was her responsibility to keep everyone safe.

She ran, heart pounding, toward Gizzy. She heard him moan as he rolled onto his stomach. So he wasn't dead. But *she* was. She'd be fired for sure.

After the ambulance took Gizzy away—a broken leg! Thank God it happened to him and not a child!—Nell had to stay for the police report. It was raining hard then, and she huddled under an umbrella with the driver of the car and the officer who answered the call. The word *accident* was used several times. No one blamed her. Outwardly, at least, but Nell knew how these things could stick on you like lint. It had to do with reputation.

By the time she got home, she couldn't help thinking *why me?* And she'd always sworn she wasn't that kind of person. *Let the Lord test me. That's when I'll know I'm worthy.*

Now she wondered if the Lord had forgotten her. Though she prayed for guidance, she felt only confusion and doubt. She had wanted to be the best Crossing Guard the Holland PD had ever seen. Instead she practically got someone killed. Poor Gizzy! How would he deliver the mail with a broken leg? What if they both lost their jobs over this?

Damn *Sally!* It was all her fault. She got Pastor Voss for a father. Probably Prudy would marry him and the three of them would become their own happy little family. Meanwhile, Nell was stuck with no church, no prospects, no hope. Only faith. And how flimsy that was!

She was about to go change out of her uniform when a movement in the kitchen window caught her eye. Her neighbor Mandy was crossing the yard, headed for the swing set. The rain had stopped but everything was still wet. Nell watched her walk with her birdlike gait toward the swing. When she reached it she put one hand out tentatively to touch the chain. The upstairs door slammed.

"Come on in now," Mrs. Veenstra called from the landing.

Mandy turned and Nell squinted. There was something on Mandy's mouth, like a streak of lipstick.

"I said come in! That's enough!"

Nell had seen this routine before, this strange cruel trick Mona Veenstra had of telling Mandy to go out and play and then calling her in. Nell had never said anything. Judge not and all that. Or was it cowardice? Mrs. Veenstra was not a woman to be taken lightly, although Sally sure wasn't shy about smart-mouthing her. As for Nell, she thought she could help Mandy by taking her to Bible School and teaching her about God's love. Now that seemed as useless as the ink-covered pages of her diary.

She stepped out the back door.

"She just came out," she said.

Mona stared down at her. "Now she's coming in." There was a challenge there.

Nell looked away. She ought to mind her own business. But if she did, Mandy would grow up with that broken feeling, always wondering *what's wrong with me? Why won't anyone love me?* And these parents—if you could call them that! They didn't deserve to own a goldfish!—they would sail through life never realizing the damage caused by their careless words. By their selfishness. Their sinful *lust*. Something boiled up in her. It wasn't fair!

"Come here, Mandy," Nell commanded.

"Don't listen to her!" Mona called.

Mandy didn't move. Nell walked through the long wet grass to her and lifted her chin. Her lip was swollen and bleeding. She had a washrag balled in her fist that she lifted to her face and it stuck, stiff and dry, to the wound.

Nell gasped and whirled on Mona. "What did you do?" The accusation just slipped out.

Mona scowled. "I didn't do anything. She fell down the

steps."

"You expect me to believe that?"

"Believe what you want. What do I care?"

Nell was stunned. She'd always tried to be kind to this… this…*witch.* Because she hadn't known! *Why* hadn't she known? How did a person live twenty-one years with her head in the sand? And how many truths had to be revealed before she opened her eyes?

"She needs stitches." She made her voice sound certain to hide the uncertainty she felt. Because though she suddenly knew Mona had done this to Mandy, she had no idea what to do about it.

"Send her ass up here and I'll take care of it."

Mandy let out a soft moan. Like a plea. There was something familiar in the sound, a helplessness that made Nell remember her own childhood, when she was about Mandy's age, and her mother had to go to the hospital for some vague female trouble. She remembered an overwhelming fear. And wanting to know *why is no one around to help?*

Then came a jolt, like a finger prodding her in the back: you're the grown-up now.

She grabbed Mandy's hand. "I'm taking her to the hospital."

"You leave her be!"

Nell clenched her teeth and pointed at Mona. "Lady, if you knew the morning I've had!"

She picked Mandy up and began running, flushed and indignant. Try to be a good person and what happens? Suppose anyone says *hey nice job!* Think you can catch a break?

"Don't worry, honey," she said, breathing hard. "We're going to fix you up." Mandy whimpered as something warm spread against Nell's hip. Mandy had wet herself. Nell tried not to panic.

Was she making a mistake? She'd already sent one person to the hospital. But that was due to carelessness. This was different. This was a chance to show what she was made of. And to think she'd always wanted to go to *Africa* to do the Lord's work! Her test was right here.

Mona stomped down the stairs. "I'm calling the police," she yelled.

Didn't she notice the uniform? "I *am* the police!" Nell yelled back.

She hoisted Mandy higher and tried to keep running but couldn't. Slowing to an awkward lope, she reached Mrs. Dekker's house. She could see Mrs. Dekker inside dozing in her easy chair.

Nell pounded on the screen door. "Can I take your car?"

Mrs. Dekker's eyes flew open and her hand clutched at her chest. "What's that?"

"It's me, Nell. I have to get to the hospital."

The old woman peered at Nell as she struggled out of her chair. Nell tried to set Mandy down but Mandy buried her face in Nell's neck and clutched her tighter.

"Mandy? Are you okay?" Nell whispered.

Mandy lifted her head. Moving her lips carefully around each word, she said, "I'm an ugly little girl."

"No! It's not your fault! I'm going to help you," she said fiercely. "Please!" she called through the screen. "Mandy's hurt." Mrs. Dekker was puttering toward the door. Before she reached it, Mona came around the corner.

"I've called the police, so you might as well hand her over."

Nell didn't believe her. "If the police come, it'll be you they're after."

"That's what you think. Mandy, let's go."

Nell hugged her tighter and stepped away. "She's going to the hospital. Mrs. Dekker, I need your car."

The old woman just stood there. "What's this all about, dear?"

"Look at her face!"

"I told you, she fell down the steps," Mona said. "Isn't that right, Mandy?"

"I want my dad."

"Your father will be very upset when I tell him this."

"Oh save it!" Nell cried. "He's going to know the truth about you. I'll make sure of that."

Mona grabbed her arm. "Who do you think you are?" she hissed.

Nell shoved her away with one hand.

"You pushed me!" Mona was incredulous.

"Yeah, not so nice, huh?" Nell scarcely recognized her own voice. Something uncontrollable had been unleashed in her. "Touch me again and you'll be sorry."

"Oh dear!" Mrs. Dekker said, rushing out onto the front porch. "Let me have a look at the poor thing."

Mona came toward Nell again and Nell kicked her hard in the shin.

"Why, you…!" Mona tried to grab Nell's hair. Nell had both arms around Mandy, but she managed to throw her elbow up. It hit Mona's chin.

Mrs. Dekker gave a cry of alarm. "That's enough! Stop this instant!"

Nell and Mona stared at each other, breathless, as a police car rolled up.

Mona really did it. She called the police. Well, good. They'd sort this out. Nell took a shaky breath. She'd hit someone! She'd never even hit her own sister or brother. It wasn't in her. Except it was.

She watched two cops get out. The driver shook out his trouser legs and hiked his belt and Nell saw that he was the same cop from Gizzy's accident. Officer Rinkema. She froze, afraid to face him again. She already had two marks against her, stealing the pastor's car, and causing Gizzy's accident.

Rinkema looked startled to see her. "You've seen more excitement today than I've seen all week," he said.

She didn't know how to take that. Before she could answer, Mona jumped in. "She's kidnapping my daughter!"

"I am not! I'm trying to help."

"And she attacked me. And threatened me. I want to press charges."

"Whoa. Slow down," Rinkema said.

Nell pried Mandy's arms from around her neck. She set her down carefully and stepped in front of her, blocking her from Mona. *That's right. Slow down. Be professional.*

"Officer, this girl needs stitches." She pointed at Mona, "She doesn't want her to go to the hospital because she doesn't want to be reported for child abuse."

"I told you she fell!"

Officer Rinkema turned to his partner. "Val, take the girl inside and check her out."

Mona started to follow but he stopped her with a glare. "You. Sit down over there and shut up."

He watched as Mona huffed across the driveway to the porch steps. Then he sighed and turned to Nell. Motioning with his head, he led her a few feet away.

"Mrs. Veenstra is her stepmother," Nell began, but he cut her off.

"Did you witness it?"

"Not exactly. Does that matter?"

He raised his eyebrows. "Are you sure you want to make a report?"

"What kind of question is that?"

"Sometimes it makes things worse."

"But…"

"Even if the kid says she was hit, she'll probably change her story later. They tend to do that."

They!? As if Mandy were part of some conspiracy of conniving little girls. Nell blinked. She had a lot to learn if she ever wanted to be a cop.

"Where's the father?" he asked.

She nodded. Here she could help.

"He works at Vroman's, on the line. He's a nice guy, but kind of vacant, you know? I don't think he has any idea what Mona's like."

"Okay. Let me talk to her. It'll probably end up with Family Services."

Nell hung back as he walked over, trying not to give in to a growing fear. Had she overreacted? Was Mandy's injury really an accident? This could be a big misunderstanding, but not the kind to look back on and laugh. *Remember that time you thought I hit Mandy? Can you imagine? Oh my!* No, Mona would never forgive Nell for this, and they had to go on living as neighbors. She'd already lost her church friends. Now she'd feel like an outcast in her own house. Not that Mona had ever been what you'd call friendly. But civil, at least. And she let Nell spend time with Mandy. Nell felt a lump rise in her throat. Officer Rinkema was right. She'd just made everything worse.

Straining to hear their conversation, she heard *never*

had any trouble like this, and *sweet kid*. Mona was gesturing emphatically, still managing to look poised, which made Nell feel more and more at a loss.

After a moment Officer Rinkema returned.

“Well, you’re right. She probably hit the kid. But she’s pressing charges against you for assault and that’s not gonna play well. I’ll have to get Van Zandt on the horn.”

“But I didn’t do anything wrong.”

“Take a seat in the squad car. This won’t take long.”

In the back of a cop car again. It didn’t seem a good sign, especially when she wanted to be up front, behind the wheel. Still, it must mean something that officer Rinkema put her in the car instead of Mona. Like they were on the same team.

He reached in for his radio. She listened as it crackled to life.

“Yeah, Phyllis? It’s Rinkema. Put Sergeant Van Zandt on, will you?”

Nell looked over at Mona. She was studying her nails, her head lifted in that snooty way she had. As if this was all such a *bother*. As if she were too cultured to raise her voice, let alone a fist. It was nothing but an act! Nell could only pray that the police would see through it.

Another burst of static, and Rinkema said, “I’ve got Nell Van Sloeten here at the scene of the domestic dispute.” There was a pause. “Auxiliary P.D. That’s right.”

He glanced at her and scratched his head. Then he turned his back so she couldn’t hear. They were talking about her. She tried to stay calm. From the moment she’d met Sergeant Van Zandt, when she went for her Crossing Guard interview, she could tell he was impressed with her. In positions of responsibility, she knew how to shine. Good eye contact, good posture, thoughtful nods, intelligent questions, and bingo! There it was, that look of respect. She imagined it was the way pretty girls felt when a man looked at them appreciatively. She had nothing to worry about.

The other cop came out and conferred with Officer Rinkema, who spoke again into his radio. Nell could see Mandy standing next door with Mrs. Dekker. She had an ice pack on her face and Mrs. Dekker was stroking her hair. Nell tried to catch Mandy's eye to give her an encouraging wave, but the officers were blocking her way. Finally Officer Rinkema put his radio away and leaned in.

"The old lady told Officer Beyer that you did hit the mother," he said.

Betrayed! By Mrs. Dekker? She'd known Nell since she was a baby. She knew Nell would never attack another person.

"She came after *me*. Maybe my elbow bumped her face, but it was nothing." Nell looked frantically from face to face. "And Mona's her stepmother. Not mother." Did Mona have them so fooled that they forgot the distinction? It was an important one. Stepmothers were known to be evil.

"Listen, you did the right thing with the girl," he said. "But these things can be tricky. You can't give someone like that anything to use against you."

He was only saying what she already knew. She'd made a terrible mistake. She never should have pushed Mona.

"Am I really in trouble?"

"I wouldn't worry about the charges. They won't stick. But..." He paused a moment.

"Listen," he said finally, chewing a fingernail. "You've been on the job, what, a week? There was that stolen car business, and the accident this morning, and—"

She knew it! The second she heard the screech of tires and

saw Gizzy's bike flip in the air, she'd known it was over for her.

"I'm trying to help people." she said helplessly. "That's what I do."

"Still. If your record was clean—"

"It's clean! I'm clean!"

He shrugged. "Sorry. Van Zandt wants you to turn in your uniform." He put up his hands. "It's probably temporary."

"But the Sarge likes me!"

He clucked his tongue and shook his head slowly. "Yeah. We don't really call him that. But go see him. Explain your situation and see what happens."

Explain? Where to start? See, my mother had an affair. And a baby. And ruined my only chance at happiness. And my father can't stand the sight of me and I don't know why. And I'm the only one who has always tried to do what's right.

"What about Mandy?" she cried.

"We'll take her to the hospital. Her father will meet us there. Come on out now."

"Can't I go along?"

"Nope. We'll take it from here."

She got out of the car and stood by helplessly.

"Family services will be out soon," he said. He motioned toward Mona. "Let them deal with her. You two don't have anything to talk about."

She felt him touch her shoulder briefly but it was no comfort. She raised her hand in a silent wave to Mandy and crossed the driveway in front of Mona, staring straight ahead and reminding herself that she did the right thing. Mona might be arrested and thrown in jail. That would wipe that prissy look off her face. Then Mandy could come live with Nell and Sally and their mother. They might even adopt her. Oh, how she could turn

Mandy's life around!

Except. How could she forget? There was too much scandal on their family now. Between her mother the adulterer, Sally the bastard child, Lenny the thug and Nell the car thief, what chance did they have? Her job with the auxiliary police department had been her best chance to rebuild her reputation, and now she'd lost that.

She went to her room and stood looking at herself in her uniform. She pulled the blue blazer off slowly and unbuttoned the starched white collar, feeling miserable and unsettled. It wasn't the job itself she was thinking about. It wasn't the school kids or the paycheck or the foot in the door. It was something else bothering her as she folded the blue slacks carefully, crease to crease, and draped them over a hanger.

Her dad would never get to see her shine.

Sally

Sally dreaded returning to school. Before her humiliation, she'd imagined gliding down the hall, in love with every person she passed, every jock and burnout and stuck up snob, every misfit and plain Jane and pimply-faced Joe. They'd have something in common. They'd all have fathers.

Now, returning to the low, meandering rat maze that was Holland High, she imagined a big neon arrow hanging over her head, flashing *Loser! Loser! Spawn of Sin!* She kept her eyes on the floor as she shuffled down the hall, studying every pair of shoes she saw. Most kids wore new ones and she imagined them at Steketees or Sears, their patient mothers pushing a thumb into the toe. *Enough room here, dear?* Then counting out daddy's money, each dollar a token of love. And were they ever even grateful? As grateful as she'd been when she put her new shoes on Saturday night? Oh, the way she'd sailed down the sidewalk in those ultra soft leather pumps, with her dad at her side! Now they were lying in Cash's garage. *Unless.* Were they tucked carefully in his underwear drawer, and was he planning some exquisitely romantic way to return them to her? Her very own Cinderella story, with Cash as Prince Charming!

But he hadn't even called. What if he hadn't given her a second thought? What if he had sex with a different girl each week? What if he didn't remember her name? Or gave her a vague look the next time they met? *Hmm. Don't I know you?*

Or, worse, what if he remembered every second, but just didn't care?

He had to care! She'd given herself to him. That meant something! And even though their....union had been far from pleasant, there was still a future for them. First, she'd get him to cut his hair, then get a better job, one that didn't make his fingernails so filthy. She'd introduce him to her friends, and if he was rude, well, she'd give them a secret look and mouth *he's just shy!* They didn't have to have sex again. She'd explain to him all that crap from the other night. The difference between love and lust, and how love was patient. He'd understand. Look how he'd cleaned himself up that night, with his nicely combed hair and fresh, pressed shirt. He'd done it for her and wasn't that worth a thousand words? Didn't that buy him a few days of silence? She *completely* understood, because she understood *him* so completely.

Her plans for the two of them—finally she'd have a boyfriend!—eased her past the crowds of sniggering faces. Probably everyone had heard about her and Pastor Voss. Her *father.* She'd *never* call him that! She could see her classmates at home, eating corn flakes or peanut butter toast, their toes tapping impatiently. *Where's the bus? I can't wait to see if Sally's at school!* Even the unpopular kids who didn't spend their weekends giggling on the phone would know what had happened at the banquet. What was it called? Collective consciousness. She'd heard a teacher ramble on about it once in social sciences class. If enough people knew something, the information became part of the universe, available to all human beings. So for the rest of her life anyone she met would think *I can't put my finger on it, but there's just something not right about Sally Van Sloeten.*

What she'd done with Cash must show too. You could always spot the loose girls. It was the way they walked, the way they slid their eyes around, sending secret signals. Could she stop herself from being that way? She checked her hips as she walked, *don't* swing, *don't* swing. She was determined to keep at least part of her downfall private. But what if Cash told? He might be whooping it up right now with his buddies, laughing about how easy she was. And would he tell them how she'd run off so fast without her shoes in the middle of the night? Wouldn't that make him look bad? Or did he hang with the kind of crowd that would find that simply hilarious?

She did WHAT? Oh boy, Cash, you sure can pick 'em!

He'd be cool. She'd be hated. Worse even than Weird Walter, who sat in class with his hands in his armpits and then smelled his fingers when the bell rang. Or fat and frumpy Lisa VanderPloeg, who chewed erasers and spit the pieces into her purse. Marybeth Van Dyke's older sister used to babysit for Lisa and said she lined the bottom of her hamster cage with the pieces to make a soft spongy floor for the stupid thing. Kinda sweet, now that Sally thought of it. At least Lisa had a hamster who loved her.

Sally lifted her head. She might as well gauge the fallout. Maybe people didn't know. Or didn't care. Maybe she'd get sympathetic looks. Maybe she'd make new friends. *My dad drinks*, someone might say. Or, *once I saw my mom naked with the TV repairman.* Something, anything, to let her know she wasn't alone. Not that she wanted that. God no. Not that. She didn't want to be a loser magnet.

"Hey Sally! How ya *doing?*" Uh-oh. Too late. Super nerd Marvin Hoekema was waving at her, wearing a dopey grin, his tongue hanging half out. The boys with him jostled each other and laughed. Freak. Probably he'd heard about Richard being a drunk and was thinking Sally could get him to buy beer for them. That's what a pea brain he was. Or maybe he knew about what happened with Cash and wanted to get in line. Jesus *Christ.* Strike me dead right now. She considered sticking a finger in one of the electrical outlets. Could she electrocute herself or did you have to be two years old for that to work?

She glared and muttered, "Shove it, Marvin," as she hurried to her locker. She would sooner die than let any of these cretins see her cry. She was fumbling with the lock when Frannie came over and put a gentle hand on her shoulder.

"Don't mind them," she said. "Don't mind anyone today."

So they *were* talking about her. "It's not even first bell," Sally moaned.

"Just remember, you're still the same person, no matter who your dad is."

The same? Every single thing about her was changed!

"How can you say such a thing?" Sally asked.

Frannie smiled. "You're still my best friend."

Frannie didn't know anything. What would she think if she knew what Sally had done with Cash? Would she still be her friend?

"I don't need you feeling sorry for me," Sally snapped.

"I don't. I mean, of course I do, but..."

She'd hurt her feelings. And Frannie was practically all she had. Unless.

She could see Debs and Patty Ann floating down the hallway, with their matching book bags and soft angora sweaters. Why couldn't Sally be cool too? Why couldn't she be part of that crowd, strutting around with Debs and Patty Ann, wearing that grownup aura of sex like a brooch on her blouse? So what if her Big Moment hadn't happened the way she would have wanted? She'd been with a boy! The first time was over and it could only get better. Now that she'd graduated into womanhood, maybe she ought to stop playing with little girls.

Sally slammed her locker. "Why didn't you come after me? Where *were* you?"

Frannie looked confused. "I tried to find you. My dad and I went out the basement door. We practically ran to your house! And I tried calling all day yesterday! Why didn't you answer the phone?"

"You just don't get it, do you?" Sally said. She couldn't leave her room. Then she would have had to face her mother, and she wasn't speaking to her mother again for as long as she lived. It wasn't so much her sleeping with Pastor Voss, though that was nauseating enough. It was all the times her mother had listened to Sally talk about her dad, knowing how desperately she wanted to find him. Just to sit there silently, what kind of a person did that?

"So where were you?" Frannie asked.

Sally let her eyes slide sideways at her friend. "You won't believe it."

"Go ahead." Frannie was waiting, her lips parted expectantly. What an innocent! If Sally were really to tell her, what would she do? Freak out, that's for sure. And then would come The Look. The same look Nell had given her when she'd come dragging in in the middle of the night. Actually, Frannie was just like Nell. They were practically interchangeable! How had she not noticed before? I'm glad I'm not like them, she thought, and for the first time since Saturday night the cloud of shame parted just enough to allow a glimmer of something else. A sort of wisdom. *I'm a woman now. Right or wrong, I'm a step ahead.*

"Okay," she said slowly. "I found Cash at the gas station and I went to his house with him."

She heard a smugness in her voice that she didn't altogether feel. Sure, it might sound cool to Debs and Patty Ann, but not to Frannie. Well, tough. Cash was part of her life now. Frannie could learn to like him, or find another friend. She tried to picture all of them hanging out together. What would they talk about? *Hey, I did five oil changes today*, Cash would say while he rolled a cigarette out of his sleeve and tamped it down on his hand. And Frannie would say *I spent the day reading Nostradamus and the book of Revelations so I can compare/contrast them for my college admissions essay.* Because, face it, Frannie had no idea how to be cool.

"You went *where*?" Frannie squealed. Her wide-eyed amazement was so annoying. And the way her jaw dropped! If she was so scandalized by that, how could Sally ever hope to tell her the whole truth?

"Catch a fly in your mouth," Sally said irritably.

Frannie closed her mouth, but kept staring, waiting for more.

"I sat in his garage for a while and then walked home at about 3 am."

"You hardly know this guy!" Frannie was practically sputtering.

"Oh Frannie!" How could she tell her that she did know him. In the biblical sense. I have *known* a man, she thought, and the unlikeliness of it, the downright absurdity, made her swallow hard. She felt crawly. Scratchy all over, like the time she got hives from eating too many strawberries.

"So what happened? He didn't even drive you home?"

"God, you sound like my mother!"

"It's a perfectly reasonable question."

"Everything you ever say is perfectly reasonable. You know that?"

"Why are you mad at me?" Frannie asked. "I just wanted to know if you were okay. If you don't want to talk about it…"

But she did! She just didn't know how. How do you explain letting yourself be used by a boy who never even said *I love you*? She slumped against her locker. What had she done? What kind of a person was she? For that matter, *who* was she?

"For your information, Cash is my boyfriend now," she said, but it came out wrong. She sounded sullen and not at all victorious.

"You *like* him?"

Frannie was so juvenile, like an immature twelve year old. *Like* him! It wasn't a matter of liking him. She belonged to him now.

"Yes and he likes me. He made that very clear."

"How?" Frannie asked, her eyes narrowing.

"He offered me a friendship bracelet, what do you think?"

Frannie recoiled. "You *didn't…*?"

She ought to just say it and get it over with. Then Frannie could hate her and she could really be free. Free to be with Cash. The two of them could drop out and leave town. Instead, she shrugged.

"You could be happy for me. I found someone. And I really need him right now. I don't even care who my dad is. Not as long as I have Cash."

Frannie hesitated. She had her arms crossed and wore a prickly, wounded look. "Just be careful."

Be *careful*. It was a little late for that, wasn't it? Where was Frannie when Sally made the decision to send that stupid letter? Off on vacation with her perfect fucking family. *Good morning Dad. I love you! Have a nice day sweetie. I love you! Sweet dreams dear. I love you!* Where was she when Sally ran from the banquet into Cash's car? Was she really looking for her? Or was she still gaping in the church, secretly thrilled by the drama?

"I've got to get to class," Sally said. But she didn't go toward her English class. She headed for the stairs at the opposite end of the hall, where she had seen Debs and Patty Ann disappear. If she hurried, she just might catch them.

This pining away for a boy was for the birds. It had been a week and Sally wasn't about to take another minute of it. After school she headed straight for the Texaco station, just to see if Cash was there. Maybe she would act like she happened to be walking by. If he was out at the pump she'd wave casually. *Oh hey! Nice to see you.* As if she had forgotten all about him. As if she hadn't spend every moment thinking of him and building him up to be more than he was.

She walked up the street with her back straight and her eyes glued on the Texaco sign. When she was a half block away she let herself look. The lot was empty. She checked both directions.

No cars anywhere. So he wouldn't be coming out. She'd have to walk by or go in. Okay then. She was no shrinking violet. If he thought he'd never have to face her again, he was dead wrong. She crossed the lot and when she got close enough she could see someone inside. She took a deep breath and pushed open the door. The bell tinkled and the person turned.

It wasn't Cash.

"Dad?" The word just popped out. Her face burned as Richard started to smile.

"What are you doing here?" she stammered. How could she call him that? Now that she knew the truth, how could she let that slip out?

"Working." He swept his arm out proudly, like he owned the place. He was wearing a faded blue shirt with his name sewn on the chest.

"But…" Why was *he* still around? Was he trying to torment her? Had he forgotten the way he humiliated himself, and all of them, in front of the whole church? And where was Cash?

"Just temporarily," he said. "Until something better comes along. I've got some irons in the fire."

"What? Why here?" It was ridiculous, but she was stuck on that shirt. Had he worked in a gas station before? Or did he get lucky and find one in a thrift store that happened to have his name sewn on it?

"This way I can keep an eye on the church, in case Voss decides to come back."

Sally squinted. "What do you mean, come back?"

"Voss cleared outta here just like he cleared outta Petosky and Blissfield." He raised his eyebrows and nodded. Like he was gloating.

"He's gone? For good?"

"Yep." He pushed a box toward her. "You want a donut? I got a cruller and a long john."

She stepped back, feeling dizzy. How could a pastor walk away from his church? Didn't he have an obligation to stay?

He's walking away from me!

It shouldn't shock her. Or hurt either. Not after everything that had happened. But why did he tell her the truth if he was going to leave?

"It's your fault!" she cried. "Announcing it to everyone like that. That's why he left."

Richard looked surprised. "Are you sorry he's gone?"

She hesitated. "I don't know." She thought Pastor Voss had been offering himself to her, for forgiveness. As a beginning to something. That she'd be the one to say, *leave me alone, I never want to see you again.* If he was gone she would never get the satisfaction.

Richard laughed. "Stop gaping, for chrissake. I could have told you he'd go."

She tried to force a smile. Because she hated Pastor Voss. She did! She was relieved that she wouldn't have to see him again.

Still. She couldn't believe it. He was so ashamed of what he did, so ashamed of her, that he left without saying anything. He couldn't accept her. Not in public, at least. He wanted her to know the truth, but let the church find out and hc slinks away like a dog in the night.

She watched Richard shove a cruller into his mouth and perch one hip on the stool, all smug and cock sure. Oblivious to her turmoil, as if all fathers were interchangeable and disposable and family dramas were only to be laughed at.

If only she could have that attitude. Because this was so

close to what she'd imagined, with Richard back in her life, working with her new boyfriend, no less! It was more than she ever hoped for. Except Richard wasn't her dad. And right now he was standing in the way of her plans to talk to Cash.

Where was Cash?

"He's not here," Richard said.

"Who?" she said, embarrassed. Here he was with that mind-reader routine again!

"Loverboy. He went to the bank with the deposit. He'll be right back."

Loverboy? Oh God. What had Cash told him?

He got off the stool and pushed it toward her. "Sit down."

She didn't move. Was she in for a lecture now? Was he going to start in with the importance of virtue?

"I know you're used to hearing this, but you're better off without him."

She swallowed. "Did he say something?"

Richard paused. "I'm talking about Voss! You're better off without Voss."

Sally was relieved. Then angry.

"Are you in some kind of father's club or something? Is that what they tell you at your membership meetings, so you don't feel like shit when you desert your kids?"

Richard was nodding, as if, yes, she was exactly right.

"I know this is all my fault," he said. "I wish I'd stayed around for a lot of reasons, most of all so old peckerwood wouldn't have gotten near your mother. But then, you wouldn't be here. Ever think of that?"

"I'm not stupid," she said.

He wiped his mouth and hands and leaned toward her. "So hey. Here's what I was thinking. See, you *are* here, and that's a good thing. And you and I have spent 16 years thinking we're related."

She scowled. "I can't see how you've given it much thought."

"There were times when I didn't, that's true. But there were times when I did."

She hid her surprise. "That must have been a tortuous five minutes for you."

"Would you shut up? I'm trying to tell you how it was for me."

"So go ahead." Her shrug said she couldn't care less. Inside was a voice shouting tell me! Tell me!

"Now I don't feel like it. Dang, you got a mouth on you! I thought Lenny was bad. How did you kids get so mouthy? If I'd been around there wouldn't be this kind of smart-assing from you all."

He sighed and rubbed his hand over his face. He was looking over her shoulder like he'd forgotten she was there. *He's tired of me. All the charm, the pretending to care, he can't keep it up. It's been nothing but a game and now the fun is over.*

If he was bored with her, Cash would be too. She ought to go.

"Here he comes," he said, and Sally turned to see Cash in the distance, still a good block away. She considered walking out to meet him. She didn't want Richard listening to what she had to say.

What *was* she going to say?

She moved toward the door but Richard spoke. "All those years, when I saw you kids, I wouldn't feel good about myself. It was nothing to do with you all. You're probably the best kind of people. But seeing you, all it did was remind me that I'm… well, I'm different. I don't measure up to you all. I wish I did, but there you go."

She turned. This sounded rehearsed. She imagined him practicing this. Maybe even writing it out. Still, she was touched. She wondered if Pastor Voss would ever talk to her like this. Was he holed up in some cheap hotel preparing a speech for her? It seemed unlikely. He was gone. But Richard was here.

Why couldn't Richard be her dad?

"So what are you doing here?" she asked. "Why don't you go back to Kalamazoo?

"Like I was saying, sixteen years is a long time to hold a certain belief. *You* know. It's your whole damn life. And I don't see any reason to twist around my way of thinking."

"What's that supposed to mean?"

"It means never mind Voss. As far as I'm concerned, nothing's changed."

"But everyone knows you're not my dad! Remember, you told the whole church. Why'd you have to do that?"

"Aw, fuck 'em. Who cares?"

"But you ruined everything!" She looked out the window at Cash. "Maybe if it could have been our secret..."

"Listen, you do what you want. I tell you I'm sticking around, and I hope that I can get to know you a little better. You and Lenny and Nell."

"You want me to just pretend you're my dad?"

Richard shrugged. "What's it gonna hurt?"

Only everything! Because now she desperately wanted it to be true, just like she wanted Cash to be happy to see her.

He was pushing through the door. "Hey," he said. No smile. Just those narrow shoulders and narrow hips that crowded out everything else in the room. Had she really been skin to skin with what was under those jeans?

"Hey yourself."

"Cash here is a nice kid," Richard said. "A real pleasure to work with."

Cash ducked his head, embarrassed. There was a long pause, then the bell behind the counter dinged loudly.

"Customer," Cash said.

Richard saluted *aye, aye, sir!* and left, leaving her face to face with Cash. Just the two of them, alone. She didn't know how to begin. *Have you thought about me? Do you still like me? Why haven't you called?*

He glanced at her. "Your dad—*Sorry.* Richard."

"It's okay," she said eagerly, thankful he was starting.

"He's pretty cool, actually. Not uptight at all."

"I'm glad to hear *you've* been having fun." She felt the sting of tears again and turned away quickly.

"I wouldn't exactly say fun…" he trailed off. She waited but it seemed he had nothing more to say. He was staring at a spot on the floor.

"So about the other night…" She faltered. *I'll sleep with you again and I'll do better!* She'd do it! She would. If only he'd like her. She opened her mouth but he stopped her with an elaborate roll of one shoulder.

"I better get back to work."

"Yeah sure." She was certain humiliation showed on her face, but he wasn't looking anyway. There was a heavy, awkward pause. She couldn't bear to leave things this way, so strange and forced. Not knowing if he hated her. Or maybe he thought she hated him. Maybe he was afraid too.

"Wanna go to the beach some time?" she blurted.

He made a face. "It's getting sort of cold now."

"It's not bad." She heard the plea in her voice. Did he hear it too?

"I'll give you a call," he said, managing another quick glance at her before disappearing into the garage. She heard him clanking some cans together as she stumbled out. Richard waved at her and she waved back, barely seeing him. She forgot to ask Cash about the shoes. Now what would she tell her Aunt Flookie? *I lost your white pumps.*

Oh Sally! she'd say. *It's so embarrassing to be related to you! How do you expect me to love you when you can't do anything right?*

Lenny

It was a perfect day for baseball. Sunny, but not too hot. A baseball cap would have done the trick of blocking the glare, but Lenny had traded his ball cap for a bandana. He could regret it all he wanted. There was no going back. He didn't want to look like a hippy with no resolve. He climbed the bleacher easily and took his regular seat up top. A few people nodded at him and he squinted back, suspicious. Let any one of these fuckers say something to him and he'd be all over it. But as the ump called the first pitch, all eyes were on the game and he relaxed. You had to love sports fans. They didn't get hung up on stupid family dramas. There was drama enough on the field.

Wild pitch across the plate and, *whoa*, the batter swung! A chorus of groans went up from the other bleacher. A few men on the home side glanced back at Lenny with rueful smiles and he flushed with pleasure. That never happened when Lenny Van Sloeten was on the mound. That kid had the best aim in the county. That's what they were thinking. He'd heard the praise often enough. Back then. Now he was just another know-it-all in the crowd.

Lenny sighed and stretched out his legs. It was the last game of the summer league, and though none of the teams were much good, he wished it weren't ending. Who knew where he'd be by the time the spring season started? If he didn't get out of town soon he might just take a bat to Voss' head. *Jesus!* He still couldn't think of that prick as Sally's father. What was next? What other bomb was about to drop? The fact that Voss had bailed him out of jail made him all the angrier. Voss probably thought he was paying his dues, somehow. Don't do me any favors, fucker. Man, *oh man!* He'd like to pop him one! Instead he'd have to keep his cool for another three weeks, until his parole was up. What would it be like working for the creep? Living practically under his roof? Lenny couldn't bear to think of it.

He started tapping his leg as the pitcher wound up. He was feeling the wind up too. He ached for the release of the ball, the complete exhalation of the follow through, the precise placement of the ball over the plate. It was better than sex. At least the sex he'd had, which wasn't much.

He had to get out. Tune in, turn on, drop out. The hippy thing was the only thing for him. He longed for some peacefulness. Something spiritual that wasn't all twisted up in religion. And the free love sounded good too. Imagine people loving him, no questions asked. Imagine him loving back. Then there was the drug thing. He didn't care much about that, but he supposed he'd try it if he had to. He needed a good mind-bending. Mind, body and soul.

Just three more weeks!

Fly ball to center field. Easy out. The Brunswick Pins were down one run. As he watched them take the field he saw a skinny guy with long stringy hair leaning against the fence. Cash. *Great.* Should he go talk to him? What would he do, tap him on the shoulder? *Hey, heard you had my sister out all night.* He'd sound like an idiot. Like some middle-aged square. Better to let his reputation speak for itself. He'd give him a good cold glare if he happened to look over. *Yeah, that's right. Mess with my sister and I'll mess you up good.* He corrected himself. Half-sister.

Lenny was so focused on watching Cash that he barely noticed as the bleacher rocked and a man came thumping over and stopped right next to him. Annoyed, he looked up. It was his dad.

"What are you doing here?" Lenny asked, surprised.

Richard motioned with his head for Lenny to move over. There was plenty of room on Lenny's right side, but Richard wanted to sit on his left. The side of his good ear. *Jesus, he remembers!*

"Came to watch a ball game, same as you."

For a moment Lenny was too stunned to move. *He actually remembers!* Then he caught himself.

"Go find another one. I was here first."

But Richard pushed him with his leg. "Scoot," he said. "I'm not leaving."

So Lenny moved and Richard sat down.

"You got some grand plan to humiliate *me* now?" Lenny asked.

"Nah. I'm finished." Richard smiled. "I don't think I'll ever top my last performance."

"It's real funny to you, ain't it?"

"Not at all. It's shameful."

But Lenny didn't detect any remorse in his dad's voice. He made a disgusted noise and moved away.

"Where were you, anyway?" Richard asked. "I didn't see you at the festivities."

"Why would I be at a Father/Daughter banquet?"

"I thought Voss had you imprisoned in the basement."

Lenny snorted again. He didn't want to talk about that night, or even think about it. If he had stayed at the church the way he was supposed to, he might have stopped his dad from grabbing the microphone. Or maybe stopped Sally from taking off with Cash. It was just that, well, when he saw the two of them coming down the sidewalk, his dad decked out in a suit, Sally glowing and grinning from ear to ear, it made him feel soft. Feeling soft scared him. So he went home. He missed his own room. He missed his mom. He figured if everyone was busy with the banquet, no one would notice he wasn't at the church. His mom would be home alone. Maybe they could sit in the kitchen together and play a hand of gin rummy.

Except the house had been empty. He fell asleep on the couch with the TV on and woke to his mom and Nell shaking him and throwing the whole story in his face like cold water. So he didn't need his dad asking *where were you?* He already knew he'd screwed up. Again.

"What about you?" Lenny shot back. "We were out half the night looking for Sally, without any help from you."

"She didn't want me finding her." He cracked his knuckles. "No, I went back to my lady friend. We shared a bottle of Jack and passed out on the couch." He gave Lenny a wry smile. "Good times," he said, and Lenny heard the sorrow. He ignored it.

"Why are you still here?" he asked.

Richard pretended to study what was happening on the field. "Well," he finally said, "I was thinking about staying around."

"What for?" Lenny couldn't ignore the sudden thud of his heart.

"Maybe try to iron things out."

"How exactly would you do that?"

"Guess I'd start by staying around."

As if it were so easy! Lenny's old churned-up feeling was back, a stomach stew of anger and confusion. He hated it. Mostly he hated the part of him that perked up at those words. Exasperated, he threw his hands in the air.

"If you want to get all fatherly, you might want to check out that kid over there. That's who Sally was with Saturday night."

Richard squinted. "Sure, I know Cash. He plays for Hamilton." Then, like an afterthought, "We work together now."

"*What?*"

"I'm helping out at the Texaco." Richard raised his hand and waved. Lenny saw Cash hesitate, then wave back, self-conscious.

"What are you doing?" Lenny hissed, yanking Richard's arm down. "He's the reason I'm on parole!"

"Yeah, I know all about that too."

"Anything you don't know?" Lenny said, trying to hide his embarrassment with sarcasm. Who was living his life anyway? Him or his dad? Lenny didn't need Richard horning his way in on everything, or acting all buddy-buddy with Cash DeVries.

"I suppose I'm wondering what your plans are, now that you're off the hook with Voss."

"I'm still working off my sentence."

It was his dad's turn to snort. "What kind of a fool are you? Voss is gone. There's nobody to hold you to that deal."

Lenny had the uncomfortable sense that he'd been seeing only the shadow of things —dim, dancing patterns on a wall. Then someone flipped the lights. "Gone? Where?"

"Who cares? He cleared out this morning."

Lenny frowned as he worked out the possibility. He'd slept until noon in the glorified closet that had been his room since June. Neither Voss nor Mrs. Dekker the church secretary had woken him. There had been no list of odd jobs left on the supply closet. Could he really be off the hook? He glanced at his dad but when he saw the way Richard was studying him, awaiting his reaction, he looked quickly away.

"Did you really think he'd wait to see if they fired him?" Richard said.

Lenny hesitated. "It's not just him. The court says—"

"Fuck that! You're done. Believe me. You served your time."

Lenny would love to believe that. "How do you know Voss took off?"

"I was at the Texaco. I saw him myself, bright and early, loading up his car. I yelled over hello, real friendly-like, and he flipped me off." Richard chuckled. "Slouching towards Bethlehem," he said.

Lenny gave him a blank look.

"Yeats," Richard said.

Lenny shrugged, his thoughts already elsewhere. If Voss was gone, would the police know that Lenny hadn't worked off his bail? Probably not. Which meant no more mopping floors or polishing pews while the stained glass Jesus stared down at him with that resigned look that said *when will you stop disappointing me?* No more sharpening all those tiny little pencils that went inside the guest registration pads. No more of Voss asking him in that mealy-mouthed way *would you mind* doing this, or that, when any idiot could see that of course he minded. He hated every minute of it. But now! It was like a weight lifting. He was free to go!

But where? Back home? That's when it hit him.

"What about Sally?"

Richard frowned. "Yeah, she's a nice kid. She doesn't deserve this."

Lenny blinked. "What? To have her dad walk out on her? Take it from me, it's no big deal." He saw his dad's jaw clench.

"So you say."

"That's right," Lenny snapped. "What would you know about it, anyway?"

"It's just a tough break for her, is all. Getting that kind of news."

Sally! Was everything about Sally now?

"She'll be fine," he mumbled.

"Sure. But I was thinking. If I stay around, well… it might help her if we just, you know, ignore the whole Voss thing."

"Are you saying you don't believe it?"

"I believe it all right. But we don't have to let old peckerwood ruin our family."

Now Lenny laughed. "Right. You took care of that a long time ago."

Richard looked at him. "You know, you could cut me some slack here. I'm making an effort."

"It's a little late, don't you think?"

"Is it?" Richard studied him, then threw his hands up. "Listen, what do you want from me?"

Lenny wasn't going to answer. He focused on the ball game but couldn't seem to figure out what was going on. "Okay," he said after a moment. "I wonder how you could let that happen, with mom and Voss."

"You mean why didn't I know that my God-fearing wife was fucking her pastor? Jesus, I'm stupid!"

"I'm not saying it's not mom's fault."

"Goddamn right! I'm tired of being the bad guy. Now you see I'm not the only one made mistakes."

See it, maybe. Admit it, never. "Yeah, you deserve a medal."

Richard was getting hot. "Maybe I do. And in case you're wondering, you are my kid. No doubts there."

"Too bad, ain't it?"

Richard stood up. "You're a goddamn smart ass, aren't ya?"

People were looking. *Here we go*, Lenny thought. He clenched his teeth. "I'm watching the game," he said to his dad. Stony cold. But he was starting to sweat too. *Please, please don't do this. Not here.* "Sit down. Or leave."

Richard hesitated, then sat. He leaned forward on his knees and chewed his lip. They both stared at the field.

"I'm not apologizing for nothing," Richard said suddenly.

"What a surprise," Lenny muttered. He could be a son of a bitch too. It was his nature, and was it any wonder? It got old, though. He wished he could find a way to talk to his dad that wasn't all sniping, but how? And what was the use anyway? What could his dad possibly say? *Sorry kid, I just had better things to do. Sorry I found you so damn boring.* Lenny didn't even need specifics. Something general would do. *Sorry for the way things went down.* Why couldn't he say that?

"You know, you kids want everything zipped up neat-like. That's how your mom has always been, expecting God to show her the way, like he's holding up some sign in black and white. In my opinion, God don't care that we fuck things up. Most times you get along by the seat of your pants."

"Thanks for the pearls of wisdom," Lenny said, bracing for his dad's anger. Why did he keep smart mouthing? He didn't want to do it. He agreed with him, that was the thing. But he wasn't about to say so. His dad didn't deserve to have it easy.

But Richard didn't erupt. Figures. There was no predicting anything with this guy. He must practice wearing a person down, that's how good he was at it. Lenny had never felt so confused.

"Well, nice chatting," Lenny said. "I'm outta here."

Richard grabbed his arm. "Hold on there. Watch this play."

Lenny nearly slapped his hand away. People didn't grab him. They knew better. He checked himself and then allowed Richard to pull him back into his seat. What was wrong with him? Where did this fucking weakness come from? He couldn't seem to make a move.

"That weaselly guy shouldn't be starting," Richard was saying. "He doesn't have any kind of arm on him."

Lenny scoffed. Here at least he had some confidence. "His ERA is 3.6."

"That's not much better than you."

"How would you know?"

"I followed your season. I read about that last game. Tough break."

Lenny had a quick image of his dad sitting somewhere with a paper spread in front of him, reading about his son. If only he had known! He might have played better.

"I choked," he said.

Richard smiled at him. "Happens to the best."

Lenny looked away. "That's all over now."

Richard nudged him with his elbow. "You can't just let it go. You've got talent. Why don't you coach?"

"Who's going to hire a coach with a police record?"

"You didn't *kill* anyone, for chrissake. One assault charge. That's nothing."

"You speaking from experience?"

"Maybe."

Lenny studied him. "You kill someone?"

Richard raised his eyebrows. "What would you think if I did?"

Jesus! Was he serious? Was this where all his own murderous tendencies came from?

Richard laughed. "Nah, but I've been arrested four times. Two D & D's, two assaults. None of them were my fault. I'm just unlucky that way."

Lenny wanted to know more about his dad's life, but he wouldn't let himself ask. He told himself it didn't matter. He was eighteen now and had his own life to live.

"Anyway, I'm leaving town," he said.

"That so? Where you headed?"

"New Buffalo first," Lenny said. "There's a farm down there."

"Aw *shit!*" Richard slapped his leg. Lenny looked quickly around the field. Did he miss a bad play? But Richard wasn't reacting to the game. He was looking at Lenny with exasperation.

"You're not into that crap, are you?"

"What?"

"Communal living. That red belly commie stuff. Is that what the bandana's all about?"

Lenny touched his head self-consciously. "It's not about anything. I'm just looking for somewhere to work, away from here."

"Yeah, I know all about the place. And I hate to bust your bubble, but there's an outbreak of hepatitis down there."

"How would you know?"

"You say that a lot, you realize that? You think I'm some dumb shit who's been living in a cave or something? I know a thing or two about life. More than you'll ever know."

"Jesus, cool it." He never should have said anything. Being a hippy was just something you did, and then you were cool. You didn't announce it in advance. Hey, I think I'll be a hippy! Like I'm going to be an accountant, or lawyer.

"For your information, I was just through there on my last trip up from Michigan City. They're not taking any newcomers. The place will be gone before winter."

Lenny tried to look unfazed. Leave it to his dad to ruin his plans even when they didn't involve him. "I'll head to Chicago then," he said finally. "Plenty of work there."

"Plenty of rioting and head busting, too."

Lenny glared. "I guess I'll go where I want to go."

"Well which is it, a commune or the big city? Sounds like you don't know what you want."

"Like you do? All the sudden you want your little family back? You want Sally to pretend she's your kid? Man, that's outta whack."

There was a long pause. "Don't I know it," Richard said, hanging his head.

Something close to pity tugged at Lenny. He tried to put the brakes on it, but it went spooling out, like a thread winding around them.

"So I guess you'll be gone by the time the series starts," Richard said.

"Maybe."

“Too bad. ‘Cause if the Tigers go all the way, I’m guaranteed two tickets to game three in Detroit.” He let loose a big shit-eating grin.

Lenny squinted at him. “No way.”

“Why don’t you come with me?”

“How would you get tickets?”

“I’ve got friends. And there’s other people I can ask, too, so you want to go or what?”

The World Series! With his *dad.* This was what he’d dreamed of as a kid. The two of them behind home plate, their scorecards in their hands, his dad raising a folded dollar bill for the hot dog vendor. *Two here!* But that was back when he still believed in his dad. He knew better now.

“I might have to work at the marina,” he said cautiously. “I’ve been pulling some shifts there. Scrubbing down boats.”

“Well, you can either work for the lazy fat fucks who can’t take care of their own goddamn boats, or you can come watch McLain throw another shut-out.”

Lenny shook his head. Imagine seeing Denny McLain in the flesh! Being that close to something so great, well, it’d change his life. “Why you asking me?”

Richard faced him. “Isn’t it about time you and I catch a game together? I mean a real one.”

The sincerity of his dad’s voice hit Lenny like a fist. He blinked hard. He had to be careful. He had to remember who he was dealing with.

“Last time we were gonna have a game together, I ended up sitting on the goddamn porch for four hours waiting on you.”

“Yeah.” Richard scowled and chewed his lip again. “I never meant for that to happen. What do you say you overlook that, and I’ll overlook you trying to take my spleen out with your bat?

We'll call it even."

Lenny didn't answer. Could they really start fresh?

His dad touched his arm again.

"Son, I'm talking about the World Series here. I know you're not stupid enough to say no."

It didn't matter what he said. Chances were that it was all another set-up. Another miserable fucking disappointment. What the hell. He nodded and said, "Yeah, I'd go."

Richard slapped Lenny's knee. "All right then! Let's pray that the Tigers bring us home!" He raised his arms in the air and yelled, "Hallelujah Jesus!"

People looked over again, but suddenly Lenny didn't care. He felt reckless. *Come on, hit me!* There was a sort of satisfaction in the promise of pain. It was a bearing-down kind of resolve that Lenny knew well. He actually laughed. His dad was waving his hands around and laughing too.

"Amen!" Lenny said. He'd never said this with any feeling before but now it just popped out of him. Was this the bubble of joy that people felt when they gave their hearts to the Lord? He felt saved.

Richard stood up. "I'm gonna go make some calls." He held out his hand and Lenny stared at it a second before he understood he should shake it. *Man to man.* It felt strange. Lenny tried to make his grip sure and firm.

"See ya," he said, and it came off casually, as if he didn't really wish that his dad would stay and sit out the game. But what would this lousy game matter when they were sitting side by side in Tiger Stadium?

"I'll be talking to you," Richard said.

"Sure, whatever."

"Hey. Don't bring the bandana to the big leagues, okay?"

he said. “You look like a freak.” He stomped off down the bleachers. “Wear a ball cap!” he called. Then he was gone.

Lenny felt dazed. The game was still on, and the regulars were still swatting flies and chewing gum and grumbling loudly. *How ‘bout an ump who knows his head from his ass?* Lenny tried to screw his scowl back on his face in case any nosy fuckers were looking at him, but it was hard. It was hard to even look interested in the game. He hardly noticed it. The World Series! Lenny Van Sloeten at the World Series? He saw Cash, sitting now, down on the first row, and had a ridiculous urge to go tell him. *Hey, my dad’s taking me to game three at Tiger Stadium!* It was stupid. The Tigers hadn’t even sewn it up yet. They still had to finish off the Senators. But they’d do it. They had to do it. Please God, if I ever catch a break, make it this one. Bless Denny McLean and Dick McAuliffe and Mickey Lolich.

And bless my dad. Bless him for having friends who can do him big favors. And make sure he doesn’t fink out on this. Or on Sally. Or me. Because this time, I swear, I’ll kill him.

Hear me, God?

Prudy

It wasn't supposed to be like this. Before she had kids, Prudy had it all figured out. She would be a patient and loving parent. Firm but fair. Her kids would love her with that whole-hearted adoration you see in a Renaissance painting. Chubby little cherubs with wings and halos, sent from God to cling to her knees. *Mother!* Serene, exalted one.

Before, Prudy would watch other women with children, thinking *my kids will never eat potato chips for breakfast, or go outdoors with unzipped coats, or crawl under the pews during church.* The joke was on her, wasn't it?

Motherhood was such a *trap.* Either you took it out on your kids, or it was taken out on you, but someone had to pay. There were women like Mona Veenstra who took out the frustrations with a smack or a pinch or a push. There were those, like Prudy, who tried so hard and still screwed up. Her mistake was in ever believing she was a separate person. She'd thought that as long as she was giving hugs, drying tears, advising, encouraging, feeding, clothing, *loving* her children, then her private sins wouldn't affect them. If she chose to have an affair—with a better man than her husband!—what right did her children have to judge her?

Sally wouldn't even look her in the face. Prudy let her be for a few days, then tried, feebly, to explain how unhappy she'd been with Richard, how she had so desperately needed someone to be kind to her. But it was like talking to a wall. She didn't know if Sally cared about anything she had to say. Whether she blamed Prudy, or Richard, or herself. She didn't know anything! Least of all how to move past this. They were stuck, marking time, and Prudy was grateful for the smallest crumbs of normalcy. Asking Sally *do you want some toast?* Having her nod and say yes.

Okay, Prudy screwed up. Still, it felt so unfair! Like no one wanted to see her side. Like the time, years ago, when she tried to tell her mother about Richard's violent moods. *I've been married to your father for 40 years*, her mother snapped. *You don't see him going for the bottle!* And the silent disapproval of Prudy's sister Bunny when Prudy told her Richard had walked out. They never knew the half of it! How Richard beat her. How he left her for weeks on end with no money. How he slept with other women. She wasn't sure they would care. Especially now.

"Tell me it isn't true!" Bunny gasped over the phone when the news reached her.

Truth was something Bunny tolerated only when it was tidy and square and clicked perfectly into the well-ordered framework of her brain.

"Oh, stuff it, Bunny," Prudy said, ready to hang up.

"Mother's in shock, you know. You have to come see her. You have to explain."

"It's not that hard to figure out."

Even Flookie—flaky, faithful Flookie, who'd known the truth all along —reproached her.

"Why did you let Sally find out now, like that?"

Prudy faltered. Flookie was right. How terrible it must have been for Sally to hear it from Phillip! Prudy knew now she had taken the easy way out. She was just so afraid of saying those words. *Pastor Voss is your father.*

"And Phillip's gone now, Prudy! How must Sally feel?"

"He told me he would resign. I didn't think—"

"*God* Prudy! What *did* you think?"

"I don't know! It's like I'm losing my mind. One minute I have it all figured out and everything makes sense. The next minute I see what a terrible mistake I've made."

Was she playing the victim? Was the spectacle at the banquet just her way of finally saying *see what a raw deal I got? Can you believe how long I lived with this?*

Or. Maybe it was a way of getting a little something back for herself. *That man you all adore? That pillar of society, that man of God? He loved me! He fathered my child!*

But motherhood is not even close to Godliness. In fact, those Renaissance paintings? Sometimes there's a little cherub carrying a bow and arrow. He's pointing it at the Madonna, ready to strike. In the background there's death and destruction. A fall from grace.

The resentment was there when Prudy found Sally bending over the toilet one morning.

"What's wrong?" she asked.

"I don't know. I'm sick." Sally heaved, producing only a mouthful of spit. Prudy put her hand on Sally's back, the way she always did. Sally shrugged her off.

"Leave me alone."

Prudy stepped back, uncertain. She'd already said these things: *Phillip didn't leave you, he left the church. He'll be in touch, when you're ready.* This, at least, was one assurance he'd given her before slithering away like a snake.

She'd already said *I'm sorry.*

Forgive me.

I love you.

What she wanted to say now was *fine! I'll leave you alone!*

She hesitated. "Should I call the school?"

Sally nodded and Prudy went into the kitchen but she didn't pick up the phone. Instead she sat at the table. That night. And that boy. What really happened between them? Sally had never shown much interest in boys. She was a good kid, level-headed and mature. But *that* night.

Prudy went back to the bathroom. "You never told me what happened with this Cash kid."

Sally's head lay on her arm on the seat of the toilet. "You never asked."

True. She'd been afraid to act like a parent.

"So what happened?"

Sally's voice echoed in the toilet bowl. "Nothing. I hid in his garage for awhile. That's all."

"Alone?"

"What difference does it make?"

Prudy clasped her hands together to steady them. "Sally. I want to make sure…" How to say it? "…that you're okay."

"I have the flu. Someone at school had it last week. It's going around."

Prudy touched Sally's forehead. There was no fever. "I'm going to call the doctor."

"I don't need the doctor. I'll be better tomorrow."

"What if you're not?"

Sally raised her head. "You think I'm dying or something? That would be for the best, wouldn't it? If I was gone everybody could forget about all this mess."

"How can you say such a thing?"

"You probably think about *him* every time you see me."

"That's not true!" Not anymore anyway. "I thank God for you every day." And every day she asked forgiveness for what she'd tried to do to herself in the bathroom. She was grateful Sally didn't know about that.

"Don't talk about God. I'm going to puke."

"Do you think it could be anything besides the flu?" Prudy asked cautiously.

Sally pulled herself into a ball. "Stop it! If you have something to say, just say it!" But she looked scared and put her hands over her ears.

Prudy stared at her. Just say it? Did Sally really think it was so easy to talk about such things? She was suddenly furious. At Sally. At everyone.

"Tell me *exactly* what you did with him!" The harshness of her voice startled her. Dread was flooding over her.

Sally shook her head violently. "I can't. I can't say it. I can't even think about it."

"Oh Sally!" Prudy cried. "Did you have sex with him?"

Sally started to cry.

"Did you?"

"Let go of me!"

Prudy didn't realize she'd grabbed Sally's arm.

"Did you do this to get back at me? Is that it?" Phillip was having his revenge on her. Why not Sally?

There was no answer, just that unbearable sobbing. Prudy couldn't take it. Falling apart was a luxury they couldn't afford.

"That boy doesn't love you," she said. "He doesn't care anything about you. He was using you."

Sally lifted her head. "What do *you* know about love?"

"You think I don't know about being used?"

The crying stopped. Barely audibly, Sally said, "Cash likes me."

"Oh *Sally*." How could Prudy blame her daughter for believing that? She'd been there herself. She knew too well the confusion that came with sharing yourself with a man, hearing him whisper all sorts of loveliness, only to have him walk away without so much as a backward glance. She was nearly forty years old and she'd never made sense of the turmoil that sex unleashed. The closeness that made you ache with loneliness. The disappointment and desperate longing for something unnamed. The understanding that you've given yourself to someone who could throw you away like an old rag. She didn't want Sally to go through it. Not after everything else that had happened.

She took a deep breath. "Is your period late?"

She wouldn't assume the worse. Nothing was certain. Except one thing. She was a terrible parent. The worst! She should have died that day in the bathroom. Her kids would have been better off without her. Lenny and Nell could have gone to live with Bunny and her husband Ollie. They could have grown up on the farm. Lenny would be strong and tanned and solid. Nell thin and smiling. And Sally would never have existed.

Prudy's stomach twisted. She loved her so much!

"Get your shoes on," she said. "We're going to the doctor."

Prudy turned and walked out, leaving Sally to rinse her

mouth and splash her face. She picked up her pocketbook from the kitchen counter and sat on the edge of the sofa, waiting. When Sally emerged she had the puffy, smeary look of a child after a nap—so young!—and Prudy had to duck her head to hide her quivering chin. She stood abruptly and opened the front door, Sally shuffling behind her. They walked in silence down the block, then turned toward the bustling morning traffic on Butternut Avenue. It was five minutes before she realized she hadn't called the school. She hadn't called Mrs. Overbeek in the office at Batt's and her shift would be starting any minute. What would happen? She was too afraid to think about it. They stopped at the crosswalk and Prudy took Sally's hand. Her only job was to be right here, holding on tight.

At Dr. Maas' office, the receptionist asked if they had an appointment. Prudy had never liked this woman, one of those too young, too perky types who have that way of giving a person a quick once-over before flipping on a smile.

Prudy steeled herself. "We need to see the doctor right away."

Flick, flick went the woman's eyes. "I'm so sorry. He's completely booked."

"He's going to have to squeeze us in. We're not leaving until he does."

The woman frowned. "Can I ask what the problem is?"

Prudy lifted her chin. "No you may not. In fact, we'll just go wait in there." Before the woman could answer, Prudy was pushing Sally toward one of the exam rooms. She heard the receptionist gasp and push her swivel chair back, but she was already closing the door behind them.

"What's he going to do?" Sally asked tremulously.

"Don't worry." Prudy was too close to panic to talk. She didn't want to raise another kid! Of course it would fall to her. Sally couldn't be expected to handle a baby. Prudy remembered how once, visiting an aunt in a nursing home, she saw an old woman pace the hallway clutching a baby doll to her breast. She stroked its back and whispered to it as if it were real and Prudy, before she realized, thought *Oh! How sweet!* But it wasn't sweet at all. It was proof of how motherhood carves a permanent hole in a woman. It's all you have, then you have nothing.

Prudy wasn't ready to let her little girl go.

Dr. Maas stepped into the room looking puzzled.

"She needs a pregnancy test," Prudy blurted. She said it matter of factly, though her cheeks were flaming. He must have heard this before! How many times? And how many times would she have to see this helpless, well *gosh!* look on a man's face? She felt herself begin to shake.

"All those times you pretended not to know that my husband was beating me," she said, "you can damn well keep your mouth shut now!"

"Prudy!" he said, startled. "We've known each other for years."

"Yes, we have."

"I've always been professional."

"If professional means you don't ask a woman the question she's *waiting* for you to ask. If it means you turn away like a coward—"

It was Prudy's turn to fall apart. She had no idea why she would, now, in front of this man. She hated it, but she couldn't stop.

"You delivered my *babies!* I put our lives in your hands. And you…" She pressed a fist to her mouth. *Just shut up! This isn't helping!*

He bristled. "Maybe it's time you see another doctor."

She sniffed. She couldn't look at Sally. "First you're giving her a test."

"The nurse can take care of that. I'll send her in."

"No! If she does it, everyone in town will know. Do it yourself."

He sighed and considered this. Then he said to Sally, "I'll put a cup in the bathroom down the hall. You will catch your urine, mid-stream, in the cup. You'll leave the cup on the toilet tank and I'll collect it. Do you understand?"

"Thank you," Prudy whispered, staring at her hands.

"I won't have the results for a few days. And I should remind you that there is always the possibility of a false negative or false positive."

Prudy nodded.

"I can examine her now," he added.

The thought of another man touching her daughter repulsed her. "No, we're going," she said. "We'll wait for your call."

Sally

Sally refused to believe there was a life growing in her. How could there be, when she felt so dead? She lay on her bed, doing nothing, seeing nothing. Wishing her thoughts would follow suit.

The doctor had called and told them what they already knew. Except. He might be wrong. He'd said so himself. False positives were possible. Look for other symptoms, he said. Breast tenderness. Frequent urination. Fatigue. Make an appointment, he said. But Sally ignored that, thinking *maybe it won't take*. Her body might reject it! The hope made her feel guilty. She didn't want to be defective. She wanted children, someday. Every girl did.

She wanted a husband too. She just never thought it would be someone like Cash. Her face burned as she remembered the way he'd acted at the station. He might be shy. Or busy. Or just an ordinary jerk. It didn't matter, because she was stuck with him now, their lives tragically entwined, like Romeo and Juliet.

Hadn't she *known* she belonged to him? This only proved it. Besides, what other boy would want her, with someone else's baby?

Face it. Cash didn't want her either! Sex didn't mean love these days. Hadn't she learned anything eavesdropping in the girls' room? She was on her own here.

She could give it away. Wouldn't that be best, to give some deserving couple a child? Because, really, *what* was she going to do with a *baby*? She put her hands on her belly and it felt warm and soft. Not different. She imagined something in there, something that would eventually want out, its face squished against the wall of her uterus like it was a pane of glass. *Feed me! Love me!* And the pain. That scared her more than anything. More than getting fat or being laughed at. Those things were bad enough, but *childbirth.* It was so…medieval. So much writhing and gnashing. Guttural, ugly animal sounds. Blood-soaked sheets in a darkened tapestry-draped room. A doctor holding a candle, shrugging helplessly. *There's nothing I can do*. Never mind that it was 1968, with sleek, modern hospitals and newfangled drugs to numb everything. Some things never changed.

Then, if you survived, there were the diapers and feedings and crying. She'd have to quit school. Get a job. Would Cash help? What would he say? What did she want him to say?

It was as if she had stepped onto a conveyor belt and, just *moments* ago, it had been pulling her toward something. Hello dad! Hello boyfriend! Hello even to the confusion of womanhood. Everything close enough to touch. Then, *hey! Come back!* All of it was disappearing. Except the womanhood part. She was left holding that like a booby prize.

She decided to keep her pillow over her face, nearly

suffocated by the heat and cotton-covered poly-fill fiber. Pretending the rolling bile in her stomach was something she caught from a dirty fork in the school cafeteria.

Her mother knocked on the door.

"There's someone on the phone who would like to talk to you."

Cash! Some feeling, bright and hopeful, flared, then went out. Extinguished by this: nothing mattered now. Her life was over.

She dragged herself from the bed and went into the kitchen.

Prudy handed her the phone. "It's Pastor Voss."

Sally froze. She wasn't ready for this.

Her mother put the receiver to Sally's ear and she heard his voice, a long way off.

"Sally?"

"Yeah?"

"Your mother tells me you're in a bit of trouble."

She glared at her mom. She told *him*?

"A bit? Uh-huh."

"And we were just discussing the fact that I may be able to help."

She pictured him bringing her a box of used maternity clothes. "I don't need your help."

"I think you do."

"Sorry. You don't get to have an opinion."

His patient sigh infuriated her.

"Sally, the church was going to fire me."

She twisted the phone cord around her finger. "Anyway, who cares?"

There was a pause. "I should have said goodbye."

"Yeah. Goodbye." Sally tried to hand the phone back but

Prudy wouldn't take it.

"Talk to him!"

Sally made an angry sound. She didn't want *him*! He was supposed to be the good guy, the respectable one. But he was all wrong for her.

She thought of the times over the years when she'd wanted to share something with her father. In second grade, when she wore the giant milk carton in the school play and shouted *plenty of me helps you run, jump, and ski!* In fifth grade gym class, when she had to do an interpretive dance and she pretended to be falling leaves, running willy-nilly in circles, flailing her arms about, and the gym teacher, a severe, bony woman named Ms. Dyke clapped and said Sally had panache. And how many times had she been with a group of girls as they pretended to be horrified—*My dad offered my date a glass of Kool Aid! Mine started smoking a pipe. Mine bought a motorcycle. He thinks he's James Dean!*—when Sally knew they talked of their dads the way they'd talk about their husbands someday. A big slice of fondness under a coating of complaints.

Why was it she could still imagine a fondness for Richard—drunken, loudmouthed, sparkly Richard—and not feel even a smidge for Pastor Voss?

"What do you want?" she asked.

"Would you like my help?"

"I'll lcavc it up to you."

Another sigh.

"What, am I annoying you?" she said.

"Yes, actually."

"Do what you want, okay? I mean, I hate to bother you."

"If you feel that this is something you can't go through with, then I can help."

She stopped fidgeting. Turning away from her mother, she spoke quietly into the phone. "I'm listening."

"I've called on many people at Grand Rapids Memorial hospital and I know of a doctor there who performs certain services."

Something in her went cold. "You want me to have an *abortion?*" She whipped her head around to see her mother giving her a level look. "You know about this?" she hissed.

Prudy nodded.

"But…that's illegal. And dangerous." She took a step backward, as if she could run from this.

Her mother touched her arm. "There are ways," she said. She had a hopeful, pleading look. Oh. She was expecting *gratitude!*

"With what you've already been through, we just feel…," Pastor Voss began.

They wanted her to believe they were saving her! Like she was special. She blinked. Where was the outrage? The disappointment? The tongue-lashing that she so deserved? This was what they thought of her! To give up on her so easily.

She struggled to find her voice. "Is God making an exception for me? I'm just curious."

"Let's not read too much into this."

Right. Maybe God's laws weren't laws at all. Maybe they were merely suggestions. And the image she'd always had of God, high on a throne, purple robes pooling at his feet, arms outstretched as he delivered his message to the multitudes, was all wrong too. God might be a short, ordinary looking guy with a goatee, chatting with a few folks in someone's living room, just another cool cat who would wave his hand casually and say *here's an idea! Try not to kill anybody, especially before they get a chance to have a life.* And some people would nod and snap their fingers. Right on, man.

But you didn't have to listen. You didn't have to do anything.

This was wonderful! She waited for the crash of relief. Willed it. They were offering her a way out! Never mind the strangeness of hearing this voice, the same voice she'd heard preach a hundred times, suggesting *abortion!* Was she going to turn this down? For what? So she could hear a few scripted lines from Father Knows Best?

"So you know a doctor," she said cautiously.

"I trust him completely. He's one of the best."

"You've sent other girls to him?"

"Well no, this is not something I'm usually involved in."

"Then how do you know he's safe? How can you trust him?"

"I've checked this out, Sally."

Her mouth had gone dry. "Just make it go away. Is that it?"

"If this solution is not something you want, we won't say another word about it."

"I'm just …" *So afraid!* There was also a sense, one she couldn't understand, that they were trying to take something from her. And there was this: Cash might love her. He'd have to, if she had his baby!

No. Someone who barely knew her would not love her.

Unless. Maybe that was the key. Maybe her only real shot at being loved was with Cash *because* he didn't know her. Her real father didn't love her and he'd known her all her life.

What should she do?

"I'm surprised, that's all," she managed.

"Take some time to think about it. I could drive you to Grand Rapids on Saturday."

"That's not much time!"

"You don't want to wait too long. Talk it over with your mother."

She looked at Prudy. Talk? Too dangerous. Better to listen. Nod, nod. *Whatever you say.* If only she had listened long ago! She wouldn't be standing here today, a stranger's child inside her. A stranger on the phone line, telling her what to do. A stranger clutching at her arm, pretending to want the best for her. If only she could go back to being normal! She'd been a fool to be unhappy. *Poor me! No daddy!* Now look at her! She'd found two fathers. The right one and the wrong one.

How was it possible to feel so alone?

Sally didn't want to come right out and admit that she missed Lenny. But she didn't understand why he hadn't moved back home. His probation was up, yet he was still holed up in the church basement. It hurt. Even Lenny didn't want to be around her. Anyway, it wasn't like she was his *real* family. They shared a mother. Big deal. It had always been that missing piece, that gaping hole in their lives, that had been their bond. Now Lenny had his dad. What use would he have for Sally?

But she needed him. Lenny, who never cared what anyone thought. Lenny, who messed up plenty. He was the only one she could talk to.

So when she woke late to the sound of his cursing outside her bedroom window, she breathed a sigh of thanks. She grabbed a wrinkled t-shirt and skirt from the floor and pulled them on, confused by the gray darkness of the sky. She found Lenny outdoors, struggling with a mountain of garbage bags. The wind was blowing hard, whipping his hair into his eyes. It was one of those strange autumn winds when it seems like the air is about to burst into tears. The kind that has you squinting at the sky, wondering *how soon until this blows over?*

"I need to talk to Cash," she said, hoping he wouldn't act ignorant. Nell said she'd seen Lenny hanging out at the Texaco with Richard and Cash. After the first pang of betrayal, Sally tried to understand. The trying was like a muscle she hadn't known she had, tired lately from overuse.

"Why?" he asked, not looking at her as he heaved two bags over his shoulder and headed toward the garage.

Sally hesitated as she held her skirt down, wondering how long it would be before the truth was obvious. She could go months without having this conversation. She could go forever. She could get rid of the baby and Lenny and Cash would never know a thing. But without them, she'd have to make this decision on her own, with only her mother and Pastor Voss advising her, and who could trust them?

"It's a private matter," she said. *Stupid.* Why prolong it?

"Then leave me out of it," he said.

"Could you just tell him to come see me?"

He flung the bags carelessly into the can behind the garage and folded his arms. "I'm not his fucking secretary. I don't even talk to the guy."

"Liar."

He shot her a hostile look.

"I mean, it's fine. I don't mind that you like him."

"You're the one who likes him."

She grabbed his arm. "Listen, it's more than that."

"Oooh," he sneered. "Puppy love."

"Lenny, I've got to talk to him. It's a matter of life and

death."

He sighed. "Good Lord, what is it?"

"Well…" She looked at her feet. There was a large chunk of mud on one toe. She bent down and rubbed it furiously. Not that it changed anything. Dirty. *Dirty.*

"What?" Lenny said, impatient.

She took a deep breath. "Well, if you must know, he and I had sex." Yes. *This* was how she'd refer to it. It was matter-of-fact. Mature. "And I happen to be pregnant."

His face jumped like a machine had been flipped on under his skin.

"*Cash* ….got you *pregnant?*" He stared at her a moment. "I'll fucking kill him!"

He kicked the garbage can so hard it flew up and bounced off a tree, littering the grass with coffee grinds and wads of Kleenex. A white plastic bag lifted, free and easy, and rode the wind into the neighbor's yard.

She took a step back. "What good will *that* do?"

He whirled on her. "It'll teach him he can't go around messing with peoples' sisters!"

"Oh *pleeease.*" But she was touched. He wasn't blaming her, he was blaming Cash.

"I'll knock him into next week!" He swung as if he had his bat in his hands, except that he wasn't carrying his bat anymore.

Wow. She liked the idea that she could have Cash beaten up. It would serve him right. Then he'd know there were people who cared about her. People who understood that she was not the kind of person to let this happen.

"I just wasn't myself, and…"

"Spare me the details," he snapped, pacing beneath the clothesline. When it bumped against his head he swatted it like it was out to get him.

“Guess I’d better get my bat,” he said finally, heading toward the house.

“Wait!” He was serious! “You can’t do that! You’ll ruin everything.”

“Ruin what? You planning a lacy white wedding? Happily ever after? I don’t think so.”

She ran after him. “You want to end up back in jail?”

“It’ll be thanks to you!”

“Lenny stop!”

He lunged at her. “What the *fuck* is wrong with you? You stupid, immature, selfish little creep!”

“I’m sorry!”

“Don’t you understand? I *have* to go kick his ass!”

“No you don’t.”

“It’s the way things go, which is something you’d know if you weren’t so stupid.”

And he was off, punching at the air.

“Don’t hurt him!” she cried.

He stopped and whirled around. “Why not?”

She hesitated. “If you go after him I’ll never see him again.”

“You’ll probably never see him again anyway.”

“Don’t say that!” She knew he was right, but *God*, did he have to be right?

“IIe’s all I havc.” Shc hatcd thc way hcr voicc caught.

Lenny stared at her a moment. At last he threw up his hands. “So what the hell are you going to do?”

She had to tell him! If Lenny found the idea of abortion despicable, then she’d know she couldn’t do it. If he didn’t, well, maybe he could convince her why it was the best choice.

With a cautious look around, she said quietly, “I have an

opportunity to get rid of ...the baby. If that's what I decide."

He narrowed his eyes. "An *opportunity?*"

Of course that wasn't what she meant. "Lenny, don't. I'll get all the preaching I need from Nell." *If* she even told Nell.

"You're the one who said it."

"What do you think I should do?"

"How the hell do I know? People don't usually come to me for advice."

"Well, I am. What do you think?"

He sighed. "You better give me some details."

So she told him about Pastor Voss and his offer to take her to the doctor in Grand Rapids. And how Prudy thought she should consider it.

"Jesus. Nothing surprises me anymore. How much will it cost?"

He wasn't against it. She felt an inexplicable pang of disappointment.

"Three hundred dollars," she said. "I think Voss is going to pay it."

Lenny whistled. "What about Cash? What are you going to tell him?"

"The truth."

"Why bother? He doesn't need to know."

"A person fathers a child, you think he'd like to know." She shrugged. "It's like having spinach on your tooth, only worse."

Anyone else would take satisfaction in pointing out what a dumb statement that was. Not Lenny. He was nodding. He knew how a person could want to do right, even while doing everything wrong. Besides, imagine not telling Cash. Imagine him parked out at the beach with some skanky Zeeland High School pompom girl while Sally agonized over committing a mortal sin. Imagine never giving him the chance to say that he was crazy about her, and that he wanted to do the right thing too.

"So will you do it? Will you tell Cash to come see me?"

He shook his head. "Nope. Sorry."

"Come on! Just this one little thing!"

"I'm not doing it. Not without kicking him in the balls first."

His face was stony. She could try to chip away at him, but it wouldn't work. She waved her hand.

"Oh forget it then. I'll take care of it." She'd call the station. If Richard answered, she'd hang up. When she got Cash, she'd do it just like in the movies. *I need to see you right away. Meet me at Tunnel Park at eight. Don't be late.* But in the movies something bad always happened.

Lenny shrugged. "Fine."

She followed him inside and watched him throw himself into a kitchen chair. He put his elbows on the table and squeezed his head between his hands. She pulled a chair out slowly and sat across from him. The thing in her belly was already like a lump between them.

"Where is everybody?" he asked finally.

"I think Mom's working an extra shift. I don't know." She rolled her eyes and Lenny saw.

"You can't really judge her," he said quietly.

She snorted. "Why not?"

"Everyone screws up."

"Nell doesn't."

"Nell lets herself down all the time. That's worse than letting someone else down."

"What are you, Dr. Joyce Brothers?"

He gave her a rueful smile. She tried to smile back, but it was frightening, hearing this kind of talk from Lenny.

"Have you told Nell?" he asked.

"No."

"Frannie?"

"No." She put her hand up to hide the sudden quiver of her chin.

"It'll be okay," he said.

She nodded vigorously. "Yeah." She didn't believe it for a minute. But she was thankful.

"I'm glad you got your dad back," she said, wiping away a tear she hoped he didn't see.

They sat in silence. At last Lenny sighed and said, "I guess I can talk to Cash."

"You won't hurt him, will you?"

He pursed his lips. She could see him imagining the fight, how he'd lay into him with a howl. But he shook his head.

"I'll leave that for you."

She winced.

"It looks like you're not the only black sheep in the family," she said.

He leaned forward and held his hand out. "Welcome to the flock." She shook it and he smiled, but it was a sad smile. He got to his feet.

"It's not your fault you know," she said. "You didn't rub off on me or anything like that."

He grabbed her and threw an elbow around her neck. "No? Guess I'd better try again." He ground his knuckles into her scalp in what they called a Dutch rub. It was one of his favorite torture methods, going back to when they were kids.

"How's that?" he said.

He wasn't being too rough, and anyway, her scalp ought to be tough from years of Dutch rubs. But she grimaced and said

Ow! because it did hurt.

It surprised her how much it hurt.

Sally waited at the bottom of the sand dune at Tunnel Park, beside the wooden-slated fence that ran along the pitted sidewalk. The place was quiet, forgotten, now that the chill of fall was in the air. Eventually she wandered, too nervous to stand still. First into the cool dampness of the tunnel, where her steps echoed off the wet, grafitti-covered walls. Then through to the expanse of gray blue water, where seagulls, shrill and complaining. swooped overhead. Finally over to the boarded up snack shop, to a wobbly picnic table worn bare by loitering teenagers. She sat down reluctantly. *Where the hell is he?*

Next to the building was a chain link fence marking the end of the park. And there was the tree Sally remembered so well. The first time she saw it, the trunk had just begun to grow into the fence, its bark bulging through the chain links, looking like a burnt waffle. Sally was always sorry for it, as if it were in pain. The tree was still there, the fence now completely embedded in its side. *Absorb and move on.*

When she heard the sound of Cash's car, she sat up straight and tried to breathe normally. He parked, leaped out, and came toward her. *Striding.* She was sure of it. It gave her the wild idea that they might go into the bushes and make out. But when he got close to the picnic table he stopped abruptly and put his hands on his hips.

"Hey," he said with a flip of his chin. As in *get to the point.*

She looked at him. "I'm pregnant."

He grimaced like she'd told a bad joke. His mouth opened, then closed. He shook his head.

"You're *what?*"

"Jeez! Why does everyone make me repeat it?"

He came closer. "Are you sure?"

"I've been to the doctor."

Now he seemed stunned. "But…"

"You don't love me, do you?" she blurted. It wasn't what she planned to say.

"Love?" Like it had never occurred to him.

"Yeah, you know. Intense feeling. Like you want to be with someone. Like you care."

"I care," he said.

"Then where have you been?"

"You know I've been working. With your dad."

She frowned. "He's not my dad."

"He calls himself that."

She was startled. "He talks about me?" Silly, she felt like she'd been given a compliment.

"He doesn't know about *us*, if that's what you mean."

Us, like they were a couple! For a moment she felt the way she had in Cash's car, driving to Kalamazoo, when she had believed everything would work out so perfectly for her.

It wasn't too late.

"Haven't you wanted to see me?" she asked.

He looked away a moment. "I thought I'd give you some time."

"Time for what?"

He shrugged. "You know, to work out your family stuff."

She stared at him.

"You know. Like who your dad is gonna be. Stuff like that."

As if she could just decide! She wished it were that simple. But she couldn't make up her mind about anything. Big stuff, such as, whom did she love? Who deserved a second chance? And little stuff, like when to use the word *dad.*

"Why are we talking about this anyway?" she said.

"I'm just saying I work with the guy now. It would be a little awkward, okay?"

"I'm telling you I'm *pregnant!* That's about as awkward as you can get!"

Cash started pacing around. "Jesus," he said finally. "Are you sure? Are you really absolutely sure?"

Sally nodded and he smacked his fist against his hand. "Damn it! I can't deal with this now." He spun in a little circle, like he was looking for a way out.

"Sorry," Sally said angrily. "Is this a bad time? Did you get a scholarship to Harvard? Hey, I know! NASA called and they want to send you to the moon. Or did you get drafted?"

"That's not funny. What if I am drafted? You're lucky I've got such a high number."

"You're right," she said. "I've never felt so lucky."

He looked hurt. "If that's the way you feel I'll go volunteer right now. Go get my head blown off. That make you happy?"

"Calm down. I didn't mean it."

He put his hands in his hair. "This is totally fucked up. I gotta get my head around this."

"I didn't think you'd take it so hard."

"Why not? You think I'm such a scumbag? You think this sort of thing happens to me all the time?"

She looked away. Okay, maybe she hadn't thought that exactly, but something close to it. Mostly she'd thought of how her own life would be ruined.

"Lots of people would like to believe it," he said, "but… I've got my job. I…I can find us a place to live."

So he had thought of her! A person doesn't say something like that unless there's been some thought.

"I'm only sixteen!" she said. But it *could* happen. They could get married with their parents' consent. Would she have to ask Pastor Voss for his permission? Or Richard? She had *his* last name. Maybe legally he was responsible for her. She might be stuck with both of them. Imagine, Pastor Voss performing her wedding. Richard walking her down the aisle. It was almost funny, except that Cash was looking wild-eyed and distraught and far from funny.

"What do you want me to say?" he cried.

"I want to know if you love me! We're supposed to be in love. That's how it was supposed to happen."

"So you want me to marry you, is that it?"

"What do *you* want?"

"I sure as hell don't want to get married while I'm still in high school! And if you say you do you're crazy."

"I just don't know how you could…" she stopped, not knowing what to call what they did. Had sex. Made love. Or, the worse, *fucked.* "How you could…do *that* with a person and then just disappear?"

His eyes searched the sand dunes, the parking lot, looking at anything but her. "I should have come sooner. I wanted to. But I didn't want you to think…" he trailed off.

"What?"

"I didn't want you to expect too much."

Oh. She *was* a fool.

"I told you I didn't want a girlfriend. You knew that!"

"That was before you..." There was that damn word again.

"Oh, what do you call it?" she asked, exasperated. "What do you call what we did?"

He looked at her strangely. So he thought she was a lunatic. So he was finding out he didn't like her at all. Didn't she know it would happen?

"You mean in casual conversation?" he said. "Like when I'm chatting with your dad?"

"You don't have to be sarcastic. I just want to know, what was it to you? Sex? A quick lay? Were we making love?"

He groaned. "God no. We're teenagers. We were screwing around, that's all."

That's *all.*

"I'll tell that to the kid," she said.

"For *chrissake*, I'm sorry! God, my parents are going to kill me!"

It seemed he might cry. Sally didn't expect that.

"You don't love *me*, do you?" he asked suddenly.

Or that.

"What if I do? What if I said I loved you the minute I saw you behind the counter at the Texaco? What if I said we should get married?"

She didn't mean it! But please, for *once*, couldn't she be the one to walk away?

"I'd say your hormones have got you thinking all crazy-like," he said. "You don't know anything about me."

As if that was all love was! Knowing facts or history. She didn't know much about her father either, but—she saw it now—she loved him. The shock of it was electric, especially since the person she was thinking about was Richard. All the years she'd spent wanting him must have somehow changed her cells, until he truly was a part of her. More biological than Pastor Voss.

Did that mean she'd decided?

And what did that mean for her baby? For her and Cash?

She tried to pick her words carefully. "Have you ever thought that these things happen for a reason? That maybe love is just choosing someone?"

He looked her straight in the face. "No," he said, and it felt like cold water. They'd never looked at each other like this. Not even in his car, when their faces were touching. Looking into someone's eyes and not having to look away, was *that* love? Because she couldn't do it.

"I'm sorry," he said, "but we're not playing house here."

He was right. He couldn't be any kind of father. Any more than she could be a mother. Anyway, it wasn't the baby she wanted. It was him. Or if not him, then someone.

"You might not need to tell your parents," she said.

"Why?"

"I can go to Grand Rapids and, you know, take care of it."

His face went slack. "You'd do that?" he asked.

"Believe it or not, Voss would take me," she said. *That's* what she'd call him. Voss. And Richard would be Dad. It was only a matter of deciding.

Cash stopped in front of her and rubbed his hands together.

"I'm not sure how I feel about that," he said quietly.

She didn't know why, but this made her angrier than ever. "Nobody is sure about anything!" she said. "But if I'm going to do it, I've got to go on Saturday. I don't want anyone here to find out."

"I'll come with you."

Maybe she *could* marry him. Wasn't he a decent guy? Why'd he have to be so decent after she made up her mind?

"No," she said. "I have to go alone."

"Why?"

"It's supposed to look like a party. Girls only. I have to wear a magenta dress."

"Jesus," he said. He seemed to consider this. "I don't even know what magenta is."

"It's like pinky-purple, I think. Or red."

"Are you scared?" he asked. "I mean, how do you know it's safe?"

"The doctor has been doing it for twenty years, I guess. The pastor knows him."

"How much does it cost?"

"Three hundred dollars."

He whistled. "Holy shit."

"Lenny gave me most of it. Pastor Voss is paying the rest."

He shook his head. "*Lenny?* This just keeps getting weirder. I'll pay him back."

"He won't take it."

"Then I'll give you the money and you can give it to him."

"Where am I supposed to say I got it?" she said.

"Say what you want. I want to pay him back."

"What about Voss? You want to pay him back too?"

He thought a moment. "Nah, screw him. But *Lenny.* Where would he get three hundred bucks?"

Sally shrugged. "I didn't ask."

"So that's that, huh?"

Panic seized her.

"Cash? What's going to happen with us?" Embarrassed, she went on. "I mean, will we go to the movies and hold hands? Should I have you over for dinner? Or do we act like, you know, nothing happened?"

He stuffed his hands in his pockets and shuffled his feet.

"You want me to buy you a teddy bear or something?"

She saw he was serious.

"No thanks."

He nodded a moment, then gave her a long look. "I've got to get to work. You want a ride?"

She shook her head and watched him go, thinking *I had sex with him!* Over and over like a drumbeat in her head. But the truth of that was already fading. Replaced by this: one day far from now Cash might pass her on the street. If she was with someone who loved her, *truly* loved her, say a husband, or maybe a father, she might point and say *See that guy? He once got me pregnant.* That someone would stop and stare. *Say that again?*

But she wouldn't. She was so tired of repeating it. Besides, the more you say a thing, the less it means.

Nell

It's difficult to hear yourself described in certain terms—irresponsible, unprofessional, lacking judgment—when you know yourself to be the exact opposite. Just as you know that the more you protest, the more desperate and guilty you appear. Besides, actions alone tell the truth. Hadn't Nell been reminded of that when her eighth grade friend Mary—the last real friend Nell had—bragged about being such a great cook, and then *right in front of Nell* put a half-eaten sandwich in the refrigerator with no plastic wrap covering it? See, Nell saw these connections where other people didn't. So she didn't say much when Sergeant Van Zandt said she was being suspended from her job for two weeks and suggested she think about the qualities required of members of the Auxiliary Police Department. She knew she'd have to find some way to prove herself.

Mandy's case was her best chance. She had an appointment at the Department of Human Services that very day.

If only she weren't feeling so down. Normally a mood like this could be improved by writing in her diary, but she'd given that up. Its orderly lined pages infuriated her, implying as they did that life's events could be strung together in a pleasantly slanted line, I's dotted, T's crossed. Writing her thoughts down would not change the fact that the house was a despicable mess, what with her mother picking up extra shifts at the plant, and Sally moping around, lazy and weepy. Worthless, actually. As if she were the only one humiliated by what happened at the banquet. Not caring that Nell had not been to church since that night. That she'd probably never go back. That she'd lost the one thing that gave her strength.

She went to the bathroom to brush her hair before heading over to the city services building. There, leaning against the faucet, was an envelope with her name on it in Sally's writing. Puzzled, Nell took the letter into the living room and opened it.

Dear Nell,

You'd better sit down because I have some news for you and it will be a shock. I have thought long and hard about whether to tell you this and I finally decided that although you are mostly a pain in the butt (here Sally had drawn a dopey smiley face) you are my sister and you should know. So here it is. The reason I did not come home that night is I was with Cash. I let things get carried away, and by that I mean that I went all the way with him. I know what you're thinking and since you will already hate me for this, let me warn you it gets worse. I am pregnant. Yes it is for sure. Mom took me to Dr. Maas. So you see I don't really have the flu. The final piece of news is that I am not going to have the baby. Pastor Voss is going to take me to a special place in Grand Rapids to have the procedure. Do not try to talk me out of it because it is what's best for me and it is my life. Sorry, Nell. I have messed up good. I don't expect you to forgive me, but you don't have to bother yelling at me either. I already know.

Love, Sally.

Nell's hand flew to her heart. The news was like the blast of a shotgun, delivering not one stinging wound, but a rash of them. Sally had sex. Sally was *pregnant*. She was planning…an *abortion?*

She sank into the sofa, seeing things she didn't want to see. A dark car and a boy's long sinewy arms. Sally's head thrown back. Revulsion flooded her, followed by this: *What was it like?*

She shuddered, ashamed and confused.

This wasn't how it was supposed to happen! First Nell would get married and have her wedding night. Then she would sit on the edge of the bed and have a sisterly talk with Sally about sex. She'd tell her what to expect when it was her time. When she was married. Nell would tell her how beautiful it was. God promised that. But there was nothing beautiful about being sixteen and doing it with a greasy long-haired mechanic.

And what was this about Pastor Voss?

Instinctively she reached for the phone. She had to talk to her mother! She had to hear it from her! *Why didn't you tell me?*

she'd ask.

She stopped. Had the pastor told Prudy about the terrible scene with Nell in his office? She imagined him and Sally and her mother sitting in the back booth of some empty diner off the interstate, crumpled tissues littering the table, their coffee turning cold in untouched cups, making a pact to keep Nell out of this. Sally saying *You know how she is.* The pastor murmuring in agreement. *Such a good heart, but her expectations are just completely unrealistic.* He and Prudy exchanging a glance.

How dare he have any part of this!

Oh, she wanted to strangle Sally! How could she *do* such a thing? She felt it personally, as if Sally had said *Oh yes, Cash, let's have sex! It'll drive my sister crazy!* Did she for a moment consider Nell or their mother or her Christian upbringing? At what point did Sally decide that nothing else mattered but her own selfish desires?

And, a baby! The idea that Sally was capable of having a baby was as surprising as seeing a dog twirl on its hind legs wearing a tutu. It was a trick you might see on television, some glassy, far-away possibility. Your own dog was never more than just a dog, fleas and all.

As for *abortion*, she couldn't even think of that without a sort of veering off, panicky feeling. No one Nell knew would ever consider such a thing. And anyone who *would* consider it was someone she didn't want to know.

She couldn't let her go through with it, that much she knew. But how would she stop her?

Nell looked at the letter again. *I don't expect you to forgive me*, Sally wrote. Tears sprang to Nell's eyes because Sally was right. Nell couldn't forgive this. In her heart she would always know that her only sister—the sister Nell was meant to have, the one Sally was meant to be—was gone. That's how final it seemed. Like Sally was forever lost.

Nell followed a receptionist down a dingy carpeted hallway to a room marked *Mrs. Van Dam, Department of Family Services.* She was here to talk about Mandy, but all of that seemed strangely distant in light of this latest bombshell. She had a folding-in sense that brought to mind the time she saw, on television, a building being demolished. Though the sound was turned down, she would swear the room she was in vibrated as, on screen, foundation and façade gave way and walls imploded in a graceful, relieving collapse.

Nell would crumble just as silently. Facing the caseworker, a harried-looking older woman with an untidy bun and a cardigan that was pilling at the elbows, only her hands trembled. When the woman motioned for her to sit down in a gray metal chair, the plopping-down sound she made was not as loud as she feared.

"It says here that Mona Veenstra has left town," Mrs. Van Dam said. "Can you confirm this?"

Nell nodded mutely. *Procedure.* That was the word Sally used. Nicer than murder, which was what it was. A roar rose in her ears.

"What makes you think the girl's stepmother is gone?"

Nell tried to focus. "I saw her leave with a suitcase and she hasn't been back."

"I understand that you live right downstairs?" Mrs. Van Dam asked. "And that you work for the police department?"

Nell winced. That life lay in ruins.

"I've been suspended, actually," she said, surprised that she sounded so calm. "Mrs. Veenstra and I had an altercation and the Sergeant is reviewing the details."

Mrs. Van Dam nodded. "And the father says he's made arrangements with you to watch the child…Mandy, is it? While he works."

"That's right." Mr. Veenstra was switching to third shift. He'd offered Nell $25 a week to let Mandy sleep on a cot in Nell's room. Nell would take her at seven p.m., already fed and in her pajamas, put her to sleep at eight, and give her breakfast in the morning before sending her back upstairs. It would be easy work for Nell. Too easy. She wanted the satisfaction of doing more.

"Tell me about that," Mrs. Van Dam said mildly.

"Uh…" Maybe not so easy. Nell would be under the microscope now, something she hadn't considered. Would the social worker make surprise visits to check up on her? To make sure there were locks on the doors, and milk in the refrigerator? What would she think of the Van Sloeten family? Here's my sister. Pregnant teen. My mother. Adulteress. Oh, and my father? Drunk. My brother Lenny? Delinquent. Was Nell so damaged that she couldn't take on a simple babysitting job?

"I haven't started yet," Nell mumbled, suddenly afraid to say anything. The wrong words from her and they might open a file on *her* family.

Mrs. Van Dam spread her hands in front of her. "Who lives in your household? What are the sleeping arrangements? What is your schedule like?"

"I have my own room. So does my mother and my sister." Nell hesitated. Technically, Lenny did not live with them, so why mention him? "Mandy will sleep in my room. It's very quiet. And..." She put on a bright face, as in *here comes the best part!...* "as I said, I have no job commitments at the moment. I don't have a social life. I don't go out evenings. My sister and mother both go to bed early." She shrugged and laughed self-consciously. "It's a pretty dull household, actually."

Her heart was pounding as Mrs. Van Dam went on looking at her. If she didn't stop staring, Nell would surely blurt out everything. Including the abortion plan. Then would Sally be arrested? Would they put some undercover cops on her tail and let her lead them to the lawbreakers who pretended to be doctors?

She *ought* to tell! But, really, what good would it do? Except for Lenny, no part of this Van Sloeten family saga was criminal. Yet. Mrs. Van Dam would only say something worthless. *Might I suggest a member of the clergy to help?* And Nell would laugh, one of those edgy, maniacal laughs. Oh, if you only knew!

"Well, we'll be watching the situation closely. If the stepmother is gone, there shouldn't be any more problems."

Nell couldn't hold back. "Getting rid of someone doesn't solve anything!"

Mrs. Van Dam looked surprised. "How do you mean?"

She swallowed. She didn't know what she meant. Maybe Sally was right. Why bring an unwanted child into the world? Just look at the stack of files on this woman's desk. Each one no doubt full of the most depressing details. Kids like Mandy—beaten, neglected, *murdered.*

Nell's own childhood hadn't exactly been a picnic. As if to remind her, a wave of doubt and loneliness washed over her. The loss of her dad had seemed, at one time, ocean-deep, pushing and pulling her. But growing up was the tide receding. She was proud of the fact that she could shake it off. She thanked the Lord for her maturity. But *Sally?* Sally wasn't equipped to raise a baby!

Wait. The answer was like an eager hand shooting up. I can do it! Let *me!*

"Can I ask you something?" Nell said slowly. "How difficult is it to adopt a member of your own family?"

Mrs. Van Dam seemed confused. "It depends. As a single woman? Aahhh..." She clucked her tongue and grimaced.

Nell sighed. Being Old Nellie the spinster, dying alone of cancer, wasn't punishment enough. No, she had to endure The System and all its stupid rules crushing an idea that was taking root, growing, spreading like a high speed film clip of a sprouting seed. Why should Sally kill the life inside her when Nell was so willing to love it and raise it and have it *as her own?*

"Are you assuming I'm single?" Nell asked.

"Well, yes, because you said..."

"But what if I was married?" She might just as soon imagine being a brain surgeon, or a rock star. What man would want her? It took only a split second for her to see her wedding, ruined by her dad crashing drunk down the aisle, hanging on her intended's arm. *Personally I never liked her much. Guess there's no accounting for taste.*

"I don't follow," said Mrs. Van Dam. "You're not related to Mandy Veenstra, are you?"

Nell didn't appreciate being grilled on the subject. "Unless you mean in the Christian sense, no," she said primly. "No relation."

"Then I'm not sure—"

Nell stood abruptly. "Mrs. Van Dam, you've been very helpful."

The real question now was what single men did she know? It wasn't like choosing a book off a shelf, running a finger along so many spines, deciding which was best to curl up with under the covers. She'd have to settle for a tattered copy. Cover torn off. Bargain basement price.

Who? Who did she know?

She turned and walked purposefully down the corridor, hardly noticing the drab aqua walls, the woman in the waiting room fanning herself with a copy of Reader's Digest, the boy in overalls with a drippy nose. What she saw was herself, holding a baby, one hand cradling the soft, pulsing head, her arm tucked tightly around the tiny bottom. She was in her own kitchen, her own house, finding fulfillment in all the ordinary things.

All she needed was a man.

Back home, Nell moved deliberately around the house, waiting for the idea to dissolve into doubt. Instead, a peacefulness descended. A clarity so strong she found herself reaching for her diary. Not to question, but to plan. There were lists to make, under headings such as: Husband Hunting. What a Baby Needs. How to Convince Sally.

She brought the diary out to the front porch. Opening it, another list jumped out at her. One she had written weeks ago, when she first found out her father was in town.

What I Want To Know:

Where did you go?

Why didn't you call?

Do you think about me?

Something caught in her throat and it came to her, momentarily, that she might be in the midst of a kind of breakdown, perhaps caused by seeing her father after all these years. She was no psychologist, but maybe that, followed by the shock of learning that the pastor was Sally's father, then the news of Sally being pregnant, was making her delusional.

As she began to write, she noticed a man coming down the sidewalk, and something about him made her look twice. The walk! The little hop, the swing of the arm. Her father! She slammed the diary shut, feeling a tingle on the back of her neck, that breath of God that comes with coincidence too uncanny to explain. She wondered if her questions had somehow conjured this visit. He must be coming to see Sally, who was at school. Or her mother, who was at work. Maybe he was looking for Lenny, but Nell had no idea where Lenny was.

She watched and realized: he was looking at *her.* More than looking. He was *seeing* her. She smoothed her skirt and waited. Okay, they'd be alone. Just the two of them. She could say anything she wanted to him. But she could feel all the questions flying away, already up in flames. Was there anything she could ask that would make him say he loved her? She'd imagined that for so long, in so many ways, but now she didn't think she'd ever hear it. Well, she'd live. Anyway, love was a funny thing. Not the steady stream of affection she'd always thought. Hadn't her own heart changed? Hadn't she felt, if only for a moment, that she could never love her mother again? Or Sally? Hadn't she seen that hate and love were not so far apart after all? Just a wispy thread between them.

What he said now didn't matter. He'd noticed her. If he didn't like what he saw, it was his own damn problem. She watched him come closer, and when he was in front of Mrs.

Dekker's house she raised her hand and waved. She felt calm, ready. She opened her mouth, said "Hi Dad," and it was like she'd been saying it all her life.

Nell took her mother's lipstick tubes, one by one, from the makeup bag in the drawer and lined them up on the counter. Candied Almond. Pink Pansy. Softest Mauve. She chose one called Persimmon and carefully applied it, then blotted her lips with a folded piece of toilet tissue.

Seeing her dad had boosted her confidence. You wouldn't even call it an official visit. *Just wanted to say hi*, he'd said. *Have yourself a nice day.* But he was sober. That alone was intoxicating.

Outside, she forced herself to step lightly and swing her pocketbook a little. See? Carefree. That's how she'd look to anyone who saw her. Not like a woman with a hare-brained scheme to snare yet *another* man. As if the debacle with Pastor Voss had taught her nothing. She'd been so foolish then. This time her eyes were wide open. For one thing, she was not in love. She'd even had to ask Mrs. Dekker *what's Gizzy's name?* It was Gerald Ten Harmsel, and that was ok. She could see it: Nell Ten Harmsel. She didn't know much about him, but she had noticed a thing or two. He carried white labels with him to replace names that were peeling off mailboxes, writing them out carefully in pleasing block letters. He liked to announce the arrival of catalogs and magazines. *Time to order spring bulbs!* he'd call. *Holiday cookie issue just in!*

Not exactly presidential commendations. But it was at least

as much to go on as her Victorian-era sisters would have had. Back then a woman got some starchy chit-chat and a few turns about the drawing room and *voila!* she was engaged. Even today, in some parts of the world, a girl might not meet her betrothed until the wedding day. Not that Nell believed in arranged marriage. But, really, there were worse things. Like being alone. Or standing by watching innocent lives destroyed.

She'd simply present the possibility of a union to Gizzy. As long as she wasn't drippy or emotional, she'd have no reason to be embarrassed. If he wasn't interested, so what? She'd keep looking. His loss.

She popped into the Salt Shaker on the way and picked out a giant wedge of blueberry pie with a crystal crust of sugar on top. As she waited at the counter for the waitress to wrap it, she took in the lunch crowd, the regulars arguing amiably about the Tigers, some girlfriends gossiping over salads and cigarettes, businessmen who tucked napkins over their ties. For a moment she had a sickening sense of being invisible, then the waitress handed her a white bag and said, *'bye hon*, and she was back in the game. She felt it again—the optimism, like a sip of something bubbly.

Pie in hand, she walked the remaining blocks to Gizzy's house. It was a small red brick bungalow near a busy intersection. Beside the front steps lay the twisted frame of his bike, a reminder of the wreck her life had become. She'd brought on his accident with a simple wave. *Hi! Over here!* Sally had done much the same and brought on a different disaster. *Hey Dad! Remember me?* Wanting to be noticed. What trouble it caused!

She took a deep breath and knocked.

When she heard his crutches thumping toward the door,

she fought the urge to run. There was only time to breathe a quick *please, God, please spare me complete humiliation* before the door opened and there he was. She noticed the black hair springing off his forehead, the bushy eyebrows that were really quite nice.

"Hi," she said. He was wearing flimsy cotton shorts, his right leg jutting out in a cast that went from the ankle to above the knee, his left leg bare and hairy. On top he wore a regular button-down shirt, so the effect was one of being *undressed.* She felt herself blush. She had never seen an undressed man before.

"I brought you some pie."

"Oh! Well...marvelous. Look at that!"

He kept nodding. A little stupidly, Nell thought. Then it occurred to her, he might not know who she was. Should she tell him? It's Nell VanSloeten. You *know.* You've delivered my mail for three years? Or maybe he'd heard The News and didn't want to socialize with her family anymore. Or he could be numb with pain, distracted by the throb in his leg.

"So…" she said, offering up the Styrofoam box with both hands.

He laughed. "I would take it, but…" He motioned down at his crutches.

"Oh! Of course." She was such an idiot, holding it out like that.

"Come in," he said. "You can set it in the kitchen."

She managed a smile. "That's right. You sit down and rest that leg."

She ventured timidly inside, past the front room, which looked shabby and cramped, a miss-mash of books and clothes and electrical parts and ….old radios? Was he was one of those eccentric bachelors, up all night fiddling with a screwdriver, hunched over a flickering light bulb, reading diagrams? And the kitchen! Dishes filled the sink and the linoleum was peeling along one wall. There was a funny smell of stale coffee and bacon grease, and on the counter sat an open jar of peanut butter with a spoon stuck in it.

She put the pie in the refrigerator, careful not to look too closely at the wrapped plates and cardboard containers lurking inside. Returning, she saw that he was easing himself into a chair. He motioned for her to sit, but she shook her head. She was too nervous. Besides, if she sat too close he might notice the largeness of her thighs. Instead, she tried to lean casually against a little half wall that jutted between the foyer and the living room. She carefully crossed her legs at the ankles and clasped her hands like she'd seen Doris Day do. She wobbled. It wasn't easy.

There was a pause before he cleared his throat.

"How's your sister?" The careful way he said it gave him away.

She felt her pose sag. "So you heard."

And he didn't even know the worst of it!

He nodded. "That's got to be rough, finding out about her dad that way. If you want, tell her I'm thinking of her. And praying for her."

A Christian man! She'd take it as a sign.

"I just wanted to say how sorry I am that I called out your name like that," she said.

He shrugged. "I've always been a klutz. This isn't the first time I broke my leg."

"Really?"

"Yeah. I did a back flip off a trampoline when I was nine. That's why I like delivering mail. If I don't walk a lot it starts aching real bad."

She would know just what to do! Soak it in Epsom salt, rub it with alcohol, wrap it in a warm towel. This reminded her that she was sort of auditioning here, whether he realized it or not.

"Why don't I get you that pie?" she said. "You should enjoy it now, while I'm here to help."

She found a clean plate in a kitchen cupboard and set the pie on it carefully. As long as she was there, she opened a few more cupboard doors and took a quick look. No alcohol. Another good sign. And there was more satisfaction in the way Gizzy wasted no time digging in. Who knew taking care of a man could be so rewarding? While he ate, Nell took the opportunity to look more closely at him. How many years had he been delivering their mail? It seemed forever, but this was the first time she'd ever studied him. His neck was beginning to fold over his collar. So he was a little fat. She was no broomstick herself. The important thing was that he had a good government job. Most likely he had a wonderful sense of civic duty. The two of them in their uniforms, what a handsome couple they'd make!

Couple. The word made her shiver. Couples held hands. They hugged and kissed and called each other *sweetie* or *honey bunch.* They had sex.

Her knees began to shake. Maybe it was the clutter around her that caused it; the memory she kept tidy and polished and tucked away crashed before her. It was that last day with her dad. Lenny's birthday, ten years ago, when she'd seen him on top of her mother in the bedroom.

"What was he doing?" she had asked her mother.

She could still see Prudy's pained look. "He wanted to do a private, loving thing that two people do when they're married," she said. "But he wasn't doing it in a loving way. He was being very mean. You saw how he was being."

"Was he trying to multiply?"

Nell was ten years old and she knew all about that. The Lord said go forth and multiply, and that was when two married people rubbed together with their clothes off.

"Not exactly," Prudy said. "He wanted to do that same thing, but not to multiply. Just for fun."

Fun? Nell still recalled the surprise of that idea. And the cold finger of fear that followed.

How could she be sure a man would never hurt her that way? She hadn't worried about it with Pastor Voss because he looked and acted so gentle. But Gizzy was a big man. A man who disemboweled appliances!

He chewed and swallowed a big bite of pie, then burped softly into his napkin. Suddenly Nell was repulsed. Men were so crude, with their dirty dishes and unwashed clothes. Their drinking problems and lustful ways! Even her brother Lenny was disgusting, always popping his knuckles, picking his teeth, or passing gas.

"I'd better go," she said, frantically backing toward the door.

"Hey, what for? Stay awhile." He looked genuinely disappointed. It was almost enough to stop her.

But Sally's baby. That did stop her. She took a deep breath, trying to stem the tide of doubt. Carefully, she perched on the edge of the chair across from him in what she hoped was an attractive posture.

"Tell me a little about yourself," she said.

He talked easily about his parents, who lived in a trailer park in Allegan, and his younger brother, who was in the Army, stationed in Germany, and for a moment Nell was lulled into thinking she was in a normal situation. Just an ordinary girl! But putting off the inevitable wouldn't make it any easier.

"*So*...Gizzy. How do you feel about marriage?" As if it had anything to do with their conversation.

"Marriage?" His eyes narrowed. He seemed to be giving her question some serious thought. "Marriage is good."

"Do you plan to get married?"

"Ah, well. That all depends."

She felt the sweat pop out on her forehead and tried to casually wipe it with the back of her hand.

"On what?" she asked.

He smiled. "I guess on whether someone would have me."

It was so simple, when it was put that way.

She looked out the window, down the street to where the streetlight blinked yellow. *Caution. Curve ahead.* She took a deep breath and quietly said, "I'd have you."

She heard the sound his mouth made as it opened. She didn't dare look at him. "Gosh," he said, "That's nice of you."

She felt lightheaded. No going back now. "Would you want to marry me?"

There was a long pause. "Is this hypothetical?" he said.

She looked at him and tried to make her voice light. "Just pretend I'm serious."

He laughed awkwardly, then fell silent. "You're taking me by surprise here," he said slowly.

This was it. She could either go all soft and make a complete fool of herself, or stick to her plan. She stood up.

"Look, here's the deal. We've known each other for years." (She would never tell him she hadn't known his real name!) "I like the way you..." Oh, this was tough. "...*are*. So punctual. Always cheerful. You're an excellent mail carrier. And you have nice eyes," she added.

“Thank you,” he mumbled.

“And I don’t see the point of all that lovey-dovey crap, if you’ll pardon my expression.” She put her hands on her hips to punctuate her point.

He leaned forward carefully and rested his elbows on his knees.

“Well,” he said finally. “You make the best lemonade on my whole route, and your flowers are very well cared for. And,” he shrugged sheepishly, “I like the way you laugh.”

Laugh? When did she ever laugh? The idea that he might see her as cheerful (watch out Daisy!) stunned and delighted her. She didn’t know what to say.

“So how about we go out somewhere?” he said. “Maybe grab some dinner?”

A date! She knew it was absurd now, after what she’d said, but she’d always wanted to go on a date.

“Ok, sure.”

“Tonight? I can’t drive, but if you don‘t mind walking over, we can go to that little joint across the street.”

It was her turn to nod stupidly. She pointed at the door.

“So I guess I’ll go now.”

He struggled to get up. She rushed over to take his arm and with a jolt realized she was touching him! He smiled and put his hand over hers.

“I’m really glad you stopped by,” he said.

“Me too.”

She handed him his crutches and he hobbled beside her to the front door. They said goodbye and she looked up to see him still looking at her. Like he was really seeing her. It was just like the moment on her porch with her father, as if she’d stepped through a door, into herself. *Come on in. I’ve been waiting for you.* What was happening, that she was suddenly a *presence?* She floated down the stairs. Not exactly carefree, but possibly as close as she'd ever come.

"Hey, Nell," he called.

She turned.

"Do you want kids?"

She did laugh then. A beautiful, tinkling sound that only comes when God has tapped you on the shoulder, singling you out. As if to say *you did it! I always knew you could.*

When the time finally came to talk to Sally, it was not the heart-hammering, *how-do-I-begin?* moment Nell had imagined. Instead, she ran into her sister in the hallway as Sally was coming out of the bathroom. Instinctively, Nell threw her arms around her and hugged her roughly, with all the finesse she'd shown in Pastor Voss' office. Sally stiffened, and no wonder. Nell was realizing what an unaffectionate person she was. She resolved to change. In the meantime, she pulled away and studied her hands.

"Sally, we have to talk."

Sally crossed her arms. "There's nothing to talk about."

"Have you thought about adoption?" Nell said bluntly. No finesse here either.

Sally sighed and walked away. Nell followed her into the kitchen.

"Well?"

"I couldn't live with that," Sally said, shaking her head angrily. "Knowing some stranger out there has my kid."

Exasperation flared in Nell. So soon! She tried to keep her voice even.

"But you can live with abortion."

"I just want it to be over." Sally opened the refrigerator and peered inside. "I'm starving."

Nell waited while Sally opened a carton of cottage cheese, sniffed it, and put it back.

"There are places you can go, to have the baby," she said. "You don't have to stay here."

"And miss a whole year of school? People aren't dumb. They would figure it out."

"That doesn't matter."

"Easy for you to say!"

"Actually, it's not."

Sally gave up foraging and slammed the refrigerator door.

"It's happening to *me*. It's my decision."

Nell sat down at the table, hoping to hide her irritation. This was not the way a person acted when she's done something wrong. Sally ought to show remorse. Humble herself! Nell had had to do it with Sergeant Van Zandt, head hung low, murmuring *I'm sorry* about twenty times. Was it easy? No. But she wouldn't dream of being belligerent.

"I'd take the baby," she said. "If you wanted to have it."

Nell could see she'd thrown her for a loop, though Sally answered casually.

"What would *you* do with a baby?"

"Take care of it, what else?"

"Nell, really! Then both of us would be ruined. I'd be the slut, you'd never be able to go to school, or have a job. Everyone would look down their noses at us!"

"They already do."

"So why make it worse?"

Nell stood, too agitated to be still. "Sally, I've thought this through! You could go away for a while. And, well, I might get married. People would think the baby was mine."

Sally scoffed. "Who's going to marry you?"

This was no time to feel hurt. Anyway, it was a good question.

Nell shrugged. "I sort of asked Gizzy."

Now Sally looked shocked. "Gizzy? The *mailman?*"

Nell nodded, wishing she could enthuse about her upcoming date. Wouldn't she have liked to share this landmark with her only sister! Cheated again!

"What did he say?"

"He said he wants children." Nell spread her hands out, as if to say *see? See how this is meant to be?*

"Children of his own, not someone else's."

"Don't you think I'd be a good mother?"

"It's not you. The kid's whole life would be a lie, just like mine. I can't do that." Sally crossed her arms again. Everything about the way she stood, the look on her face, said *leave me alone*. Nell wanted to scream. That's right! Open up to a near stranger, *bare yourself!* But shut the door on a sister who only wants to talk!

"Sally, please. It could work!"

"I want to go to Hope College. Frannie's dad is going to get me in."

"You could still do that. Just later."

Sally gave a harsh little laugh. "Come on, Nell. You don't want me to go to college. Just because you haven't gone, you want to ruin it for me."

Nell had to bite her tongue. *She* ruined it! Was she in

the backseat of a car panting like an animal with a low-life mechanic?

"It's not about that."

"Then what is it? You love Gizzy?"

"You're so immature!" Nell snapped. "You think love is such a big deal?"

Sally gave her a wide-eyed stare. "Yeah."

"That just shows how childish you are. Anyway, why wouldn't I love him? What's wrong with him?"

"Nothing. Except a broken leg."

Nell's hand slammed the table. "Exactly! And whose fault is that?

"He was in an accident."

"Like I said, you're so childish."

There was a pause while Sally looked at her. Then, in a low, suggestive voice, she said, "In some ways I'm older than you. In fact, in one very big way."

Nell jumped up. "Anyone can do what you did," she cried. "The hard part is what comes after." She thumped her chest. "*I'm* willing to do the hard part."

"What about *my* hard part? I'd have to deliver it! Then just hand it off. What if I can't do it?"

They were shouting at each other. Just what Nell didn't want. She thought of the list she'd worked on so carefully: How to Convince Sally. Number one was *stay calm*. What a waste of time that wretched diary was!

She took a deep breath. "You *can* do it." she said, more quietly. "Please think about it."

Sally grew quiet too. At last she heaved a sigh, as if she were giving up. It made Nell freeze, expectant.

"I'm going to Grand Rapids," Sally said, her gaze level and

sure. “It’s for the best. You’ll see.”

She walked out and Nell didn’t try to stop her. She felt as if someone had thrown a blanket over her. A quilt, maybe, each square representing the work she’d willed herself into taking on. Gizzy’s filthy house. His ill-concealed burps. Her fear and fascination surrounding sex. The bedtime stories she was planning to read to Mandy. Little acts of civic duty to impress the local police. The salvation of her sister. Raising a *child.* The temptation to hide, to take cover and ignore all of it, was suddenly too strong. She was giving up.

Lenny

Lenny was not a team player. That's why none of the scouts wanted him. How they spotted it, he didn't know. He'd never known how people marked him with just a glance.

Anyway, the way he figured, whatever it was that marked him meant that leaving town was a waste of time. Ever since that day in the bleachers with his dad, he'd known he wasn't going anywhere. And when Sally told him her doctor visit was going to cost three hundred dollars, well, his old plans were a train leaving the station.

He pulled a sock out of the small chest of drawers that was in his basement room and took out the roll of bills he had hidden inside. Two hundred twenty seven dollars. Six months of working at the marina. He threw all his clothes into a duffel bag, tied a clean bandana on his head, grabbed his Slugger, and pulled the door shut behind him.

It didn't take long to walk home. He was a little unsure about where to put his things. Should he reclaim his room? Or crash on the couch? The fact that he hesitated bothered him. He no longer knew what to do. He was stepping into the outfield here, with no choice but to wait and see what would come his way.

Once the money was put in an envelope and left on Sally's bed, he picked up his bat and walked aimlessly back toward the church. He sat on the front steps, across from the Texaco, and studied the sky. It was a brilliant blue day, breezy, with cotton ball clouds tumbling over one another.

He waited. And thought.

Here's the thing about baseball: it can drag on for hours. Ho hum. Death by boredom. Then comes the crack of the bat. Physics in motion. Some molecular magic sends the ball deep to center field, but someone bobbles it and the second baseman misses the relay throw. Do you turn on the guy because of one error? Do you tear up his trading card? Even if you're not the greatest team player, you know enough to stick with him. You join the crowd as it roars and comes alive, and who knows? Maybe it's only that sudden energy, the perked up shoulders and stamping feet, that leads to bases loaded in less than five minutes. Who's to say what brings about the change? The point is, you can't ever give up. The optimism is there all along.

Sally

How many hundreds of girls had sat in a car beside their fathers to be driven to a football game, or sleepover, or dance class? How many of those girls had rolled their eyes over the same tired exchange: Drop me here. Not *too* close.

Give me a kiss, hon.

Dad, please!

Little pieces of father-daughter speak that Sally would never know. The same way she could never know that her first time catching a ride with her father would be *this*—going to an abortion. The worst part was that she was dressed like she was going to prom, in a starchy, purpley-pink dress.

"You look nice," Pastor Voss said after she'd settled herself awkwardly, her skirt balled carelessly in one hand so she could shut the door.

She scowled at him. He couldn't bother to shave? She thought of Richard and the night of the banquet. At least he had cleaned himself up.

He must have read her look. "Sorry. I've been living out of a suitcase."

Deliberately, she turned her face from him and watched the row of wood A-frame houses sliding away, not wanting to hear anything about where he'd gone or how he was living. When she first heard the news that he had left town, it was like a little trap door in her closing and blocking off a route that, given time, she might have considered taking. But now that she was sitting beside him, she felt only a curious flatness.

"How long until we're there?" she asked, and even her voice was flat.

He puffed out his cheeks and exhaled loudly. "*Psshew.* About thirty-five minutes, I'd say."

She waited to see what else he'd say. He remained silent and she tried to fix her mind elsewhere. There was the parking lot of Charlie's Market, where an old woman struggled in vain to unstick two shopping carts, and a scrappy-looking kid hopped on one foot, holding something smooth and brown in his baseball cap.

You never knew about people. Still, she felt certain that he didn't like her much. She considered asking him about it, but he'd only lie. *I like you. I ... well, I love you, of course*. Then she'd feel worse. This is love?

She thought again of Richard. It bothered her that she kept wondering things like, where was he right now? Would Lenny tell him where Sally was going, and why? Would she ever tell him herself? Or, for that matter, would she ever see him again? And the most disturbing of all: why did she care? Why was she wasting time feeling mushy over someone who didn't belong to her?

Whistle, *whoosh* was the sound of Voss' breathing. Sally found it odd and unpleasant and it made her cringe. Richard would be chatty, at least. For all his bluster, his hooks and barbs would be just the thing to pin down this empty, floaty feeling that had descended over her recently.

It must be the pregnancy. One moment nodding off, eyelids made of lead. The next swallowing hard against a rolling, churning storm in her stomach. She preferred the relative peace of this flatland. In this state, when she thought of the fetus inside her sapping away her life force, leaving her a useless, hollow shell, she wasn't overcome with fright. Besides, the nothingness ought to be familiar. She'd been seeing it for years in Pastor Voss' face when he looked at her. She'd heard it in Richard's voice when he announced to the world that she was a bastard child. She was nothing to them. And now, she was nothing at all but a receptacle for some errant, poisonous seed. The sooner she could have it extracted, the sooner she'd return to herself.

"Why couldn't my mom come?" she asked in a thick voice. Her mouth was dry and tasted of bile.

He let out a heavy sigh. "This is tough on her."

Sally smiled weakly and shook her head.

"It's complicated," he added.

"If she thinks you and I are going to make up for lost time or something stupid like that..."

"Honestly, I don't know what she thinks." She heard the edge in his voice and studied him a moment. No. There would be no making up. She may as well ask.

"Why are you doing this?"

He seemed to think. "You deserve a chance."

"Why?"

This made him move uncomfortably in his seat and make

a sound as if he would speak. She practically leaned toward him. Nothing. Again she was amazed that a man who delivered sermons every week could be so tongue-tied. *He really knows nothing about me!* She didn't know why, but this scared her. The floaty feeling intensified. With it came a disturbing darkness around the edges of her sight, as if she were a horse wearing blinders to keep from being spooked. She focused on the grainy vinyl of the dashboard. *I'm okay. It'll be over soon.*

But would it? She had set out to find her dad, to find a missing piece of herself. Instead, she felt parsed out, divided into too many pieces. There was the old Sally, unwilling to take her dear Uncle Ollie to the banquet, insisting on having everything just *so*, no matter what. There was the part or her that loved her sister and her brother and knew that the risks they'd taken for her required a courage that was at least equal to her own. And the part that hated them for it. And then the new Sally, who, whether she liked it or not, belonged to this sweating, sighing lump beside her.

How she longed to be anywhere but here! In another time, worlds away, she might be at Frannie's house, with Frannie's mother and father and nine-year-old brother Justin. They'd be pulling boxes of Chef Boy-ar-Dee mix from the cupboard, preparing for the Valkema Friday night ritual of pizza, Pepsi, and, for the grown-ups, a game of Rook. The Dorns would come, from down the street, or Mr. and Mrs. Dc Vricndt from church, and Sally, suddenly shy before these social, smiling creatures, would help Frannie fill their plastic tumblers with ice cubes and set soda cans beside each plate. Until they were eight years old, Frannie and Sally spent these evenings playing Barbie dolls, absorbing themselves in the minutia of Barbie's world: Barbie would *never* wear heels to a garden party! Well, she'd never accept another date with Ken either, after seeing him with *Skipper!* These nights, Sally felt safe in the bubble of childhood, buoyed by the presence of capable, God-like adults.

She wasn't a girl anymore. Just a few months ago Mr. Valkema had invited her and Frannie to join the adults in the card game. Sally had held the cards reverently, fanning them out the way she saw the others do. She had listened patiently as Mr. Valkema tried to explain trumping and bidding, but it was just so *boring*, and, with a single, flickering look at Frannie, the two of them had given up and rushed upstairs, laughing *Gawd!* Flopping dramatically on the bed. If *that* was what grownups called *fun*. Well, no thanks!

Only later would Sally remember sitting at that table and realize the honor of being invited. The Valkemas had seen it first, before she'd seen it herself. She was growing up. Speeding along in Voss' Galaxie 500, in this separate and alien universe, she recalled something else: Mr. Valkema saying to Mrs. Dorn *is that a new hairstyle, Regina?* Mrs. Dorn blushing and giggling like a girl, her fingertips brushing her bangs. Sally saw it now. They were *only people*. People who had known each other since grade school and still thought of one another as the child, then the teenager, each of them had been. Bald spots, hanging jowls, burgeoning waists —those didn't cloud the truth: no one really changes.

She understood, too, that being grown-up isn't who you are. It's what you do. That's why her mother couldn't come to Grand Rapids with her. This was one of those grown-up moments when you can't hold mommy's hand. It *has* to be hard.

"You know..." Voss said tentatively. "What you just asked. Well. I once knew a woman who became pregnant, and she was so afraid to have the baby that she tried to end the pregnancy herself, with a knitting needle."

Sally was listening to the faint, rhythmic thwacking sound of the tires on the highway. It was so soothing. She wished he would be quiet. "Hmmm," she said.

"Imagine that," he said.

She didn't answer. Vibrations were rising from the pavement, up through her legs and into her hollow belly.

"Imagine it," he repeated, fervently, so that she realized he wasn't being rhetorical.

"I'd rather not." Then, in spite of herself, "What happened?"

She saw him swallow.

"What would you say if I told you that the woman was your mother? The baby was you."

Sally went on looking at his Adam's apple. It was like a large walnut stuck in his throat, bobbing about. Watching it, she thought she might gag. She put her hand over her mouth.

"Do you see?"

"Don't speak to me," she said sharply. She understood now that she had to protect herself from these people, these reckless, childish people masquerading as adults. As *parents*. She felt ferocious, like a mother bear protecting her cub. But she wasn't protecting her baby. She was only protecting the part of herself that still believed she could get through this. *She had to get through this!*

"You asked why I'm doing this," he said defensively, his expression open and wounded.

She shook her head and groaned softly. She couldn't take one more word! Her mother *loved* her. Before she'd ever seen Sally's face, or held her in her arms, she'd loved her. That was the kind of woman she was.

But oh, the clarity! Sally could see how her mother

would feel, pregnant with an unwanted child. She knew the desperation. She felt its stranglehold on her even now, tightening by the second. Still, to pick up something sharp, and put it *there*. She squeezed her eyes shut, trying to block the thought of it.

"What else you got?" she said, her heart pounding fearfully. He was no different than a bully on a playground. The only way to end this was to push back. "Come on! Get it all off your chest."

His voice was so low, he might have been talking to himself. "I drove her to it. And then I hated her for it. Part of me hated you too, I guess. And another part…" he stopped and grimaced. "….*didn't*."

There was a long pause.

"Do you see?" he said again.

But the question of her mother's love for her was a black hole Sally was falling through. Dizzy and confused, she only knew that when the pain of it hit her, she'd die. She held fast to her knees and felt them shaking. *It's not so bad*, she told herself. *Not so bad.* It didn't change her situation, or stop her from straightening her own life out. Once this was finished she could walk away from her mistakes. Like her mother had tried to. Like Richard did. And now Voss. Yes, just like *them*, said some internal voice, weighted with disapproval. She felt her jaw clench. So what? Why not me, too!

Voss put a hand on her arm. "Sally, you shouldn't have lived. But you did. And you're all the more precious to Prudy because of it."

"*Precious?*" She was incredulous.

"That's how she feels!"

The word conjured all things baby: knit booties, downy soft sleepers, crocheted caps, plush stuffed puppies. Aside from the day Prudy took Sally to see Dr. Maas, Sally hadn't allowed herself to think about a *real baby.* Now, images flashed before her like a giant accordion-folded photo sleeve flipping open. Prudy holding a baby, her lips pursed against chubby infant cheeks. (Was it Sally or Lenny or Nell? They had all looked the same. The *same!*) Lenny holding the tiny pigtail he'd cut from Sally's head, defiantly staking his claim as big brother. Nell, five years old, smiling shyly, with baby Sally cradled stiffly in her arms. There was comfort remembering, comfort Sally didn't deserve. Or want. Not now, when it was too late for her. She'd made up her mind.

"I don't understand!" she cried. "Are you telling me to reconsider?"

"No! I'm saying your mother doesn't judge you. And neither do I."

"But you do! You always have!"

"I was wrong! Haven't I said that?"

She stared at him. "No! Never!"

He looked flustered. His hands began massaging the steering wheel, and his words, when they finally came, were choked. "All anybody wants is to get the Lord's attention. We try to do what's right. When that doesn't work, we screw up. Just to test him, I suppose. I don't know why. I really don't."

What did he mean? Was she making a mistake? Or fixing one? She searched his face but it was twisted as he fought against something. Only the tremor in his chin told her. Not only did he not know anything about her, he didn't know anything *period.*

And yet. Sally was suddenly and inexplicably grateful. He was trying to tell her something, however bumbled and impossible to understand. He was letting her see his uncertainty, his confusion. For the first time, looking at him, she saw herself.

"You sound sort of like a real person," she said, begrudgingly. "For once."

His laugh of relief filled the car, startling her. He swiped a finger under one eye and said, "Sally, I am truly glad to know you."

He shook her hand then, and his touch made her wonder, fleetingly, what other discoveries might be made. She hesitated, wistful. If only he weren't so… Oh, he was just so stiff and flat, like a face on a milk carton! One of those missing persons you stare at every morning until you can picture every feature inside your eyelids, so familiar that you come to believe it's someone you know. But, really, are those people ever found?

They exited the highway and merged into slow moving downtown traffic.

"Here we are," he said, a moment later. "I'm dropping you at the Carmichael hotel. A car will come for you."

She stared at the building before them, a stately red brick affair, with smooth white columns and a gold-edged revolving door that shone in the late day sun.

"I'm going alone?"

"There will be other girls. You'll all go together."

"But why can't you drive me? I thought—" That he'd be waiting just outside the door while she did this. Providing moral support. Immediately she saw the joke there.

"This is the way it's done. The less you know, the better."

"That sounds so ominous! Am I going to be arrested?"

"Try to relax. It's very safe."

Somehow she knew, hearing him say that, that it was not at all safe. She was breaking the law. And putting her life in a stranger's hands. She could *die.* She could bleed to death and she would have no idea where she was. She drew a deep, shaky breath. She wanted her mother! Just to lay her head on that sloping valley between her mother's neck and breast, her arms about Prudy's soft waist, just to feel safe. Would she ever have that again?

"You have the envelope?" he asked.

She felt for her purse, nodding. The car door opened and a man in a burgundy uniform offered his hand.

"Go on," the pastor said gently. "I'll see you later."

She took the gloved hand and stepped out.

"Good evening, miss. Lovely night, isn't it?"

Surprised, she looked around. She hadn't noticed, but yes, the sky was awash with a pink, pearly light, like the underbelly of a seashell. The air was humming with the sounds of insects and birds and cars and the conservations of passers-by. So much life!

She watched the pastor's Ford pull away and willed herself to climb the steps and push her way inside. Beside the revolving door stood a gray-haired woman who smiled at her.

"Right over there please." She pointed to a group of girls standing awkwardly in the lobby and Sally joined them with slow, self-conscious steps. There were five of them, plus Sally made six. Nobody acknowledged her, and she said nothing, though they all stole glances at one another. First she noticed their dresses, each a solid color, like hers. Vivid red, pale lilac, buttery soft yellow, a sea foam green, and one truly awful orange. The girl in red was fresh-faced and pretty. She had pierced ears and wore tiny diamond chip earrings. *Wealthy.* The yellow girl was enormously large, with ankles that bulged over the backs of her pumps. Miss Lilac had a lovely, soft-flowing dress, though she was angular and rough-looking and kept tossing her black hair so strenuously that Sally wondered if it was a nervous tick. The girl in green was another beauty, the porcelain, fragile kind, and she was chewing gum with teeny rabbit chews. Orange disaster would have been the most ordinary of all, except that she had heavily penciled eyebrows punctuating her face. What a statement *they* made, though Sally just knew she had not drawn them on herself. *Here!* they said. *Be pretty. Be normal.* This girl didn't stop looking at the floor and Sally was disappointed. She wanted to catch her eye, but maybe that wasn't *done*.

They stood for what seemed an eternity, pretending to admire the paintings on the walls and the thick Oriental rugs, swaying slightly to the sound of piano and violins, a perky waltz that emanated from the very walls, when the girl in red startled the group with a dramatic sigh. Throwing her arms up, she said, "I wish we could *dance.*" She looked at each of them expectantly, awaiting a reaction.

"What?" she said, wide-eyed. "It's supposed to be a *party.* Remember?"

"Shut up," Sally said in a low voice.

Miss Red scowled and elbowed the large girl beside her. "What's with *her?*"

When this got no response, she whispered loudly, "It's called *acting.*" Her face fell into a pout. "I'm going to be an actress."

Sally looked at the orange girl and saw a tear slip down her cheek. She sighed and turned away, wondering how long they would have to wait. She had to go to the bathroom. Then, thankfully, the woman was rushing toward them, beckoning wildly.

"Come now! The cars are here!"

They were loaded three girls to a car and Sally's stomach

lurched again. She was so sick of riding in cars! Cars were supposed to mean freedom and fun, but she knew that, for the rest of her life, every time she rode in a car she'd feel nauseated and trapped. And when the driver, a large-nosed, faintly attractive young man, turned and held up three blue bandanas, saying "Cover your eyes, please. It's a very short drive," she wondered what would happen if she began to scream.

"Give 'em here," said the dark, bony girl, who was sitting in the middle. She tied one around Sea Foam Green's eyes, then put Sally's on quickly. Sally tried to thank her but her mouth was too dry to speak. A moment later the girl took Sally's hand and squeezed it hard. They rode that way, holding hands, never speaking a word, until the driver told them they could look.

The car was slowing before a large Victorian house. They were hurried out and up the steps so quickly Sally became dizzy. A foyer, a coat rack, a gray tweed overcoat, a woman's khaki blazer. Colorful medals in a framed box on the wall. Flowers on a table. A parlor with a gargantuan fireplace made of stone, a deer head mounted beside. A woman, with gray hair like the first, greeting them in a strange voice. British? A table in one corner covered with refreshments.

"Weak herbal tea," the woman said. "Fruit juices. For *after*. Cookies and biscuits and sweets." She turned and smiled gently. "Piece of cake."

Sally stared at her dumbly, not sure if she was referring to the procedure or the dessert tray. It was all so strange! She hadn't expected these *grandmothers*, if that's what they were. She tried to get a closer look. Maybe they were wearing wigs. Under cover, just like Julie on The Mod Squad! But no one else seemed worried about being thrown against the wall and slapped with handcuffs. Girls were sitting on the couch, reading magazines, or chatting quietly with one another. Several stood in line at the refreshment table and waited to be handed a cup of tea. Slowly, moving as if through water, she joined them. She didn't want the tea, but it would ease the wait.

Soon a nurse in a white dress and white cap appeared and called, "Miss Periwinkle, please." And on it went this way, more nurses coming at intervals to pull another color from the room. Each time a different girl was called, Sally's knees went weak with relief. She still had time! She could find a phone if she had to. Call a cab. Ride anywhere, away from here, and jump out at a light before the driver discovered she couldn't pay. It was the same feeling she'd had at the Stuckey's, when Cash ditched her.

"Miss Magenta?"

Sally smiled, suddenly calm. This was it. Her way out. She'd been thinking of it the wrong way. She was lucky to even be here. Lucky to have family willing to pay for this. And these people, why, they were so friendly, so helpful! They were performing a lifesaving service.

She followed her nurse down a wide, carpeted hallway to a back bedroom. Inside was a hospital bed covered in a white sheet, and some metal trays beside. So professional. You might say *elegant*. On the windows hung beautiful blue velvet curtains, thick and plush, with gold tassels along the top. There was even velvety wallpaper that looked soft to the touch.

Really very lucky!

"You can change in there," the nurse said, motioning toward a large closet. "Everything off and leave the gown open to the front."

Sally stepped into the largest closet she'd ever seen, big enough to fit the entire Young Miss collection from Steketees, with built-in shelves for shoes, and hanging rods on every side filled with pink padded hangers. She took her dress off and hung it carefully, then put on the gown.

"Come on," said the nurse, and Sally could hear impatience in her voice, but she froze. The closet was safe and warm and reminded her of the forts she used to make from sheets when she was a kid. She wanted to crawl into the corner and pretend she lived here.

She couldn't go through with this.

She could. She *would.*

She managed to climb onto the table, feeling the white paper crinkle beneath her bare bottom. It was comical, in a way. She was sitting on a giant paper *napkin* and she was very naked. And there was a bright light hanging over the table that would soon be pointed right at her like a stage light. *Drumroll….* Intro*duc*ing…. It would shine on her most private parts while a strange man examined her and touched her and *—oh!*

"I'm going to be sick," she said.

"That's right," said the nurse in a soothing voice, handing her a bucket. Sally put her head in it. Nothing came up, but her mouth would not stop salivating.

When she was able, she put the bucket down and lay back. The nurse covered her with another white paper sheet.

"The drapes are nice," Sally said, as a distraction. She looked at them a moment longer, noticing how they blocked out every particle of light.

"They seem a little out of place," she added. Cloak and dagger came to mind. The cloak was on her and the dagger was hiding beneath the white cloth on the table beside her.

"I suppose so," said the nurse. "I never thought about it before."

Never thought about it? So it was possible to work in a place like this, performing one abortion after another, and not question every detail? To not ask who pays the mortgage? Who buys the cookies? What if the doctor is arrested? Or I am? Should I pray for these girls' souls? For my own? To think only *hmmm, wonder if Meijer still has those pork chops on sale.*

"What's your name?" Sally asked, curious about this sort of person, and wondering how she might become one.

"Beth Anne."

Sally stifled a groan. She disliked people with two names. Like Patty Ann. And a girl called Mary Paige who was Lenny's age and used to call him on the phone, treating Sally like she was so *dumb* if she answered the telephone.

"Does the doctor live here?" Sally asked.

Beth Anne gave her one of those patient, tight-lipped looks. "Hon, let's just get you comfortable."

Hon? Sally hated that too.

"What's his name?"

"You can call him doctor."

Beth Anne didn't get it. Sally didn't want to call him anything. She only wanted to know if he was a Michael or a Thomas or a David. She liked *Paul*. It was solid but sensitive. She hoped he was a Paul.

With a tap on Sally's legs, Beth Anne directed her to put them into the stirrups. The simple act of lifting and bending made something in her unhinge. Her heart pounded fearfully and she gripped the edge of the bed. Closing her eyes, she turned her head to and fro. She felt feverish, overcome by a painful, bruising wish to go back in time, before she mailed that letter. Before she climbed into Cash's car.

"What will he think of me?" she whispered, not sure who she meant. Richard? Cash, or Pastor Voss? Maybe Lenny. Maybe all of them.

Beth Anne patted her arm, startling her. "The doctor?" she said. *Yes, him too!* "Why, he won't think a thing. Will you, doctor?"

Sally's eyes flew open. There stood a man in a white coat, his hand on the open door.

"Nope," he said with a grin. "We're not allowed to think." He chuckled heartily.

Oh. He was one of *those.* The kind who think a dumb joke will put a person at ease. Sally's cheeks burned as the doctor turned and, serious now, took a pair of rubber gloves from a small cardboard box on the bureau. The room grew very quiet. The only sound was her own thumping heart and the squeaky pull and pop of rubber as the doctor put on the gloves.

Stepping close, he said, "Move your bottom down please. A little more."

She fought another wave of nausea and did as he asked. When his hand touched her *there*, she flinched.

"Relax. You'll feel some pressure."

Cold metal pierced her and she clutched at the white paper beneath her, her breath coming in short, noisy bursts. A tear rolled down her cheek and landed in the corner of her mouth. Its saltiness brought to mind oceans and earth and all things natural. There was death in nature. And destiny. Her mother knew it, too. Clearly, she saw her mother doing this to herself, trying not to feel the poke of cold metal, wondering if the roar in her ears was the voice of God. Trying desperately to make out his words. Failing. What she felt then wasn't hate. It was something sad. Sorrow, perhaps, though this was a word that made Sally think of church hymns, or the book of Job. Too ancient a feeling for sixteen.

She squeezed her eyes shut again and felt the doctor lean over her. His foot kicked the plastic bucket underneath the table. "Nurse," he said, and his voice had a reaching tone to it that let the nurse know he needed something. Sally heard the rustle of her dress, then the sound of the bucket being dragged. *That's right. Move it over. Catch whatever's about to spill from me.*

"I never meant for this to happen," Sally whispered.

"Of course not," said Beth Anne. "You couldn't know."

Sally frowned. Did she mean Sally couldn't know she'd end up here, as in *we never know what the future holds?* Or that she was too stupid to know the birds and bees?

If only she'd listened to her mother! But she was listening to her mother now. Prudy wanted her to be *here*, doing *this*. The two of them knew what it was to be unwanted.

She steeled herself. "Carve away," she said. It was her turn to make a joke. Horrible! *Horrible!* But she felt like a giant turkey on a platter. Scoop out the stuffing! Remember to be thankful! She imagined a Thanksgiving dinner with an empty seat where this child would have been. It wasn't so different from the empty seat she'd been seeing for years—the place where her father would have been. *Richard.* No. Get it right. *Voss.* She tried to drop *him* into that seat. It wouldn't work, and she suddenly realized why. Richard was the one choosing her. *I hope I can get to know you better*, he'd said.

A sudden swell of tenderness moved through her. Tenderness toward all that was imperfect. The tree at Tunnel Park with the bulging, scarred bark. The way Nell sometimes backcombed her hair when she was dressing up, how even though it didn't look good, it looked, well...sweet. Lenny's deaf ear that made him wrinkle one side of his face and say *whassat?* How her Aunt Flookie always said the wrong thing at the wrong time, and how it made her funny and surprising and alive. Her mother's fried potatoes, burned to a near-black crisp, the kind a restaurant would never serve.

Her floaty feeling disappeared, replaced by a sharp, expectant focus. Recent events became curious objects in her hands to be turned over and inspected. Lenny coming home holding a World Series ticket in his hand, *laughing.* She had never seen such a wide grin on his face. It was as if a door had been cracked open, making her wonder what was on the other side. And *Nell*, saying what she'd said about the baby—though it was pure craziness (as unthinkable as Sally lying on a table with a mysterious doctor's hands between her legs), it too made her wonder.

What was she doing? Who was this *she,* anyway? Who did Sally *want* to be? Certainly not her mother, scared and alone. Waiting so long—years!!— for love, but instead being tossed aside. Why did people do that to each other? Why did they throw away love given willingly and without question? And what was that word?

Precious.

A prickly warmth washed over her, along with the urge to wiggle, squirm, rise up and *go.*

"Can you take that thing out of me?" she said.

"It won't be long now," the doctor said. From the corner of her eye she saw his hand, strong and capable, stretching toward the tray.

"No. *Stop.* Can you stop?"

Beth Anne made a clucking sound with her tongue. "There are no refunds," she said. "And no rescheduling."

But Sally was sliding away, gathering the white paper gown in her hands, fistfuls of courage. Beth Anne began moving about briskly, clearly annoyed, but the doctor only stepped back and shrugged.

"Call me when the next one's ready," he said.

Sally ducked into the closet and changed so quickly that when she heard the soft thud of the padded hanger hitting the closet floor she didn't bother turning around to pick it up. Then she was *out*, past the rainbow of dresses, through the heavy front door, into the yard. The sun was nearly gone, throwing its light against the clouds. The autumn air was cool and the wind was rising, raising an eddy of leaves around her ankles, fiery orange and red, rich green and tarnished gold, each leaf changing—dying even —but lovely. Lovely, too, were the branches, each one stark and bare, that let them go.

Epilogue

Mr. And Mrs. Gerald Ten Harmsel
are blessed with the arrival
of their daughter,
Maggie Prudence
born June 21, 1969
at Grand Rapids Memorial Hospital
6 lbs. 7 ozs.

It's hard to know what to say to a sister who practically hands over her life to you. *Gosh, you shouldn't have! How very kind. Could you pass the butter?*

What the Van Sloeten sisters will never know is that they are each thinking the same thing. Their arrangement is a leap of faith, but if either of them has doubts, they aren't admitting it. How can one more family secret hurt when there is JOY surrounding them? If they were in church, they might raise their hands in praise. Even now little Maggie is reaching a tiny arm upward. *Here I am! Look at me!*

If it's a weekday at the Van Sloeten house, a letter might arrive from Hope College. Gizzy will pull it from his pocket at the dinner table, a devilish grin on his face. Everyone will gather around, watching Sally's reaction.

I thought it was a federal offense not to put it in a mailbox, she'll say, causing him to laugh.

It's a stupid rule, isn't it?

If it's a Sunday dinner, and warm enough to eat outside, they'll sit around the picnic table watching while Aunt Flookie pushes little pieces of watermelon into Maggie's mouth, her long red nails flashing like daggers while Nell tries not to cringe. Lenny will show up late, Richard likely on his heels. Seeing him, Prudy will hand Nell a glass of lemonade to give him. *Go ahead*, she'll say, motioning with her head. She'll excuse herself and go inside, where she'll stand at the window watching, waiting patiently for him to finish and leave.

Returning, she'll ask the three of them *how's your father?* It's a glossing over, perhaps. It's also a question that, stripped of an old and tiresome weight, causes something in each of them to rise. Like a muscle, once clenched, releasing and expanding with vital blood.

Richard will come by often enough. Once or twice, he'll try too hard, calling *Hello loved ones!* from across the yard. Sally will be reminded of the way Lenny and Nell once said this as a joke. She has always known that they laughed because they wanted it to mean something. Well, why can't it? It's more than hello. Easier than *I love you*. It's something more obscure. Some space in between, found only when you choose to look.

ACKNOWLEDGMENTS

I'd like to thank Jerry Cleaver and The Writer's Loft workshop in Chicago for helping bring these pages to life. Thanks also go to Cyndi Dale's Write of Passage class for lighting my way. And Dr. Larry Stoler, Katie Oberlin, Barbara Starke, and Cynthia Hutchison have my gratitude for not only calling me a writer, but making me believe.

ABOUT THE AUTHOR

Tammy Letherer was born in Holland, Michigan and now lives in Chicago with her three children. She writes fiction and non-fiction, and can be found at TammyLetherer.com. This is her first novel.

Made in the USA
Lexington, KY
24 May 2012